WHAT REVIEWERS ARE SAYING ABOUT THE SEVEN DEADLIEST

"The Seven Deadliest *breathes new life into the exploration of sin… original from first page to last. The words of* **Foster, MacLeod, Lansdale, Kirk, Mason, Thomas,** *and* **Taff** *lead to a new kind of wonderful hell.*"

—Michael Bailey, Bram Stoker Award® winning editor of *The Library of the Dead*

"*[Our] reading slump is over… breathtakingly good.*"

—Kendall Reviews, via Twitter

"*Each author was randomly given one of the seven sins as their theme on which to base a novella. Each is horror driven and the writing… oh, the writing is exceptional! …This is a book you don't want to miss… it's that damn good.*"

—Cat After Dark Reviews

"*Forget the ready-made horror trappings implicit in the notion of the Seven Deadly Sins. Forget, even, that you're dealing with seven of the best writers in today's horror fiction. Focus instead on these seven intense, soul-crunching stories, showing you all the ways the sin can affect the sinner. Imagine these stories as rotations of tales around the campfire, all meant for you; turning the page just means looking at the next person. The Seven Deadliest serves up such surprising, chilling, intimate stories of our darkest fears and greatest regrets, told in the close manner of friends, I didn't want any of them to end. A stunning achievement for all the writers.*"

—Paul Michael Anderson, author of *Bones are Made to be Broken*

THE
SEVEN DEADLIEST

ALSO AVAILABLE FROM
Cutting Block Books

EDITED BY
PATRICK BELTRAN
AND D. ALEXANDER WARD

VIRGINIA

THE
SEVEN DEADLIEST

Cutting Block Books
an imprint of Farolight Publishing,
a division of Farolight Entertainment, LLC
PO Box 1713
Herndon, VA 20172
www.cuttingblockbooks.com

First Cutting Block Books trade paperback edition: May 2019

Inset Layout and Design by Bailey Hunter
www.facebook.com/BaileyHunterDesign

Cover art by Bailey Hunter and Francois Vaillancourt
www.baileyhunterdesign.wixsite.com | www.francois-art.com

Published in the United States of America
1   3   5   7   9   1 0   8   6   4   2

Library of Congress Control Number: 2019937326

ISBN 978-1-7320090-3-5

For the horror fans who support, via your purchases, every small press like ours—we couldn't do it without you.

And for my daughters three—the joy of being your dad is enough to banish all the shadows.

—P.B.

For my fellow readers and sinners, whose company I always enjoy. To borrow from St. Augustine's Confessions, may we someday be made righteous, but not today. After all, we have far too many succulent stories yet to devour.

—D.A.W.

TABLE OF CONTENTS

FOREWORD

OUR FAVORITE SINS

by Mercedes M. Yardley

Mmm, the seven deadly sins. What a deliciously intimate topic. There's such a ripe lushness to the subject matter, isn't there?

I live in Las Vegas. Sin is our currency. Every day I walk down the street and see a town of neon and excess. It's the best and the worst, the highs and the lows. People laugh and celebrate. They drink until they vomit and pass out in the street. They cover themselves in sequins, feathers, and whatever they could fish out of a dumpster behind the gas station. They drip with diamonds and despair. Spend all of your money, drink as much (and then some) as you can handle, eat desserts covered in real gold foil, and be a celebrity. Look, taste, partake, touch. Use your eyes, your hands, your tongues, and your teeth. Perhaps these sins will break you. Perhaps they'll liberate you. Either way, for good or ill, they will, at least for the moment, make you feel alive. There will be consequences, yes, but wouldn't most of us do nearly anything in order to feel alive? So many believe it's a gamble worth taking.

We are familiar with the seven sins, because we have all been lectured about them at one time or another. Mother, or Father, or friends, or guardians, or headmasters, or law enforcement has, at least once, sat each one of us down.

"Now, James," they'll say, for so many of us are named James. "Your pride will be your downfall." "Keep your anger under control, Maria. Nobody likes a hothead." So many people want to tell us what to do, don't they? They say they want to keep us safe. They insist they're doing it for our own good. We have heard, "Put some of that food back or you'll get fat," or "Be wary of the green-eyed monster. Jealousy isn't a good look for you." Looking, living, and sometimes simply *being* are enough to call down sin upon ourselves. "What are you wearing? You can't go outside in that. Cover yourself up so you don't entice others," they'll say. Or perhaps something even more harmful that so many have heard more than once: "Remember your place, and stay there."

Oh, my darlings. These hurt. They damage. Remember your place. School your feelings. Don't do these things, say these things, or even *think* these things, because the road to Hell is littered with the bones of those who indulged in sin. You don't want to do the wrong thing, do you? You don't want to be A Bad Person. Surely nothing in life is as horrific as that! Heaven forbid.

We aren't children anymore, and our multifaceted lives aren't divided into something as simple as Good and Bad. Genuinely Bad People are terribly difficult to come by. There are shadows of Good flitting in the dark. As we grow and develop, we learn to process, think and analyze. We learn to read subtleties like tone and gradation and nuance. After all, there are seven virtues, too, but nobody seems to be able to remember them. They aren't pounded into our skulls the way sins are. It's all right if you forget to be Good, but don't, even for a second, even glance at what has historically been considered Evil. Cover your eyes, child. Run, boy. Save yourself.

What happens when you no longer believe in Good and Bad, black and white? What if you really look at these famous sins and examine them for yourself? Perhaps you'll find these sins can be flipped on their heads and explored so deeply and passionately that they become something else altogether. The famous sins are reborn. They become something else than what you expected.

That's what you're going to find in this book. Patrick Beltran and D. Alexander Ward have put together the most compelling exploration of this topic that I have ever read. They found seven highly talented, unique authors who tackled each topic one by one.

John C. Foster introduces us to a woman named Claude who desperately wants to be one of the elite. That hungry, brazen want can bring out the horror in all of us.

Bracken MacLeod explores a holy father's wrath, and makes us wonder if it can, in fact, be righteous. More than that, he makes us wonder if it even matters.

Kasey Lansdale takes an unflinching look at the similarities and differences between pride and vengeance.

Brian Kirk explores how generosity and jealousy can be insidiously intertwined, and even virtuous actions can bring about rot.

Rena Mason's beautifully nuanced look at sloth is both heartbreaking and chilling.

Richard Thomas writes an intricate and complicated tale that examines lust in a clinical setting.

John F.D. Taff wonders what happens when, instead of stuffing ourselves with things we hate, we instead devour the things we love?

These stories take everything you think you know about the most famous of sins and force you to reexamine them. They're magnificent jewels that you hold up in front of you, turning them slightly to catch the light. They're gems that you've seen before, set in royal crowns or your old diamond ring. They're the fine cufflinks, lapel pins, or brooch that you remember your grandparents pulling out for weddings when you were a child. Now you look at them with fresh eyes, seeing the flaws and cracks that you never noticed before. You notice that if you hold wrath up to the window, its color deepens and darkens into something that stirs your soul. You want to decorate your room in avarice. You've never seen anything so beautiful and horrific as sloth. You're going to bathe in pride, jealousy, and lust. Gluttony tastes like strawberries that began rotting yesterday, but are still slightly desirable. You want to paint your face in the deadliest of sins.

Join me in this wonderfully complex, thoroughly entertaining collection. Sit down while these authors whisper in your ears, saying, "My darling, let me tell you a little story about my favorite sin."

—Mercedes M. Yardley
Bram Stoker Award®-winning author of *Little Dead Red*
Sin City, USA
March 2019

GILDA

by John C. Foster

"Claude is such a beautiful name for a girl."

Gilda's words rose towards the ceiling on wisps of smoke from smoldering tapers.

"We're growing stale," she added. "It's about time we had new blood."

Ceiling fans revolved cosmetically, and even with a breeze from the lagoon it was a muggy night. White linen curtains billowed at the edge of my vision and the jungle serenaded us with a chorus of frogs and cicadas.

A rifle shot popped in the distance.

The year was 1980 and Gilda was seventy, but spoke like an actress from the forties. Earlier in the evening she said, "I can handle a stain on my reputation, but not my dress." It was easy to think of her patter as an affectation, but Gilda was an Aztec temple of a woman and those who knew her insisted that the movies copied Gilda.

Stories were her business and she was at the top of the heap. There wasn't a war she hadn't reported, a scandal she hadn't uncovered or a bestseller list she hadn't topped. When the last American caught his helicopter out of Saigon, real estate in Thailand went for a song and Gilda snapped up the hotel in which we were relaxing. East of Chanthaburi, the former French plantation was within spitting distance of the slaughter in Cambodia and the purchase only added to her reputation.

Stories were the business of everyone in the long, high-ceilinged lobby. But this wasn't a noisy gathering of the National Press Club with disheveled reporters crowded around an open bar. This was a very exclusive function. The group was small. Its meetings took place every two years.

The Whiskey & Ink Ladies Drinking Society numbered only five at any one time, no boys allowed. If things went right, I would be initiated into WILDS at the end of the visit. I was a legacy, all that remained of Ava Wood, a founding member of the society and first of the old ladies to die.

The three crones surrounded Gilda with bourbon soaked laughs like acolytes around a holy woman. Though all of the chairs were made of the same bamboo and orange cushions, hers was somehow grander than the rest.

There was no one else in the hotel save a servant who seemed as much shadow as person, silently leaving the objects of her desire in the dumbwaiter whenever Gilda needed a refill or a fresh cigarette. He was some kind of butler or bodyguard and moved with a limp. She called him Mam, a funny name for a man. I suspected it was Viet or Cambodian, but wasn't sure how to ask without looking like a fool.

I felt the weight of their rheumy gazes and forced myself to sit up, aware of sweat darkening the shirt beneath my arms. "Mother named me after the actress, Claudette Colbert."

"Lovely." Marie stroked her painted nails along my forearm, and her many bracelets clanked.

Hysteria fluttered her fingers. "Ava always had a flair for the dramatic." Her name was actually Hystria but she'd gained the nickname covering the Chilean coup d'état of '73. "Did she tell you why she named you after a star?"

"Remember that blonde Swede on the Paramount lot?" Wilma jabbed her cigarette holder, long and black like a stage magician's wand. "He asked Ava if she was a virgin and she said, 'only on my mother's side.'"

"No, no, no!" The others silenced her.

"Last time it was all about your stories, Wilma," Hysteria said. A charm bracelet on her wrist tinkled with tiny bells.

"Let's hear one from Claude!" Marie cooed.

I lipped a Viceroy and held a candle to it to buy time. These women covered movie stars and collapsing governments, the Moon Landing and the Lindbergh kidnapping. "All mother really said…"

Mother said that Marie wrote turgid prose, Hysteria never met a cock she wouldn't suck and that the frightening rumors about Wilma were mostly true.

"Yes?" Wilma, Hysteria and Marie leaned in with glittering eyes.

"All mother said was that Gilda always went first, then one of you would try to top her."

Marie's smile went brittle and Hysteria went still. A length of grey ash crumbled to dust at the end of Wilma's cigarette.

The queen brushed her sweat-dampened hair back, revealing the infamous left ear. Gilda never hid her disfigurement as another woman might, and she never told anyone how the lobe had been snipped off as if by garden shears. A smile drew the skin tight along her jaw line and I understood why mother had always envied her looks, injury or no injury. It was a long jaw, almost a man's jaw, and gave

2

the impression that if she opened her mouth wide she might bite like a lioness. Wider still and she would swallow you whole.

"Who knocked on my door at two a.m.?"

The rustle of fabric heralded the turning of three heads towards Gilda. The tip of Marie's tongue was very pink as it wetted her lips. Wilma lit a fresh cigarette and sulphur punched the atmosphere. She dropped the burning match in a glass ashtray on the round table beside her and blew a smoke ring. "Well?"

Gilda drew her feet up to sit cross-legged in the chair, despite the protesting bamboo. Decades dropped away as she took on the aspect of a girl telling stories around a campfire.

"That's how it starts," Gilda said, her voice throaty with confession. "The greatest story I never told." She turned her attention to a pocket and produced the white twist of a joint. Placing it between her lips, she leaned towards Wilma, who extended her wand and offered the glowing coal of her cigarette as Gilda inhaled.

"Who knocked at the door?" Hysteria asked.

"You can't stop there," Marie pleaded.

Gilda grinned around her marijuana, the teeth stretching up miles before they rooted themselves in gums. "I'll tell you, but there's a price."

"What?" I was determined not to play the wallflower.

Gilda's gaze spoke of rituals completed. "You have to wet my whistle, dear." She winked. "Give a tug on that cord by the dumbwaiter." She extended a thin finger towards the bar. "Mam will send up another round."

As I moved away among islands of bamboo furniture, the conversation faded into clucks and I saw myself gliding towards my own reflection in the long mirror behind the bar. I wondered if the women hated my unwrinkled skin, my auburn hair untouched by grey. The lighting was low enough that what I saw in the mirror was only a suggestion of myself and I felt insubstantial, as if I might blow to tatters in a strong wind.

Licking sweat off my lip, I located the dumbwaiter and pulled on the cord swaying beside it like a snake from a branch. A muffled tinkle of bells sounded from below and I lifted the sliding door, grunting with effort and using both hands.

The dark maw of the dumbwaiter drew me like a magnet and I leaned inside. I expected some kind of light from below but it was as black as a mineshaft, and I wondered if Mam was blind. I imagined his horribly disfigured face, napalm scarred, as he performed menial tasks in a stygian kitchen.

When the drinks materialized I jerked back. They rose so quietly that I hadn't heard the mechanism. Mam made no more noise than the shadows in which he hid.

After slowing my pulse, I weaved my way back towards the island of light around the gathering, determined not to play servant.

They will test boundaries, mother had told me. Don't let them.

Gilda's voice summoned me like a beacon. "The guy says, 'You give me a rubber check and I'll give you the steel' and I says, 'Just give me the scotch.'"

All four of them broke into laughter and I noticed that Hysteria yipped like a hyena. She turned my way, lips peeled back over yellow teeth. Gilda wasn't the only one who could bite.

"Next round is on Hysteria," I said, dipping to place the tray on the glass table.

Hysteria tucked a dollar bill into my collar, her charms tinkling. "Thanks, doll."

The chair creaked alarmingly under my weight as I sat down, and an honest chuckle broke the tension. Gilda stretched her hand towards me, the smoldering joint tucked between the knuckles of her index and middle fingers.

"Sweet strains of jazz cabbage to set the mood." Gilda winked.

"It never does anything to me." But I took it and inhaled until the smoke clawed my lungs like Gilda's chipped nails. Another laugh went around the group when I coughed out a great gout of smoke. "Sorry," I squeaked and handed it back, red faced and laughing myself.

Wilma sipped a martini, catching the toothpick to pull an olive free with her front teeth, as nimble as if they were tweezers. She slid it into her cheek, where it made a lump, and she said, "Tell your story, Gilda."

Marie pushed the bracelets up her arms as if she were preparing for surgery. "Tell your story."

Hysteria licked the rim of her martini glass. "Tell your story."

I picked up my glass, a cold trickle of gin spilling on my wrist. "Tell your story."

Gilda nodded.

"It started with that knock on the door."

⸺

Arnold Didion sat up and the blanket slithered to the floor.

What was that?

He was on the living room couch in his Fruit of the Looms, objects around him burnished by a glow from the smoldering coals in the fireplace.

The door rattled in its frame and Arnold bit back a gasp, gripped by a chill that had nothing to do with the season. The brass clock over the mantle caught the orange glimmer from below and he thought the hands read 2:00 a.m. The house shuddered and sparks swirled up from the fireplace as wind whistled down the flue.

It was still dark outside, and white fingers of snow tickled the window panes. He slipped to the floor and moved with the quiet swish of his socks across the pine boards to the window. Where he expected to see the headlights of a car in the driveway, he saw only the pale snowscape beneath a blanket of night.

Arnold's skin crawled as he leaned close enough to the window to fog the glass. With Rose long dead, there was no one whose dire circumstance would warrant knocking at his door in the middle of the night.

The door rattled again and he sprang back from the window as if he'd been spotted. A flush of anger warmed his face. He'd be damned if someone would frighten him in his own house. He felt his way by touch across the living room and eased open the glass door of his gun case. Of the four long guns inside, only the twelve-gauge was kept loaded, and he took its comforting weight in his big knuckled fist.

The next knock charged him with a strange mix of emotions, fear swelling large beneath the anger. He spat into the fireplace for luck and strode to the door.

"Who is it?" He bellowed, pleased that his voice boomed out big and thick. He thumbed back the hammers on the shotgun as he waited for the door to shudder, half-planning to fire straight through the wooden panels.

"Mr. Didion?" The voice was small and barely audible.

"What?" he called out, beginning to feel foolish.

Whatever the visitor said, the words were unintelligible. Arnold yanked open the door.

If the stranger was surprised to see a big man in nothing but his undies with a gun in his hands, he didn't show it. His features were bland, his hair combed over a bald spot in a way that reminded Arnold of salesmen. In a belted coat unsuited for the New Hampshire winter, the man was as unperturbed by the snowdrifts on his shoulders as he was by Arnold's warlike posture.

"What?" Arnold managed to force out through a spit-dry mouth.

"This is yours, Mr. Didion." The man raised a briefcase in his right hand.

"Who are you?" Arnold's free hand crossed half the distance. "I don't own a briefcase."

The man drew back the case and suspicion flickered across his features. In the night gloom, the stranger's eyes glittered like jewels deep inside a cavern.

"You are Arnold Didion?"

"Of course. This is my house."

"Excellent," the man smiled and offered the case again. "This is for you."

Arnold snatched it before it could be taken away, afraid the man wouldn't release his grip. But release it he did, and Arnold felt the heavy weight of the briefcase pull at his shoulder.

"Good night, Mr. Didion." The man descended the roughhewn granite steps with the help of a cane. He kicked up drifts of powder with his wingtip shoes as he walked down the unplowed driveway and Arnold thought to call out, to complain of a mistake. Hell, to invite the man inside to warm up.

But he did none of those things. He closed the door instead and set the briefcase down on the coffee table, shivering as goose pimples broke out on his arms. He scooped the blanket from the floor and slung it around his shoulders before taking two logs from the stack and setting them on the fire.

Couch springs offered a rusty protest as he sat, resting the shotgun on the floor beside him. Fire crawled lustily over the new logs and he clutched the blanket around himself like a primitive hunter in his cave.

5

He had never before owned a briefcase and had no idea why a stranger might deliver one to him in the middle of the night. In the middle of a winter blow, for Christ's sake. New England pragmatism swept aside thoughts of forgotten relatives and inheritances. Rose liked to read about that kind of nonsense, but he knew that kind of thing didn't happen in the real world. Not to Arnold Didion.

Probably some kind of lawsuit. A summons. He wasn't sure if a summons usually came in a briefcase, but he knew those fellas could show up anywhere and you were obliged to take it.

Right?

Pure foolishness is what all this was. His thumbs pressed against metal catches designed for smaller hands, but with a moment of wrestling, the stiff locks released and he lifted the lid of the briefcase.

"Holy shit."

He picked up a bound stack of cash and riffled it with his fingers. Twenties. They all looked like twenties. He wondered how many twenty dollar bills were in a stack and how many stacks were in the case, but his eyes skipped off the sight like a rock on a pond as a roaring sound filled his ears.

He was rich.

———

"There was a hundred thousand bucks in that briefcase," Gilda said. "More than Arnold Didion had ever seen in his life and he had no idea where it came from."

"Someone just knocked on his door and gave him the moolah?" Marie clapped her hands and her bracelets jangled. "Why does everyone else get all the luck?"

"It wasn't lucky, was it?" I asked, but Hysteria talked over me.

"You're trying to tell me that a stranger gave him a hundred big ones with no strings attached?"

Gilda waved her quiet and cocked her head at me. "Speak up, doll."

"I said, it wasn't lucky, was it?"

Gilda saluted with her martini and took a sip, taking time to roll the liquid around her mouth before continuing. "Oh, it was lucky alright."

She winked.

"But not good luck."

———

Arnold Didion didn't know what to do. He was afraid to spend any of the money, sure that carloads of revenuers were already on the way. Vehicles would scream up his driveway, red bubble lights flashing. A cigar chewing man with a badge would scream, "Where's the loot, Arnold?" for all of his neighbors to hear and Arnold, pinned in the spotlights, would have to say, "I spent it."

But he was afraid to keep it too, because as soon as the little bagman realized his mistake, a line of black sedans would splash up his driveway, Tommy guns poking out of the windows as the bagman shouted from a running board, "You lyin' cheat! Give us the dough or the boss will skin you alive!"

Arnold moved the briefcase three times that first day and twice more the next. Under the bed—even a child would look there! In the oven—too much chance he would cook it like a meatloaf. In the coal bin—anyone could follow the black trail of his footprints in the cellar. And on and on, even trying in the middle of the night to bash through the frozen earth behind his house with a pickaxe.

After a few days of this, Arnold was a frazzled wreck, his eyes red-veined, grey whiskers furring hollow cheeks. Not accustomed to dishonesty, he worried himself into a frozen state and planted himself in a rocking chair facing the door with a bottle of rotgut in one bony fist, sippin' and waitin'. Waitin' and sippin'. When knuckles politely rapped on the door at 2:00 a.m. on the fourth night, he heard the sound as thunder and imagined sawdust blowing out of the doorframe.

Blitzed almost to immobility, Arnold managed to stagger to the door and yanked it open just as a great, whiskey powered belch blew from his mouth with all the heat of the dying Hindenburg.

The little man with the cane was unruffled, however, and offered a neat smile. "Mr. Didion?"

"The case," Didion slurred. "You come about the case."

"Why yes." The man smiled as a teacher might at a bright student. "I came—"

"It's here, it's here!" Didion stumbled away from the door and began tearing up his living room, so drunk he forgot that the briefcase was beneath a couch cushion. "I knew you'd be back! I didn't spend a red cent, no sir! I'm an honest man and—"

Another mighty belch burned a path up from his belly and he stopped, clenching his gut and grimacing at the taste of guilt.

The little man limped inside with the help of his cane, a concerned look on his face. "I'm afraid you misunderstand me—"

"Not a dime is missing from that briefcase!" Arnold's eyes lit with triumph as he flipped couch cushions and lifted the briefcase over his head. "It's all here!"

"Mr. Didion." The visitor raised his right hand and Arnold saw that he held another briefcase, identical to the first. "I brought your briefcase."

Arnold blinked. "Mine?"

"Of course."

Arnold lowered the case from over his head and hugged it to his chest. "Is this still mine too?"

This time the tips of small, square teeth were revealed by the visitor's neat smile. "Yes." He offered the new briefcase and Arnold reached out to take it. With a briefcase in each hand, he looked like a hobo playing at traveling salesman.

"Mine."

"Yes."

Arnold's horselike teeth showed themselves in a smile. Happy, yeah, but he was still ready to give the bagman the bum's rush. "So long."

The visitor tightened the belt around his raincoat, but hesitated.

"Mr. Didion?"

"Yeah?" The word was truculent.

"May I trouble you for a glass of water before I go?"

Relief flooded across Arnold's features. "Fella, if I got it, you can drink it."

Two days later, he shot Tom Frasier's son.

⁓

Gilda set down her empty martini glass, chewing an olive. "I'm drowning in eel juice, ladies." She yawned wide enough that I could see pieces of olive mashed on her molars.

"Hah! That cliff hanger's straight out of a cheap detective book!" Hysteria laughed.

"You're the expert," Wilma jabbed.

"They were best sellers," Hysteria shot back.

"Wait a minute." I slugged back the last of my cocktail and tried not to slur. "That's it?"

Marie clapped her hands, and the bangles sounded like a steel drum band. "She wants to know if that's it?"

Hysteria was sulking but Wilma fixed me with a look, gesturing with her wand. Grey ash drifted my way.

"The last time we met, Gilda's story took two and a half days," Wilma said through thin lips. "Your mother's took six."

Gilda stood and the other women rose as well, bleary eyes fixed on me until I joined them.

"Bloody Marys and bloodier stories at breakfast," Gilda said with a twirl and swept from the room.

They looked smaller when she was gone, the three crones. Smaller and drunker, with sunken eyes. Junkies who didn't score.

"Perchance to dream," Marie plagiarized as she hurried after Gilda, hoping for a last word. Hysteria hiccupped and shrugged before following.

Every curtain in the lobby billowed inside at once, as if the hotel were besieged by the four winds. The frogs tried to make their croaking point but the cicadas shouted them down.

Wilma crossed thin arms and stared at me. I blew my nose into a cocktail napkin.

"Be sure you want it, kiddo." Wilma stalked away after the rest.

⁓

It was an elegant bedroom built for a different age, lavishly employing teak and rosewood for shiny plank floors and ornately carved furniture. The mirrored vanity was framed in bamboo. French doors opened onto a shared second story terrace facing the lagoon. Despite the hour, the room was lit in blue tones by a full moon that seemed so much brighter than it ever was at home.

The French doors were open to allow the sluggish air to make its muddy presence felt and along with it, mosquitoes buzzed and flitted. Lit tapers on either side of the doorway added their pungent smoke to the general smogginess of the air.

The bed was unbearable.

Beautiful and canopied, shimmering drapes of mosquito netting cascaded down on all four sides, keeping out insects and fresh air alike.

I barely managed to doze in the stifling dark, my t-shirt and sweatpants drenched with perspiration. Moisture pooled in the hollow of my throat and my sweat stank of gin. Christ, these old broads could drink. Mother had warned me, but it was one thing to hear her whispered stories and another thing to match them martini for martini.

After an interminable hour my stomach lurched and I tasted acid. I'd been drinking whiskey for months in preparation. The Whiskey and Ink Ladies Drinking Society. Why the hell were they drinking gin?

"Oh shit." I scrambled from the bed and became tangled in the netting, desperate enough to tear it free and run like a sheet-draped ghost, if necessary.

As if sensing it had won the point, the bed released me and I made it into the bathroom just in time to give back a bit of what I'd imbibed.

Be sure you want it, kiddo.

Yeah, I wanted it. I wanted what they had. I wanted the stories, the access and the money that flowed from knowing Gilda. From being in the inner circle.

From being one of the five wild women.

I ran tepid water in the sink and cupped my hand beneath the faucet, rinsing out my mouth and splashing my face. I peeled off my sweat soaked t-shirt and skinned the sweats down my hips, kicking them off my feet so I could scoop handfuls of water onto my chest and belly, the back of my neck.

Frogs and cicadas outside. I was goddamned sick of them. Heat and alcohol and the incessant jungle chorus robbed me of sleep. Tomorrow night I would ask for a sleeping pill. Maybe more of Gilda's jazz cabbage.

A sound drifted to me as I returned to bed, something working against the natural rhythm of the jungle.

Thump-thump.

I went still beneath my blanket of humidity and strained to listen.

Thump-thump.

Clearer this time. All of the women were staying on the same floor. Was someone trying to signal me?

I leaned out of bed and rapped my knuckles twice on the teak nightstand.

The response was quick. Thump-thump.

I repeated my double tap.

Thump-thump. Immediate. My knuckles had not yet descended before it came again.

Thump-thump.

Thump-thump.

Growing louder.

Approaching.

I looked at the line of light beneath the door. Thump-thump. It was definitely out in the hall. Not someone signaling, someone walking…

Thump-thump.

I looked at my bag beside the dresser. If I could get to it…

Thump-thump.

A shadow darkened the light beneath the door and I froze, afraid to move, afraid to breathe.

Who was outside?

Goosepimples rose along my bare flesh and my sweat grew cold, the stink of fear supplanting the reek of gin. My bladder felt full to the point of sloshing and if I had been breathing, I was sure I would see it mist in the air as the temperature plummeted.

I swallowed and held completely still.

Eventually, the shadow moved away from my door and I made out the clean line of illumination from the hall lighting.

Thump-thump.

Moving away.

I slid from the bed into a crouch, doubled over on fingertips and the balls of my feet as I scuttled to my bag.

I risked the sound of a zipper as I opened an inside pocket and my fingers closed around the comforting grip of a French MAB Model A in .25 caliber. I'd picked it up in Bangkok before making my way towards Chanthaburi and the old plantation.

Sweat trickled into my eyes and stung me into action, propelling me towards the door. Staying down on one knee, I reached up and turned the knob, wincing at the pop of the lock disengaging but too afraid to hesitate.

I pulled open the door and leaned out.

The long hall was immaculate, the teak floor as shiny and clean as that in my room, the lamps all glowing with comforting yellow light, everyone's door closed.

The hall was empty.

Closing my door, I crept back into bed and slipped the pistol beneath my pillow. The digital clock on the nightstand told me it was 2:00 a.m.

⌣

In the morning it rained.

Barefoot, I stepped out onto the terrace to enjoy the cooler air, but was unsettled by the sight of an enormous spider web between the support beams and railing of the terrace. It stretched five feet in diameter, nearly my own height, and I craned my neck to see if the spider was scuttling across the ceiling or down the wall behind me.

I was too uneasy to remain on the terrace and picked my way down wooden steps to the beach, a thin stretch of white sand trucked in to add a touch of luxury to the lagoon's shoreline. The surface of the water danced with the downpour.

The jungle was alive with the clamor of fat drops splashing against wide green leaves. My t-shirt was soaked through in seconds and I tilted my head back, eyes closed and mouth open. The relief was palpable and the cool thudding against my forehead eased my discomfort.

With a sense of daring that was absent back home, I peeled off my shirt and let the water wash down over my shoulders and breasts. Monkeys screeched from the treeline and I grinned, throwing my arms wide to embrace their cheers.

"That lagoon looks it was left out in the rain."

I turned with my arms crossed over my chest as Gilda strolled down from the hotel, shoeless in a pair of linen culottes, already unbuttoning her flowing, white shirt. She dropped it on the ground and slipped thumbs into the waistband of her pants, shucking them without a thought. Her body was lean and leathery in the manner of tan women, but nothing about her struck me as weak. It was as if the years had sucked away only non-essential fluid and flesh to leave a perfectly working machine at her command.

If she was feeling the gin, she didn't show it.

"You coming in?" She smiled and it struck me as genuine. Just us girls.

"I was worried about—" I made a vague gesture at the water.

She laughed. "All the bad stuff is on land, honey. Snakes and spiders in the jungle. People in the hotel. Out there it's perfect."

She strolled by me and into the water without hesitation and I was struck by the elaborate, colorful tattoo covering most of her back. It was wings, the feathers blue and red and gold, the detail exquisite. I remembered a story I'd covered in Tokyo and thought Yakuza thoughts.

As the water reached her thighs, she sprang into a flat dive, the splash a happy counterpoint to the raindrops. When she surfaced she shook wet hair out of her face and shouted, "C'mon!"

Modesty be damned. I slipped off my sweatpants and underwear with one move and cantered into the lagoon, laughing in spite of myself as I kicked up water. It was warm and smooth and in a moment I was deep enough to dive. Hands outstretched, I cut beneath the surface and shot through the water, enjoying a transient perfection that was as close as I'd ever get to flight.

I broke the surface and swiped the heavy flop of hair out of my eyes as Gilda stroked towards me. "People ask me why I bought the place," she said, droplets spraying from her lips. "And I don't know how to explain to them what it feels like to walk down here in the morning and swim in this piece of heaven."

"It's kind of…"

"What?" She challenged.

"Magic."

She floated on her back. "You understand."

I tilted back so that I floated beside her, blinking my eyes against the downpour. It was easy to surrender to the moment, the susurrus of soothing noise, the warm caress of the lagoon. When she spoke, the words were muffled because my ears were below the surface.

I lifted my head. "What?"

"I said Arnold Didion didn't believe in magic, but he did believe in luck." Water sparkled like diamonds from Gilda's eyelashes. "And he was lucky to have only winged Tom Frasier's boy, and not too badly at that."

"Should we be starting without the others?"

We were facing each other and treading water.

"You wanna wait?" She asked.

I looked up at the hotel and saw someone watching us from the terrace, though rain and distance conspired to keep their identity hidden.

"No."

Diamond eyelashes. Pearl teeth. "You're just like your mother, maybe a little more so."

"What happened to that Frasier kid?"

⌣‿⌣

Arnold Didion told the sheriff, "I saw a man with a rifle and panicked. Tried a warning shot—"

"And winged him," the sheriff finished. He didn't miss the old man stink radiating from Arnold, and his quick eyes had picked out empty bottles on the counter, but the Frasier boy was a hooligan out jacklighting deer and maybe a little buckshot in the ass was just what he needed. "Tom Frasier is embarrassed as all hell and the kid ain't in no position to press charges, so I think we can chalk this one up to bad luck and call it a day."

On his way to the door he paused. "Everything alright around here? You don't look so good."

"Black dog is barking," Arnold lied. "You know how it is."

The sheriff knew his share about depression and figured a man who lost his wife had a right to mourn. "Alright then, you might feel better with a shower and laying off the sauce for a night, get your color back."

When the door banged shut Arnold collapsed onto his couch and cried like a man lost. Day after day he moved the money like a squirrel hiding his nuts and the only thing that gave him a moment's peace was brown and came from a bottle. Now he'd nearly killed a boy, never mind he was a juvenile delinquent.

This money was nothing but bad luck and he was determined not to open his door again should the little man arrive, nor could he keep the Judas silver in his house.

"Frank," he said into the phone once he composed himself. He had details written down in shaky hand so he wouldn't forget what he wanted to say to his late wife's brother, a cop in Boston's North End.

"Alright now," Frank said when Arnold was done, his voice thick with a three pack a day rasp. "You don't tell nobody about this, right? You don't tell your neighbors, that tin badge sheriff, nobody. I'll pick up the dough, put it into evidence down here until we can get in touch with the New Hampshire State Police."

"They gonna arrest me, Frank?" Arnold sobbed, flushed with shame.

"For what?" Frank said, calming. "You did the right thing, calling me."

His hand was too unsteady from a week of drinking to risk a razor, but Arnold managed a shower and clean clothes before his brother-in-law arrived. He opened a couple of windows to air out the place but needed a knock from the bottle to steady himself when he saw Frank Ricci's tan sedan turn into his driveway.

"And you didn't touch a dime?" Frank said, seated on Arnold's couch with both cases open on the coffee table before him.

"Not one red cent," Arnold said. "I'm no crook."

"Of course not." Frank wore black rimmed glasses and he plucked them from his nose to rub the lenses on his patterned tie. "But anyone would be tempted."

"Not me," Arnold insisted and Frank nodded, closing both cases and slapping the locks shut. He stood, a squat man only shoulder high on Arnold. "I'll let you know if anyone'll have any questions for you, but I've got your statement so I think your part in this caper is done."

"So you do think it's some kind of scheme?"

"Definitely, even if I don't know what it is yet." He picked up a briefcase in each hand. "Remember, no news is good news, but keep your lip zipped, alright?"

"Alright."

Frank Ricci lifted his chin in place of a wave as Arnold closed the door behind him, and as Frank walked to his car, Arnold could hear him humming a tune.

———

Aromatic trays of food had been set out on the bar and I was dizzy from the exotic perfumes of spicy shrimp and rich soups. Sharp odors of garlic and ginger and peppers made my mouth water. There were sautéed vegetables and long noodles shining with sauce, and I added things to my plate almost at random. Again I imagined Mam as blind and working in the dark below the dumbwaiter, because only a person reliant on other senses could create such a symphony of enticing smells.

Daytime sounds of birds and monkeys came to us through the open doors, familiar noises now, and though the heat was already squeezing drops of perspiration from my pores, I was better equipped in a loose linen shirt and shorts, my feet bare.

"Going native?" Gilda said as I passed her, me on my way to our gathering spot around a table, she on her way to fetch another Bloody Mary from a chilled pitcher on the bar.

"And then there were four." Wilma nursed her own Bloody Mary as she lounged in a chair, the black cigarette holder sticking up at an angle from her red painted lips. With her hair pulled severely back and lanky figure snugged into pencil skirt and a black silk shirt, she looked like an aging model several decades late for a photo shoot. In the light of day, her makeup had to work harder and had less success.

"Hysteria never could hold her booze." Marie wore a muumuu in mauve and orange that clashed with the cushions on our chairs. The bracelets this morning were jade and bone, and the bags beneath her eyes were purple, as if she'd been boxing. "Giggle juice gives her the fits."

"Probably still in bed, weeping about lost youth." Wilma pressed the back of a wrist against her forehead. "I could'a been somebody. I could'a been a contender."

"Should somebody check on her?" I asked, pulling a grilled prawn from a wooden skewer. It crunched between my teeth and tasted as good as it smelled.

Wilma waved her wand towards the door in invitation.

I shrugged. "You have lipstick on your teeth."

For all I knew, Gilda sat up all night with one of the others like old sorority sisters reliving their salad days, passing a joint back and forth as she introduced them to Arnold's brother-in-law... or maybe told them something else entirely. Gilda might be telling each of us something different so that as the plot unfolded, we heard a different story.

I considered asking if either of them had been up and about in the night, but instinct kept me quiet until Gilda swept back towards us with a frost-rimmed glass filled to the brim with red liquid.

"Of course," she said, settling into her chair and pausing to sip from a jaunty straw. "Frank Ricci didn't go anywhere near the police evidence room."

⌒〜⌒

Frank knelt in the cold basement of his apartment building, a flashlight on the floor providing the only light. The pile of junk concealing the trap door to his floor safe was rigged on a hidden pulley and square of plywood so that he could swing it out of the way with ease if he needed to get to the safe in the hurry.

He was fighting not to laugh out loud and had forced himself not to skip away from his car when he parked it at the curb. Two hundred grand would take care of his problems with the bent nose crowd and set him up for a big win.

He was humming "We're in the Money" as he turned the combination lock and lifted the safe door, waving away dust. The cupboard was bare, so to speak, and he popped the locks on the first briefcase to start piling in stacks of crisp bills without further ado.

"Hah!" He lost control of his mirth at last when he realized that he had so much money, he couldn't fit it all into the safe. "Mattress it is." He thundered up the stairs until he reached the third floor, pushed past the racks of dresses cluttering the hall (the lady in 3B stole from her job at a department store) and banged through the door of his apartment, breathing hard and sweating bullets but smiling like a kid at the circus.

The phone was waiting for him.

"I've got a bellyache," he told the receptionist at precinct. "I've got your money," he told Lou the Florist. He hung up after a few more calls to tie up loose ends and changed into a fresh shirt and red suspenders before tromping down the sidewalk to push his way through the door of Conte's Corner Club. "Scotch, gimme the good stuff." Enjoying the way heads turned as he bellied up to the bar.

Frank was the kind of man who could never lose his gut, no matter how hard he exercised. He always sported a five o'clock shadow, even when he shaved twice a day. To say he wasn't used to female attention was an understatement. When the blonde cozied up on his right side, he bought her a champagne cocktail. When the brunette sidled up on his left, he bought her a kir royale. When they dragged him over to Charlie Bianchi's table he bought a round and put ten thousand smackeroos on Red Rooster to win, place or show.

"A pitcher, a pitcher, my kingdom for another pitcher of Bloody Marys," Gilda said, sliding back in her chair and curling her feet beneath her.

Wilma stood and smoothed her skirt with the flat of her hand. "I have to powder my nose." Beads of sweat were carving lines through the makeup on her face.

As she walked away I imagined how a pencil skirt was supposed to fit a woman. All Wilma could give it were hip bones, never mind the seam down the back of her stockings.

"You should'a known her back in the day," Marie said, reading my mind. "See that rock on her hand? Big enough to pitch in a major league game."

"Four different guys gave her a buzzer like that," Gilda added.

"Were you ever married?"

"Not even this much." Gilda held her finger and thumb a centimeter apart.

Marie tapped my arm, bracelets rattling like knucklebones. "You're the only one still rosy cheeked after last night," she said. "Be a doll?"

"For fuck's sake," I pushed out of my chair hard enough that it screeched back. I cut a weaving path across the lobby towards the bar as they chuckled behind me and Gilda said something about an interview opportunity with "the Prime Minister" in Rome.

Was that how it happened? Gilda tossed out leads as the women distracted each other to get the goods for themselves? Mother was never clear about how she had benefited from Gilda's largesse, just that our travel and homes and my schools wouldn't have happened without it.

I carried the empty pitcher to the dumbwaiter and placed it inside, giving the rope a tug. It descended into darkness. I leaned inside the black shaft and heard music drifting up from below.

Mam, singing alone in the underworld. "We're in the money, that sky is sunny…"

⌒

Frank woke up to the thunder of guns and promptly vomited. Fortunately, he had passed out alongside the toilet.

He moaned, holding his splitting skull together while his stomach did the Twist. Drums beat his brains to mush as he tried to piece the evening together.

He'd lost his shirt. Literally. His cheerful red suspenders were looped up over his white undershirt, the worse for a dark stain down the front. He remembered being at a table and that blonde, Mama Mia…

How much did he bet?

A second bout of retching put his face into the bowl, where the echo of his guts unspooling drowned out a fist on the door.

He leaned back and fetched his glasses from the toilet, groaning as he rinsed them in the sink.

This time he heard the knock and realized it had been going on for some time. Charlie Bianchi?

He crawled into the hallway until he could stand on unsteady feet in his slippery socks. The windows showed night and streetlights outside and he had no idea of the hour. He stuck his head out into a cold wind but didn't see any hard guys in long coats and fedoras milling about on the sidewalk.

The door rattled.

He had no idea where his revolver was, lost along with his shirt and shoes. So he snatched a baseball bat from the hall closet and made his way to the door, one hand trying to hold his unruly guts in place.

"Who is it?" He placed a hand against the first of three deadbolts and tried not to sound like a corpse. "Who's there!?!"

"Mr. Ricci?"

Even muffled by the door the voice was trim and small, officious even. He couldn't imagine any of Bianchi's goons sounding like that.

"I wanna know who's knocking on my goddamned door!" More cop in it this time. He sure wished he had his gun.

"I have something for you, sir."

Frank looked through the peephole and threw back the deadbolts. He opened his door and saw a little man with a neat mustache, leaning on a cane. Behind him was a hallway filled with clothing racks and nothing more.

"You alone?" Frank barked.

"Of course, may I come in?"

"No so fast." Frank jabbed the end of his bat at the man's belly. "Open up that raincoat."

The man leaned his cane against a wall and did as asked, struggling to undo the belt with one hand, his other occupied with a briefcase.

Holy shit, Frank thought.

The little man made like a bashful flasher and opened his coat one side at a time.

"C'mon in, friend." Frank smiled.

The man closed the door behind him before holding out the briefcase. "This is yours, Mr. Ricci."

"You sure?"

"Quite."

Frank took the case in his free hand and hefted it. Something inside clanked. "Heavy."

"Yes," the man said. "I wonder if you could do something for me?"

"When have I denied you anything?"

"Right." A tight smile showed the tips of small teeth. "Kindly take this," he produced a white envelope from a pocket. Already addressed. "Put a stamp on it and put it in a mailbox."

"That's it?"

"Why yes."

"Arnold never mentioned you asking him for any favors."

"Who?"

"Guy you was giving briefcases to before me."

The little man tipped his head to one side quizzically, in the manner of a dog. "The briefcases are for you. Only for you."

Frank frowned but plucked the envelope from the man's hand, careful to touch only the corner. He was thinking about fingerprints.

"Alright, I'll mail this thing."

The man nodded and showed the tips of his teeth again. Frank imagined him nibbling on a carrot.

"Good night." The man opened the door and stepped through, closing it behind him without another word. Frank could hear the tap of his cane and rustle of hangers as he brushed past the clothing racks.

"Chump." Frank leaned his considerable posterior against the door to make sure it shut and padded to his kitchen table, pushing aside a stack of newspapers to make room.

The briefcase locks popped open at his touch.

"Sweet Mary, mother of God."

The briefcase was piled with more sparklers than he'd ever seen in one place. A jewelry store without the velvet. Chokers and rings and earrings. Faceted emerald brooches and fat ruby necklaces. Strings of creamy pearls and shining pendants. There was a sapphire big enough to tip a mace, a hand mirror backed with silver, ivory trinkets and gold enough to make a pirate blush. He undid the drawstring on a tiny leather bag and a galaxy of diamonds spilled across his palm.

Frank dragged a chair across the scratched linoleum and sat down, air whooshing out of him.

His problems were over.

⌒

Storms painted the afternoon black and the old plantation shook with thunder. Gilda dozed in a hammock on the terrace, oblivious to the fury raging only feet away. Lightning slapped the vision from my eyes and I shook my head at afterimages of Gilda outlined against the conflagration, as if great forces fought for her attention.

Another enormous spider web waved and shook against the beams over the hammock and with my vision dazzled by lightning it was easy to think that the webbing and hammock were one great construction spun by the old storyteller herself.

I left her on the terrace and headed back inside, tracking wet prints across the lobby and climbing the stairs on the balls of my feet. Lilting strains of Edith Piaf drifted from inside Marie's room and I glanced through the half open door to see the old woman asleep on top of the bedclothes, one shoe dangling from her toes, the other on the floor.

Her mouth was open as she snored, an aging hanger-on suffering from the booze. I slipped inside, unsure if my attentions would be welcome, but I couldn't leave the shoe dangling from her toes like that. I pulled it off as gently as I could and bent to place it beside its mate.

The French doors were closed against the storm and the room smelled of powders and age. Flowers drooped in a vase and added the cloying perfume of their corruption.

Did I want this, sucking at the gilded teat? Did I really want what WILDS had to offer?

Piaf crooned from the large metal flower of an old fashioned phonograph and I approached, entranced by the scratchy perfection of the music. When the music ended I lifted the needle and returned it to the first song, hoping to lengthen Marie's rest if I could.

Closing her door behind me quietly, I made my way down the hall until I reached what I believed to be Hysteria's room. I raised a hand and hesitated, worried about Wilma's acid tongue if I knocked on the wrong door.

In the end it was the sense of emptiness in the room beyond that convinced me to rap my knuckles against the wood.

The knob turned beneath my hand. "Hysteria?"

My answer was silence.

I felt around for the wall switch and turned on a light. The room was empty. The bed was made and the floors swept as if no one had stayed there at all. The adjoining bathroom smelled of bleach and there was no sign of dampness in the bath or sink.

Hysteria was gone. Just gone.

I had just left her room and closed the door behind me when the hall plunged into darkness.

⌇

The lights were out across the entire plantation.

In my darkened room, even the walls were sweating. I opened the French doors and the wind howled inside, scattering papers. I closed the doors and choked on my own perspiration.

Lightning slashed across the lagoon.

The note was folded over twice and tucked into my pack of Viceroys. TAKE THE MOPED IN THE GARAGE AND LEAVE.

In the storm? I'd bog down before I lost sight of the hotel. Lightning would knock me out of the saddle like a sniper's bullet.

I shook the cellophane wrapped package and a metal key tumbled out onto the vanity.

Leave. Sure. And let the jackals take my turn?

I ran a cool bath by the light of perfumed candles, hoping the storm would let up before they burned down. I found my pistol by feel and carried it with me to the tub, wrapping it in an unused wash cloth to keep it dry as I placed it on the soap dish.

A sigh escaped when I slid into the cool embrace of the water. I decided to drink less when we gathered next, no matter how much hooch the old broads sucked down. Maybe I'd introduce them to the modern wonders of coffee.

I lit a joint hoping to relax.

I dozed.

A spindly black leg quested up over the side of the tub, followed by a second. They waved about, tapping gently, relaying information to something below, as yet out of sight.

How big was the owner of those legs? It was silent, this intruder. The only sound was the beat of my heart.

Thud-thud.

The legs were spiny with hairs. Waving and finding purchase. Another leg grabbed hold. Another.

Thud-thud.

A large spider pulled its bulk onto the edge of the tub to regard me.

Eight eyes, dancing with orange candlelight. Eight sprawly legs thick with fur, rippling with constant movement. A body the size of a rat's with coarse brown hair like the threads on a coconut. Its abdomen was bloated and larger than my fist.

Thud-thud.

Something whistled between my teeth and I was unable to scream.

The joint tumbled from my lips and the shock of the smoldering tip striking my breast galvanized me into action. A shriek of abject terror ripped itself free, scoring a bloody passage up my throat to explode into the world.

19

I pushed back as I flailed for the pistol on the soap dish and batted it into the water. My heels slipped and my head dunked below the surface. I slid towards the spider and panic undid me.

The shadows outside my door took swirling form and my heartbeat became the crash of feet as someone rushed into the bathroom, swinging a shoe like a hammer to impale the spider with a stiletto heel. The creature cracked and wriggled as it was lifted, spiked through and spurting thick fluids. The legs scratched and flailed but couldn't reach back to the human who'd done it in.

I was pressed into the corner, half out of the tub, muscles locked with terror. My rescuer was between me and the candles by the sink so that I was unable to make out any details. I moaned in horror, as close to swooning as I'd ever been in my life.

My rescuer took the thing away and I heard the wail of the storm as the French doors were opened. They banged shut a moment later.

When she limped back inside, Wilma bent to remove her remaining stiletto pump and leaned her lanky frame against the doorway.

"You owe me a shoe."

I sank into the water and wept.

⌣

Night fell without moon or lightning to reveal our path and the power was still out. Though the fireworks were over, the rain continued, unrelenting.

I lit my last candle and dried the MAB Model A with fresh towels, ejecting the magazine and popping the shiny bullets free with my thumb. Each one received attention before it was pressed back into the spring loaded magazine. Movies told me I should take the pistol itself apart and dry it piece by piece, but I didn't know how.

I hoped it would fire if I needed it.

Following the small flame of my candle, I entered the gloomy hall and heard nothing over the drumming of rain against the roof. I knocked on Marie's door. "Marie?" I knocked again. "It's Claude."

Her door was unlocked and I pushed it open. I held the candle over the bed and saw that it had been made since my last visit and that Marie was no longer in it. Nor were her shoes beside the bed where I had placed them.

"Hello?" There were no suitcases in the room and the Edith Piaf record had been taken from the antique phonograph. I crossed to her bathroom but found it empty. My nose stung from the heavy application of bleach and I knew that Mam had erased her presence.

Back in the hall I touched the pocket on my cut off shorts to make sure I had the key to the moped. Assuming there really was a moped. Up until I found the note, I hadn't realized there was a garage.

The soles of my feet squeaked on the stairs and the candle flame bent over with a flicker. I paused, shielding the tiny fire with my hand until it had recovered, careful not to snuff it out with my breath. It occurred to me that the candle wasn't much help, but would make me a wonderful target. I remembered the rifle shot in the jungle. Our location gave new meaning to the word remote.

There were two sources of light in the lobby bar, a line of candles along the bar itself, and another cluster creating a soft glow around our usual table in the middle of the airy space.

I followed my nose towards the orange flare of a cigarette hovering in the shadows near white curtains. The sound of the rain grew louder as I approached. The sense of wet fresher. The doors were open beyond the curtains but the cloth itself was sodden with moisture and hung dead without a breeze to give it life.

"Where's Marie?" I asked.

"Resting her liver." Wilma stared out at the rain.

"Where's Hysteria?"

"Maybe she went for a walk."

"In this?"

"Maybe she needed a shower."

"With her suitcases?"

"I need a drink." Wilma's heels tocked across the wooden floor as she headed for the bar where ten whiskey sours were lined up in ranks with a bowl of ice cubes for those so inclined.

"And then there were two," Wilma lifted a candle and lit a fresh cigarette, posing. Rumor had it that Andy Warhol once exhibited her nudes.

"Is it always like this?" I pulled out a stool and gave it purpose.

"It's always the same."

"How?"

"It's always different." Wilma sat, crossing one long leg over the other, her hair done up in a chignon, her lashes thick with mascara. She had a face built for the dance of candlelight and shadow, and I believed the bit about Warhol.

I knocked back a whiskey without benefit of ice. My throat burned and my eyes watered as I plunked the glass on the polished bar.

"Did you leave me a note?"

She plucked a single ice cube from the bowl and placed it in a glass, allowing the liquor to cool. "What did it say?"

I grabbed a fistful of ice and plunked it into another glass, splashing the bar.

I sipped. "What happened to Frank?" I asked, coughing into a fist.

Wilma blinked like a big cat on a tree branch. "You know what happened to Frank."

"Do I?"

"Don't play cute. You don't have the tits for cute."

"Thanks for noticing."

We smoldered and drank and when I opened my mouth to ask, Wilma already had a cigarette for me. I stuck it between my lips and leaned over to light it from a candle as she held back my hair.

21

"Ava was a good friend," Wilma said.

I let the smoke trickle from the corners of my mouth. "She said the same about you."

She laughed. "No she didn't, she said I was a bitch." Long lashes lowered in a blink. "She was right. But she was still my friend."

We clinked glasses and Wilma poured a little on the floor along with a flow of Gaelic. "Ar dheis Dé go raibh a anam."

"Godspeed," I added, studying the glowing cherry of my cigarette. "Where's Gilda?"

Wilma looked around the big, gloomy space. "Writing the end of the story."

"I thought the story had to be true."

Wilma stubbed out her cigarette. "It will be."

I tipped my head to listen to something just below audibility, a sense of whispering ghosts. It grew louder but remained undefined as I approached the open shaft of the dumb waiter.

"I think she's down there," I said. "Someone is talking. A woman."

Wilma picked up two glasses. "Let's go down."

And just like that, it clicked. They will test you, mother had told me. The power outage, the spider, the disappearing women, Wilma playing at friends and now voices in the basement.

The ancient bitches were hazing me.

"Where's the cellar door?" I asked.

Wilma nodded her head at the bar. "Grab some glasses, she'll want you to give her something."

"Me?"

Wilma paused in the doorway. "Your turn is coming up."

~——⁔

We made our way by the fickle glow of my single candle, and I carried a whiskey sour in my free hand. I'd written a series of investigative pieces on Los Angeles gangs and even witnessed a young member being "jumped in"—violently assaulted by a group to see if he had courage. Whatever these women had in store for me, it wouldn't be as bad as that and I was determined to show them that I had the grit to be a part of it.

If the price of entry into the Whiskey and Ink Ladies Drinking Society was humiliation, and my pride the coin, I would pay it willingly.

I wanted what these women had while I was young enough to enjoy it.

A dead neon sign reading SORTIE hung over a door behind the bar and we discovered a dingy service corridor leading to another, unmarked door.

The candle flame wavered when we opened the door and a putrescent stink wafted forth. It was the stench of a root cellar where the jars have broken, their contents rotting in the dark.

"Gilda always liked atmosphere," Wilma muttered.

I went first with the candle, Wilma making a precarious descent in her heels behind me. The stairs were slick stone, unlike the rest of the hotel, and Wilma said that the cellar had been built with soft limestone mined from a local quarry. Stone that seemed to melt in the flow of water from the storm above, the walls giving the appearance of drowning in sweat like the heaving ribs of an overworked racehorse.

I stepped down and stopped in shock. The basement was flooded with several inches of rainwater and the floor was greasy beneath it. My small light did nothing to reveal the space and I looked up at Wilma as if she would tell me it wasn't worth it.

"Well?" she challenged.

I splashed forward without responding and with no sense of direction, straining to hear past the gurgle of the flood. "This is fucking ridiculous." I wished I had shoes or a sense of reference. Every splash of my feet kicked up the stink of corruption.

Wilma was behind me. Behind her was only blackness. The stairs had been consumed by the dark.

Thick, amniotic liquid dripped from the ceiling overhead and I told myself it was only rain, though it made my skin crawl. I bent my march to the right, thinking to find a wall and work my way along it. So far there had been no other occupant of the basement. No old furniture or building materials. No rusting file cabinets or china cabinets with broken glass. When substance swam out of the darkness ahead of me I increased my speed, kicking up a filthy spray in my eagerness to be tethered to something. Anything.

I stopped short when I saw the wall.

The great limestone blocks were covered in a network of webs, stretching away from my weak light in either direction. Individual strands were as thick as ropes, hairy with fraying. It was the work of a thousand spiders over a thousand years. They rippled with movement from the dripping water and I remembered the spider crouched on the edge of my tub. "Jesus."

My sweat turned to ice water.

"In some of the villages they harvest and eat them."

I glared at Wilma. "When are you guys gonna spring it?"

"What?"

"Whatever the plan is."

Wilma shrugged her shoulders, careful not to spill the cocktails. "I don't know about any plan, but I think the voices are that way." She nodded to her left. I flinched at a drip on my shoulder, waiting for the touch of a long, hairy leg.

We splashed through the dark until I was sure we had moved beyond the boundaries of the hotel. How big was this place? I tried to imagine what purpose was served by this subterranean expanse. Storage? Smuggling? A light derailed my musings and I aimed towards it.

"...Frank found out that each delivery came with some kind of price, a small task usually. A drink. Use of the bathroom." Gilda's voice scratched through the wet splatter. "But on the fifth visit, he learned that the price was higher than he wanted to pay."

I blinked against the glare and made out a row of four chairs up ahead, the world's smallest underground theater. Marie and Hysteria occupied the middle two chairs and had their backs to me. They ignored our splashing approach, riveted on the performance before them. As always, they focused entirely on Gilda.

I squinted at the light bleeding past the audience, unable to see whatever stage Gilda had erected. It was if the footlights were aimed outward to blind the audience rather than illuminate the performer.

Cheap trick, Gilda. Cheap but effective.

"Frank needed the money by that point," Gilda continued. "Needed it like a junkie needs the needle and he did what the little man asked. He put a shovel in his car and drove up to New Hampshire, to a small graveyard he knew all too well. He found his sister's humble gravestone hidden in tall grass, and worked in his fat man's undershirt by the light of the moon until he was drenched in sweat.

"The grave was shallower than the six feet the funeral home had promised, but that was alright by Frank, sweating and heaving for breath as he scraped away the last of the dirt from atop the casket. A couple of hard stabs from his shovel broke the clasps and he tossed the shovel out of the hole, guts all atwist, but doing what he needed to do to get the next briefcase.

"He stole his sister's mummified remains, stuffing the rags and bones into a double-strength trash bag brought for just that purpose. They went into the trunk of his car along with the shovel before he headed out on well-known roads toward Arnold Didion's property. He drove with his headlights off and parked half a mile away, carrying the trash bag through the bramble until he reached the Didion property and found the well in back.

"Frank worked quietly at prying up the wooden cover and set it aside gently, one eye cocked on the house for any sign of a light snapping on behind a window."

"'Dump the remains in the well and you're done,' the little man with the mustache had instructed and Frank did just that, sick to death at what he was doing but more sickened at the thought of an end to the briefcases.

"He left and wept and drank himself to sleep when he returned home, not even the sight of a new load of jewelry able to rouse him from his funk.

"Arnold Didion woke up the next morning none the wiser and set about his morning ritual, but he tasted something funny when he brushed his teeth and noticed it again in his morning coffee. He called the man who had drilled his well, and the fella came out with his gear to inspect it. The inspector's dip line brought up human bones."

I churned towards the makeshift theater with no effort to be quiet but stopped when Gilda talked through the commotion. Wilma put a hand on my shoulder.

"...break down and had to be taken to the hospital. The call was picked up by a local reporter on his police scanner, who remembered a crackpot letter he'd received some months ago without a return address. That letter had accused a local widower named Didion of heinous desecrations. Grave robbing. Necrophilia. When the reporter, name of Cormier, informed the police, the story blew through town like wildfire in dry brush. Before long everyone knew the local law was interrogating Arnold Didion for defiling his wife's corpse."

Neither Marie nor Hysteria bothered to acknowledge my appearance as I moved alongside them, holding my hand up to shield my eyes from the painful glare. Blinking away red suns, I made out a single flashlight resting on a crate, aimed right at us. Gilda's voice echoed from the dark beyond the ray of illumination, but I could hear a smile when she continued.

"When that story broke, so did Arnold Didion, and he hanged himself from a cross beam in his living room, the same room where he opened that first briefcase."

I refused to sit in the chair waiting for me, or to even look at the other women.

"How the hell do you know all this?"

Wilma sat quietly in the empty chair at the far end of the row as Gilda spoke.

"I picked the story up off the wire and thought I had my hands on a New England gothic. The kind that would land me in Esquire with all the thunder of Truman Capote," Gilda continued. "In a story like that, you look for interesting characters. It didn't take long for me to find brother Frank Ricci and put in a call. Turns out ol' Frank didn't want to commiserate… one could understand… so I paid him a visit at his apartment. I was the one who found him, dressed in a new suit with shiny new suspenders sitting on the couch with his gun in his lap. Coroner said he'd put the gun in his mouth before pulling the trigger and the .38 round blew off the back of his head."

"Tah dah!" I stepped forward through the light and put her cocktail on the crate, taking the flashlight in trade. "Damn good story, Gilda." I played the flashlight in an arc past the crate. "Why'd you wait 'til now to spill the beans?"

The storyteller was nowhere to be seen.

"Gilda?" I called out.

There was nothing beyond the crate but another crate standing in the rising water like a wooden island. "Gilda?" I saw a boxy object with a red LED light atop the crate. "Hey, it's a tape recorder."

Wilma shrieked. "Oh my God!"

I spun and Wilma jittered through the beam of my light, splashing away from the chairs with a keening wail.

This is it. This is the gag.

Movement caught my eye and I swung my light over to the chairs where Marie leaned forward as if to rise.

"Okay Mar—"

The words stuck in my throat.

Marie had no face!

"Holy shit!" I stumbled backwards and sat hard on the wooden crate.

She bent as if to follow—

—and toppled forward into the flood.

The light shivered and shook as I waited for her to push up out of the water, but she remained on her belly, muumuu fluttering around her in the agitated flood.

Terror glued my tongue in place as I aimed the flashlight at Hysteria, who stayed still through the ruckus. It was her, I was sure of it, but I couldn't make out a single feature on her face. I brought the flashlight towards her with tentative steps.

I made out the familiar bump of her nose and the glimmer of her eyes, but a low moan leaked from my lips when I realized why I couldn't see more.

A spider web. Skeins of webbing stretched from her chin up over her entire face and hair to hide her features like a woman's veil. As if the spider had crawled around and around to wrap her head entirely.

My knees went weak and I sagged, the moan rising into a desperate whistle of air.

A nightmare stretched its legs up from behind the old woman's shoulder.

First one, then another. Black and spiny with whiskers. I was in the tub again, frozen with fear as it pulled its bloated abdomen across her shoulder to sit beside her face, pulsing on its long legs as if preparing to spring across the distance.

"Claude, run!" Wilma screamed.

I heard the sound of bodies colliding and swung the flashlight around. Wilma was struggling with an unknown assailant. They fell out of the light and I heard a splash followed by a terrible sound. A butcher's sound.

Wilma's shriek was abruptly cut off.

I circled away from the spider's feast and pinned Wilma's killer with my light. "Stand up, you sonofabitch," I shouted.

She looked away from the blinding light and I saw her cruelly amputated ear. "Gilda!"

Her head whipped towards me and her pupils shrank inside eyes bulging with malice.

Even then I didn't understand.

"Where's Mam?" I spun, casting the light around for her servant. "Where is he?"

"Mam?" Her laughter drew my light like a magnet. "He's with the loot, doll, for there lies the Fourth Circle of Hell."

"What?" I continued angling to my left, feet sliding across the slippery floor.

"He is lame of foot," Gilda said. "Yet winged, for he is slow to arrive but quick to depart."

"What the hell are you talking about?"

"You kids have no grounding in the classics." Gilda bent to tug a machete from Wilma's corpse. "The price is okay at first, but eventually it gets bigger than you want to pay."

"You're telling me this is really happening." My head swam. "You have the briefcase."

"Cases," she emphasized the plural and sloshed towards me, linen blouse and pants hanging heavily against her body. "At this point I can't let them stop. I can't."

26

She pointed the heavy blade at me. "When he said the price was my best friends, I figured you owed me, don't you think, Ava?"

Lips peeled back from long teeth and her face narrowed. I grappled with the idea that she was insane. She didn't know who I was or what she was doing.

"C'mere, girlie," she hissed. "I want to whisper in your ear."

I tugged the gun from the back of my waistband and shot her. The bullet punched her in the shoulder and she rocked, a dark spurt of fluid arcing out from the wound. She opened her mouth to speak so I shot her again and she sat down with a splash.

"I'm sick of your goddamned voice," I said, taking two steps forward. I pulled the trigger and missed. She laughed and my forth bullet drilled a third eye in her forehead.

She flopped back into the water and that was the end of Gilda. Roll credits.

＿〜＿

I sat in the gentle caress of candlelight and waited for the rain to stop. While I waited, I got drunk.

After Wilma and I had depleted the earlier battalion of cocktails on the bar, Mam must have replenished their ranks. How, I didn't know, because the dumbwaiter didn't lead to a kitchen, but to what I half believed was a portal or place or even the Fourth Circle of Hell itself. I resolved in a drunken fashion to read Dante, though I didn't expect to like it.

I ejected the MAB's magazine and checked my ammunition status. One bullet remaining. I opined that fortifying the bar was as wise as fortifying my spirit with spirits, and carried a stool down the narrow service hall to wedge beneath the knob of the door that led below. I wedged another stool against the door marked SORTIE, because exits had a terrible way of becoming entrances and I was in no mood.

I chased a room temperature whiskey sour with cool water from the melted bowl of ice and noticed that I could see myself in the mirror, wild haired and bug eyed. Light was drifting in through the windows.

I had made it to the dawn.

When the rain ended I celebrated with another cocktail for breakfast, and it struck me that such a fine hotel should have better service. My old friend the rope who wanted to be a snake was amenable to several tugs, and I shouted into the dumbwaiter. "I want shrimp and noodles! And bring me juice!"

I hipped my way up onto a stool and grabbed the bar before I could topple over, grinning like an idiot as the whiskey had its way with me. "Whiskey and Ink Ladies Drinking Society." I spat a gob of 80 proof saliva on the floor.

Thud-thud.

Mam was limping towards me with the help of a single crutch. He wore the faded clothes of a local villager but I recognized the trim mustache and the bad comb-over. It made sense that he would dress for the location. Thailand was no place for a trench coat.

"Claudine Wood?" He showed small teeth in a smile. I could see him sitting among the monkeys of the jungle, nibbling fruit with those teeth.

"Call me Claude." I straightened up on the barstool.

His eyes narrowed. "But you are Claudine?"

"Yeah, yeah, Claude is just my nickname."

"Excellent!" He lifted a briefcase from his side. "This is yours."

I took the briefcase and the weight jerked my arm towards the wooden floor. "Thank you."

As he turned away I asked, "Nothing you want from me?"

Another tight smile. "Nothing else."

I imagined the briefcase filled with my brunch order and stifled a laugh as my thumbs found the brass catches. When the lid sprang up my breath whooshed out and my jaw dropped open.

I couldn't eat it for breakfast.

But I was set for life.

AFTERWORD

Writing "Gilda" was enormously enjoyable, in part because I had to step out of my usual process to do so. Normally I discover the beginning of an idea (Say... Why does a sunset mimic the colors of a bruise?) and mull it over for a period of time until some inner claxon sounds and demands that I start writing. But this story was written by invitation with a tight deadline. After saying, "Yes!" I worried about crafting a piece that would be worthy of standing alongside the other stories in the book. It also presented a challenge with regard to the particular sin that fell to me, avarice. At first I thought that it wasn't an idea I've dwelled on (unlike wrath or gluttony) and I was struggling to get a handle on it, until I realized the protagonist already existed in my own history. Lo and behold, Claude was born. A young woman willing to pursue financial and career success with an unhealthy level of vigor, much as I was in my 20's when I moved to Los Angeles. The name itself was drawn from a co-worker at my very first job in L.A. as a nod to the desperation of those years.

A different kind of fortune struck at that moment, as two ideas found each other in the murk of my subconscious. Like most writers, I'm continuously generating the fragments of story ideas, many of which go nowhere. One such idea was originally called "Diner's Club," about a group of storytellers with a particular fetish, an all female take on Peter Straub's Chowder Society, if you will. But I was never able to develop a strong enough central hook for what I imagined as this rather vicious group of old women gathering in an exotic locale to swap tales. As soon as this fragment of an idea bumped into the concept of avarice, lightning struck and the bones of the entire story laid themselves out for me.

Once I had the characters and structure, I needed the embellishments, the details that would lift this story up and set it apart, and research into the notions of avarice and representations in literature turned up a treasure trove of material, some of which became the mysterious servant Mam...which is short for Mammon, and the references to Hell that came from Dante. The noir tone was natural for a story about people putting themselves in jeopardy because of their own terrible decisions, and helped me position Claude as both hero and anti-hero.

I hope you enjoyed reading "Gilda" as much as I enjoyed writing it and remember, if someone knocks on your door with a briefcase full of money, don't take it!

WRATH

A SHORT MADNESS

by Bracken MacLeod

"*It is difficult to fight against anger; for a man will buy revenge with his soul.*"
— Heraclitus

Anger is a short madness.
— Horace

PROLOGUE:

I say, "This is my confession. I repent and ask for absolution."

PART I: RECONCILIATION

WEDNESDAY

I stepped into the small, stuffy room and closed the door behind me. I tugged at my collar, trying to loosen it a little. It was likely no one would be seeing me for the next two hours, but I couldn't take it off. I walked around the screen and took my seat, flipping the switch on the wall that lit the green light outside the door, letting my parishioners know I was ready to receive their confessions. Ready. Though it was time, I never felt *ready*.

Other priests I knew felt enlivened by reconciliation. One told me that he saw it as evidence people were trying; they were seeking the grace of God and hadn't given up on their faith. Another said it gave him humility. Listening to people own up to their feelings of spiritual inadequacy reminded him of the work he needed to do to resist his own sinful nature. But what was a gift for others felt like a burden to me. No feelings of grace or humility kindled in my heart when I heard people lay themselves bare. Instead, those admissions felt like a burden. Just walking into the confessional reminded me of Giles Corey asking for more weight. Eventually, he knew the stones would crush him, but his conscience gave him no choice but to bear them. And the weight of these confessions grew heavier and heavier still, until I felt pressed nearly to death.

Someone entered the room. I waited to see if they'd walk around the screen to sit in the chair opposite mine, making their contrition face to face. When I heard the creak of the kneeling rail, I leaned back and settled in to listen blindly instead. Few people ever chose the chair over the rail. Anonymity was merely a mutually agreed upon illusion, though. I recognized all of my regular parishioners' voices. I recognized them by their transgressions and anxieties *outside* of the Confessional as well.

I was jealous of my wife's accomplishments at work. I diminished them in front of her to make me feel better.

I had impure thoughts; I imagined making love to my neighbor while I masturbated.

I went a month without visiting my mother in the rest home. When I finally went, I resented her for being there.

I despair of God's mercy. I doubt that He will ever forgive me.

I took a breath and began the ritual. "May the mercy of God touch your heart, so you may know your sins and have the courage to confess them."

Margaret Fleming, kneeling on the other side of the screen said, "Bless me, Father, for I have sinned. My last confession was about three months ago. Last week, somebody was walking in the street and it was slowing down traffic a bunch. I was so mad, I yelled out my window at him." She hastily added, "I'm sorry for this sin and all the sins of my past life. I repent and ask for absolution."

I knew there was something else she wasn't telling me. Something that made *this* the sin she wanted absolution for. But, I gave her the benefit of the doubt and didn't press. "We all get angry sometimes. It's natural."

"I... I called him the enword, Father Price. The effword enword."

A lawyer friend of mine (not a Catholic) confided in me once over a glass of whiskey that he only ever got to see people at their worst. Even when they were doing something constructive like buying a house or starting a new business, they still behaved badly because of the stress involved. He'd said that it had to be refreshing getting to see people who were trying to get into Heaven. There *was* a sort of truth there. I saw them laugh and dance at weddings, and weep and comfort each other at funerals. But then, at confession, I heard them at their worst. Their very worst. They admitted to being full of anger toward their friends and resentful of their parents. Breaking vows of marriage and professional honesty. They told me about stealing and fighting and fucking their neighbors' husbands. About abusing their children. It frightened me that they sometimes said the things they did with

31

such calmness in their voices. And then they asked me for forgiveness, knowing that in most cases I couldn't refuse to give it. They accepted that *God's* forgiveness was unlimited, but it was me they wanted to hear it from, since I was God's instrument. That was my other conscious illusion. I granted them God's absolution, though I hadn't believed in any god for a very long time. They walked out of this room feeling reconciled with their Creator, as though their souls were clean, but I knew nothing had really changed. They were still the same lying, cheating people they were when they walked in with heavy conscience. And I'd see them again, because if there was one thing I absolutely still believed from Catholic doctrine, it was that we all fall short of perfection.

I was glad that Margaret had chosen the rail instead of the seat after all. In years of sitting in a confessional, I'd heard all manner of sins, venial and mortal, and I was rarely surprised, but I hadn't expected this from *her*. I'd thought better of Margaret; she'd seemed truly nice. She *was* nice, and very often even kind as well. She made cookies and brownies for parish bake sales and donated hand-me-downs to the winter coat drive. She put money in the collection box and she said her prayers. But deep in the core of her, there was something cruel and bigoted. Her mother, Gloria, still complained about "forced bussing" in the Nineteen Seventies—that is, school desegregation. There seemed to be a piece of her in Margaret. If there was any glimmer of hope, at least she recognized that she'd done something wrong.

I said, "If you're ever looking for examples of wrath, look at traffic. We are so easily vicious behind the wheel. Did you try to make amends?"

"No. Of course not. I don't know who he is. He was just some... guy walking in the street." Her voice gained a hard edge. "I drove off. I had to pick up my kids. I'm not even sure he heard—"

"Have you made amends some other way?"

"What? I've prayed for forgiveness. I said the act of contrition and made my confession, Father. What else?"

I took a breath. I wanted to recommend that she volunteer somewhere she could serve people who might have once been hurt by the kind of word she'd said. Something to help her to get a perspective outside of her insular, white suburban community. But then, I knew how my congregation talked about me. The *liberal* priest from the city—a bleeding heart.

"I want you to read a book."

"A book?"

"Yes. I want you to read *Kindred* by Octavia Butler. It's a good one, trust me."

"How is that going to—"

"Every time you see... *that word* in the novel—nigger—I want you to say an Our Father." She gasped as if she hadn't just confessed to saying it herself. Though I hated the word, I said it so she couldn't have the bloodless confession she wanted. She had to face what she said, instead of some sterilized euphemism—the "enword." I continued. "And if you ever repeat it again in anger—or *at all*, for that matter—I want you to re-read the book—the whole thing—and do the same. You can find it at the library if you don't want to buy it, but I encourage you to get your own copy." I didn't say because I knew if she did what I said, she'd be reading the book more than a couple of times. I didn't know if she liked science fiction, but I made a guess that the book would be more personally meaningful to her than *Invisible Man* or *The Fire Next Time*. I *hoped* it would be anyway. That was more important than the prayer. "That is your penance," I said.

"But..." she hesitated. Perhaps she caught the hard edge in my tone. For my first penitent of the day, she'd hit a nerve. "Yes, Father," she said. At that moment, I doubted she'd read the book. But I hoped she would.

"Now say the Act of Contrition." I listened as she did and then said, "Through the ministry of the Church, may God grant you pardon and peace. And... I absolve you of your sins, in the name of the Father, and of the Son, and of the Holy Spirit. Amen."

Through the screen, I could see her crossing herself before she got up to leave. She didn't say anything else. I wondered if she'd be all smiles the next time I saw her after Mass. I took a drink of water from the glass on the table next to me and waited for the next penitent to come in.

The door opened again and another parishioner knelt at the screen. "Forgive me, Father..."

Ugh. Tony Tremblay. It was going to be a long two hours.

⌁

I turned off the green light and drained the last trickle of water from my glass. Though I'd taken a break an hour earlier to go to the bathroom, I'd "broken the seal" as my lawyer friend put it, and had to go again. I walked around the screen divider and left the confessional, almost running into a boy standing right outside the door. I recognized him, though he wasn't a regular church goer. *What's his name?* I thought. *Adam, Andrew, Alex... Aidan! His name is Aidan. Aidan Flynn.* He looked scared at first, and then guilty. He turned quickly and started to walk away.

"Hey, Aidan. Can I help you?" I tried to sound welcoming and nonchalant.

The kid froze. His ears flushed red and his shoulders hunched up, like he'd been caught out doing something he shouldn't.

"Uh, no. Huh uh." He took a hesitant step away. I thought if he managed to take another, he'd build up enough momentum to break the spell of whatever had compelled him to come this far in the first place. I'd seen kids who wanted to come to confession, but had trouble working up the will. No one wanted to admit to their sins. Least of all young teenagers like him, already struggling with doubts about personal worth that teachings about Original Sin planted like bitter seeds in fertile soil. I remembered being a boy, and how hot shame burned—how hard it was to work up the nerve to verbalize my slights, while imagining the most vivid torments of Hell. I could almost imagine this kid waiting in the pews, trying not to be seen until everyone else had gone and it was his turn to walk through the door, all the while, screwing up his courage to stand exposed before the judgment of

Almighty God. And then, the time had passed. If he was like I'd been, he'd spend the next week agonizing over his unreconciled sin, afraid of being hit by a bus or some other freak accident that would send him directly to divine judgment. If he wasn't like me, maybe it wasn't that bad. But then, he was the *only* teenager who'd shown up that day.

"Aw, shit," I said, knowing the unexpected profanity would grab the boy's attention. I patted my pockets. "I think I left my iPhone in there. Sorry, I gotta go find it. Bishop'll hang my skin on the wall if they have to buy me another. See you later." Despite the urgings of my bladder, I reentered the confessional. The door clicked shut behind me and I walked around the barrier and turned on the green light. After a moment, I heard the click of the door latch. It clacked shut again and though I hadn't heard any footsteps, the kneeler creaked slightly under the boy's weight. I flipped the switch that turned the light outside from green to red and said, "May the mercy of God touch your heart, so you may know your sins and have the courage to confess them."

Aidan stammered. "Uh, bless me father, for I have sinned. I guess, it's been, like... I don't know how long since my last confession. I don't really do it much, you know."

"It's okay. You're here now," I said, and settled back to listen. Though confession weighed heavily on them, I found young people's sins slight and their remorse out of proportion to the seriousness of the offenses they admitted to. If there was any joy I took in reconciliation, it was telling a child they had nothing to worry about—that their souls were not tainted.

I waited to hear Aidan tell me that he'd back-talked his mother or shoplifted something. I did my best to project a sense of calm forgiving through the screen. "What do you want to tell me?"

"I have kind of a question first."

"Okay. I'm listening."

"Father Price, is it a sin to, like, keep a secret? Like a *big* secret?"

"It depends, I suppose. If someone trusted you with something very personal, and repeating it would hurt them or your friendship, then I don't think so. That's what I do here. People tell me things in confidence, and I respect their privacy and their trust in me. If I didn't, no one would ever come back and I would have failed at a very important part of my job."

"Yeah, but what if you're *not* a priest?"

"It's... complicated." I paused for a moment to collect my thoughts. "If someone was planning on hurting themselves, for instance, it might be a good thing to tell someone else who could help, if that person wasn't willing to seek it out on their own. If you know a person who needs help—someone who might hurt themselves or someone else—it's not a bad thing to try to prevent that from happening."

The boy took a deep breath. I waited. After a moment, Aidan said, "What if someone already got hurt, like really bad, and the secret is about who did it?"

"Well... that's different, isn't it?" My stomach knotted at the mention of secrets. I had once delighted in being the man my father couldn't be: a man people came to for comfort and spiritual nurturing. But my faith had *always* been delicate, like armor made of glass. I stepped into it, and though I could see right through it, I pretended it was thick enough, hard enough to hold me and keep me safe. And while cracks appeared throughout the years, it held. Right until The Boston Globe Spotlight reports shattered it, leaving me dressed in shards. I said, "If someone has asked you to keep a secret about something they've done that's illegal, that's not right, and it's not fair to you. I know it's difficult. But you can tell me, and together we can discuss what the right thing to do is."

"The Bible says to honor your parents, right?" He was taking the long way around to admitting what he'd done. I remained patient. We'd get there; I had to let him find the way.

"It does," I said. "That commandment *is* about obedience, but... it excludes immoral actions. It's a direction to be a good member of society and a good Christian; you don't have to be obedient to a parent or any other authority who is asking you to do something wrong. Does that make sense?"

"I don't know. Maybe."

I heard Aidan shift on the rail. It sounded like he might be getting up to leave. I wanted to spring up out of my seat and grab him, say he couldn't go until he confessed what had been done to him, and by whom. I wanted to know so *I* could do the right thing. So I didn't have to look in the child's face on Sunday and wonder if he was going to be all right, or if he was still in danger.

The boy blurted out, "I think my dad killed someone."

I stifled a cough. It wasn't what I'd thought—what I'd feared because it was what I'd been through. It was something else. I tried to relax, but my memories and my bladder had me perched on the edge of my chair. "I doubt it's as bad as that," I said.

The boy knelt quietly for another painfully long moment before saying, "You remember that lady and her kid on the news? The ones that got hit by the guy who didn't stop?"

I felt the bottom fall out of the room. Yes, I remembered them. I'd known Justine Neville.

I said, "They arrested someone for that. They caught the man who hit them." He had been an auto mechanic on the other side of town. Had a family—wife and three kids. People said he ran a good shop and didn't charge too much. But the talk about him changed once he was arrested. It got worse when they revealed he wasn't the man they knew. He'd said he'd moved to Ripton from New York, but in reality he was someone else from someplace else entirely, living under an assumed name. Paolo something. Paolo was sticking in my head. Not that it mattered.

"It wasn't that guy. It was my dad."

"How do you know?"

"I saw him washing his truck with the hose. He never washes his own truck. He always takes it to the car wash. And he was like *really* washing the front, but not the back so much. Like there was something on the whatdoyoucallit?"

"The grille," I whispered.

"Yeah, the grille. And the bumper. Then, when he saw it on the news, he freaked the fuck out... sorry, Father. He, like, *really* freaked out, you know? He went out and washed his truck again. Then, they arrested some other guy with the same kind of truck. I saw it on the news and it looks just like my dad's."

I remembered it wasn't long after the revelation about his immigration status that Paolo somehow "found" a loose piece of metal in his cell and sharpened it enough to slit his own throat. How hard would it be to cut your own throat? People slit their wrists all the time. But that didn't come with the uncontrollable panic of not being able to breathe. Blood was frightening. But if you got cut, you just slapped a bandage on it or went to the E.R. for stitches. A *throat*. How terrified would an innocent man have to be to do *that*? Of course, people would say he wasn't actually innocent. He was here illegally—he'd broken the law. But that wasn't running a mother and her child down in the street. And Aidan was saying he was innocent of *that*.

"I guess that means my dad killed *him* too, right?" the boy said, like he'd read my mind.

Finding the right thing to say was beyond me at that moment. I couldn't breathe.

Aidan started to cry.

I heard a sound in the room like someone else coming in with us. No one did of course; the red light was on. I tried to focus and tell Aidan it would be okay. But I didn't believe it. Nothing was okay.

PART II: REVELATION

SUNDAY

I waited at the bottom of the steps greeting the people who'd come to Mass as they filed out of church. Some paused to shake my hand and make small talk. A couple mentioned how much they enjoyed my homily, though I knew not all of them really meant it—it was just a thing they said. There were always some who didn't like it when I touched on social issues; they'd rather hear about how wonderful the next life was going to be, than how they had to work harder to make this one livable. They were usually the ones who avoided me after the service. That morning, I'd been preaching to one person in particular. Though I knew that hint-dropping wasn't going to make Rory Flynn jump out of his seat and run to confess what Aidan had said he'd done, still, I wanted to see even a hint of something in his face. Whether it was remorse or guilt, didn't matter as long as I could see him wrestling with what he'd done. But the elder Flynn's glib expression didn't change at all throughout my sermon. Not even when I read Proverbs 28:13 aloud. I'd practically shouted it like some Baptist revival tent preacher. "He who conceals his transgressions will not prosper, but he who confesses and forsakes them will obtain mercy." He didn't react at all. Not even to nod like the other fakers. People who came to Mass to satisfy their spouses or grandparents often pretended to listen while they thought of sports or errands that church was keeping them from. Like them, Flynn had that practiced look that seemed attentive while his mind was somewhere else, far away. Most of the time, that look didn't bother me; I understood. I wanted to see Flynn sweat. But the man hadn't felt even a little heat.

Maybe he'd been unmoved because he hadn't actually done anything. I reminded myself that I didn't actually have *proof*—only the suspicions of an imaginative boy who'd seen his father washing his truck. But I *believed* Aidan. Unlike me, he feared Hell; he believed that bearing false witness against his father could send him there. Aidan had no reason to lie, and every reason in Creation to tell the truth. He was worried for his soul. And that made Rory's inscrutability more frustrating. His son was right there, filled with anguish, and he didn't feel a damn thing. That made me want to climb down out of the ambo, grab his lapels, and shake him. That made me angry.

Another parishioner took my hand and quizzed me about the upcoming yard sale. Her children, two boys, bickered with each other, shouting and tugging at her in an attempt to get her to intervene in their disagreement. She ignored them while she suggested much more deserving charities than the ones earmarked for the proceeds of the sale. "You know, people will bring better items to sell if they thought that the money was going somewhere they can *see* it doing good." I tried to listen to what she had to say, but was losing patience. One of the kids shoved his brother and she grabbed his little arm and jerked it. The boy yelped and had to take a quick step to stay on his feet.

At that moment, Flynn came walking out of the doors, his wife and son trailing behind like an afterthought. He walked over to Rich Matthews and the two of them began laughing about something I couldn't hear. Only his obnoxious laughter carried. The swell of anger that had grown in me during the service came crashing down again.

"Are you listening to me? Father Price?"

I snapped back to the woman in front of me. She paled and took a step back. I wondered what my face looked like at that moment. I tried to soften my expression but wasn't sure I succeeded. My mind was clouded, though I remembered her last confession very well.

Sometimes I think about sending my kids to live with my ex. It's not that I want them to live with him—he's a terrible father—but I want them to push his new wife like they push me. I want her to feel as tired as I am.

"Yes, Karen. I hear you," I wanted to placate her, if only to shut her up, but had no interest in hearing who she'd rather donate the money raised at the yard sale to. I told her, "We've already let the recipient organizations know we'll be making a donation ahead of time. If you don't like them, perhaps you can take your boys to the park instead. I'm sure they'd love to have an afternoon with their mother's *full* attention." I looked at the children and added, "Wouldn't you? Perhaps a playdate with some friends from school. Wouldn't that be nice?" They immediately began barking names of kids that they'd like to play with at their mother, turning the idea of an intimate day in the park into a party. I ushered her away, giving the children the big smile I withheld from her. She walked off looking more than a little upset with me for putting the idea in her boy's minds.

I stared at Flynn and Matthews as they laughed loudly again. I wanted to go tell them to shut up. What I really wanted to say, was "Shut the *fuck* up." I wanted to shout in Rory's face about taking responsibility for the lives he'd ruined. But I couldn't.

I looked at Aidan staring quietly at his cell phone, waiting while his father socialized. He looked pale and shaken. While my sermon had no effect on the elder Flynn, it appeared to have badly discomfited his son. I took a step to go reassure the boy, but hesitated, unsure of what to say. I'd walked right up to the line of betraying the sanctity of the confessional by directing my sermon at his father. More importantly, I felt like I'd betrayed the boy's trust in me. What was there to say to fix that?

Out of the corner of my eye I caught a glimpse of a last, straggling churchgoer who appeared from the shadows of the doorway at the top of the steps. I turned, relieved to have another hand to shake instead of having to make amends with Aidan. Shame burned at the back of my throat. I told myself I could talk to him in a minute. Greet this person first. Use the time to think of something to say.

The woman stumbled, taking the steps too fast and off balance. Her ankle rolled and she tumbled down. I lurched forward to catch her, but was too late and she sprawled flat on the path in front of me. Her black hair was a mess and hid her face, though she was unmistakable. Except, it couldn't be her. I knelt and reached out to help. With her open wounds and jutting bones, I couldn't find a single place where my hands wouldn't cause her pain. The blood on her skin was wet and bright in the sun. And there was more than there should have been after a fall down the steps—even one as bad as she'd taken. Much more.

I heard a loud laugh behind me and I turned ready to bellow at whoever thought this woman's suffering was funny. But no one was looking at us. Rory and Rich were still joking and their wives were chatting with each other and Karen was gesturing with a thumb over her shoulder at me while talking to someone else, but not a single one of them seemed to have noticed what happened.

I turned back to the woman. She was pushing up from the ground. Her arms trembled and one of her wrists shifted under her weight, distorting at an angle no joint could make. I grabbed her arm and helped her to her feet. She slumped against me, heavily. I wrapped an arm around her waist and held her close. Her head lolled back and she opened her mouth. Instead of speaking, blood cascaded from her lips, spilling down her chest onto her uniform and plastic nametag.

JUSTINE

Her tongue probed at the gaps where her broken teeth had been. My stomach tightened and I clapped a hand to my mouth. She smiled with her split lips and caressed my cheek with a blood slick hand. It smelled like iron and the sweet perfume she always wore.

She whispered to me. "Conccceals his transgressionssssss."

I struggled to hold on to her, pull her closer, but she slipped out of my arms like smoke, and I let out a small cry of despair as I imagined her falling again. Falling under a truck as it mowed her and her child down.

She was gone.

Never there.

My chasuble and stole were stained dark with her blood. I touched my cheek where she'd caressed me and my fingers came away wet and red.

Aidan came over and said, "Are you okay, Father? Did you trip?"

I looked again at my clothes and hands and felt like I might be going mad. "She... I was..." He looked at me with concern, but not horror. Covered in blood as I was, it should've been *horror*. I cleared my throat and took a deep breath. "I'm fine, Aidan." I reached out and placed a hand on his shoulder, meaning to say something else, but the dark stain I left on his dress shirt stole my speech. He didn't seem to notice. "Everything's fine," I choked out.

His father stepped up and grabbed Aidan's shoulder, covering the bloody mark I'd left there. "It's time to go," he said. "Your mom wants to go get brunch. You hungry?" The elder Flynn looked me and added, "Nice sermon; real inspiring," before pulling the boy away to go. Aidan stared over his shoulder as they walked toward the parking lot. I raised a hand to wave, knowing that I looked... like I'd been hit by a car.

⁓

FRIDAY

I ran my toothbrush under the tap and set it on the counter next to my razor and comb. I rinsed and spat and lingered in the bathroom, not looking in the mirror, but straight down into the sink basin where there was no reflection to remind me what I looked like. I flossed and stepped over to the toilet. I pissed, zipped up, and sighed at the knowledge that there was nothing left to do in the bathroom. Not unless I wanted to take *another* shower. I'd spent the week trying to wash her blood off. I showered and showered, and the red stains lingered. I could only get so clean and no more. Though it seemed like only I could see the blood.

I turned off the light and walked out of the bathroom.

My bedroom in the rectory was simple and didn't have space for deep shadows. The lamp next to my bed was bright enough to read by and cast what I'd once thought of as a warm glow. Now, it seemed like it invited shadows. Like the bathroom mirror, I avoided looking into the dark corner at the far end of the room. Where she stood. I blinked, trying to banish her. But she persisted. The darkness came with her, a spreading degradation that grew deeper and blacker. She wasn't a dream I could wake from.

Justine Neville had worked at the drug store over on School Street. She'd always been kind to me when I went in to shop. She flirted with me. While I didn't wear my collar out, she confessed that one of her co-workers had let her know I was a priest. She joked that I was going to either save or damn her soul—she just couldn't tell which one yet. "Would you like to give me your e-mail address, Father Price?" she'd asked me once, winking as she said, "Father."

"Please, call me David," I replied. "And it's already in the system."

"It is, but *I* don't have it."

I blushed and said, "You don't want to go on a date with a thirty-nine-year-old virgin."

She'd said, half under her breath, "You let me know if you decide you don't want to be a forty-year old virgin." I skipped a step and stumbled toward the doors. Looking back, she was smiling. I kept walking, though I should've stopped. I should've turned around and gone back and given her my cell number. I should have done a lot of things. Instead, I left.

Off and on, I found reasons to go back. Buying necessities that weren't necessities, and picking up things for the rectory that were already stored away in cupboards and closets. I looked forward to seeing her and would wait in a longer line to be rung up at her register, waving other people ahead of me if another checker called out for the next shopper. She always made it a point to touch my hand when she passed me my shopping bag. It was a slight gesture, but it made me tremble inside. I shook a lot of hands, but no one ever touched me like *that*. As if I were a man first, and not a priest. And underneath the teasing and the flirting, there was something really there, maybe. Something that could've gone further, if I'd ever gotten up the courage to leave my job—and that's how I'd looked at it for years, not a calling, or a vocation, but a job. I didn't leave my job. I didn't call Justine for a date. I didn't do any of the things I dreamed about.

I hadn't known she was a single mother until I read about the incident in the paper. That's what they called it. An *incident* involving a truck and two pedestrians. Not an accident. She had been walking home from picking up her son at daycare when someone ran them both down. The media had described it as "road rage gone wrong," as though that ever went right. Witnesses said they'd seen a pair of men shouting at each other at a red light. When the signal turned green, one of them tore up the street and around the corner, hitting two people in the crosswalk before speeding off. The other driver had gone in the opposite direction. Other motorists stopped to help, but no one had gotten the plate—all anyone knew was that it was a red truck. The kind with a silver ram on the back gate. The driver never even slowed down after hitting them.

Justine's two-year-old son, Kerry, got to ride in a helicopter, though he never knew it. He lingered for a day in the hospital before dying.

After that, I never saw her at the store again.

Since Aidan's confession, the darkness had split open and Justine stepped through. She lurked in the periphery of my vision like the aftereffects of a camera flash. I tried to ignore her in the pews during service, across the street when I went running... standing in the corner of my bedroom. Everywhere else, I could pretend that she was someone else. Not the image of a woman broken under a truck, but just another person out for a run, coming in to hear the word. But in my room, she was as exposed as I was. She was Justine. The woman I'd fantasized going on a date with. The person who flirted and made me feel like a desirable man. The woman who never needed a thing from me—not a prayer or a good word to a bishop. All she wanted from me was a moment of fun banter while she worked a dull job—a smile and a kind word. Now she wanted something else. What that was she couldn't say. Or wouldn't.

I tried to ignore her, pretend nothing was different. I draped my robe over the back of a chair and pulled back my bloodstained bedsheets. I climbed in, pulled them over me and turned out the light. But I could feel her looking at me. I took a deep breath. The air was stale and tasted like copper.

"Why me?" I asked the darkness.

41

She was silent. I knew exactly why.

"What do you want me to do?" I asked.

She slipped into bed next to me. Her arm across my chest was cold. It was what I wanted. I tried to hold her hand, but I couldn't find a way to grasp it.

"Kill him," she whispered.

PART III: WRATH

SATURDAY

Rory Flynn parked in the lot behind Hautala's Lounge. He climbed out of his red truck and headed for the entrance. He held the door open for a woman who came stumbling out. She said something to him I couldn't hear from inside my car. He laughed. It was the same obnoxious laugh he let out on the front steps of St. Francis, loud and broadly gestural. The kind of laugh you couldn't ignore or speak over. He ran his free hand through his hair. I could see his artificially white teeth gleam in the light above the door from a half block away as he smiled at her. She touched her own hair, mirroring his gesture before brushing past him. She passed into shadow and all I could make out was a dark shape in the distance, but I could tell she looked back at him. And he lingered, watching her. When her shade fully disappeared into the night, he went inside. I wondered how hard it had been to make the choice between craft bourbon and her. I wondered if he knew her. Their exchange seemed to be a continuation of something larger. I didn't know if he was having an affair—he didn't come to confession—but it wouldn't surprise me if he was. The kind of man who could run down a mother and child in the street wouldn't have any compunction about fucking around on his wife. But then, his buddies were waiting inside. He was faithful to *them* at least.

I waited a couple of minutes. When I was sure he'd found himself a seat and a glass, I got out of my car and tried to look inconspicuous. There was no way to stay in the shadows in the lot, though. Flynn had parked under a light, and his truck stood out like a big red beacon, like a warning—come no closer; there's danger here. I was beyond caring how exposed I'd be. Fuck Rory Flynn and fuck his big red pickup. I didn't put stock in Freudian interpretations of vehicle sizes, but it was hard to argue that Flynn wasn't compensating for something. I'd have said, self-doubt and character deficiency, but that assumed he recognized his own flaws. I hadn't seen any evidence that he did.

The behemoth was bright and clean. It wasn't a work truck. There wasn't a speck of dirt on it, and no chrome toolbox behind the cab suggested that the thing served any purpose other than plumage and intimidation. There was a step on the side for the driver to climb in. A step, because it was too big to just get inside. I had to fold myself into a contortion every time I got into my Kia Rio, and if I turned to look for traffic at a light I hit my head on the door frame half the time. But he needed a God-damned step.

I leaned over to look at the grille. I didn't know what I was looking for, and knew I wouldn't find anything anyway. Still, I wanted to see it up close. There was no damage to the thing that I could see. Flynn's truck had a big, black grille guard on the front—thick steel bars like the business end of a battering ram. It was the sort of thing that made me nervous when I saw one in my rear view mirror. I shuddered to imagine what something like that would do to a body. I doubted it was much different than what the front of a pickup truck like this would do without it, but it still seemed almost monstrous. I touched it. Nothing special happened. I don't know what I expected. There was no revelatory vision that showed me the truth of Rory's guilt or innocence. No flash of pain communicating what Justine might've felt as the truck barreled into her body. I got nothing from it but cold. Leaning closer, I squinted and tried to see inside the black honeycomb grille, hoping to catch a glimpse of a scrap of fabric from a Rexall Drug apron or a piece of fluff from a favorite stuffed animal. There was nothing there but plastic and steel. The truck kept Rory's secrets. There was no "evidence" to be found. That had been washed away long ago. So, what was I doing there?

I was doing what I told people to do every day: I was searching for answers that couldn't be seen.

I straightened up and turned back toward my own car. Unlike Flynn, I hadn't parked under a streetlight—purposefully so—but still, I could see a spot of deeper darkness sitting in the passenger seat. A shape like the one Flynn had lingered to watch walk away in the dark. Except this was no flirty blonde with an easy smile and an unspoken invitation to follow. My shade was silent and dour. She was angry and wanted blood. And, Heaven help me, I intended to give it to her.

A couple came stumbling out of the bar, laughing and leaning on each other. I jerked out of my paralysis and staggered an involuntary step forward, trying to get away. If they recognized me, or even noticed I was there, they didn't let on. The pair headed away in the opposite direction, continuing to laugh and carry on as they held each other up. I looked at my watch. Flynn wouldn't be coming out for a while. There was still time to back out.

I looked at my car again. The shadow still sat there, waiting. I took another step toward it. And another. Eventually, I made it across the street and found the shape in the passenger seat was just a shadow from a tree falling across half of the car. At least, that's what I told myself when I climbed inside. Despite that, I couldn't bring myself to look at the passenger seat. Instead, I stared through the windshield at the door to Hautala's, waiting for more people to come out. Waiting for one in particular.

I'd brought a Thermos full of black coffee, thinking it might be difficult to stay awake until closing time, but it wasn't. I didn't feel tired at all; I could have stayed up all night without caffeine, riding the energy of my anger. Of course, I didn't have to. The bar, like every other in Ripton, closed at two in the morning. I'd been following him since nine, when he walked out his front door. At around one a.m., I started the car and let the engine idle. After a while, when people started to leave, I put it in gear and pulled forward so I could see better. I didn't want to make a mistake. I didn't want to hurt the wrong person. I very badly wanted to hurt the right one.

He came staggering out at ten-to-two with a pair of his friends. They were laughing and roughhousing. Flynn gave one friend a shove and staggered back, taking a hard, unintended step off the curb. He nearly fell in the street and my heart raced. I almost put it in gear and jammed the gas at that moment, but his pals caught him before he landed in the gutter. I didn't want to kill all three of them. I doubted I could if I tried. And leaving them alive meant getting caught if they saw me and could remember the details of my car or plate—or my face. I cursed myself for not wearing a ski mask or even a hat. But on a warm late spring evening, it'd look more suspicious than just sitting in the car outside a bar all night.

They righted him and I could hear his laugh through my windows over the sound of the idling engine. I squeezed the steering wheel tight. I felt my knuckles pop but I didn't relax my grip. I wanted to be squeezing Rory Flynn's fucking neck. Throttling him until my hands hurt and his eyes came bulging out of their sockets and I felt him thrashing underneath me. And then I imagined holding on longer, squeezing tighter until I felt his windpipe collapse and his vertebrae grind against each other and smelled his bladder let go. I wanted to kill him with my hands because it was a cowardly fucking thing to run someone down in the street. But there was no other way. I didn't know if I could beat him in a stand-up fight. And I wasn't an assassin. I didn't know how to break into a house. I didn't know how to kill a person and get away without having to murder everyone else in it. I didn't know how not to leave a trace. All I understood was that Rory Flynn was never going to be punished in this world, and that there was no other. He'd live his whole life having gotten away with it if I didn't do something right now.

So, I put the car in gear and stood on the brake.

A cab pulled up to the curb next to them. Did the driver see my car and wonder why I had been sitting there for so long? I could've been competition—a MyRyde driver waiting for my app to summon me to pick up someone at the bar. It was too late to print out one of those company logo signs people put in their back windows and install it as a diversion. I'd failed again in even the most rudimentary kind of deception. I didn't look like anything other than a man who'd been sitting in his car for close to four hours, waiting. And when they came to find Flynn lying broken in the street, people would say things like, "There was a car parked right over there all night," and "It was there when I went inside and was still there when I came out again. And I saw a *man* sitting in it both times!" My master plan was less than masterful by a long shot. It didn't matter. Flynn deserved to pay for what he'd done. And if that meant I paid too, that was the price of rendering his judgment.

Flynn's pals got into the cab. I saw Flynn shake his head, "no." He wasn't going with them. They urged him again and I willed him to refuse. *Say no say no say no. Just refuse their generosity and walk away.* He held up his keys and I could read his lips when he said, "I'm fine." He slammed the taxicab car door too hard and a second later the cabbie pulled away, carrying his responsible patrons away. Flynn, alone on the sidewalk, swayed a little on his feet and then took a step toward the lot. Not falling-down drunk, but drunk enough to kill someone.

He hadn't had been drunk when he hit Justine and her boy. Just full of rage. I wondered how his compared to mine. His had been deranging; mine was focused. He hadn't intended to hit Justine and her boy. I was pointed right at him.

I took my foot off the brake.

The car crept forward. My foot hovered over the gas pedal. I could jam it down, steer the car up onto the sidewalk and run him down. I could do this. It's what I'd hoped for—he was by himself, drunk and senseless, and I had a clear shot at him. I could hit him and get away. There might even be a moment to back up and run him over again before anyone could make sense of what that sound was outside and come running to see. And then it was home to wash the car. I thought of Aidan's confession. He knew what his father had done because he washed his car. I never washed mine by hand either. I took it to the drive-through. I enjoyed reliving the pleasure of being a child inside my mother's car when it went through the carwash tunnel like an amusement park ride. It never got the car quite clean enough, but the trip was worth it.

That's when I realized a washing wouldn't do it. I wasn't driving his truck or even a decent-sized sedan; I was in a low-to-the-ground subcompact that would hit him at the thighs and throw him up onto the windshield. It'd break his legs for sure, but unless I really got up to speed, chances of killing him seemed slim. And whether or not he died, the impact would definitely wreck my little car.

I watched Flynn take an awkward step, right himself, straighten his clothes, and then with a measured intent, walk carefully toward his pickup truck. With purpose in his stride, he walked confidently into the parking lot and out of the path of my car. I'd waited too long. I'd failed. Though I imagined I'd have another chance to set up exactly this scenario some other night, I knew I'd never do it. I was plagued by doubt and hesitation, while he had the confidence of a man who knew that even when he did wrong, he would be just fine. He never felt like he had to atone for anything. And I had no ability to hold him accountable, because I was a coward.

I pressed down on the gas and steered toward home.

Behind me, I heard the roar of his V8 engine and a squeal of tires as he peeled out of the lot, taking the turn onto the street too fast. I pictured him rolling the thing and killing himself right there without me. Then his bright headlights filled my rear window and blinded me.

He rode up on my bumper and I braced for the collision that would ruin my car and my body and leave him without a scratch. At the last second, with his truck so close it felt like his headlights were shining out of my back seat, he honked and swerved around me. His engine roared like a monster and my shoulders tightened in response. My little car rocked in his wake.

Tears stung my eyes and I felt weak and utterly vulnerable. I pulled over and breathed deeply for a few seconds, trying to calm my heartbeat.

Her voice whispered in my ear. "Home."

I knew where he lived; I'd followed him to the bar from his home. And the fastest way to get back there was straight ahead.

He'd turned right at the end of the block instead.

⌁

I turned onto Flynn's street, pulled over to the curb, and stared at his McMansion standing in the center of the cul-de-sac. It was a straight shot from the street into his driveway. If he'd beaten me, there would've been a light on, but the windows were dark. While it was possible that he was navigating his house in the dark to avoid disturbing his sleeping family, it somehow seemed more likely that I'd gotten there first.

He'd turned right instead of going straight when he left Hautala's Lounge, because he was following the call of the woman he'd run into on the sidewalk out front. I imagined her saying something like, "Swing by when you're done." After he'd drunk his fill with his friends, he took her up on the offer before going home to his wife and son. Because he could.

Or maybe he was already asleep in his bed, and I had missed another opportunity.

I pulled around the cul-de-sac and drove back toward the intersection at the end of the street. It was closing in on two thirty and all the houses were dark. I pulled up to the stop sign and rolled down my window. I shut off my engine and listened to the sounds of the nighttime. A soft breeze rustled the tree branches overhead and somewhere in the distance I heard a dog bark. I wondered if it was a stray or if someone was out walking it in the middle of the night, tired and anxious for the thing to do its business so they could both go home and get back to bed.

I'd give him an hour. If he didn't show up by three-thirty, he was probably already home and I was a fool. Except, whether he was sound asleep in his own bed or fucking someone in another, I was already a fool. I was a fool for thinking that I could hold him accountable.

Then, through the breeze and the calm of night, I heard a faint engine rumble. Throaty and loud enough to carry through the outskirts of the city. I listened for a little bit to make sure it was coming closer.

I opened the jockey box and pulled out the small flashlight I told myself I bought for emergencies. Most of the time, those emergencies were simply that I'd dropped something that had landed underneath the driver's seat. I clicked it on. A thousand lumens lit up the inside of the car like an explosion. I doused it immediately; a blue afterimage hovered in my sight like a ghost. The thing was brighter than I ever needed, but at the time I bought it, it seemed like a fun thing to have. A light bright enough to cast a beam in the sky, like a spotlight summoning people to a Hollywood movie premiere. It was an indulgence that seemed silly in hindsight, though at that moment I was glad to have it.

I restarted the engine and pulled forward. I turned the car to the left and stopped in the middle of the intersection. Then, I turned off the engine again and got out. The sound of Flynn's truck was growing louder.

While the low branches of an elm tree near the corner shaded the streetlight above me, the intersection was still lit up well enough. I took a few steps back and tried shining the flashlight up at the sensor on top of the light. Even with my flashlight focused down to a tight beam, the streetlight wasn't going out. I gave up and doused my light again. I went to hide in the shadows of the opposite corner.

After a few minutes, a truck turned the corner at the far end of Effdey Street and started toward me. With the bright headlights shining in my eyes, I couldn't be certain it was Flynn's truck; I put my faith in the now familiar sound of that engine. That sound had been roaring in my ears since he tore around me to get to his girlfriend's. It had to be his truck. It *had* to be.

I ducked behind an elm in someone's yard. The engine grew louder and more terrifying. This was the sound that Justine and her son heard in the moment before he ran them down.

Come on, you fucker.

He was going fast and didn't seem interested in slowing down for the four-way stop. That suited me. I ran through my list of explanations. *I sometimes drive at night to think. My car died and I didn't know what to do. I'd gotten out to push it clear of the intersection when I saw him coming. He didn't even slow down, officer. I was barely able to jump out of the way before...*

The woman stepped into the road without looking, pulling the child along behind her. She screamed, but the sound was nothing compared to the truck's howl and I cried out incoherently, not mute but rendered speechless by what I saw. Just a long, loud cry of terror.

I lurched out from behind the elm and dashed toward her. The sound of screeching tires was shrill as a chorus of angels. My legs felt boneless and I stumbled into the road, half upright and entirely out of control. The headlights lit me up bright and white and cold like Heaven, blinding me to everything but it. I put up my hands, dark against the stark brilliance. They were worthless against the monstrous consequence bearing down on me.

I stood frozen in the street waiting to feel the push bar and grille slam into my body. I waited for the feeling of being hurled through the air, weightless and then landing, devastated, on unyielding asphalt. Or perhaps, I wouldn't feel any of that, but rather a merciful blinking out.

And then everything went dark. But not silent.

The screeching chorus of tires reached a higher pitch along with a racing engine suddenly flooded with gas, and became a symphony of scraping metal and shattering glass. I heard a sound like the slamming of a great door. The percussive sound of it splintering and breaking and then another crash. The musical conclusion of the last cymbal trill of safety glass and the engine winding down like a sigh before dying. And then, the soft breeze returned and I heard the muted sound of rudely awakened dogs barking behind locked doors.

I opened my eyes to see Flynn's red truck resting on its roof, warped and ruined, and wrapped around the oak I'd hidden behind a moment earlier. He hung half out of the window, a dull white ball inside the cab pressing against him. The airbag hadn't done any good. He was contorted, arms reaching in impossible directions, and his neck turned at a right angle, unblinking eyes looking directly at me standing in the middle of the street, untouched.

I looked around in a panic for the woman and child, but couldn't see them.

My legs still felt rubbery as I staggered toward Flynn. A black pool spread out from under him, glinting red in the streetlamp's glow. Windows in living rooms all along the block began to light up. I ran to my car. Despite wanting to stay and watch them pull Rory from the wreck—wanting to see them lay a sheet over his body and lift him into an ambulance that drove away without its lights flashing—I climbed in my car, started the engine and drove away.

In the distance, I heard a siren wind up. It reminded me of a single soprano voice intoning the first notes of Górecki's *Cantabile-Semplice*.

〜⌣〜

Epilogue

I say, "This is my confession. I repent and ask for absolution."

The headstone is silent. I reach out and touch it. My fingers trace over the letters engraved in the granite.

Adam Linden Neville
Born, May 19, 2017
Taken, June 28, 2019
Beloved Son, Loved Forever

I set the small stuffed bear I bought at Rexall in front of it and wonder what happened to the one I left before. It doesn't matter. If this one vanishes, I'll buy another. And another.

"What are you doing?"

The voice from behind startles me, and I feel shame burn in the hot blush of my cheeks. I turn around to say "sorry," and freeze. She's shorter than I remember. Her face is different, uneven, but still beautiful. Her hair is cut differently, but the same deep black. Now framed in white at the temples.

Too young to be going gray.

"Father Price? Is that you?"

I swallow. "I, uh, I'm just David now. I left the priesthood. I'm sorry, Ms. Neville. I'm so sorry for your loss." I stand and take a step to go. She stops me with her free hand—the one not holding her cane.

"It's Justine."

I reach for her hand, expecting her to pull away. She lets me take it. Her hand is solid and I don't pass through. Her fingers are cold, and I wrap them in my hands to warm them, though mine aren't much warmer. They're finally clean though.

"*You're* the one leaving the stuffed animals?"

I nod. "They keep disappearing."

"He would've been upset if they got cold or rained on, so I've been taking them to put in his room." She laughs once, softly. It's not a happy sound. "He would have liked them."

"I'm glad you have them."

"I miss seeing you," she says.

"Me too." I let go of her hand and take another step to leave.

"Wait." she says. "Can I get your e-mail address?"

This time, I don't walk away.

AFTERWORD

You're Gonna Carry That Weight a Long Time

When John Taff asked me if I was interested in writing for a seven deadly sins themed anthology, I tried to give him an out—a couple of times, actually. I told him that I wasn't religious and didn't have what one would consider "doctrinal" views on the deadly sins. I also told him that transgressive neo-noir is my voice and that maybe he wanted someone who'd be a little less love the sinner *and* the sin. He insisted that he wanted me onboard for exactly those reasons. Because I love and respect John and I wanted to work with him, I said yes. Then he gave me my sin: anger (or more archaically, wrath) and I almost choked, I was laughing so hard. (He insists that was randomly chosen.) Could I write about anger? Have I ever *not*? I started to think about how to write again about my most familiar emotion.

When I started to plot out the story, I realized I didn't want to write about the direct experience of feeling one's own anger. Instead, I wanted to tell a story about someone whose job it is to help people cope with their feelings, because it's a hard thing to be the person who offers to help someone else shoulder their pain. Back when I was a lawyer representing victims in abuse and discrimination cases, I almost only ever saw people in pain and often struggling with very righteous and hard-earned anger about what had been done to them. I say "struggling" because the constant drumbeat in our culture is that anger itself is bad, no matter how justified you are in feeling it. It's "toxic" and we should work to rid ourselves of it as soon as possible. By a kind of transitive principle, if you allow yourself to feel it or, worse, cultivate it, *you* are bad. But these people who came to me for help weren't bad people; they were good people who'd been done wrong. They deserved to feel their feelings without shame.

And I was their advocate.

Part of my job then was to listen to them tell their difficult (and often embarrassing to relate) stories in detail—a kind of confession—so that I could recount what had been done to them in litigation. I never got to offer absolution, though. At the end of a plea deal, trial, or a settlement no one lifts the burden from your shoulders and magically heals you. Often, people are left with the same anger and resentment they had at the beginning, but sometimes with a little more money in their pocket, or the knowledge that their abuser couldn't hurt anyone else—for a while anyway. But what had been done to them couldn't ever be taken back or dispelled. And if we lost, at best, that person never got to hold her abuser accountable for what he'd done. Sometimes, their feelings of being victimized intensified if we lost.

So, it was my job to take that anger and turn it into a weapon to effectively slay their dragons. I'm more than fluent with anger; having spent a lifetime surviving very intimately with my own, I knew how to swing that sword. There's a difference though, between feeling your own anger until you've worked through it, and collecting other people's like currency to spend later. That weight gets heavy if you don't get to unload it. After a while, carrying it all pushed me down, and I had to get out from under or be crushed.

That feeling was what I wanted to write about.

I didn't want to tell the story through the eyes of a lawyer, though. We've all read it, and frankly I'm bored with reading about tortured lawyers. I wanted to consider someone else's experience—someone who doesn't get to take that collected energy and spend it in a fight. I wanted to write about a person who lives *without* catharsis and explore how it affects his relationships both with other people and with himself. That's when I thought about priests and confession.

I began reading about Catholic priests and how they manage the emotional burden of hearing their parishioners' confessions. Surprisingly (to me, anyway), the resources I found all described very positive experiences—like David's colleagues express in the story—but from my own history, I suspected that was not universal. Out there somewhere, someone's struggling with the burden of what people lay on him in that little room. I wanted to tell his story, for no other reason than that I know what it's like, as the Beatles sang, to carry that weight for a long time. I suspect more than a few of you out there know what it's like as well.

I hope this story made the burden a little lighter on you, for a while anyway.

(For Jonathan)

Pride is shiny, bright as all time. Pride needs the prideful to feast like a lion.
—Ancient Folklore

*A woman especially, if she have the misfortune of knowing anything,
should conceal it as well as she can.*
—Jane Austen

CAP DIAMANT

by Kasey Lansdale

It was as cold as one might expect it to be in Quebec City mid-October. George de Roche pushed up the collar of his sea coat and adjusted his watch cap to combat the wind, and trudged onward. As he went he glanced up at Cap Diamant, and though it was dark, there were lights on the mountain where the moon illuminated strands of quartz and made them shine.

The port was a flurry of activity, filled with evening traffic as throngs of sailors, soldiers, and townsmen flocked to tie one on with the ladies of the night. The clopping of hooves echoed across the cobblestone path as George made his way to the village tavern, the tinge of sea salt still in his nostrils.

The last thing he wanted to do after disembarking ship was watch idiots hooting and hollering at one another, putting on a show like animals in heat. But it was his brother Jean's birthday, and they'd set aside this evening to celebrate. They were going to have fun if it killed them. They too would soon be counted among the idiots.

They were all waiting on him. Drinks were already on the table. George sidled up and slid into a spot on the bench. His middle brother, Samuel de Roche, was sitting to his left, and his friend, Leo, who worked with Samuel at the butcher shop, was on his right. Jean's mate from the print shop, Alix, sat across the table from him, beer in one hand, redhead in the other.

"Put a smile on ya, Big George, it's cause for celebration," Alix said. "Jean has turned nineteen."

"He's not the smiling type," Samuel said. "Come on, brother, give us a grin, for Jean."

"It's all right," Jean said.

"No, it is not," said Samuel. "Smile, Big George."

George managed one, but it looked more like the bared fangs of a wounded animal.

It was a joyous occasion, however, and George knew that—if for no other reason than Jean had made it to nineteen, which was no small feat considering the amount of pneumonia and flu that had circled around as of late. Illness had ravaged the townspeople, including a number of their friends. Even their mother had suffered a bout with the flu, and was only now, after coming close to death, successfully recovering. It finally felt like all of that death and sadness was behind them.

"Here, little brother, have a shot," George said, picking up a bottle of whisky and pouring a healthy shot into a glass.

He was trying to get into the spirit of things.

George slid the tiny glass in Jean's direction as the amber liquid sloshed over the edge and onto the wooden slats of the table. Jean reached for the glass, held it up and nodded, then slammed the acrid liquid down the back of his throat to everyone's delight.

"Here, here," Jean said, face wadded up in response to drinking what may have actually been paint thinner. "I think my lungs just folded."

George knew that Jean had never acquired the taste for whisky, and was glad of it. He had certainly had his own battles with it.

George watched the people buzz around as Jean and their friends drank their booze and spoke of this and that. The seamen in the pub were dressed in their starched denim shirts and bell-bottomed trousers, and George saw Samuel glance first at him, then at the other sailors.

"Don't even think about it," George said. "The sea is a tough mistress."

"It beats a butcher shop," Samuel said.

"Mother needs you here."

"What about you?" Samuel said.

"I'm already lost, but someday you'll own your own butcher shop, and I'll be a broken back sailor."

"There's barely enough room for one butcher shop," Leo said.

"I didn't say there would be two," George said, grinning sincerely this time.

"Oh, that's the cut," Leo said. "My family teaches him the trade, and he takes us over."

"I'm joshing," George said. "Your Uncle Ray has been like a father to us, has he not, boys? More than once he's brought us fresh meat at no cost, merely because my mother is a struggling widow. It couldn't have been easy raising three boys alone. Our father, Satan damn him, went away long ago, and I can't say as I miss the sonofabitch any."

"He has indeed," Jean said, and raised his glass. "To Ray Byrd. Long may he live."

They clinked their glasses together, and drank.

When they had lowered their glasses, Samuel said, "Jean. That fantastic blonde has her eyes on you, she does."

Jean turned slowly and looked. She was on the far side of the room, but there was no question who Samuel meant.

She wasn't like most of the women in the pub. She wasn't a working girl. She was out of place. She was smooth of skin and long of leg, and wore a dress the color of fresh blood, laced sandals, and sparkling gold earrings.

"Stop daydreaming about her, little brother" Samuel said, go talk to her, or I may change the focus of her eyes."

"Jean's the pretty one," Alix said. "No one wants to look at you."

"That's right," Leo said. "You could hang Jean for a picture he's so cute."

They all laughed and Leo and Alix touched their glasses in delight of their own humor. The redhead in Alix's arm giggled.

George noted the way the woman was focused on Jean. Like a duck that had spotted a fat beetle. It made George uncomfortable, but damn it, she was something beyond reason. He had never seen a woman so beautiful, and he couldn't exactly explain why. He had seen as fine a face, as fair a skin, as blonde a hair, and as long of a leg, but there was an aura about her, and George had the uncomfortable feeling that had her focus turned to him, he would have become as weak as Jean obviously was. He seemed to be melting into the bench on which he sat.

"I think you should leave that one alone," George said. "She's not one of us."

"Oh, hell," Jean said. "How can I?"

"I think you should leave her be," George said.

"Don't ruin it for him," Samuel said. "It's him she's interested in, not us."

"What do you care who she's interested in?" the redhead said. "I'm right here."

"You'd be happy with anyone looking your way," Samuel said, "as long as they have money."

"That's not very nice," said the redhead, and lowered her head.

"Don't let him get to you," Leo said. "He spends too much time with butchered meat. And George, all he knows is the sea and fish."

George grunted.

Samuel wasn't paying attention. He was trying to catch the woman's eye, but without success. He said, "See how she looks at Jean? And just him? And look at that smile."

And smile she did, and when she did, Jean let out a loud breath and went silent.

George felt cold discomfort. Colder than the outside wind. It was as if Jean had breathed his last, and the devil had walked over his grave.

They looked at the woman. Her eyes were still focused on Jean, and she still had a smile on her face, shiny and inviting in the lamp light.

Jean gathered his courage and stood up.

George started to say something else, then thought perhaps he was merely jealous, and held his tongue.

"Jean's never been good with the ladies. Too shy. But tonight, maybe he can put that behind him. And if not, well, I'll take my chances with her," Samuel said.

⌒

Jean glanced over at Samuel as if to scold him, but Samuel cut him off. "Quit stalling Jean," Samuel said. "Go."

Since the whole table was now involved, Jean's pride obligated him to approach her if he wanted to maintain any semblance of masculinity. He'd have to go over and introduce himself at the very least. Jean smoothed down the folds in his jacket, checked the shine of his shoes, and with all the dash-fire he could muster, made his way over, trying to equal his brother George's self-assured rolling gait.

She wasn't doing much but sitting there, far as anyone could tell, but when he sidled up next to her, her presence was like a bonfire. It heated him up and burned him deep.

He cleared his throat as he towered over her. She glanced up at him with those electric green eyes and he felt his throat tighten and his chest burn as though he'd drunk a barrel of that cheap whisky.

She seemed amused by his timidness, like a cat toying with a terrified mouse. The corners of her coral lips turned upward and into a partial smile. Up close, she was even more stunning. She was an incomparable beauty, and she knew it. Her long blonde hair draped lovingly across her petite shoulders like a beautiful Greek nymph.

"Good evening ma'am," Jean said, tugging at the navy scarf tied around his neck.

Hardly original, but it was what he had. She said nothing, just continued to stare. She was no longer smiling. Jean thought: Could she have been smiling at someone else? Could she be teasing me?

"Can I buy you a drink?"

She looked at her near empty glass, picked it up, put it to her lips and tilted her head back, gingerly finishing the last of it.

"I suppose that would be all right," she said, as she gently set the glass on the table. Her voice was like a song, like ocean water washing over smooth rocks.

In that moment, Jean realized that he hadn't brought enough money for another drink. He'd intended to stay just long enough to finish one on his own and high tail it out of there, but he couldn't back out now, and he didn't want to.

"And what is the lady drinking?"

"Jack Rose."

"My pleasure… I'm Jean, by the way."

Jean looked at her, waited for her to fill in the lull with her name. It came slowly, and beautifully, rolling from between her lips like spring water.

"Éloïse."

58

Her name was as beautiful as she was, and when she moved, the red, silk print dress she wore molded to the curves of her perfect figure. The pin across her collarbone was filled with rhinestones, and the way the light caught them made it appear as though the night stars danced across her ample bosom.

He could have stayed there all night, staring down at her, but he could tell she was growing restless, and excused himself to fetch her another drink. He walked back to the table where his onlookers watched, leaned over George and whispered into his ear, "George, I need some money."

"You've got money."

"I do, but I haven't it with me. Please George, I need it to buy a drink for Éloïse."

"Éloïse, is it? If you ask me, she ought to be named trouble, because that's what she is, Jean. I'm no hawkshaw, but I can see it in her eyes."

"Well, trouble as she may be, she's waiting on me. I'll pay you back tomorrow. I'm working extra at the shop this week."

"Fine," George said, slipping his hand into his pocket. "But if you don't pay me back, there's going to be an anointing."

George pulled the wad of bills from his pocket and extended his hand toward Jean. "Thank you," Jean said, taking the money.

"Sometimes what looks like beauty is the work of the Devil, and everything appears to sparkle in hell," George said. "Be careful."

"She's just a woman," Jean said. "A fine looking woman."

"Ignore him," Samuel said. "He's jealous. Hell, boy. It's your birthday. Go get 'em."

Jean patted George on the shoulder, started back to Éloïse.

George said nothing more, but continued to watch Éloïse, making no attempt to mask his disdain. She turned her attention directly to him for the first time, and in that moment, George felt as if he had been stabbed with icicles. It was such an intense feeling, he averted his gaze.

By that time Jean had made his way back to her, and she had her attention on him.

Jean leaned close to Éloïse, placed his lips near her ear, whispered something. She appeared to be more reciprocal of his presence now, which emboldened him.

"Shall we take a walk somewhere more quiet?" she asked.

"What about the drink?" he said.

"What about it?"

She let her thick lashes tickle the mounds of her rosy cheeks and smiled.

⌒⌣

George looked up as Jean and Éloïse walked past toward the tavern door. Jean looked over his shoulder and winked at him. What Jean didn't notice, was that Éloïse had turned as well. She looked directly at George, narrowed her eyes and licked her lips. George felt his blood run cold.

At that very moment, someone cranked up the Edison at the back of the tavern, and *Let Me Call You Sweetheart* began to fill the air.

⌒⌒

By now it was twilight, with dawn breaking over the horizon. It was the quietest Jean had ever known the city. It was early enough that even the crickets still slept. A thin veil of fog began to lift and fade into a warm orange glow. And in that moment, just as Jean was about to remark on the stillness of the world at this early hour, a series of loud caws echoed from the wooded trail in the distance. He jumped, startled by the sudden sound.

Éloïse didn't seem to notice, and carried on the winding pathway.

"Where are we going, exactly?" Jean asked. She'd invited him for a walk, but this wasn't exactly what he'd had in mind.

"There's a spot in the woods near the water where I like to sit sometimes. You can see my house from there," she said, and pointed toward the mountain.

"Is it much further? My mother will be expecting me home soon." The moment the words escaped his lips he wished he could reach out, grab them, and stuff them back inside his mouth. She glanced back at him, mouth stretched into a wide grin across her porcelain white teeth. Though she was smiling, Jean couldn't help but notice that she didn't look happy.

Finally, they reached the woods where the crows had called out to them from a distance. The entire murder of them seemed to have awoken, for the trees were alive with sound now.

Éloïse continued through the forest, not looking back to check on Jean until they reached a riverbed where she finally stopped and leaned up against an old, towering sugar maple. The roots were thick and twisted, big enough for Éloïse to sit on. Behind her was the shadow of the mountain, the scimitar moon seeming to rest on its peak.

"I used to ride horses along this river, with my family." she said.

"When?"

"'Twas another lifetime," she said.

"I used to play here when I was a boy," Jean said, "but these days, I stay closer to town. My mother has not been well and…" He trailed off. "Here, please, let me put down my coat for you to sit upon." Jean peeled his jacket from his body and draped it over the damp bark of the tree root.

Jean could feel the conversation was getting off track.

"Do you still ride?" he asked.

"Not since the accident."

"Oh no, I'm sorry, were you hurt?" Jean asked.

"No. *I* wasn't," she said.

Jean turned away from the river and peered out towards the tree line. It was full on morning now, and it was true that his mother would in fact, be looking for him. The boldness he'd felt back at the bar had faded and his eyelids grew heavier by the moment.

"Let's go to my place," she said.

When she said that, Jean lost all concern for what his mother might be thinking. He felt overcome with excitement. He looked across the top of the tree-lined forest and pointed upward.

"There? How do we get there?"

"Follow me," she said. "I have the boat tied just around the bend."

The wind picked up and shook the trees like a hand had reached out and fanned their tops. Golden yellow and vibrant orange leaves wafted through the air and danced to the ground.

The dome over the bed was high up and made of glass. The center of the dome was a round mirror, and there were lights behind it that made it appear magnified, and all around the mirror the glass was clear and the sky could be seen. They had watched the sun fade into the mountainside through the glass hours earlier, and now the stars gave the impression that they were mere ornaments to enhance the glory that was Éloïse, and at the top of the mirror the crescent moon seemed to sit in just a way that it reflected across Éloïse's delicate forehead and into a heavy gold crown.

As she lay there, nude, she looked up at the mirror in the center of the dome, observed her smooth, whale-bone white body and her golden hair, flowing like a waterfall of honey over her shoulders, her legs long and skin supple. Her eyes shone like emeralds, and she thought: *I am as Aphrodite, the goddess of love, the most beautiful and desirable woman in the world, and the universe is mine.*

Jean looked up at this same mirror, admiring Éloïse, too captivated to notice that his image remained unseen atop the smooth, leathery blanket draped across the bed. It was akin to the hide of his work horse Marguerite, heavy, and sewn together in various sized patches.

He tried to squeeze in closer to her, but she spread her arms out into a stretch, keeping him at bay, and pushing him out of view of the mirror.

"Before, you said there had been an accident. What happened?"

Éloïse stayed in her splayed out position, her lips twisting into a smile.

Jean thought she might be withholding, but here in the comfort of her bed, with the glow of the moonlight shining down on her, she seemed almost anxious to tell her story.

"It was a long time ago, but I once loved a man, I would have done anything to make him happy. He left me all the same for some…" she paused, took a breath and continued, "some peasant. A short, fat, brown headed blob of a woman. Oh she was sweet enough I suppose, was able to give him a child, but she would never have what I have."

Her words were cold, and she smiled up at her reflection as she continued to admire her naked self.

"As you saw, the trip up can be precarious if you haven't a boat or if the fog hangs too low on horseback. One morning, he left me here, in this very bed, to go see *her*. He tried to sneak back in the early hours, when the ground was wet and the sky dark and I lay sleeping, but he fell from his horse and broke his back."

Jean didn't respond; he was too captivated by her image.

He felt her hand touch his face, and then she turned and placed her mouth against his.

⌒

After work each day, Samuel searched for his brother, not worried at first, merely concerned, but by the third day he felt frantic. His mother was beside herself, and hadn't slept since Jean had failed to return home. Her concern and fear soaked into Samuel like blood into a sponge, and when he wasn't working and looking for Jean, he was comforting her. Her small body shook as if with a chill, even when she sat before the fire. Her knitting lay abandoned next to her chair. She hadn't picked it up once. It seemed to him she had become frail and truly old overnight, her hair gray, her face lined, her spirit sapped.

He hadn't told her about the woman in the tavern, not wishing her to know that he had pushed his brother to pursue her. He tried to comfort himself by believing Jean's first real experience with a woman had intoxicated him, and that he was shacked up somewhere.

He wished George were home. He would know what to do, where to look, but he was back at sea now, so it was all up to him.

Samuel tried the tavern at night, looking for the woman, but he didn't see her and no one seemed to know her, though everyone remembered her.

On the fourth night, having gone to the tavern, having sat there for hours, drinking very little, watching, he gave up and started home, knowing his mother would still be up, waiting beside the fire.

As he walked toward his mother's house, he came to a turn in the street, and as he did, he was certain he saw Éloïse come out of another tavern than the one where she had met Jean. He couldn't see her face, only her shape, but he remembered her by that. The way she moved, even walking, was reminiscent of how her body shifted in her seat that night, and the way she walked when she went away with Jean was registered in his mind as surely as his own face. He saw that walk now, and was convinced it was her, and he followed.

She moved swiftly, and he found it work to keep her in sight. Out of town and into the forest she went, taking a narrow trail toward the river. She was almost to the river when he caught up with her, touched her shoulder.

She spun, and yes, under the hood he saw her face. The light from the moon was bright there where the trail widened out of the trees, and he saw her eyes, which seemed unnaturally bright, even in moonlight, and then his eyes latched to hers, and she smiled.

It was a smile that was for him, and in that moment Jean, his mother, everything in the world was lost to him, and the only thing that mattered was that smile, that face, those lips. She spoke to him, and he spoke back, and by the time he reached the boat and climbed in beside her, he had no idea what they had said or why he'd been out in the first place. What he did know was that her presence made him feel powerful. Wanted.

The river was silver, the moon was bright, his heart was on fire.

⌒

George returned from sea in the spring, only to discover that his brothers Jean and Samuel were lost, and that his mother was deathly ill. He went to her, there in her little cottage, lying in her bed, ragged quilts pulled up under her chin, a fire blazing in the stove. She looked at him, and for a moment she rallied. She reached out and touched him, smiled thinly, and said, "Find your brothers," and then she was gone. As if all she had been waiting for before leaving this life was the touch of his hand, a moment to pass her last spark to him.

Ray Byrd was there. He had long been a good friend of the family, and George was certain he had always been sweet on his mother. When George arrived, he'd left the bedroom, went into the other room to sit before the fire.

George continued to sit by the bed holding his mother's hand, feeling the warmth seep out of it, until it turned cold. He placed her hands across her chest, and pulled the blanket over her head, and went out into the main room. He walked over and stood by the fire.

Ray looked up at him. "Is she…?"

George nodded.

"I'm sorry, son, truly. She was a fine woman. Ah, when she was young there wasn't a lad in town that wasn't crazy about her. What a beauty she was. I swear it again. The men were crazy about her, and she never really knew how lovely she was."

"My father wasn't crazy enough about her. He left."

"The man you call your father was a fool, as all men are fools when it comes to women. But it's not as you might think."

Ray seemed to be chewing something over in his mind. Finally he said, "Your father, both your brothers, and now your wonderful mother, all gone."

"Nothing says my brothers aren't alive."

"They are not alive," Ray said.

George turned and looked down at Ray, a large man gone to seed, his hair thin and white.

"You say that with some authority."

Ray nodded. "I looked for them as best I could. To appease your mother, and myself. But all I could find in way of evidence was the woman."

"The woman? You don't mean the one Jean met in the tavern?"

"I suspect I do. Sit down, George, and listen to what I have to say. Your mother is gone now, and a bit of time to reflect will not dishonor her. Sit, please."

George sat, and when he did, Ray began.

⌣

"She appears now and again, and on her own time schedule, but I think it's because she comes to a point where she has to feed." Ray said.

"You're confusing me, old man."

Ray looked at George and smiled. "First, let me tell you this. Your brothers were both handsome men, as you are, but did you ever wonder why you looked nothing like them?"

George was slow to answer. "It crossed my mind."

"Now, I tell you this with sincerity and respect, because I have kept up with you. You were her first son, and you are my only son."

At first George felt angry, but it passed almost immediately. It felt right. He had always been different.

"We were to be married," Ray said. "It happened before. You, I mean."

"But why didn't you marry?"

"The night before the marriage I went to celebrate at the tavern, the same where you last saw Jean and Samuel. And she was there. Let me tell you, I loved your mother, but I lusted for this woman. She was as shiny as pride itself, and I think that's exactly what she was. And for there to be pride, there have to be those who wish to bask in pride's reflection. Women are pride because we make them that way. We want the young ones, the pretty ones, the ones whose voices are soft as silk. We want the warm ones. We want the one that is better than the next. And women, that is the burden we have given them. And bless them, for they have embraced it, whether they meant to or not. They have become pride because we want them to. We give them their worth in their beauty, and little else matters. It starts when they are but children. They battle each other over who is the most beautiful, the most perfect, and we feed it, George. We, meaning men. 'By water, by land, woman and man, the same game is played, from here to the end.'

"That is the reason there are sirens. They wish to beguile men. They wish to punish them for what we have made them. Sirens. The succubus. The goddess of pride, Hybris. All are reflections of man's desires and lustful images, and women comply. Until in some, pride is all they are, and yet, they know too what fosters their strength, and their weakness. Men. And we become, perhaps rightfully, their prey."

"Are you trying to tell me that woman is… one of those things you named?"

"She is all of those things. When a woman loves a man who throws her away for a shinier, or prettier, younger woman, she becomes them. Sometimes, they leave for a woman who is none of those things, and let me assure you, that is almost worse. For some women, this opens a place for the bad to slip in. A bit of a spell, or even an accidental situation, can cause her to be overtaken by pride, and then she's no more of this earth. Éloïse may have been around for a hundred years, a thousand, and what she has become has been around since Lilith, Adam's first wife, was expelled from the garden. Her spirit, it is multitude, and in some cases, it is beyond just a glimmer of pride in a beautiful woman. Sometimes she makes a house in a willing soul."

"How would you know such a thing? I've heard stories at sea about the like, but that's all they were."

"I know because I did not marry your mother, and left her to feel abandoned. Something I have been trying to correct all my life. I've watched over you, boy. I've helped with money and goods when I could. Where do you think all that fresh meat you ate while growing up came from? How do you think a widow paid her bills? Oh, you boys helped, and you especially. But it wasn't enough. I wanted to help her. Not only because I loved her, but because I lost her. And I blame my pride for that. You see, pride feeds pride. Men, they measure themselves by the beauty of their women. And on the night before we were to be wed, when I went into that tavern, there she was."

"It couldn't be the same woman."

"It's the same woman, son. And she is not of this world. Sometimes she looks a little different. Hair color, color of skin. Long and lean, short and light. But she has that pride, and it sticks out of her eyes and into your soul. I couldn't resist her. But fate took a hand. When I saw her in the tavern, I forgot I was to be married. I forgot who I was for that matter. I was a wheeled toy on a string, and she was pulling me along. Out of the tavern we went, through the woods to the edge of the river. She had a boat there, and we took it across, and started to climb the trail up Cap Diamant toward her home. The moon was shiny, and the house was too. Built of great timbers and massive stones. The glass in the windows reflected like animal eyes in the depths of the forest. I knew it was too late. That she was already sucking a bit of my soul by me just being in her presence, and yet, I wanted her so. I knew too that once she made love to me, that I would be little but a shell, my essence sucked into hers, left to twirl and dance with all the other souls that were there. The things she fed on from time to time, from need to need.

"Well, we climbed that trail to her house, and we stood at the portal, about to go inside, and then a strange and fortunate thing happened. A great owl screeched, and when it did, it broke the spell, just for a moment. An owl can do that. Their feathers, their cries, even their dung is used in spells; they have nature's power. It was a minor break, but it was enough, because in that instant I saw the house on the hill was no longer made of firm timbers and solid stone. It was made of burnt sticks and tumbling rocks, and there were no windows, just dark squares where they should have been. That house was long abandoned, eaten by fire. And Éloïse? She too was broken down and ravaged. Her hair was as thin and stringy as an ancient mop. Her skin was bumped and savaged. Her body was like a sack of twisted sticks. Only her eyes were still hot with prideful glow.

65

"I turned my head. I knew right then, if I had gone through that portal, had that owl not called, my soul would have gone some place rotten, and the pride inside of me, the pride of being with a woman like that, would feed her, keep her alive.

"I tumbled then, startled myself into imbalance, and down the hill I rolled. And it was a good thing. I rolled long and hard and came up with this limp. Worse right then, but I was thankful for the pain it gave me, because it made me rational. I reached the boat and started across. The sky turned black, sacking the stars. Lightning burst. Thunder roared. The rain cut me like razors. Finally, I reached the far shore.

"By the time I had limped my way painfully home, the moon had dipped and the sun had risen, and I lay in bed three days, delirious. I don't even know how I got home. It was all a blur. But I had ruined it with your mother. Last anyone had seen of me was in the tavern, leaving with that woman, and your mother's pride, though another form, a better definition of it, wouldn't allow her to marry me. And in a short time she married a man who had sought her before me. And when you were born, the timing was close enough, and no one ever thought to consider you had been created before the marital bed."

George sat silent, considering.

"I know it's a lot to take in, and I know you must consider me a crazy old man. But that's how it was."

George lifted his head. "No. I believe you. I do. I believe you're my father, and I believe you about Éloïse, as insane as that sounds. Because she caught my eye too, old man… Father. She caught my eye and had she not already chosen Jean, had she not turned her attention on him, I might well have gone with her instead. I knew then there was something wrong about her, or too right about her. I have to find her, though. I have to find Jean and Samuel."

"You won't find them," Ray said. "Not as they were."

"Then I have to find her, destroy her."

"That's pride itself speaking, boy."

"No. It's vengeance."

His mother's funeral was private, at the church. She was buried in the church cemetery, and though the priest didn't know her well, he threw in a handful of psalms George had mentioned were her favorites.

As George and Ray stood at the grave, George said, "You said you have some advice for me."

"You shouldn't go. I know why you want to, and I don't blame you, but you shouldn't go. You're dealing with something that isn't of this world."

"I'm going, with or without your advice."

"I thought you might." Ray sighed. "Come to the house and let me give you what I have. For years I planned to kill that monster, but truthfully, I never could bring myself to do it. I know I was lucky to survive. You will be lucky to survive."

"I'll survive."

"The confidence of a man without knowledge. That's what you have."

George walked along with Ray, who limped painfully toward his house. It was a short walk, not far from the church, and once they were inside, Ray collapsed in a large overstuffed chair. There was sweat on his face.

"I have to gather myself. I am a shadow of what I once was. Time and age have done that to me, along with her."

"I understand, but the sooner, the better."

"It has to be at night."

"I prefer daylight."

"Preference has nothing to do with it. She is a night creature, like a bat, like a weasel in the wood."

"Tell me what I have to do."

"Guns will do you no good. It would be like shooting the mist. A knife won't help either. Nothing that would kill a human will work, not without the special touches. You can go there by day, and wait until night, but when you enter her dwelling, you can count on there being mirrors."

"Mirrors?"

"Pride, son. That's what she is. Vanity and hubris, and mirrors constantly affirm her beauty. Mirrors made with glass. But silver that reflects, that isn't comfortable for her. Silver is known as a protection against evil. It won't necessarily protect you, but it will assist you. I have several bags of turmeric for you as well. You must take that with you, and when you enter through the main portal, you must seal it with a line of the powder. To be certain, seal all the doorways and windows with it. That way she can't escape, and you can. If you're lucky."

"I don't believe in luck. I believe in action."

"Good enough. Now listen to me…"

He took the mountain trail, and not the river by boat. If there was a boat, it would be on her side of the river. Ray gave him a map that led to the top of the mountain. The cliffs were adorned with diamond-like crystals and gathered on the peaks were fluffy beds of snow. Ray gave him the bag of turmeric, and a round silver platter; like the shield of Perseus, the old man had said… His father had said. And he gave him an axe blessed with a wash of Holy Water.

"You'll be covering quite a few religions," Ray told him. "Better safe than sorry."

"Will it work?" George asked.

"In theory."

"That's thin."

"That's why I prefer you not go."

But go he did, a sea bag of items from Ray slung over his shoulder. He climbed up Cap Diamant with the sun high and the wind cold, and by the time he was near where the map indicated he was to go, the sun was dipping behind the mountain in a burst of crimson flame.

The sky was still bathed in red light when he reached the peak of the trail. The dying day was pushing light through gaps in a stack of crumbling ruins on the top of the mountain trail. Great timbers that were partially burned lay on the ground, and huge stones had been tumbled about by time. Only the frame of the house remained, except for a massive single room in the middle of the ruins. There was a door and walls and the ceiling was a dome.

George tugged at the door, but it was stuck. He put his shoulder into it and it moved. He stepped over the threshold, paused to dig from the bag and apply a line of the turmeric at the doorway. He pushed the door shut, moved into the room and was astonished to find it was indeed covered in mirrors, as Ray had predicted. The walls were a series of mirrors, even behind the bed, and the ceiling had a mirror in its domed center, and there was glass on either side of the mirror there, and through the glass he could see the last of the dying red day giving way to darkness. There was a bed, and on the bed was a covering that spilled over the sides and draped over the foot end of the bed and touched the floor. In the last of the light he saw that it was made of leather. He reached out and touched it. And then he saw that there were patterns in the leather, faces, human faces, and there were too many to count. And then he let out with a cry, for there, at the top of the covering were two faces he recognized. His brothers Jean and Samuel. He moved to the top of the bed, reached out and touched them, then recoiled with horror. They were not patterns of faces, they were indeed faces, somehow through witchcraft or some other unnatural means, they had been mashed flat into the covering, and yet clearly visible—or were, for by that point the last of the light had faded and the room was a thick, stifling shadow.

George pulled a candle from his bag and lit it. He dripped a bit of the hot wax on the headboard of the bed and placed the candle there, sticking it in its own wax. He did this on the other side of the bed, and throughout the room wherever he could find a spot to place a candle, until he ran out of candles. The room was lit now, though the light flickered and moved with a gentle draft.

On the far side of the room he found a door, and he left that one as it was, so that she would have an entryway. Ray had explained that to him. To trap her here, he first had to allow her inside. To keep her out would only delay her, not destroy her.

He went throughout the rest of the house, or rather what remained of it, stopping at the window frames that were left, guessing at others. It was all guesswork, which didn't give him tremendous confidence, and Ray had told him there were no guarantees.

He returned to the domed room, stuck the bag of remaining powder into his pocket and waited. As time passed, his fearlessness gave way to discomfort, and then the hairs on his neck lifted and the top of his head felt cold.

Purple shadows covered the glass in the dome, and they became thinner as the moon rose. There was a chair at a table in front of a mirror on the far wall, and he took the chair and sat it at the foot of the bed. He took the axe from his sea bag, and he took the silver platter—onto the back of which had been affixed a handle, allowing him to hold it like a shield. He placed the open sea bag at his feet. He took a deep breath, and waited.

George sat there a long time, and then the candles ceased to flicker. They gave light, but it was a dead and lifeless light. The air grew stale and the shadows in the corners grew darker. The mirrors became shiny, as if greased, and breathing the air was like breathing in water; it made him feel as if he were drowning.

And then he saw movement.

Something on the far side of the room.

He turned in his chair.

There was nothing there.

A flicker. He jerked his head to find the source.

Nothing.

He stood up, strained his eyes to see into the dark corners of the room, but still nothing, at least nothing he could discern.

And then he saw it. The room in one of the mirrors, but in that mirror he could see her. He glanced quickly about, at the other mirrors. All they showed was the room. But in the one across from him, she was inside the mirror, moving gently forward, her hair lifted on a wind he couldn't feel, and she was looking at him. He felt weak, as if his legs were turning to water. The closer she came the weaker he grew, and then he remembered, do not look her in the eyes.

It was not too late, but he realized he was within moments of her owning him, using him and sucking out his essence, his face being placed into the bed covering, along with his brothers and all those foolish men.

He lifted the silver platter, looked into the reflection it made. The mirror and her image were warped. She seemed wide and rippled, and her eyes were flat in the platter's glare.

George felt his legs strengthen. His heart beat fast. She was stepping out of the mirror. The room was as cold as ice and felt damp, smelled sour. The stench increased and an acrid liquid rose in George's throat.

And then she moved. It was impossibly fast, but he could see her coming in the platter, and then she was there, upon him. He lifted the handle of the axe and swung, making contact. It hit her across the face, tearing the flesh and she screeched. Smoke rose from her singed skin and the smell of burnt death filled his nostrils.

She moved backwards, very quickly, back towards where she had emerged, disturbingly on all fours, like a wild animal. Her hair flashed around her like yellow fire, and then melted back into the mirror, and then… the mirror was just a mirror, and all he could see was himself and the contents of the room.

He wheeled about, glancing left and right. Trying to make out things in the platter's reflection.

He saw her shape, still on all fours, move from one mirror to the next. She was traveling between reflections, and each time she traveled he saw something different about her. Her long dress was hiked over her knees, and he could see scales on her legs, like a fish, and her long, forked tongue moved out of her mouth like a reptile tasting the air.

From mirror to mirror she went, faster and faster, circling the room. She could spring from any one of them at any time, and this caused George to feel that running might be the better and wiser part of valor.

But he held his ground, turning and watching from his chosen spot, the chair behind him, the bed behind that, the mirrors on the wall. It all became a blur as he turned topsy-turvy trying to keep up with her movement from mirror to mirror.

And then she was gone.

Or at least not visible. But he could feel her presence as surely as he could have felt a boulder resting on his chest, a fever in his brain, a stake through his heart.

She was there, but unseen. He lowered the platter and continued searching the room for movement. He took steps backwards until his heels hit the foot of the bed and he stopped, stunned by what he had seen. He dared not even blink. His eyes cut from to side, frantically searching for any sign of her. Still nothing. He could feel his body shaking, from the cold, from the fear. His shoulders were drawn up to his ears, his teeth and fists tightly clenched. He dared not turn his back.

In that moment, a crashing sound echoed from one of the mirrors overhead and all at once she was on him, her legs wrapped around his body, clinging to him like an animal in heat. Her arms flailed about, her outstretched hands and twisted talons clawing at his eyes as she hung there, spittle slinging from both sides of her grey, upturned lips. He grasped frantically for her hands, desperately trying to pull her off of him, causing him to drop the platter and the axe in the struggle. George flung himself backwards toward the bed, landing on top of her wiry body. She writhed and moaned but still she came at him. Tearing at him, ripping slits into the flesh of his bloodied shoulders.

George tossed his body side to side and was putting up a pretty good fight until he thrashed his head to the right and there was Samuel, smiling back at him in a twisted leathery grin. George screamed, and she let out a gurgling laugh. He tried to sit up and roll himself off the bed but she reached for him and yanked his head backwards, biting through the lobe of his right ear, and in that moment everything grew still as a ringing sound reverberated through him. He saw images of his mother, his brothers, and the father he had just now begun to know. The throb of the pain rumbled through his head as her laugh cut through him like the midday heat in the depths of summer. He clenched his eyes closed, desperate not to look at her. He could feel her crawling out from beneath his weight and moving on top of him, straddling his ribbon-cut body. He could feel the warmth of her breath moving in closer to his. He tried desperately to sink his body deeper into the mattress. He let his arms go slack and he strained with every muscle to make space between them. She rolled her head side to side, like a predator sniffing out its prey. He kept his eyes clenched tightly closed, and then he felt the pull of dragging wind from the unhinging of her jaw. The stink of rotten meat wafted through his nostrils and he gagged. He had to concentrate hard to not vomit from the stench alone. He was trying not to breathe, trying not to look directly at her, when he remembered something from before.

George reached his limp hand into the pocket of his pants and scooped out a fistful of the fine, orange powder he had tucked inside earlier. His eyes still clenched, he tossed it upward, hard as he could and heard her begin to hack and wheeze, felt her begin to writhe in pain. She let out a screeching sound then continued her coughing fit, allowing George enough time to lunge her from atop his body and roll to one side of the bed. He stood, and with eyes still to the floor, he could see his axe and shield a few feet away. Pure animalistic fury was driving him now. The pain he'd felt pulsating down his ear and neck was non-existent. He was now working off adrenaline. She shot up from the bed and turned rapidly, launching herself into the air like a condor in flight and landed on all fours, backwards at his feet. Her swollen, distended belly lifting and falling as she breathed heavily from exhaustion. The sounds of snorting and snarling echoed around him. He lunged toward his axe and shield only a few feet away and scooped them up, regaining his advantage—at least that's what he told himself. Like a dog waiting to attack, he watched through the reflection of the shield, both horrified and amazed as she looked up at him with that gaping, cavernous hole of a mouth. Rows of teeth lined her black, rotten gums and through the reflection she appeared almost shark-like. She let out another guttural yell and George brought the axe down in the direction of her screams. He missed, and she began to thrash uncontrollably. She scuttled from one side of the floor to the other, until finally she darted backwards, back towards the mirrors from which she had come. The sounds echoed throughout the room as she fled. The clicking of her claws and the cut of her screams swirled around him, blending into one another, and with the mirrors on every surface, she seemed to be everywhere.

He scanned the floor near him with the platter. She was everywhere alright; he could hear her, except she was nowhere to be found. He held up the platter overhead to look into the columns of mirrors and still, he could not pinpoint exactly where the sounds were coming from. George reached for the remains of the chair that had been crushed during the battle, and tossed them in the direction of the sounds, though it was impossible to tell. He continued doing this until he noticed something shift. He could see her then, her shape moving from one mirror to the next, like a wild animal.

George rushed the mirrors where he had last seen the shift, raised the axe and dropped the blade to meet with the reflective, shiny surface. Shards of glass went everywhere, and he tried to ignore the singing pain from the pieces that flew up and cut through his flesh. One by one he began to move about the room, trying not to let his gaze linger in any place too long, smashing mirrors. Her shape fled after every crash. He tried to keep up with her, but there were so many mirrors. She was too fast, and he was losing a lot of blood.

George was stooped over now, his breath heavy and labored. Still with the platter in one hand and the axe in the other he continued to scan the room. Every mirror now shattered, and still no Éloïse. He made his way back over to the bed and collapsed. George began to weep, the tears filled his eyes and ran down his pink face, mixing with the blood and sweat. The salty liquid burned as it made contact with every gash, every wound. He lay there, the crook of his arm covering his eyes as he continued to cry. He had let down not only his brothers and his mother whom he loved so dearly, but now his father. He was exhausted, and the rage that had washed over him had now turned to sadness. He had to pull himself together. Ray was still out there. Ray still needed him.

He wiped the sweat and tears from his face with the back of his arm and sniffed, and just as he was about to sit up, he saw it. The mirror in the dome overhead. There was something he couldn't quite make out. He grabbed frantically for his platter and poised it at an angle to look. There was something dripping down—it looked like black tar. It oozed and rolled its way down until it stretched the height of the room. Once closer, George could see the gooey, wet reflection of Éloïse and her liquefied flesh peering back at him through the platter's surface. He saw the corners of her putrid mouth curl and he knew this was his final moment.

He grabbed for his axe which lay beside him, and in tomahawk style, lunged the blade upward to the dome, shattering the glass of that final mirror and sending the gooey blob crashing down onto the bed beside him. He ducked his head to hide from the axe and falling shards. When he lifted his gaze, he saw her, sprawled out on the bed, across the human blanket where his brothers lay in eternity. She was no longer ooze, but shattered bones and a rolling skull, rotten and blackened by pride and vanity and time. George stood up and grabbed her skull from the human bedspread, held it high overhead and threw down his arms with all his remaining might. The skull went hurling towards the ground, smashing it into ruins. George stood over the debris, panting. He noticed one chunk of her eye socket stood intact at a distance where it had rolled. He walked over to the remains and placed his heavy boot atop the bone and let all his weight fall upon it. He felt the sweet release of the bone being ground to powder beneath his foot as he twisted his heel from side to side. He stomped his way through the remains and towards his sea bag. He scooped up his sea bag and pulled out the remaining bag of turmeric powder and proceeded to sprinkle it on everything. The bed, the bones, the shattered mirrors, the faces of his deceased brothers... until he had nothing left.

Dawn was on the horizon now, and the shimmer from the cliffs reflected onto the earth as he made his way out of the house and back outside. He coughed and spat, clearing himself of the darkness that had seeped into his fatigued body. He reached into his left pocket and pulled out a matchbook. He plucked one match from inside and scraped it against the heel of that same boot he'd used to crush the skull of the demon, Éloïse.

It sparked, and he delicately set the match at the doorframe and watched, waiting for the already dilapidated structure to catch fire. He smiled as the fire climbed upwards and the dome folded into itself. The wood crackled and spit as the flame rose, and just as quickly, the wood and the remaining beams collapsed into a pile of steaming ash and embers. Black smoke billowed out towards the sky. He watched as it continued to float towards the heavens, and in the smoke he could see her image. Her flimsy, rotted spirit swirling its way around the thick, dark clouds like a tornado.

He heard the loud, screeching call of an owl overhead followed by a popping sound. The flame surged and licked the skies, dancing from side to side and then shifted into a deep greenish-blue color. He looked upward to spot the creature who had called out to him, and just like that, saw the lifeless image of Éloïse as it looped around the funnel cloud of black smoke one last time.

Éloïse was gone. Just like Jean and Samuel. Just like his mother. The remains of her home lay in burnt ash before him as the smoke continued to swirl above, though now it had turned to a crisp bright white. As white as the owl who had called to him earlier that night, delivering him from evil, and had then disappeared into the sky.

He glanced down upon the St. Lawrence River winding gently around the base of the mountain like strips of foil, glimmering in the dawn. It looked lively and never-ending, stretching out as far as George could see. He thought for a moment about the river, about the loss of his mother, his brothers, and the gaining of a father. About the glint of the quartz from the cliffside, and how the crystals hung there like diamonds. He thought of his time at sea, and the vastness of the ocean and how the tide is ever-changing. How rocks, in time, can be washed over and smoothed. How the tug of the river and the ocean, like pride itself, could pull a person under. How that same life-force can drift you gently back ashore if you stop fighting, and let it carry you.

He wondered if Éloïse had at one time stood in this same place and had these same empirical thoughts. He remembered the gorgeous woman he had seen that night at the tavern. How she turned out to be nothing more than a sad, vile sack of bones and flesh, and for a brief moment he pitied her. A woman like that, she would have always been seen a certain way, always a prize to be won. Though in that same breath, his compassion jolted back to anger as he thought of his deceased brothers. His sweet, naive siblings who would never know the joys of love, of a family all their own.

George continued staring down at the water, the magic of it, and in the distance he could see where the ocean and river waters merged and carried on throughout the city. The constant flow that was the life and heartbeat of this town. A language all its own. He could see the church house down below, and though it was too far to make out exactly which grave belonged to his dear mother, he could see the rows of headstones set in perfect alignment, one after another, and he felt at peace. She would never know the fate of her lost children, but George took comfort in knowing that Ray could rest easy tonight.

George inhaled a deep, satisfactory breath, and became suddenly aware of the sweat and blood-stained clothes he was wearing. The smell of fear had permeated his skin, but none of that mattered now. Finally, he would be the most attractive of all the de Roche boys.

AFTERWORD

"It was Pride that changed angels into devils; it is humility that makes men as angels."
—St. Augustine

Pride, the sin from which all others arise. In the fall of 2017 I traveled for the first time to Quebec City with my boyfriend to witness the changing of the leaves. I was struck by the unique beauty and peculiarity of the city, as well as its openness to celebrate Halloween in every public square. Being raised in the deep South, you still get the random cracker here and there that thinks Halloween is about worshipping the devil. Even if it were so, I suppose it's good to believe in something.

There were decorations everywhere, and on a walk through the city center we came across a public park I found particularly engaging. High from the trees, strung up amidst the branches were the ghost-like figures of witchy women and sunken-faced ghouls. The grass was still a rich green, and piles of fat pumpkins littered the lawn. Beneath one notable display stood a framed piece of paper describing the local folklore of "The White Lady."

As we wandered throughout the city, down the horse trails across the cobblestone paths, I couldn't help but feel transported back in time, feel a part of this woman's story. I decided to take the concept of this White Woman, and place her in 1900s Quebec.

A woman who wore a long white veil and lace wedding dress, waiting for a man whose love was strong enough physically and mentally to make it to her side at the mountain's peak, though none ever did. Various suitors came towards her, then fell to their death on the ascent. That's how the story idea started.

I liked the idea of her, desperate for love, wearing that gown, enjoying the proverbial game of cat and mouse. It felt like a good comparison to modern-day dating. Without the death. Though sometimes you hope for it.

That's where the pride comes in. We all have our pride, our vanity. It can be a good thing, keeps you from settling on things that maybe you don't need to settle for. But it can also keep you from ever being happy. It can keep you thinking you're too good for everyone and everything, and then one day you look up, you're left empty and alone, confused why nobody loves you. Beautiful, wonderful you, standing on top of a crystalline mountain in a wedding gown, waiting for a groom who will never show. That's what I hear, anyway.

I hope that what the reader gets out of this story is that first, Quebec City is beautiful, and dare I say I think she's a humble city. Secondly, that it's easy to get wrapped up in your own bullshit and forget that everyone has stuff. Even the so-called pretty people. Even the ones who seem to have everything easy. Pride can be a gift. It can give you a reason to get up in the morning, a goal to strive for. Everyone wants something to be proud of. For someone to be proud of them. It's human nature, and it's a powerful feeling. But with that power, you gotta wield it carefully. You gotta know that it's fleeting, like time and beauty. In an instant, everything you know to be true can be gone, and what you can hope for is that you're left with the goodness you chose to put out into the world reflected back at you. It's easy to see the world through our own looking glass, but maybe, just maybe, this story will give someone an opportunity to see something from another point of view. Even if they don't agree with it, maybe it'll encourage them to have the humility to explore another mindset.

And if not, well, a lot of people die in this story. Enjoy.

CHISEL AND STONE

by Brian Kirk

"For wherever there is jealousy and selfish ambition, there you will find disorder and evil of every kind."
—New Living Translation, James 3:16

"Do not neglect to show hospitality to strangers, for by this some have entertained angels without knowing it."
—New International Version, Hebrews 13:2

Wealth does not bring prestige. I think my dad told me that the day of my rehearsal dinner, which he had not been invited to attend. This was Paul's third wedding and he'd wanted to keep the festivities… intimate, I believe was his word. Though classy is what he had meant. His family, friends, and business partners had been there, sipping vintage champagne, nibbling hors d'oeuvres with pretentious names, dressed like penguins preparing to mate. Intimate was Paul's way of saying he didn't want to have chuck steak on the menu, or serve Coors Light at the bar. Risk having my dad repeat the same dull fishing stories. My mom giving a long, meandering toast and cry.

Don't forget where you came from. That one was definitely Dad. As though I should take pride in my little hometown best known for being one of the last counties to let blacks into the schools. Like I should honor the Confederate flag and its history of hate simply because that was my heritage. Recall with fondness the many nights I'd tucked my little brother into bed after Mom and Dad passed out on the couch, snuffing their lit cigarettes before they fell to the shag carpet.

Can't say that I blame him. Paul, I mean. There's nothing wrong with being discerning about the types of people you associate with. One drop of oil taints the well. Or, as my dad would say without an ounce of irony, all it takes is one fart to clear a room!

No, wealth does not bring prestige, but it sure feels like it at first. Before I'd met Paul, the fanciest dress I'd worn had been rented for my senior prom. Baggy around the hips and tight on the breasts with faded stains that could have come from spilled mayonnaise, but I doubt it. The nicest car I'd ever ridden in was a souped-up Camaro with a muffler so loud it sounded like some furious devil. Paul was the first man to take me outside Louisiana—a week of spa treatments and wine tasting in Sonoma and Napa Valley where I'd gotten wasted on chardonnay and vomited seafood risotto onto one of the sommeliers. Hey, you can take the girl out of the country, but you can't take the country out of the girl! I'll credit Mom for that one.

Our courtship had been my initiation into high society. Celebrating monthly anniversaries with diamond earrings, multi-course meals, and long weekends at one of Paul's several homes. My gradual makeover occurring in increments, like furnishing a living room on a layaway plan. Don't listen to law enforcement—crime does pay. It just pays high-priced attorneys like my husband Paul. My last paystub was from Red Bull for two weeks of work and was for less than it takes for Paul to pick up the phone. I'd met him while sampling product at some event he was attending and he'd—how does the saying go?—swept me off my feet. Swept me into his limousine is more like it. But I've come to love him. Or maybe it's the lifestyle that I love. Sometimes I feel like my profession is being married to Paul, so maybe I just love my job.

It does fade, though. Five years removed from Louisiana—we live in Texas now—and I'd become bored with wealth and its superficial excess. Cooped up by myself in a house with five bedrooms. Paying $1,400 a month just so I could sit in temperate air. Tri-weekly lunches with the same pre-approved women with our empty aspirations and circulating lies.

Money, I've learned, brings security. And security becomes a cage. After seven years of captivity I wanted to rattle the bars. So, without thinking, as though gurgling up from my stifled subconscious, I repeated that same line my dad might have said the day he was snubbed from our rehearsal dinner, "Wealth does not bring prestige," and I could tell it snuck through Paul's tough exterior, landing with a surprising sting.

"Come again?" Paul said. This was just after the Landrys bought the dilapidated estate across from us and began demolition. We were on our front porch watching the work crew while sipping from a bottle of riesling recommended by the wine buyer at the country club. There is something inherently satisfying about watching old structures get torn down.

A bulldozer cracked one of the foundational beams and I waited for the shouts of warning to fade as the eastern wall canted to the side. "My dad said that,"

I said, and Paul grunted—the two men had never struck up a bond. Paul took Dad pheasant hunting once and blamed their lack of success on the lingering smell of alcohol and those aforementioned farts that could clear a room.

"Your dad said, 'prestige?' Why do I doubt that?"

It was a fair point. "Maybe he said happiness," I said. Relieved laughter came from the bulldozer driver who had nearly buried himself under two stories of debris. "It's not like it's an original saying. Happiness, prestige. Same thing."

Paul cut a cube of aged Gouda and brought it to his nose. "Happiness is not the same thing as prestige. Those are two different things entirely." He took a tiny bite and chased it with a sip of wine, beads of sweat glistening along the base of the glass. Slow and meticulous, my Paul, except between the sheets where he pumps himself breathless inside a minute, crushing me under his two-hundred-plus-pounds until he musters the energy to roll off. "Happiness is a feeling of inner joy or contentment. Prestige is an image of success projected onto others. We have that in spades. So happiness is what you mean to say in this context. Are you saying you are unhappy?"

This was the wordplay that made Paul so effective in court. The Miranda rights had been written to protect the innocent from men like him. Whatever you say may be used against you. That was Paul's specialty, twisting words around like Bugs Bunny bending a shotgun barrel until it was pointing back at the shooter. Pull the trigger and kiss your face goodbye.

The estate across the street had stood for seventy years and by this time tomorrow would be rubble. "We could always be happier, I guess."

He nodded. Not in agreement. More by way of processing. Careful to lift his chin to avoid fat rolls from forming around his neck. He'd been fitter when we met. His bachelor weight, as I've come to learn. "So you're saying there's an unlimited supply of happiness. A gradient without end that we can continue to climb until, what? What does infinite happiness look like?"

I can remember farther back than most people. Back even before I learned how to talk. When thoughts were vague sensations and compartmentalized images like panels on a quilt. I remember breastfeeding—people think I'm making this up, but I swear I'm not—held so snug against my mother's breast I could hear her heart beating, and my whole body thrummed with an all-encompassing sense of contentment, the blissful drowsiness felt when waking from a nap outdoors. Nothing traumatic separates me from that little girl—the line is straight and untroubled—but that feeling of basic contentment has been replaced by an ever-present anxiety that buzzes like a hornet in the pit of my chest. A biological warning of danger from some threat I can't see.

"Infinite happiness?" I said. "A lazy river filled with champagne, obviously."

He sipped wine through a smile. "Mine would be milk chocolate. Floating on a custard-filled donut."

"Like that kid from *Charlie and the Chocolate Factory*?" I puffed out my chest and sang in a terrible German accent. "Augustus Gloop. Augustus Gloop. The great big greedy nincompoop."

He frowned as he failed to get the reference, which shouldn't have surprised me. His father had probably lulled sweet Paul to sleep by reading case briefs. That's what you get having a federal judge for a dad.

The workers across the street yelled something in Spanish just before a window shattered and then cheered like their team had scored a goal. "Maybe even happiness isn't the right word," I said. I always felt smarter than my friends growing up, most of whom graduated from LSU with degrees in leisure management. Topics of conversation typically varied between hunting, drinking beer, football, fighting, and having sex—subjects I've found to be intrinsically linked. I never met anyone like Paul before I left Louisiana, and talking with him was a challenge I enjoyed. "Fulfillment, maybe? Take the Hendersons for example."

The way Paul stiffened silenced me. He set his glass down and turned in my direction. "What exactly are we talking about here?"

This was like being put on the stand, him with his arms crossed. The look of fierce concentration as he waited to pick apart my words. Usually it was enough to make me back down—say if I were pushing for a yoga retreat to Tulum, or for tickets to a Carrie Underwood concert or something. My life was filled with enough luxuries I had no problem caving on certain extravagances that were outside Paul's comfort zone. But this was different. I had begun to feel empty in our material existence. Unfulfilled. Worse, I think—and this was what really set the next series of events in motion—I had become jealous of our neighbors across the street— the couple next door to the new Landrys' place, in fact—who appeared to have struck a gracious balance between wealth and fulfillment through philanthropy. You could only take so much, it seemed. At some point you had to start giving back.

"Nothing to get defensive about, jeez," I said, wishing I hadn't used court language. Now I'd unconsciously put him in prosecutor mode. "I'm just thinking about some of the things Alyssa talks about at lunch, is all. And thought it was maybe something we could talk about."

Alyssa Henderson was part of my tri-weekly lunch crew, and for the last year or so all she'd talked about was the foundation her hotshot hedge fund husband Eric had started and tasked her with running. Alyssa couldn't tell you the first thing about stock dividends, but was a self-proclaimed expert at providing aid to inner city dance academies and grants for Montessori schools, as she made clear to us by boasting all about the "amazing" and "unbelievable" and "life-changing" work her foundation was doing. "We're so fortunate," she'd say, which none of us could argue while eating crab cakes on a work-free Wednesday afternoon. "The least we can do is give to those less fortunate than us." Another iron-clad point that I heartily agreed with while my face burned with shame.

Yes, I still could have backed down to Paul at this point—should have backed down in retrospect—but I didn't. "What I'm talking about," I said, walking down the road of no return. "Is trying to find a greater purpose in life. Maybe by giving back in some way like Eric and Alyssa do through their foundation." A support beam cracked with the sound of gunfire and we both watched as the canting wall collapsed to the ground, raising a great cloud of dust into the air. "Using some of our money—" Referring to his money as *ours* always irked him. "To make a difference. You know, like a legacy project."

Paul was capable of masking all emotion under a face of stone. Could win a staring contest with a wall. "The Hendersons build ballet studios in places where half the population is on food stamps. I wouldn't call that saving the world."

Speak of the devil and the devil appears. The front door to the Henderson's opened and Alyssa rushed out with her five-year-old daughter, Alexandria, to come see what had caused the thunderous crash. We could hear the excited squeals from little Alex as she pulled her mom out for a better look. She was another unspoken source of jealousy. Paul already had three kids from a prior marriage and had made it clear he didn't want more. Had tied his tubes years before we met. Back when I was in my mid-twenties with no interest in having kids interrupt my active social life—thinking step-mom status would satisfy me, not realizing how difficult it would be to endear myself to girls who had stopped trusting their father's taste in women. I'm only eight years older than Paul's oldest daughter and the most motherly advice I've offered was to lighten her dark arm hair. She looked at me like I had a pentagram tattooed on my forehead, and I've kept my mouth shut ever since. God forbid I'd urged her to sugar her bikini line or, worse, anal bleach.

"True," I said, and smiled. What Paul had said *was* funny, and even eased my jealousy some. "But that doesn't mean we couldn't do something better. Something truly worthwhile that genuinely helps people and makes a real difference in the world."

It took several minutes for Paul to pit an olive and cut another cube of cheese. His movements may be slow, but I know his mind was whirring as he came up with counter-arguments. I watched Alyssa hoist Alex up on her hip and point towards the demolition site, teaching her more useful lessons than which bronzing lotions worked best.

"So, Mother Teresa," he said. "What exactly do you have in mind?" Wait, had I just presented a compelling case? No objections so far, your honor!

"Let me think about it," I said. Which has always preceded the most deadly of endeavors known to mankind.

⌒⌒

I'm not very political, but you can't help but be inundated with outrage over the government these days. My Facebook feed has become a battleground for warring factions. Turn on the TV and you'll find some talking head shouting about securing our borders while another screams about the rise of Xenophobia. Growing up in the rural South, I was exposed to a fair amount of bigotry and racism. Hell, my dad's an unapologetic racist who uses the "N" word as though there's no more suitable term. My mom claims tolerance, but thinks equal opportunity is prejudice against whites and presumes all black men shot by police had it coming. I've seen the bad hand many minorities have been dealt, born in poverty-stricken ghettos pockmarked with stray bullets. I didn't win the lottery being born in rural Louisiana, but at least it was in a white neighborhood among working families. Could just as easily have been one of the mostly black neighborhoods that seem more like farm systems for prisons. Or, God forbid, somewhere in the war-torn Middle East fearful of deadly shadows passing overhead.

Being pretty doesn't hurt either, and even that was outside my control. Let's keep it real, I wouldn't have caught Paul's eye had I been either ugly, overweight, or had some speech impediment, other than the Cajun accent I've learned to hide around my new friends. He likes to look at me—okay, more than just look if we're keeping it real—and I like the lifestyle he provides. No laws are being broken, but I can't say it feels fair. Not when the innocent struggle from cradle to grave due to a lousy roll of the dice or the color of their skin.

And that's where my thinking mind went: how to use our wealth—Paul's, I mean—and influence—Paul's, once again—to fix some of the injustices against poor minorities or people fleeing war. Maybe it was an attempt to whitewash the guilt I felt for my racist upbringing, I don't know. But I couldn't think of anything more worthy of my time. Or Paul's, as it turned out. It would do more good than teaching underprivileged kids to twirl and dance on their toes, that's for sure.

We were home watching the news when the idea struck. It was a segment on the new vetting processes being placed on refugees trying to enter the country. Paul's father was adamant that the orders being handed down by the president were unconstitutional. And Paul who, while lacking a bleeding heart, always sided with his liberal father, agreed. Personally, I couldn't have cared less about a stale old document written centuries ago, but the program we were watching showed pictures of young kids who had been caught in the crossfire of civil war. Little boys and girls barely five years old with faces covered in soot and smeared with blood from flying shrapnel. Sunken eyes, glazed by the horrors they'd seen that would forever alter the way they viewed the world—their innocence another piece of collateral damage.

"God, that's awful," I said. And maybe it was God who heard me, or more likely the devil considering how things went, because I was immediately struck with the idea for what we should do. "That's it," I said. "That's our cause right there." And just saying it lifted a weight of guilt and indecision that was pressing against my chest. "We've got to help them somehow."

In my mind, I was picturing living centers for displaced families. Apartment complexes that would house people escaping war while they looked for a more permanent place to live. A way to keep families together and provide a safe environment for kids to recuperate from the trauma of having bombs dropped on their neighbor's house. Stepping over dismembered limbs as they shopped for food.

But that's not what Paul had in mind. He was more interested in actions that allowed him to flex his judicial muscles. Which is what led us to Guantanamo Bay. A detention center in Cuba holding presumed prisoners of war, many of whom had been incarcerated for years without ever receiving a trial of any kind.

"Let Europe deal with the refugees," Paul said, more animated than I'd seen him since our early dates when he'd been trying to win me over. "I'm not interested in running a damn Airbnb. It's justice I want."

He also wanted recognition, which winning early release for prisoners of Guantanamo Bay was sure to provide. Making him a hero within his small circle of progressive attorney friends so far removed from average, everyday life it was like two separate strains of humanity. What do they say about marriage? It's an exercise in compromise? Not that I had much leverage in this particular negotiation, but arranging for the release of innocent men who were casualties of war sounded like a fair compromise to me. A starting place, if nothing else. There was also something powerfully sophisticated about the idea that excited me, and it certainly played well with my lunch crew. My husband with his political pull. Actually, his father's mostly, if we're still keeping it real.

It took nearly a year for Paul to maneuver through all the political obstacles and government interference. His father, who was even more excited by this endeavor than I was, got him access to the right people. Finally, when it was clear he wouldn't be deterred, the pentagon allowed Paul to review the cases for five of their lowest risk prisoners. Men who had been swept up in a fishing expedition at the age of eighteen and detained without trial for the last eleven years. Paul flew out to meet with the officials and discuss conditions of release. He called five days later with the most startling news I'd ever heard, "I've got one of them. And I'm bringing him home."

I naturally thought Paul meant he was reuniting the freed man with his family. But his family was dead, his home destroyed. He had nowhere to go, so Paul was bringing him back to Texas to stay with us until we could get him set up somewhere else. So much for his aversion to Airbnb. But this was much more in line with my original idea, and I was ecstatic. The whole operation had been outside my sphere of influence, and now I'd have a chance to play a direct role.

"Oh my God, Paul. You're incredible! Tell me everything." He did and I wish I'd never asked.

⌒

News spread fast. A mixture of trepidation and support. Paul was due home the next day and Alyssa was with me on the front porch, watching the final pieces of the Landrys' place come together. This being the new home replacing the old one that had been torn down. A beautiful 4,500 square-foot palatial estate with a custom stone exterior. I always figured those exterior stones were fabricated in a factory, but here they had a huge supply of stone slabs in the front yard with a single worker using a chisel and hammer to hand cut each one, fitting the finished pieces together like some prehistoric jigsaw puzzle. Alexandria was in the yard playing with a large hoop that made bubbles when she swung it in the air. If that's not innocence, I don't know what is.

"And you're not worried? Not at all?" Alyssa said. She was sitting in the same seat Paul was when we had our fateful conversation. We weren't eating cheese, but we were drinking wine, and Alyssa had consumed just enough to loosen her tongue. "I mean, I still don't get it. Why?"

I try not to think about what Paul told me about the prison, but I can't help it. It's all I see every time I close my eyes. Dark hallways with metal doors. Look through the little crosshatch window into the sparse cell and see a man—not some abandoned dog waiting to be adopted—someone's father, son, or brother sitting naked in the corner with his head in his hands and who knows what running through his mind. Alone, cut off from friends and family. The only human interaction coming in the form of extreme interrogation. No trial. No chance to plead his case. Treated like a homicidal killer without consideration for whether or not it's true. *Dog bites,* Paul had said. *All over his arms.*

"Hell yeah I'm worried," I said, though anxious was the proper word. "But I believe we're doing the right thing." The *just* thing, as Paul would say. "Imagine if someone you knew was stuck alone in prison for some crime they didn't commit. Wouldn't you want to help?"

The sound of chisel on stone made me think of men working a chain gang. My God, we are terrible towards each other. Crime and punishment both. "Yeah," Alyssa said. "If it was someone I knew. And I knew they didn't do it. How can you possibly know this man wasn't planning some terrorist attack? I mean, Jesus—" I found it strange that she invoked His name when condemning my act of charity. "That's where they send the very worst of the worst, Tracy. And you're bringing him here? To our neighborhood?" She whispered this next part. "With children running around?"

Alex skimmed over the grass lawn as manicured as a putting green, a shimmering bubble stretching behind her. Blissfully unaware of the kids her own age who right then were crying out from underneath mounds of smoldering rubble.

"He's got nowhere else to go," I said.

"How is that our problem?"

Alyssa had been one of the most enthusiastic supporters of the idea when I first mentioned it last year. Back when it seemed like a storyline from one of her favorite TV shows. Things had changed now that it had become reality. The worker set down his chisel and held the jagged stone up to the sun. Deemed it perfect, and nestled it snugly into its place on the wall.

"He's an innocent man," I said. "Jee-wiz." My version of Jesus. "Have a heart."

I shouldn't have said that, it gave her permission to be angry. "Please, cry me a fucking river," she said. A river? Keep this up and I'll cry you Niagara-Fucking-Falls. "You want to do something good? Feed the homeless, Trace. You don't go goddamn messing with convicted fucking terrorists and bringing them around our kids. I mean, Jesus!"

"Again, Alyssa," I said, trying my level best to stay calm. "He's not a terrorist."

"Right, they locked him up by accident, I forgot."

We sat in strained silence while the worker retrieved his hammer and chisel and approached another slab. "Even if he was innocent," Alyssa said, with a cynical edge. "How about now? I mean, won't he want revenge? I know I would."

Maybe life would be different if we actually looked for the best in others. "It's temporary," I said. "Just until we can get him set up somewhere else. Look, I understand why this scares you, but it's important to me. To us. It's something we feel called to do." Rather, it was important that I maintain the moral high ground throughout this ordeal. That was the original point of all this, even if it had expanded into something more.

Alyssa exhaled a frustrated gust of air. The chisel clinked, clinked, clinked. Alexandria chased a bubble half her size. "Well, I hope you'll at least keep him..."

Her bottom lip was trembling. Doing good never felt so bad.

"Locked up?" I said.

She drained her glass of wine and stood. "Come on, Alex girl. Time to go."

Alyssa grabbed Alexandria roughly by her upper arm and led her home. Wishing, I bet, our new president would build the wall he'd promised on the street between us. The Kaisers' rescue dog barked from behind their gate a few houses down and it made me think of the man I'd be meeting tomorrow. Those bite marks on his arms.

⌐⌐

His name was Zahid Bari. Thank God it was something I could pronounce without sounding like a fool, unlike those stupid hors d'oeuvres we'd served at our rehearsal dinner. Though I couldn't help but say it without using some lilting accent that was more Indian than Arabic. Paul and a small team of lawyers from his firm helped speed Zahid through customs and brought him to our house sometime after midnight. I had spent the last few days setting up his guest room, which was basically a studio apartment over the garage. Dressing the bed with the finest linens sold at Nordstrom's. Loading the bathroom with an array of soaps, shampoos, shaving cream, and the plushest toilet paper I could find. Can you imagine the indignity of using a bucket and wiping with your hand? I get stage fright going in a stall next to somebody. I'd suffer constipation before I squatted in front of a guard.

I pictured Zahid coming home like some Arabian prince returning to his palace after a long and harrowing journey. A romanticized fantasy that shattered the instant I saw him. I actually thought we'd wake that first morning and get acquainted over eggs and Belgian waffles.

He came in wrapped in a wool blanket. Shivering as though hypothermic despite the summer humidity and internal thermostat being set at seventy-two degrees. I could smell him across the room. The bottom of the garbage can after weeks of rancid trash has leaked from the bags. *Maggot food* is what came to mind, and I actually gagged at both the thought and the smell. His wiry hair was a kid's on Christmas morning. His face a patchwork beard cropped with a dull blade. I'd seen eyes like his in dogs at the pound you knew would never find a home. The fingers clasping the blanket were long and grimy, as were the nails. And my first thought was how relieved I was that he'd come at night so that no one else could see him—especially Alyssa, though I later learned she'd been spying through her window along with all the other neighbors within eyesight. Forgive me for saying this, but he looked more like a wild animal than a man. Even to me, he looked dangerous and it made me realize we all harbor racist thoughts whether we like it or not.

Paul and his colleagues ushered him up to his room where they stayed with him most of the night. Shaken, I wrapped the bowl of hummus I'd set out in cellophane and bagged the sliced veggies. I didn't see him again for a few days, and by then the neighborhood was already in an uproar over this murdering terrorist who couldn't even make it out of bed.

I shuttered all the windows and stayed indoors myself. Barricading us in. Three days after Zahid arrived, Paul assisted him downstairs. I felt like a terrible host who had failed to provide an official tour, and was desperate to find some way to make him feel comfortable.

"Get some water, hon?" Paul said. "Maybe some toast?"

I peeked through the shuttered blinds and saw that a sign had been posted in our yard.

TERRORIST FREE ZONE!
PROTECT OUR KIDS! SEND HIM HOME!

It seemed like southern hospitality hadn't spread to Texas. At least not to my silver spoon neighborhood.

Zahid was wearing a t-shirt from a Hilton Head resort, his collar bones jutting out like hanger wire. Hunched over, shuffling in Paul's cotton slippers. Arms wrapped around his stomach as though he'd just been sucker punched. Then I saw them, the puckered scars scattered up and down his arms—a mix of neat, round holes, and jagged strips from ripped skin.

"Coffee?" I said, and Paul shook his head. Water and toast, then. Just like they serve in jail.

We sat at our round glass kitchen table. I was wearing an athletic tank top with spandex pants, which I now realize was grossly inappropriate. Zahid took small bites of bread and sips of water. Thin as my anorexic friend Betsy who went to rehab to put on weight.

"Welcome to our home," I said, speaking in that silly accent that is really no sillier than any other. "We are so, so honored to have you."

I'd never seen eyes so haunted, staring straight through the glass table. I turned to Paul, "Does he speak English?"

He nodded. "In time."

Zahid looked both older and younger than twenty-nine. The lined face of a man with the stilted mannerisms of a child. Grey at the temples and chin. "Would you like some butter or jelly?" I said, and he just kept on chewing as though he couldn't hear or understand me. Each bite producing a dry crunch. Crumbs catching in the trenches of his cracked lips.

Something broke inside me seeing him like that. Perhaps some untapped motherly instinct—or, more likely, a basic human one. I reached across the table for his hand and he jerked violently away, his chair screeching across the floor. "La!" he said. "Kif!"

"That means 'stop,'" Paul said in a stern voice. Wearing his courtroom suit. His watch probably worth more than Zahid could make in a lifetime. Had I really thought I could help this man, or had I hoped he could help me? I thought again about those dogs in the kennel destined for a needle, too broken for a home.

I forced myself to lose the phony accent, speaking with the Cajun one that came most naturally. "I just want you to know," I said. "That you're safe here." Thank God the blinds were shut so he couldn't see the signs. "Our home is your home, and we'll make sure no one hurts you any more."

It was impossible to tell if he heard me. I think he sent his mind away long ago to escape the pain.

⌒⌒

There was so much I hadn't prepared for. The first was Paul returning to work. The thought of me and Zahid alone in this large, empty house. My only formal training is in the field of hospitality, but serving Red Bull vodkas wasn't going to help Zahid feel more at home. I should have done more to understand his culture before he'd arrived, but all I had to pull from now was stuff I'd seen online. Mostly footage of hostages kneeling behind hooded men holding knives.

I needed to establish common ground, and I found that through food. Regardless of our differences, we all need to eat. So that became my early mission. As my Grandma would say, *Put some meat on them bones.* The problem was that he was terrified of being in the same room with me. He would begin trembling any time we crossed paths. And I didn't want to leave trays of food outside his door like they did at Guantanamo Bay. I wanted to break him from that association as soon as possible, and the best way to enter a cold pool is to dive in.

If you find a Southern woman who can't cook, then you've come across an imposter. Hell, we coined the term Comfort Food. And that's what I set out to make. Biscuits and gravy. Fluffy scrambled eggs and fried green tomatoes. Chicken jambalaya and red beans and rice. No pork, which was a shame. My country ham is to die for. And bacon? Please, that's God's most perfect meal. I figured he couldn't stay in his room forever—foolish considering the last eleven years—and hoped the aroma would draw him out. Thankfully, I was right. I caught him watching from around the corner, like a kid spying on his parents after bedtime. I was fearful of spooking him, so I pretended I hadn't noticed as I placed the food in serving dishes, the steam curling up like a finger calling him forward. Spend eleven years eating institutionalized slop and try to resist rich Southern food, you can't. I spaced the dishes out on the kitchen counter buffet style and then retreated to the table off to the side. Sat and began playing Solitaire on my tablet.

He came shuffling around the corner in that same Hilton Head t-shirt, baggy sweatpants slung low on his waist, wearing Paul's favorite slippers. I hate that I keep using the canine reference, but I can't help it. He was so much like an abused dog, cautious and fearful of being hurt again. The way he eyed the food you'd have thought the ramekin of eggs contained an IED. Growing up, my biggest fear had been getting a huge zit on my lip the day of a big date. My how our little planet harbors many worlds.

I waited until he reached the kitchen counter and began inspecting the food, looking lost and confused. It was time to put on the charm. I set my tablet down and stood, my movements slow and meticulous—taking my cues from Paul. I was wearing pants to cover my legs and a long sleeve blouse buttoned up to my neck. My hair pulled up in a bun. I approached like a server at a high-end restaurant. Polite, respectful, subdued.

"Hungry?" I said, trying to blind him with my smile.

He flinched and began apologizing profusely as he rushed back towards his room.

"It's okay. It's okay," I said. "Please don't go. Please, stay and eat. I made this for you."

He hesitated at the corner. So skinny; he had to be starving. The devil should have used this meal during his temptation of Christ.

"Please, come eat." I began scooping the food onto a plate, making it clear it was for him. I set it down and he still wouldn't come. I was the cold water. He was the boy cringing every time he dipped a toe in. I'll tell you one thing, my daddy may not have taught me much, but he didn't raise me timid. I approached him with a hand outstretched. Got to him before he could retreat and grabbed him gently by the wrist and led him back into the kitchen. Stood him before the heaping plate of food and handed him a fork. "Bon Appetit," I said. Then, clarifying, "It's for you. Please, eat."

I made myself a plate so he didn't feel awkward eating alone. Poured us both some orange juice. Then I watched with satisfaction as each bite got bigger than the one before. It wasn't long before I served him a second helping.

I had never been so lost for words, but the silence was killing me so I just said the first thing that came to mind. "How's the bed? Is it comfortable?" Thank goodness Paul wasn't here to make me feel dumb.

Zahid paused mid-bite, nodded. Then, miracle of miracles, he said, "Yes. I thank you."

A thousand pounds of pressure lifted from my shoulders. "You're welcome," I said.

The eggs could have used a touch more salt, but Zahid didn't seem to mind. "I want you to feel comfortable here. Whatever you need, just let me know."

He ate, swallowed, nodded. "I thank you."

"First time in Texas?" I said, stupidly. But, hell. How do you build a bridge across the Grand Canyon without a degree in engineering?

"First time, yes." He turned, almost looked at me, and then averted his gaze.

I set my fork down. "I know how strange this must all be for you. But you're free now. You can do anything you want. You're never going back to that place."

He started shivering, thinking about that prison I assume. His shivering intensified, and I wished I had said something else. That I had a manual or a script written by someone experienced in these things, if such a person exists. He dropped his fork and hugged his body and tried not to cry, his face bunching from the strain, but he couldn't hold it in and the tears came in a torrent as he crouched to the floor and began rocking on his heels.

I didn't know what to do, so I stood there like an idiot. Trying not to stare. But it's not like this is something I could ignore. So much for brunch being my great olive branch. I squatted down beside him. How long since he'd felt a tender touch? Those scars all along his arms. Who knows what others lie hidden under clothes, or inside his tortured psyche. I placed my hand on his back and his whole body spasmed. "It's okay," I said, though it wasn't. He needed a therapist, not my empty assurances. "I'm here for you. You're safe." I wrapped an arm around his shoulders and pulled, fighting his resistance until he fell against me. Collapsed into my arms, balled up like a Texas armadillo sensing danger. I sat there with him cradled against my chest long after the food went cold. Rocking him like a child, running my hands through his hair as I whispered sweet nothings and made soothing sounds. Fighting like hell against the tears straining my eyes. Summoning strength for us both.

This became our ritual. Our rite of bonding. And it got better each day, his clothes filling out as he dined on 80/20 skillet burgers, and baked beans, and tater tots, and skyscraper nachos, and cheese pizza, and fried chicken, and crème filled donuts, and brownie sundaes, and rib eye steaks. "I thank you. I thank you. I thank you," spoken each day with fewer tears and the growing promise of a smile. He had not yet gone outside, however, and I didn't want my home to become a luxurious prison complex. But the neighbors hadn't stopped protesting with their stupid signs and I was worried about the way he'd be treated when they finally met. This was not the same as cold water.

I took him out at night. Paul was handling the situation from a legal standpoint, working to get Zahid a work visa, while leaving the rehabilitation efforts—as I came to think of them—to me. I gave Zahid a Texas Rangers baseball cap by way of disguise and loaded him into the car in the garage. The plan was to take him on a nighttime tour of Dallas. Up to the top of the Reunion Tower with its ball of lights. Maybe a stroll through Highland Park Village, or grab some fast food and eat in an empty park. Baby steps, you know. Though we never made it out of the car. Zahid would begin trembling any time we came near a crowd of people, and the highway completely freaked him out. He sat ramrod straight in his seat, fingers curled around the handrail as he kept pumping imaginary breaks with both feet. So I ditched the city with its loud gridlock and took him out to the quiet of White Rock Lake instead. Found a place where we could park looking out over the water with the city skyline in the distance. Turned Pandora to my Ryan Adams station and kept the volume low.

This is among the most peaceful places I know, and he was nervous the whole time. Head on a swivel, knee pattering a bass drum.

"You okay?" I asked. Another stupid question. Look at him, Tracy. Yeah, he's splendid. "Do you have any lakes back home?"

"No," he said. He was breathing shallow and his voice was shaking. "Much sand. Very dry."

Of course, he comes from the freaking desert, dummy. "Pretty, huh?" I said, and he looked at me. "Out here, I mean." And he nodded.

"Big," he said with a sweep of his hand that showed he meant more than the lake. "So much. Very rich," he said. "So much is possible here."

And yet I had felt stifled in the face of all this opportunity. In this moment, however, I felt completely alive. Looking out on this view with a renewed sense of wonder. Grateful I could come here whenever I wanted, gazing at the brilliant skyline, and sit in peace.

"Ready to go home?" I said, not wanting to push too hard on this first venture out, and he nodded.

"Yes, I thank you." To think that I was giving this tortured man a place to call home. All of Alyssa's ballet studios combined couldn't amount to that one act of goodwill. And maybe this was just the beginning. I was feeling good as we rounded the turn onto our street, and Zahid had visibly settled down. Then I saw the pocket of neighbors in front of our house holding signs, all standing to attention as soon as they saw my car and started blocking the driveway.

"Oh no. I'm so sorry Zahid, ignore these people," I said, as though there was any way to ignore the angry faces crowding the car and pressing against our windows. Eric and Alyssa were on either side—I'm assuming they left Alexandria alone in bed—with expressions of such rage I hardly recognized them.

"You're not welcome here!" Alyssa shouted.

Eric was less diplomatic. "You fucking terrorist fuck!"

Zahid slouched down in his seat. "What are they doing?" Trembling like he did the first night he arrived.

"Go home to Allah, you goddamn Muslim! This is Jesus Country!"

I tried reversing, but we were blocked on all sides. Then the chant started. Like they'd been rehearsing. "Go home! Go home! Go home, you Muslim scum!" These were people we smiled and waved at every morning. Shared meals with at the club each day. Is it fear? Do we all revert to animals when afraid? I smelled urine and heard the spill of liquid as Zahid pissed himself, sinking further down in his seat.

I began honking my horn to drown out their crazy chant. Accelerated in spurts to clear the front end and maneuvered onto our driveway and into the garage. The closing door sent my neighbors into a frenzy. They started hammering on the door and shouting in victory as though the Cowboys had just won the Super Bowl. All that pent-up rage over someone they hadn't even seen. Which makes for the most frightening of monsters, I suppose.

Paul was at a window calmly looking out. "Can't say I'm surprised," he said, giving me a look like I had brought this on myself. Like driving an innocent man around town had suddenly become a crime.

"Well I sure as fuck am!" I shouted, trembling like Zahid but for different reasons. "What about human fucking decency! This is insane!"

Led by Eric and Alyssa, our neighbors trampled over our perennial beds for a look through the windows. "We want him out of here!" Alyssa shouted, the queen of philanthropy showing her true colors. "Listen to us Tracy! We don't feel safe!" she said while brandishing her fists in anger.

Paul sighed. "I'll handle it," he said, exiting through the front door and leading the crowd away from the house. They circled him, shouting angrily, but I knew they'd soon be cowed by his courtroom demeanor. He was a master at dealing with a raucous press.

I rushed Zahid up the stairs to his suite. His shutters were all open and the windows peered out over the front of the house. Offering a clear view of the Landrys' new construction across the street and the Hendersons' beside it. Which means he had seen the signs before. Had been watching the neighbors for days as they circled our house and planted their signs and sneered and pointed and conspired in hate.

I closed the shutters, covering the windows with horizontal bars. They were forcing me to turn my house into a prison, to treat our honored guest like an inmate, and it infuriated me. The hell this man had already been through and was still being made to suffer. All for what? Where he'd been born? The religion he'd been taught as a boy? Had my parents been Pentecostal Christians I'd have handled snakes and spoken in tongues and not thought twice about it. He was eighteen when they took him, if not younger! Just because he fit a profile, or was in the wrong place at the wrong time.

I was shaking, my heart filled with such anger—such vicious hate—for my neighbors below that if I could have ordered an airstrike on them all right then I would have. Not one real offense had been committed and we were primed for war. If there's anything more deadly than our own imaginations I've yet to see it.

Zahid was sitting on the bed in his piss-stained pants, staring vacantly at the floor. I rummaged through the drawers and retrieved a change of clothes and handed them to him. I didn't want to leave him alone, so I put my face in the corner while he changed. Turned back when he was done, and sat on the bed beside him.

"That was terrible, I'm sorry," I said.

He was gone again. Had sent his mind away.

His beard had filled in since he'd been here, as had the sunken cheeks of his face. His collarbones no longer jutted up through the fabric of his t-shirt. It was so hard to see past the damage, though. To picture him at a nightclub with a modern haircut, trendy clothes, maybe a chain necklace, a hearty laugh and carefree smile. Busting moves with his buddies and hitting on chicks. I wanted this for him. He deserved it, and that became my goalpost. Assuming that's something he ever wanted.

I put my hand on his back and he arched away.

"All I can say is I'm sorry," I said.

His hands were clasped with such tension I'm surprised he didn't snap a bone. "Everything I have is gone," he said. "Your people took everything from me."

My people.

Me.

I nodded.

"You say Jesus," he said. "Did Jesus kill women and children? Did Jesus bomb mosques and hospitals? Take men from their families and torture them? Make them do disgraceful things?"

Whatever strength I had summoned left me and I began to weep. "No," I whispered.

"No, but your people did that in his name. You say my religion is evil. Tell me who is evil."

"I can't," I said, not wanting to engage in a philosophical debate about religion. Point out that his religion calls for things that are evil as well. Who is it that we're worshipping, anyway? Who do we believe made up all these barbaric rules?

My eyes were drawn again to his arms. The inhumanity of all this was described in those scars. Man and dog are allies. How could we turn such a sweet and loving animal into a weapon of war?

"It doesn't make sense," I said. "Any of it. All of it. Life is a battlefield, it seems, and I hate it." I may have just bastardized a Pat Benatar song, but I feel she would have approved of it here. "Everyone is at war."

He looked at me through mannequin eyes. "You know nothing of war. You know nothing of pain. You know nothing of suffering. You have everything you could want. Home, money, food, safety. And still you want more. Always you want more."

His face was calm while his hands were balled into knots of rage. A pressure cooker ready to pop. I stood before the situation could escalate. Walked to the door and turned. "I want what you want," I said before leaving. "I want peace."

I shut the door slowly behind me, but heard this before it closed. "With your God, there can never be peace."

⌣

We were back to square one, if not even further back than that. Zahid refused to come out of his room. I was forced to leave food out in front of his door like I'd wanted to avoid. It was like he'd placed himself in solitary confinement, and was threatening a hunger strike. All because of my asshole neighbors, especially Alyssa with her phony brand of philanthropy. *Give back to those less fortunate*, my bleached ass. The only shelter the Hendersons cared to provide was for their taxes. And to think I'd wanted to be like her.

I stayed inside most of this time as well. Paul, however, had to go to work and interact with the community at large. He was shouldering the brunt of their outrage, and I hadn't really considered the toll it was taking on him. Local news stations had picked up the story and supported our neighbors' point-of-view, taking statements from Paul and twisting them around while portraying Alyssa and others in a sympathetic light. An act that was meant to bring prestige to Paul and his firm was producing the opposite effect, causing friction with many of their clients and sabotaging their cases. Creating guilt by association in the judges' eyes.

I wouldn't have ever called our bed a pillar of hot passion—I have my battery powered friend for that—but it had grown even colder as the stresses associated with Zahid piled up. "I've done my job," he said from the far side of the bed in the silent dark. "I gave him the gift of freedom. What he does from here is up to him. It's time for him to go."

"Go where?" I said. Paul hadn't spent the time with Zahid I had. He might have been nearing thirty, but his emotional development had been arrested the moment he was locked up. He didn't have any money. Any connections. Any idea how to live in this world. Sending him away was sentencing him to death. "He's nowhere near ready to go out on his own, and you know that."

"This wasn't part of our agreement," Paul said. "I told you I wasn't interested in running a bed and breakfast. This has to come to an end. For the sake of us all."

For the sake of his financial interests is what he meant to say. His continued membership at the club. I was too angry to sleep so I got out of bed. "You're the one who brought him here," I said from the doorway. "He's not a fucking Amazon package, Paul. You can't just return him because he didn't meet your expectations." I shut the door before he could reply and went for the nearest bottle of wine.

Fuck this. Fuck everyone. The lessons we teach our children we ignore as adults, and the hypocrisy makes us small. I took half the bottle down in two glasses, welcoming the numbing relief. Another glass and I decided to check on Zahid. I knocked softly and entered when I heard him say, "Come in."

It was dark in his room. The only light was coming through the windowpanes where Zahid stood in silhouette, looking outside. I came up behind him and peered over his shoulder, my breath catching in my chest. Five men were standing in a straight line on the street just beyond the curb, staring up at us. Their heads covered in the black hoods executioners wear. I pulled Zahid back from the windows and closed the shutters.

"I'm calling the cops," I said.

"Cops?" Zahid said.

"The police. They can't threaten us like that. That's—" terrorism, I wanted to say.

Zahid grabbed my arm. "No, please. No police. Please." His grip was painful.

"Zahid, I have to. It's different here. They'll help keep you safe. Keep us safe."

I found my cellphone and placed the call and returned to Zahid's room to wait for the patrol car. It came minutes later and I watched from the windows as it pulled up alongside the group of men and stopped. The men turned and approached the passenger window and leaned down to talk, pointing back at our house. Maybe a minute passed before the patrol car started up again and continued down the street, leaving the men behind. Never even bothering to turn on the flashing lights. I closed the shutters, casting the room in total darkness. I was the only person on the planet willing to protect this poor man.

"I won't let anything happen to you," I said, the washout of adrenaline was mixing with the wine to make me sleepy.

"They fear me," he said. "Who should be afraid?"

I sat on the bed, my head buzzing. After a couple of minutes I felt him sit as well. "I want you to feel safe here. I wish there was more I could do." I leaned back, rested my head on the pillow. Eyes open, eyes closed, the darkness was the same. *Just until he falls asleep*, I thought, and that's the last thing I remember.

I woke to a hazy light, my arm wrapped around Paul, though something felt strange. My position on the bed and the feel of the sheets. Paul's ribcage. My eyes jerked open just as the cracked door was being closed from the other side, and listened as the footsteps faded. I jumped from the bed, Zahid sitting up behind me, and rushed out the door. Paul was dressed for work and striding down the stairs.

"Oh my God. Paul, wait!" I said, still wearing my thin nightshirt with no bra. My flannel pajama pants. "Paul, please! Stop and listen to me!" He continued on, walking faster to stay ahead. Out through the garage and into his car and onto the road before I could stop him. I called his cellphone, but it went straight to voicemail. This, I knew, was the last straw. The final bit of coerced evidence needed to get the verdict he was looking for. I got dressed and drove around looking for someplace for Zahid to go. Driving aimlessly, really. Just needing to be away from the situation for a while. I returned later that afternoon, and retreated to my room, waiting for Paul to return from work. He never did.

⌒⌒

Two days passed and Paul had yet to come home. Yet to answer my calls. Meanwhile the protests waned, which either meant they had grown weary or Paul had assured them Zahid would be leaving soon. The air in the house was oppressive, and I had to escape it, which I did by driving laps around White Rock Lake. I was ashamed for sleeping with Zahid, even though nothing had happened, and never would have even crossed my mind. I could tell Zahid was upset, too. How could he not be after seeing those hooded men issuing their silent threats?

Who knows how much he'd seen looking out his windows? A question that would haunt me the following day.

The news came with a wave of storm clouds like some dark omen. Eerie timing considering we'd been in a state of severe drought for several months. It was the first time Paul had called since he'd left and it was to tell me that Alexandria had gone missing. Not just missing. Abducted. That was the immediate claim, though there was no evidence of breaking and entering or foul play of any kind. She was just gone.

My mind went immediately to those hooded men. The news stories had been attracting people from outside the neighborhood. Who knows what crazy or perverted psychos the stories had stirred up. Filling them with rage and drawing them here with no release valve to vent through. And that's what I told Paul right away. That's the only thing that made sense. The timing was too coincidental.

"You're not getting it," he said, his voice distant and cold. "This isn't some random incident. That's not how these things happen."

I had to go outside. Our 4,000 square-foot home was closing in. The worker across the street had left with rain on the way. Abandoning his rock quarry with the stonework nearly completed. "Don't go there, Paul," I said. "He hasn't even left the house." I imagined Zahid upstairs staring out through the windows. In his isolated cell, looking out onto the street for weeks, and seeing what? Alexandria playing out in the front yard? Her parents with those hateful signs?

"Tracy, this is outside our control," Paul said, taking a measured breath that failed to calm him. "Our goddamn neighbor's daughter has gone missing, and we have a fucking terrorist living in our goddamn house!"

The first raindrop fell heavy on the overhang. Thunder rumbled nearby and the rain fell in sheets, forcing me to plug my ear to hear over the noise. "Pull your fucking head out of your ass, Tracy," Paul said. "You don't know him like you think you do. Enough's enough. This has gone too far."

"Too far for who, us? How much further must this go on for him? How much more punishment should he endure before he's had enough?"

"That's not up to us," Paul said. "You need to distance yourself right now." I could hear the insinuation as he said, "You've gotten *far* too close. What the fuck were you thinking, anyway?"

All I'd done was cook the man meals—fallen asleep by his side—and that was somehow too much. "Fuck you," I told him. "Fuck all of you."

I went back inside and up to Zahid's room. The heavy rain drummed against the roof, trying to make up for its long absence all at once. He was by the windows again; his lookout tower. *Maybe some lives are write-offs*, I thought when I saw him. *Cursed from birth or forgotten from above.* He turned as I entered and I saw surrender in his eyes. The total absence of hope.

There was no time for small talk. "I need you to be honest with me," I said, as though I'd know the difference. Paul was right, I didn't know this man at all.

A black Lincoln town car pulled up in front of the Hendersons. Four suited men exited and took a long look at our house before approaching the front door.

"What is it?" Zahid said.

"Paul just called." I pointed across the street. So close, and in Zahid's direct line of sight. "The little girl who lives there has gone missing."

Zahid looked. The front door opened and the four men were quickly ushered inside.

"There?" he said, and now we were both pointing.

I nodded. "Someone took her, he said."

His hand fell. He lowered his head as though it had grown heavy.

"I need to know. Have you seen anything?"

Muscles bunched along the sides of his jaw as he shook his head. Wearing the same sweatpants, that same Hilton Head shirt.

"Are you sure?" I said. The pause went full term before he nodded, the rain pounding overhead, obscuring the view outside.

"Zahid," I placed a hand on his arm, feeling the puckered scars. "Do you have any idea at all what happened to that little girl?"

"Only God knows what happened to that girl," he said, his breath frosting the glass. "If she is gone, it is because He took her. Maybe it is for all the children they took from my country."

Had that been a confession? To use Paul's terms, he had the motive and, with me driving aimlessly across town, opportunity as well.

"Those men are going to come and talk to you," I said. "If you tell them what you just told me they are going to take you to jail. You need to know that."

"Everywhere is prison for me," he said. He pulled his arm away and turned from the window. "I do as God wills. My rewards will be in Heaven."

I'd welcomed a killer into our home, and endangered my neighbors' kids.

⌒⌒

I felt like a foreigner in my own house: unwelcome and unwanted. Paul bought this beautiful home through hard work and now preferred to sleep in his office—I assumed—rather than stay here with me. Zahid remained in his room despite whatever I had cooking on the stove, and refused to talk whenever I visited, which wasn't often. I was not afraid of him, but wasn't comfortable either. Every waking moment—which was all day and night because I couldn't sleep—was troubled by constant anxiety. I'm surprised my hair wasn't falling out in clumps. I desperately wanted to talk to Alyssa. To comfort her in any way that I could. She was a friend, and I could not imagine the pain and terror she was experiencing right then. I could feel the collective blame of every friend and neighbor directed at me and it was like being buried alive. Add to that the blame I placed on myself and I had to fight the urge not to harm myself. To punish myself for my naïve stupidity. I wanted to pull my hair or slap my face and scream in the mirror until my throat split open and I choked on my own blood. No matter what happened, I'd be moving. There was no way I could stay here after this.

Paul came home, finally. He'd been meeting with Homeland Security, who were working with the FBI. They were collecting evidence and would soon be coming for Zahid. Putting him in shackles and back into the interrogation room, getting him to talk—by any means necessary, I presumed. I was somewhat surprised by how unconcerned Paul seemed about having Zahid in our house at that time, but I suppose he knew it would all be over soon. He was more concerned about the storm. It had been pouring rain for two straight days now, and our area was under a major flood warning. Dirt from the Landrys' new construction was getting washed down the street in a mudslide. Paul was pacing in front of the windows, watching rainswept debris clog the gutters and collect in the road.

Neither of us slept that night. I wondered what was taking the FBI so long to come and interrogate Zahid. Paul kept getting out of bed to check the storm, cursing under his breath. I was happy for the rain as it kept the protestors away. Especially those psycho men wearing their executioner garb. I was sill not convinced that some maniac hadn't been driven here by the news and taken Alexandria. Even as a botched frame job. I also wanted so bad to talk to Zahid again, but that was strictly forbidden while Paul was home, and I understood why. It was clear he thought something more had happened that night I slept in Zahid's room. What a fucking mess. Or as my father would have said, *Like sitting in a barrel of snakes.* Oh to be back in those simpler times.

Paul was up at first light, and I was right behind him. Nothing is less comfortable than a sleepless bed. I'd never seen a legal case consume his attention as much as that rain, and it began to worry me. I was clearly missing something. Or maybe he was just waiting for the Feds to arrive. His agitation continued to climb, and when we both saw water draining out of the Landrys' foundation, he rushed to put a rain jacket on.

"The Landrys' is flooding," he said. "Stay here."

Like that was any of his concern. Even if it was, it's not like he was going to empty the house of water like a rowboat with a bucket. His behavior was scaring me. "What are you doing?" I said.

"I'm going over there." He grabbed me by both shoulders, glaring into my eyes. "You stay here. Make sure Zahid doesn't leave."

This made no sense. I felt like we were under some threat I couldn't see. Paul rushed out in the rain, and ran across the street faster than I'd ever seen him move. With him gone, the house suddenly felt very empty, and I felt unprotected and vulnerable. Panic rose in my chest, triggering my instincts to fight or flee. So I went chasing after Paul, wanting to be near him for whatever he feared was happening.

I held an arm across my chest as I hurtled through the rain. My hair getting drenched in the downpour. Paul had already entered through the front door and I went in after him, unconcerned about getting water on the new gleaming hardwood floors. I tracked his footprints through the spacious living rooms to a door that led down to the basement. The carpeted stairs muffled my footsteps as I descended, and floodwater was rising a few feet up from the ground floor. I froze when I reached the bottom and heard him scream. He came wading back through the water towards me. It came up past his knees "Jesus!" he said when he saw me. "Move! Call the fucking police! Go! Go!"

He tried to pull me with him, but I clung to the railing. I had to know what he'd seen. He reached for me when I moved past him, ordering me to stop. But I hardly heard him anymore. At some point fear focused everything down to primary senses, and I just heard my ragged breathing, the splash of water, and the white noise in my brain. Through a doorway and I was in the boiler room, stormwater up to my groin. I heard Paul splashing behind me, yelling unintelligibly, or at least my mind had stopped trying to interpret what he said. There was a storage closet in the far corner that was cracked open, the gap widening as I watched. Then, as some weight pressed against it from inside, it opened all the way and a tangled mass of cloth came floating out. No wait, I saw hair. *Maybe*, my panicked mind pleaded, *a doll.*

But it wasn't a doll. A little girl was floating face down in the dark floodwater. Wearing a grey dress I'd seen before with a bow sash belt, white stocking legs and feet bound with tape at the ankles. I rushed towards her and turned her over and I was looking down into the pale and bloated face of my neighbor's darling girl, Alexandria. Who, just weeks before, had been blowing life-size bubbles in my yard while I drank wine.

Her eyes were open. Silt water leaked from her nose and mouth. The time for CPR had long passed and I knew the girl was dead in my arms. Her wrists were bound with the same silver tape as her ankles. Soggy bread and bags of chips floated out through the storage closet door. I bent and lifted her out of the water, hardly feeling the weight of her waterlogged body. Rather than go up the stairs, I opened a side door, stumbling and nearly falling as the release of water pulled at my legs.

I carried her body up the sloped yard to the street, not knowing where I was taking her. Just wanting to get her above water as though that mattered any more. I heard doors slamming like thunder. Screams and shouts from up and down the street. Paul ran towards me, having come back out the front door, and tore the child from my arms. I stumbled, seeing neighbors coming our way from all directions.

Paul was shouting, "We found her! We found her!" Pointing to the silhouette of a man in the window above our garage. "He took her! Oh God, I'm so sorry!" Paul fell to his knees in the rain with Alexandria cradled against his chest. Heroic pose of the first responder.

But he knew exactly where she'd been. Had been watching the rainfall with rising dread. Waiting until it was too late. Was this to save his business, his reputation, or just to get back at me? Penance for my night of exhaustion.

"Where the hell is he?" someone shouted. I looked and saw that it was Eric. His face a brutal shade of red with veins bulging across his forehead and neck.

Men and women were screaming in shock. I saw teenage faces viewing death for the first time.

"There he is!" another man shouted, pointing at our window where Zahid stood motionless, watching the congregation build as all eyes turned his way. Eric was the first to pick up a large rock from the stone quarry. "I'm going to fucking kill him!" he yelled. And others followed his cue, grabbing chiseled stones from the ground.

I had neglected to close the front door in my haste to follow Paul. Its opening was an invitation to enter. I didn't see who it was that stormed through first, followed closely by two men, the last one being our neighbor Charlie who hobbled in on his arthritic hip. I was frozen with indecision. Paralyzed by fear and a type of premonitory vision of what was to come. Standing among the growing mob, many of whom were now carrying large, heavy stones. I rushed over to Paul and kneeled in the mud beside him.

"Goddamnit, Paul. Do something! They're going to kill him!"

His spotted scalp was revealed by the rain, tunneling in the deepening grooves of his face. "There's nothing more I can do!" he said, cradling the young girl like the daughter we never had. "Nothing can save him now, don't you dare try," he said. "You'll only make things worse."

What could possibly be worse than this? I thought as the men reappeared at the doorway, manhandling Zahid who didn't appear to be resisting. Still dressed in the Hilton Head t-shirt and sweatpants. Perhaps the last uniform he'd ever wear.

"Murderer!" the mob cried when they saw him. "Evildoer!"

The men threw Zahid to the ground where he landed in a puddle of rain. He rose to all fours, and then lifted himself onto his knees, scanning the men and women forming a circle around him. I started to stand and Paul grabbed my shirt. "Tracy, don't. If you love me you'll stay here."

I ripped my shirt from his hand. It was plastered to my torso and I wasn't wearing a bra, but that was the least of my concerns. "This has nothing to do with love," I said, rising and shouldering my way through the small crowd.

I heard Alyssa before I saw her, unleashing a banshee cry as she hurled the first stone, hitting Zahid square in the chest. He didn't even try to deflect it, just grimaced as his eyes went to that distant place where pain couldn't follow. Eric wound back and stepped into his throw, hurling a softball size rock that caught Zahid in the jaw, collapsing him back onto his heels.

The crowd murmured and pressed forward. I pushed people out of the way, hardly recognizing their familiar faces. Two more stones hit Zahid while he lay dazed in the grass, blood sluicing from a gash on his chin. And then I burst through the front row and, without thinking, threw my body over his. Within moments, hands grabbed the back of my shirt, my arms, my hair, and tried to pull me off but I wouldn't let go.

"Stop!" I screamed. "What is wrong with you! All of you, stop!"

"Get her! Kill her! Kill them! KILL'IM!" A frenzied chant that blurred into a single deadly command. And the stones began to fall. Landing on my back like hobnail boots. My shoulder and legs and the back of my head. Zahid was moaning underneath me, and then I heard some warbled cry that I assumed was caused by my damaged brain but turned out to be a police car. It's the only thing that saved us, though that's the wrong term. It's all that kept Zahid and me alive.

I'm in the hospital, recovering. The only person who has come to visit me is Paul, and that was to make very clear legal threats should I get any strange ideas regarding the disappearance and accidental death of Alexandria. I'm waiting on my parents to come, but that's not for another day or so. I suspect I'll be moving back in with them, and that comes as a relief.

Zahid is recovering as well, though his physical injuries are less severe than mine. I have no idea what's next for him, and doubt I ever will. I keep thinking about the last thing he said to me. *My rewards will be in Heaven.* And I hope he's right.

Before Paul left he asked what happened that night I spent in Zahid's room, and I wonder if that's what caused everything that followed. He didn't seem to believe me when I told him nothing. That I simply passed out. Or maybe it's just a truth he can't let himself accept. "I don't get it," he said. "Did you think you loved him? That your love would heal him? Save him somehow?"

No, that's not what I thought. Even then I knew my love alone wasn't enough. It would have taken more than just me to heal Zahid. Make him feel at home. In fact, it would probably have been more merciful to let him die. No, my love could not have saved him. But maybe, if I don't let the anger building inside take over, there's someone else my love can save. Me, if no one else.

AFTERWORD

The deadliest animal is not man. It's a mob—which is a lifeform all its own. Walk door-to-door in just about any town, and you can expect to be relatively safe. Come back during a town meeting and, depending on your race or personal beliefs, you'll want to watch your back. It's the same with discourse. Sit in a room with someone who opposes your viewpoint and you should be able to have a civil discussion. Should, being the operative word. When opposing factions meet on the street, however, it starts with screaming and soon devolves into violence with broken bodies littering the road.

Ideas also become exponentially more powerful as they aggregate, and are subject to the same form of perceptual bias, like a Rorschach blot. Where some people see a butterfly others see a bird of prey. What's beautiful to one person is vile to someone else, perhaps even threatening.

It's hard to determine the reason ideas mutate when they reach critical mass. Or why some good ideas can have such bad results. Take religious cults, for example. Read the mission statement for any such cult and it probably sounds rather appealing. Utopian, in fact. Why, then, do so many end in mass suicide and bloodshed?

I think the foundational intent behind an idea might be at least partly to blame. The cult leader says he wants to create a society built on peace and spiritual unity, but really he just wants to have sex with all the men's wives. In some cases, their daughters as well. The core idea might have merit, but the underlying intent is corrupted so the entire enterprise collapses.

Kindness is like that. Do someone a favor without expecting reciprocation and it feels really good. Do the same favor because you expect something in return, and you'll go mad if you don't receive reciprocation. Many so-called acts of kindness have ultimately ended in murder.

My story *Chisel and Stone* features a woman who wants to do something altruistic—free an innocent man from the horrors of Guantanamo Bay—but her true motivation is rooted in the deadly sin of envy. What she really desires is the esteem of her rich housewife friends who perform charitable acts for tax purposes. Now take that good idea based on bad intentions—a deadly sin, no less—and expose it to the scrutiny of a frightened and angry mob. That's a powder keg ready to blow.

Is there a lesson here? Maybe. Sometimes I feel like Earth is a classroom. Its curriculum is terrifying and I'm afraid to graduate.

SLOTH

"Hard grind got us the glory, the saying goes—but sloth will slide us back into the sea. And these days, the rising waters feel so near."
— Jessie Burton, *The Miniaturist*

CLEVENGERS OF THE CARRION SEA

by Rena Mason

Daniel Whittaker pushed his little sister out the window. His heart leaped with the fading of Gretta's screams. Four stories down she fell, each one represented a birthday she'd celebrated. Lifetimes went by until he heard her no more.

Smoke flooded Danny's lungs and singed them, tightening his chest and shrinking his breaths. He stuck his face out into the cold and gulped back coughs, not taking in air to focus on her shrill baby voice were it to sound again, ached to hear it once more while everything burned behind him. His breath shot out in ashen fumes, a failed dragon whose fire had sputtered out.

"Gretta!" His voice a raspy whimper.

"Come on, boy. Jump!" Voices rose from below. They said nothing of Gretta.

Walls around him groaned and popped. Flames lashed his calves and backside, and he imagined his parents whipping him onward with a glowing fire iron.

He couldn't hear his mother and father anymore.

Danny hadn't gone downstairs when he'd heard them calling out for help. He had lain in bed, gasping for breath while their shouts became shrieks, hoping all the noise would just stop. When they fell silent, relief washed over him, but in that same moment his and Gretta's hacking brought fear and realization. Guilt struck him in a wave of heat, and he'd gotten up and run, leaving Gretta behind. Then she'd screamed. Once. Twice. It took all his will to go back into the raging fire. After battling flames, he'd yanked her from the floor mattress with raw palms. He'd felt his way over stairs and crawled, dragging her ahead of the blaze that had chased close behind. Oh, how his shoulders had ached, the muscles stretched so far apart he thought they'd tear from their sockets as he'd pulled his way up with one arm, hauling his sister with the other.

"Gretta, help me! We have to get upstairs."

She'd wailed and nothing more. He'd bit his lip until the sting and salted tang of blood kept him from leaving her there.

On the last floor, he'd headed toward a window at the end of the hall. The only way out. His little sister jumped up and clasped her arms then coiled her legs around him. He thought he might've broken some of her bones lugging her over the steps, and then when he had to peel her off him. Gretta hadn't wanted to go first, but the men below told him to throw her down. He couldn't trust her to jump on her own, and he wouldn't leave her to burn. Not after all he'd gone through to get them there.

His back searing in a way no amount of patting would extinguish, Danny raised his feet and perched in the window frame, bracing his hands against the sides. A crack loud as lightning tore down the hall with a rush of scorching air. It blasted him from the building, swaddling his body with heat and filling his ears with thick silence. His stomach floated up to his neck; he couldn't force it down.

Cool wind blew his hair to the sides, then his gut wrenched with a fast-sinking pull, but he stretched his arms out and willed himself up. He imagined flying toward a pale moon. Soft crunching sounds encroached the quiet and grew louder as he rose into the night sky. Did the fire burn him that badly? Was his skin crinkled and flaking off? He put those images out of his head and pictured the stars above, the way they'd twinkled last year when he was eleven, before the rash, the bumps, scabs, and scars had blinded him and Gretta.

Snapping replaced the strange crackling that had grown in his ears. Splintered pain shot through his insides, and he screamed.

He hadn't been flying after all.

⌣

Jump! Don't think. Leap across those tracks. Life is over now anyway, isn't it?

Margaret Fitch's boot heel scraped a low mound of dirty ice as she backed from the platform's edge. Her foot rose off the ground in a moment of weightlessness. A raw breath froze the back of her throat as she reached upward, righting her balance with a grasp of solid nothingness. Not far from where she stood, an attendant with a keen way about him stiffened his shoulders and scrutinized her.

Snow gusted off the train in listless fans against ashen clouds as passenger cars rushed past, pulling into Grand Central Station. Frost jetted from the tracks and nicked Margaret's face, but she refused to turn away. The uniformed man raised a whistle to his lips and blew, then shouted over people disembarking, forgetting all about her, the eighteen-year-old woman who—more than he might have considered—almost ruined his day.

From Manhattan, she would travel to Chatham, then on to Albany via the Boston and Albany Railroad. The next day Margaret would board the Pettit family coach and ride to Clinton County where her fiancé, Andrew Pettit, awaited her arrival. She hadn't seen him since they were children—after his mother had caught them examining one another the way innocents do, turning it into something perverse, thus faulting her and sending her away to school.

Margaret stood unmoving while city folk jostled around. Their conversations centered on the rioting and fires in Brooklyn, and something about smallpox. Elbows and shoulders nudging past became potentials for disease, so she moved near a lone stanchion and waited to board.

The clomping of thick boots came up behind Margaret, so she glanced back at a woman draped in thick, navy wool. Heavy fabric swathed the lower part of her face, covering her mouth, which she spoke through.

"You're smart to separate yourself."

Margaret ignored the woman and edged nearer the platform, but the woman's voice followed her, grew louder, became more agitated. Strange crunching sounds rose between her words as if she chomped biscuits between talking.

"It's 1894! Times of modern medicine. How can this foul sickness still exist? It came from abroad, don't you think?"

"I beg your pardon, but—"

"All the immigrants coming through Ellis Island. It's reprehensible," the woman said.

Margaret's stomach shot up her throat as she lurched forward then floated in the air, stopping when her body struck the hard, icy ground. A long metal rail guided her line of sight into a dark tunnel lit with a faint star. Crackling filled her ears to a deafening pitch, and the ground trembled under her cheek. A loud whistle sounded before everything became a blinding, white haze. In the sudden miasma that surrounded her, she heard a boy's voice.

"Can you help me?" he said.

⌒⌒

Red light shined behind his eyelids and gentle crunching sounds woke Danny. His limbs wouldn't move as he drifted on an easy tide that crackled warm against his skin. The fall must've killed him. A twinge of guilt tightened his chest; a part of him hoped Gretta and his parents floated nearby. Danny knew if they were here too, wherever this place was, then they'd all died in the fire. A bad thing to wish for, but at least his family would be together.

Was this Heaven? If not, he'd gone to Hell for not minding his father about extinguishing the candle flame. Its little bit of warmth made him feel safe. Had he burned them all up? Maybe he was there because he'd ignored the yellow flags and took Gretta to Bushwick where he'd gambled away the halfpenny he'd made boot-blacking at city hall. They'd gotten smallpox soon after that.

Bittersweet liquid trickled into his mouth as he ebbed and pondered. Thirsty, Danny swallowed it, igniting pain at the back of his throat that flashed hot white pulses through his blindness. Dead weight writhed across his belly, pushing his backside down, plunging him into the complete darkness he'd known since he'd lost his sight. He gasped and sputtered.

"Dr. Beauchamp, he's waking!" A woman's voice echoed through a large space.

Slapping footfalls grew louder, but beyond the clacking shoes, Danny heard distant shouting.

Gasping, someone clanged against metal, rattling Danny.

"It's a miracle." A man spoke with a gruff French accent.

The odors of onion and a meaty stink rushed across Danny's face. He couldn't remember the last time he'd eaten, and his stomach growled. Warm fingers and hands pressed and prodded him all over, and then they shimmied his body in jerky motions. Pain exploded from everyplace they touched. Danny grunted, inflaming his throat again. No white stars burst behind his eyes this time, only the black abyss that was all his to see forever.

"I'm sorry, young man. I know it's painful. The nurse is going to give you something for that." The doctor's voice shifted to the right. "Anne, one-sixth grain of morphine through his IV. Slowly, please."

Dr. Beauchamp directed his voice back down at Danny. "You're lucky to be alive. Your sister Gretta is doing fine. We're taking good care of her. You're at the Kingston Avenue Hospital, in Flatbush."

A boom and a crash came from near where the doctor had run from. Glass shattered, and screams echoed.

"Dammit, bar the doors!" the doctor said. "Don't worry, Danny. We'll keep you safe."

The doctor patted Danny's head then yelled orders that faded with quick steps away from the bedside.

The nurse, Anne, spoke again. "We're going to get you, Gretta, and some of the others away from here. It's too dangerous for you who… Dr. Beauchamp has a place up…"

Danny floated from dark depths and bobbed on waves. A white glow shone above. Faint crackling filled his ears. "Hello?" he whispered, worried he might be pulled under. "Can you help me?"

A woman's voice, not the nurse Anne's but one more tender, spoke out through all the chittering around him.

"Is someone there?" she said.

"My name's Danny, miss. I'm lost," he shouted. "Please, find Gretta."

⌣

Margaret woke in a hospital with her wrist bound and draped across her waist in a sling. A nurse rushed past, but Margaret moved too slowly to get her attention.

"Help," she said. Her voice a pathetic whimper.

"She's awake," a man said behind her.

The man came around and stood next to the bed. She couldn't mistake the dark hair, hawk eyes, and sloped, pointy nose, but the features made his face handsome, nothing like the severity in which they affected his mother's appearance.

"Andrew?" she said.

He squeezed her free hand, raised it to his lips and repeatedly kissed it with a maniacal temperament that made unease creep up her arm. But she was too weak to pull her hand away.

"There's a lost boy," she said. "His name is Danny."

"Nurse!"

"Where's your mother, Andrew?" Margaret said.

"I told her I'd come and bring you home. I came as soon as we'd heard the news of the accident," he said. "Besides, I didn't think seeing her would make you feel any better." He grinned down at her and winked.

"You're probably right," she said.

"You know, a part of me likes seeing you helpless like this." He glanced down at her chest and bound arm.

"What?" Margaret couldn't have heard him right.

The nurse came over, carrying a tray with a syringe on top. "Are you ready to take her then, Mr. Pettit?" She smiled and gazed at Andrew as she spoke.

"Soon," he said. "She's worried about a lost child."

"Danny," Margaret said. "He said his name is Danny, and he told me to find his sister, Gretta."

The nurse looked confused at first, then flustered as her eyes darted back and forth between Margaret lying in bed and Andrew standing at her side. "There are no children here by those names, miss, and I'm very busy at the moment. Please, sir, if you'll help me turn her, I'll give her some morphine Dr. Ford prescribed for the journey, and then you can be on your way."

Andrew rolled Margaret toward him. His eyes reflected a spectral likeness of her as they lowered their gaze. The expression in his stare as the nurse raised her hospital shift made her wary. He kept a gentle hold against her back as he pressed himself closer to the bedside, forcing her face toward his groin.

"Want a better look?" he said.

"What was that?" the nurse said.

"Nothing," Andrew said.

"All done." The nurse pulled Margaret's shift down. "Do you need help dressing your wife?"

"Www…" Margaret's mouth went dry, and her lips wouldn't move to talk right.

"Not at all," he said. "Her maid Helen is waiting in the coach, but I can manage this alone."

Andrew smiled down at Margaret as he pulled the curtains around the bed closed.

Margaret's heart raced, and her breaths quickened. Images of domination rose from a dark corner in her mind. Sounds of laughter reverberated, scandalous whispers echoed, and humiliation shot to the forefront of her memories. She knew now why she'd forgotten the details of her dismissal.

Margaret shivered at his touch.

"You used to sneak into my room at night," she said. Or at least she thought she'd said it. Mostly she struggled to stay awake, making sure he wasn't molesting her.

He held her head upright and looked into her eyes. His jaw muscles clenched.

"So, you do remember. I'll never let her send you away again, Maggie. I promise you that." He leaned in and bit her earlobe then whispered, "I love hurting you too much."

⌣‿⌣

Margaret sat on a chaise at the foot of the bed and ate toasted bread and cheese, while her new maid, Helen unpacked.

"This dress!" Helen held it up against her rounded, protruding gut and turned to Margaret. "It's lovely, but the color. I've never seen anything like it."

"It's called cramoisi."

Helen smoothed the silky fabric over her belly. "Cram… What? Cran… Berry. No. Red, but deeper. Like old, dried—"

"Blood?" Margaret said.

Helen jerked her hand away and checked her fingertips as if the word had left a stain. "Where did you get it?"

"I did seamstress work for extra money. The tailor had the roll hidden in the back of his shop. He told me it was too bold for his customers and out of fashion, but I fell in love with it."

"A wise fellow then. This color's shocking and not fit to be worn by any proper lady." Pinching her fingers together, Helen picked it up off the floor and tossed it back into the trunk.

"I worked six months without wages, so the tailor would make me that dress. I did plenty of other jobs and got paid for some too. Even assisted a surgeon during—"

"Please, enough. Not a smart choice on your part. As scandalous as Andrew marrying you in the city on the day you were released from the hospital was. It'd be nothing compared to you wearing this out in town. Mrs. Pettit would never approve of your working, or this color fabric. You best keep your jobs to yourself and this dress out of sight."

"I couldn't. It's too beautiful. I worked long and hard for that gown, and I won't hide it. I won't hide who I am, and to be quite honest, I remember very little about what happened in the city after I left the hospital. I was on medication and not at all in my normal state of mind. Andrew had no right—"

"You were promised to him ages ago, but Andrew dashed your mother's wedding plans, and that's why she's so upset about the whole ordeal. Trust me, Maggie. At least until you're more settled in the community and in this house as Mrs. Andrew Pettit, you'd be better to step down a bit."

Margaret gazed at the dress, her eyes following the darker, floral lines of the brocade. It represented everything that wasn't Pettit. Her heart sank, and she lost herself in shadowed pools of crimson as the maid left the room.

Helen knew Mrs. Pettit better than anyone. Margaret didn't need a fancy French education for that.

Hours later, she woke in the dark, and in that moment, when no lights in an unfamiliar place is most disorienting, she heard the boy's voice call out again.

"Hello?" he said. "Can you help me?"

"Danny is that you?"

Blinking and focusing hard into the darkness to see anything at all, Margaret reached out and felt her way toward the dressing table. Sizzling sounds came up from the floor. Persian silk fibers no longer padded her step; the rug wriggled underfoot. Every footfall crackled. Tickling sensations crossed her bare feet and writhed between her toes. She kicked out, smacking her ankle into her trunk in front of the bureau. Margaret winced and squinted her eyes through the pain as she fumbled for the Diamond Match Company tin she saw Helen use earlier.

Cold metal against her fingertips gave her some calm, and her vision eased back in gray hues as familiar shapes formed in the darkness.

"Where are you?" Margaret struck a match and saw nothing out of the ordinary.

The next day, Margaret watched Helen add hot water to the bath while she had her feet propped up on the tub's edge, recalling the tickling sensations she'd felt there in the night.

"Are there any children in the house?" Margaret said.

"Not here. Mrs. Pettit wouldn't allow it. Any little ones belonging to staff live in town."

"I thought I heard a child's voice in my room last night."

"You were travel weary and are still recovering from your injury. But you look much better today. Probably just something you ate. Finish washing up, and I'll help you dress for tea. You must be excited to see Mrs. Pettit and Andrew again."

"Yes. Yes, of course." Feeling overexposed at the thought of Andrew, she pulled wet linen over her chest.

"This is the dress Mrs. Pettit says you're to wear to your wedding party. Isn't it grand?" Helen stepped away from one of the armoires carrying a Portland Blue dress patterned after Wedgwood.

"It's lovely." Margaret said, thinking how it would make her look fragile and on display.

"Please don't tell her I showed you."

"You can trust me. I won't."

Helen nodded and put the dress away. "Thank you, Maggie. You were always a sweet girl. A stubborn handful when you were younger, but you've grown up to be a fine lady. You and Andrew got me into loads of trouble too back then. Sneaking here and there, playing hide and seek and other silly games."

"I remembered why she sent me away."

"You were both so young and unnaturally precocious. Andrew turned melancholy after you left. Like something of his got taken away, giving him a reason to be angry with his mother. The light left his eyes, and nothing would stir him. Weren't 'til Mrs. Pettit promised you to him in marriage that he came around again."

Margaret wondered if any light had ever existed in his eyes. "I wasn't hers to promise away."

"Forgive me for saying, miss Maggie, but you were. Your parents' will left her in charge of everything, including you. But now you've got me on about sad things, and on a happy day. Stop this nonsense and get out of that tub so I can fix your hair."

Helen quieted and prepared the dressing table with a brush, pins, and elegant silver combs. Dew drop tears clung to Margaret's bottom lashes. They fell as she stood, rippling before settling back into a tub that might someday overflow with all the sorrow from her eyes.

Nausea and a bit of vertigo overcame Margaret as she followed Helen downstairs for tea. Mrs. Pettit wore black muslin, making the old woman's dark, beetle eyes burrow into her pale face, which from the side, appeared slightly crescent-shaped. Gray hair pulled into a tight bun sat on top.

The old woman glared at them as they entered the room.

"That will be all, Helen," Mrs. Pettit said.

Andrew stood up with an energy and excitement that calmed Margaret somewhat. Mrs. Pettit took on an expression of disapproval at his enthusiasm.

An older gentleman with a strong resemblance to Mrs. Pettit rose from his seat as well. A priest.

"This is Father Greer," Andrew said.

Margaret shook the priest's proffered hand.

"Sit down, Margaret," Mrs. Pettit said.

"Forgive me. Please do, Maggie." Andrew kissed her cheek then pulled out a chair.

Margaret sat the way she'd been taught, following proper etiquette, knowing Mrs. Pettit observed her every move.

"We're so happy to have you home with us again. Aren't we, Mother?"

The old woman's face remained stoic, exaggerating her blanched features.

"We will discuss your post-wedding party arrangements. Margaret, you'll be doing volunteer work under Father Greer for St. John's church to introduce you to the community in a more proper way." Mrs. Pettit gave Andrew a wicked glance, then glared at Margaret for the remainder of the tea.

⌒

Now his wife, Margaret lived on Andrew's floor of the house. Her once older, bully sort-of-brother was now her husband, and he took great pleasure in disgracing her behind closed doors. When he wasn't, Andrew worked long hours and traveled to the city often. Being alone with Edith—who never relented voicing the importance of Margaret's duty to bear Andrew children—became far worse than what she had to endure with Andrew, so his absences during the month since their marriage left Margaret both thankful and angry. She spent much of her time at St. John's Church, but even Father Greer had already run out of menial tasks for her to do.

"Perhaps a change of circumstance and scenery?" he said.

"I don't think—"

"Forgive me, not a change in your own circumstances, but that of others."

Margaret turned away. Used to hard work, she didn't want more of nothing to do.

Father Greer cleared his throat. "There's an orphanage in Essex County."

"You want me to help children, when all I need do is have my own to ease my mother-in-law's relentless torment? Father, I find that rather unfeeling and somewhat cruel. Especially for a man of the cloth."

"As often as you're here, child, I've watched you avoid the Sacrament of Penance and you've never confessed your sins. You've done so much for us, yet I don't recall seeing you pray once. His light is not in your eyes. But maybe surrounding yourself and caring for these, these... special children, will bless you. The Essex orphans receive little charity, barely surviving on what they're given."

"I understand your meaning, Father. And I want to help but—"

"Good. I'll write Dr. Beauchamp straight away."

"A doctor cares for them? I'd think that quite a blessing. What makes these children so special?"

"They're blind." Father Greer tugged at his collar. "Frederick Beauchamp grew up in this area but chose to practice in the city after his education. Smallpox caused a panic, and the people not affected… Well, they tried to get rid of the sick by rioting and setting fires to the dwellings of those infected."

Margaret gasped then said, "How awful."

"Frederick, his nurse, and an assistant fled with the children to his family's farm. The place was nearly a crumbling ruin when he left, and I'm afraid it's even worse now. He's put everything he's had into making it livable. I like to think of them as special, because they're survivors twice over."

"Which hospital did he work at in the city?"

"I believe it was Kingston."

"I was there! After my fall. Perhaps that's why…" The nurse didn't mention the smallpox and riots. Andrew would've thrown a fit if he'd known children with smallpox had been in the same facility that had treated her. Even as sedated as she was, the more she thought on it, the more she realized the hospital seemed to be recovering from a chaos when she'd awakened.

"Why what?"

"Um… why would the doctor make such a sacrifice?"

"Who else would have them? As well as being blind, they're badly scarred."

"Those poor souls," she said.

"Indeed. So now you see why they're in such need. I think your efforts would do them good. Maybe this act would right you with God and see you fit to bear children of your own."

"A test," she whispered. Anger renewed its force in the pit of her belly.

Father Greer rose from the pew as did she. "I'll get a letter to Frederick, I'm sure he'll be happy for your help. I think it best you come and go from here. Edith—"

"What's she to do with it? Does she know about these children?"

The older man's eyes softened as he focused on the statue of the Virgin Mary. "She was against having the children brought to Essex County."

"They're not contagious, are they?"

"No. The children are harmless. But to look upon them… It may frighten you."

"I have a stronger constitution than that. I did some anatomical sketching for a surgeon in Paris. But please, don't tell Mrs. Pettit."

"I understand. Edith would disapprove. She's been a dear friend to me over the years, but we don't always agree on matters, and I can imagine she isn't the easiest woman to live with."

"Not at all." Margaret laughed. "So I want to help these children all the more. You should know that about me by now."

His wide smile exposed teeth that jutted a touch, impressing an equine look to his face. "Yes. Come here tomorrow, your normal time, and I'll ride with you to the Beauchamp property and make the introductions."

112

"Thank you, Father."

"It is very gracious of you, and I will not forget your generosity. Even if it doesn't work out, I know the children will be happy to meet someone new."

"I promise to put forth all my effort."

"Make that promise to God. And pray for these children as well as caring for them."

Being orphaned herself, Margaret would give everything she could to help them, do anything if it would better their lives—but she would not pray. She remembered all the praying she did as a child. The hours then days that turned into years that came to nothing. So, she would not pray now.

Nor ever again.

—⁓—

Icy gusts lashed Danny's cheek, waking him. Glass panes rattled. They sounded old and thin. Whistling accompanied their tinny vibrations.

"Gretta?" he said.

"Danny, you're awake. I'm Anne, the nurse you met at the Kingston Avenue Hospital."

He couldn't quite recall but nodded. "Is my sister here?"

"Yes. You're both safe now. Gretta's with the other children. I'll go and get her."

"Please, miss." A frigid draft went straight to his bones and he shivered.

"Oh, you must have a chill. I'll get another blanket, and then bring Gretta in. We put boards over the windows where the glass was broken, but I'm afraid they're not doing a very good job of keeping the wind out."

The nurse slid him upward, then propped pillows behind him. "How are you feeling?"

"My backside hurts," he said.

"I can give you some—"

"No. No more medicine, please. I want to know Gretta's here. The medicine, it makes me think slow and gives me bad dreams. Worms. They feel so real. I can't, don't, want to go there ever again."

"All right. Be calm." Anne straightened blankets on top of him. "I'll get Gretta now."

"Thank you," he said.

"Danny!" The pitter-patter of little footsteps intensified within a short distance, and then a whump and rush of air came next to where he lay. He gasped and groaned in pain as little hands batted the bedding over his chest. Chilly, small fingers groped his face, tickling all the scars.

"It is you," she said.

Her baby voice brought tears to his eyes as she chatted on. "They told me you were alive, and I didn't believe them, but nurse Anne and Dr. Beau are so nice, I knew they wouldn't lie."

"Mom? Dad?" he said. Danny knew in his heart what had happened to them, but he wanted to hear it. Maybe coming from Gretta, in her way of talking, might lessen the pain.

"They're all burned up." Gretta burst into sobs and rested her tiny head on Danny's chest.

He lifted his arms, wincing at the pain, and held her the best that he could; together they cried.

Anne's voice came from the other side of the room, "I'll leave you two alone for a bit."

Danny heard creaking just before the door shut.

"Where are we?" he said.

"Dr. Beau's house."

"Not at the hospital?"

"No. We're in the top part of New York, by Canada. It took us lots of days to get here."

"Why'd they bring us here?"

"Not just us, silly. There's Timothy Wells, Blake something… I can't remember his other name, but that doesn't matter, does it, Danny? Jacob, Tina, Will, and Marion. That's six, right?" Gretta counted to herself, pressing her fingers on the blankets covering him.

"Yes. That's six. Good job. But who are they?"

"Nurse Anne has been teaching me to count with my fingers. They're like us, and can't see either. Dr. Beau said we had to leave 'cause bad people burnt us."

"The fire! That's how it started? They wanted to kill us?"

Gretta's head nodded against him. He thought he'd forgotten to put out the candle after his dad had told him to. Maybe it wasn't his fault after all.

"Just bad people wanted to." Then she whacked his arm.

"Ouch." Danny gasped.

"You threw me out the window!"

"I had to. You know I did."

"But if you went first, maybe you wouldn't be broken now."

"Better me than you."

"You're right." She rubbed his arm where she'd hit him. "Mom and Dad would've wanted you to since you're the oldest. I love you, Danny."

"I love you too."

Gretta squeezed him, and he grunted instead of crying out in pain.

"I can't wait for you to get better and meet the others. You'll like them. I know you will."

"Is there another woman here?"

"Frances? She's—"

"No. A woman named Margaret. I think she can help me. Us, I mean. I have to find her. She's in this place where I can see."

"Danny, you can't see anything. And neither can I!"

114

A slow squeak sounded as the door opened. "It's me, Anne. I brought you another blanket. And Dr. Beauchamp, too. Come on, Gretta. It's time for your lunch. Let's leave Dr. Beau and Danny to talk a while."

"Okay," Gretta said. A slobbery kiss dabbed his cheek before the weight of his little sister lifted off him. "I'll visit later. Maybe you can meet the others then."

"There will be plenty of time for that," Dr. Beauchamp said. Danny remembered his gruff accent.

Footfalls faded and then the door creaked shut.

"You sure my parents are dead?" Danny said.

"I'm sorry, yes." Dr. Beauchamp patted Danny's arm. "We had to get you out of the city quickly. There were riots, people setting fire to the places where smallpox patients were."

"But we don't have it anymore. We survived."

"I know, but some people, cowards, were afraid and panicked. You came to us in bad shape after your jump. You're lucky to be alive."

"How bad?"

"Your left leg is broken in several places. From the bruising on your chest, I think maybe a couple ribs might've broken too, and your left arm. I had you in traction at the hospital. Something I've been experimenting with. We had to be very careful moving you, so I thought it best to keep you drugged. The pain would've been intolerable, even for a grown man. But you've been so brave, and you're only twelve. Anne told me you don't want any more medication, and I think that's very brave, but maybe now that you know Gretta is safe and that you're both being taken care of, you can take it without worry. It will help you rest while you're still healing."

"The strange dreams though."

"That's a normal side effect, as well as thinking slow, and feeling itchy as if bugs were crawling on you. You may think you're seeing things that aren't there. If you get scared, try and remind yourself that it isn't real. Anne and I are here, and another woman named Frances too. We won't let anything happen to you or Gretta, or any of the other children while you're in our care."

"Will we be staying here very long?"

"This is your new home now. It was where I grew up, and I think you'll be comfortable here. Once you're feeling better and can move around and know the place, I'm certain you'll like it. It's my family's farm."

"Do you have animals? Gretta would love them."

"Not yet. All the children have asked the same thing." Dr. Beauchamp laughed. "But we will by spring, I promise. You need to get some rest now. I'll send Frances in to help you eat a little bit. She worked at the hospital, too. She came with us to help. Then I'll send Anne in to give you some medicine. Is that all right?"

Danny nodded.

"I'll come back later. Let Frances or Anne know if you need anything."

"Thank you, Dr. Beauchamp."

"You're welcome, son."

Danny's heart pinched at *son*, and he bit his lower lip, fighting back sobs while he waited for the door to squeal shut again. The rough blanket Anne had brought scratched his face but also shielded it from the raw sting of his tears. He waited in sorrow, dread, and anticipation for Anne and the medicine.

Hours had passed, maybe more—or less—he didn't quite know. Food in his stomach and pain medicine coursing through his veins, Danny kicked his way up through depths of crackling white. He spread his arms and swiped weight aside as if opening endless drapes. Lighter than liquid and crumbly, a living sea writhed around him while some behemoth roiled in the deep. The waves it made threw off his balance in a place where he could breathe and *see*, which soothed the fear in his gut.

He lowered his head and watched churning russet colors part. His body plummeted a good way down before his feet struck a slimy black surface. Danny waved his arms to stay upright while his soles slid over ridges, skimming crimson goo between his toes and over his feet. The monstrosity glided fast in one direction and began to thin under him. Then it disappeared, and he dropped, reaching out toward the thing to grab hold and keep from sinking. Pain seared his palm, and he screamed as his body was dragged through layers of caramel and ivory. Sweetness of a wrong kind filled his mouth and he coughed, balled up and vomited, freeing his hand from impalement. Pink froth coated his skin from the tips of his fingers down to his wrist, along with bits of the sea. Up close the milky water wriggled. Worms. No! Maggots crawled over and through the bloody foam, popping the bubbles.

Danny cried out into closed lips, puffing his cheeks, then threw up some more. The crunching all around him became unbearable. He thought of what Dr. Beau had said about the itching sensation of bugs on his skin. A thunderous rumble came from below, agitating the larvae into a frenzy. Oh, please, don't be the monster again. He clenched his wounded fist at the thought, squishing the feeding maggots.

"Hello?" A woman's voice traveled through the squirming wrestle.

"Help," Danny shouted. He listened hard for a reply.

"Who's there?" she said.

Packed tight, squiggling walls folded in around him from all sides, pushing against him as the rumbling intensified.

"Please, miss Maggie. Help me. It's coming. Gretta!"

"I can't see where you are. It's too dark."

"It's here!" Danny screamed again, his mouth filling with sweet little worms.

⌣

Andrew lay with Margaret that night. His rough desires had waned somewhat, and he spent time conversing with her afterward. She didn't mention the orphanage.

He told her he'd leave for the city in the morning and wouldn't return until the following week, then went back to his room.

Margaret fell into a deep sleep only to be woken by rattling floorboards a short time later.

"Hello," she said.

The same boy she'd heard before cried out for help. Margaret flung the covers back, then felt her way to the foot of the bed. Hard as she tried, her eyes wouldn't adjust. Darkness clung to her face.

"Who's there?" she said.

He shouted something was after him, his words echoing through her room.

"I can't see where you are. It's too dark. She struggled to find him. Fear in the child's voice suffused everything; even her skin quivered. With her arms outstretched, Margaret reached for the matches on the dressing table. The rug rippled underfoot, and she tripped and fell. Pain shot through her knee and her sore wrist. She rolled over, clutching it.

"Gretta!"

Margaret couldn't make out the rest. Then the boy screamed.

Every hair on her body raised at his howl. She lay on the floor and cried until only aches remained. Moonlight peeked through drapery seams, expelling the heavy darkness that only moments before had blinded her.

Horse hooves trotting away woke Margaret later that morning. She swung her legs out from under the bedcovers. A crimson rose had bloomed across her knee where it had struck the floor, confirming she hadn't dreamed about the boy calling for help.

Navy linen floated into the room, Helen right behind it, holding a dress. The one Margaret wore for her work at the church.

"I'd prefer the gray wool today, please, Helen. I've got a bit of a chill."

"I hope you're not ill." The maid peered around the dress sleeves. "I've been told you're to stay at home if you're feeling the slightest bit out of sorts." Helen rushed over and placed the back of her hand against Margaret's cheek.

"I'm fine. Really. Don't make a fuss." Margaret swatted her away.

"Well, you don't feel feverish. My, what happened to your leg?"

"I fell out of bed last night."

"You should have rung. I'd have come and helped you."

"It was nothing. I thought I heard something is all."

"Not the little boy again? You sure you're fit to be leaving the house today?"

Margaret grabbed Helen's hand. "I need to get out of here for a while. Please, don't tell Edith."

"I'll keep my mouth shut." Helen pointed her head down toward the mattress. "About that, too. Looks like your monthly's come."

Margaret sighed and got out of bed, her nightgown sticking to her backside. She couldn't blame Andrew; he was gentler than he'd ever been.

"I'll run down and get a rag for the Hoosier belt. You tidy up. If I get the linens started before Mrs. Pettit sees, it'll stay a secret you're still without child."

"Thank you."

⌇

The landscape, the priest's overcoat, and the hem of Margaret's wool dress compounded the drab mood. Father Greer spoke very little as they rode to the Beauchamp farm, and Margaret wondered if maybe he was reconsidering his plan.

"Is it far to Essex County?" she said.

"Just over an hour. Not a bad ride. Even better in warmer weather."

Margaret shifted on the seat. The Hoosier belt cut into her waist, so she moved again.

"I brought blankets for the trip back, but I'll get them out now if you're cold," he said.

"It's fine. Just getting comfortable."

"I'm glad you dressed warm. I feel a storm coming. They don't keep fires lit throughout the house either. Not enough money." He clucked and tugged on the reins.

Horseshoes thumped a tiring rhythm, so Margaret counted trees to stay awake. Father Greer didn't speak again until the farmhouse came into view.

"It's gray, too," Margaret said aloud.

"Just old and in need of some handiwork. Frederick told me he has plans to fix it up when the weather improves. He's a strong, capable man. Folks around here always wondered why he'd want to live in the city after his schooling when he had such a nice property here. Caring for these orphans now though, no one here will see him for what ails them, and he gets little charity."

"That doesn't surprise me."

"Not everyone in these parts is like Edith, although many take her lead, which saddens me."

Father Greer pulled his horse around to the front of a barn that jutted from the ground in a slant, leaning like a gravestone. Ravaged by time, its slats had turned gray, deadwood. Dirt blown over decades had filled the woodgrain, giving the barn's exterior deep wrinkles. The planks had large gaps between them, big enough a man could fit his arm through. Margaret hoped no animals lived inside.

One of the barn doors hung off kilter, lending it an ashamed expression.

After tying the horse to a feeble hitching post, Father Greer helped Margaret from the carriage.

"Shall we?" He buttoned up his coat. "It's cooling down for that storm. We won't stay long."

As if Father Greer had commanded it, miniscule flakes, scant and sparse, fell from mid-sky, melting before they hit the ground.

Although the farmhouse's exterior fared much better, it was an obvious relative of the barn. Yellowed flakes of white paint topped its gray stone base in irregular strips. Boards crisscrossed broken window panes as if someone had taped the house's eyes shut to keep hidden what lived inside.

A young woman with short dark hair opened the door as they stepped onto the porch.

"Hello, Father. And you must be Margaret. Please, come in. Frederick's out searching for Daniel." The woman looked past them, her head darting from one direction to the next as she scanned the landscape before shutting the door.

"Margaret, this is Anne, Frederick's nurse, as well as his wife," Father Greer said. "Anne, this is Mrs. Andrew Pettit."

"Forgive me," Anne said. "It's a pleasure to meet you."

"Likewise," Margaret said.

"Where has the child gone?" Father Greer didn't remove his coat, so Margaret followed his lead.

"We have no idea. He shouldn't even be, couldn't possibly be, out of bed." Anne turned to Margaret. "He has a broken leg on the mend. Daniel wasn't in his room when Frances went up to bring him his breakfast. The whole house has been in chaos since."

"Is there anything we can do to help?" Margaret said.

"I'm not sure." The nurse turned away, wrenching the fabric of her apron.

"Surely the boy couldn't have gone far," Father Greer said. "I'm certain Frederick will be back with him soon. Have faith, Anne." Father Greer put his hand on the nurse's back. "Why don't you introduce Margaret to the other children while we wait for their return."

"You don't think we should go and help Frederick look?" A pained expression crossed her face.

"I think it best to wait. He'd worry if he came back and we were gone."

"You're right, Father. Thank you." Anne's shoulders relaxed, and she smiled at Margaret. "They'll be happy to meet you, albeit they're a bit anxious with this morning's events."

"Prepare yourself, and hold fast, Maggie," the priest said. "Remember they can't see you, but they can hear quite well."

Margaret nodded, wishing he hadn't called her Maggie in front of Mrs. Beauchamp. But why put on airs at an orphanage for children blinded by smallpox? Father Greer had good manners and would never introduce her as Maggie to anyone in town. She forced her mind to wander while her gut twisted. She bit the inside of her lip, bracing for the horrors she would soon see.

"They're in the sitting room with Frances, playing games. This way." Anne headed down the hall from the entryway, Father Greer walking behind her. He turned back to Margaret.

"Stay close to the door in case you need to excuse yourself."

"I will," Margaret said.

Anne entered a plain room with a low ceiling, followed by Father Greer. Low flames struggled to rise from a single log inside a small fireplace opposite the door.

Margaret stepped in and her body tilted to the left. Old floorboards squeaked and curved down with her weight. She shifted and balanced her footing, looking for joists where she could stand that might be more solid.

On the other side of Anne and Father Greer, some children sat while others lay scattered around in a circle next to the fireplace.

"I've someone new here who wants to meet you all." Anne stepped aside.

The children raised their heads. Margaret held her breath and covered her mouth in case the children could hear her silent scream. Their little faces pocked and pitted with dark mottled skin. Many eyes looked but didn't see her, glazed over in white, their lids scarred down, appearing stretched and pinned. She bit down on her hand and inhaled through her nose. Father Greer grabbed her arm and turned her toward the door. Margaret pulled away from him then pinched her cheeks and focused on cracks in the ceiling, slowing her breathing.

"Hello, children. My name's Mrs. Margaret Pettit. But my good friends call me Maggie. I'd like for you to call me Maggie, too."

The older woman, sitting near them stood up. "Well, it's nice to meet you, Mrs. Pettit. My name is Frances. Children, what do you say? Why don't you introduce yourselves and tell this nice lady how old you are?"

Margaret lowered her head and nodded thanks to Frances. The woman smiled, tight-lipped.

"I'm William, and I'm eleven." He appeared to be the biggest child, and probably the oldest.

The girl lying next to him spoke next. She swiped stringy, dark hair away from her mouth. "I'm Tina. They call me Tiny Tina, and I'm five-years-old." She held up her little hand and wiggled her fingers and thumb.

"I'm Jacob, and I'm five, too."

"Timothy Wells, miss. I'm seven." He reached out and nudged a boy seated next to him. "This is my friend Blake Jameson, and he's nine."

Blake smiled, curling the edges of dappled ridges around his mouth, giving him a pained expression.

Sitting farthest away, a waif raised her bony hand. "My name's Marion, and I'm eight-years-old."

A little girl with curly blonde hair turned around and cried. "I want Danny to be here," she said. Her voice, less than childlike, almost babyish, floated like bubbles from a face of red, scarred flesh. A cruel fate for one so young. Margaret balled her fist against her chest.

"He told me about you," the child said.

Frances stepped over and took the child by the hand, pulling her up to stand. "Come now, Gretta, your big brother will return soon with Dr. Beau. Be a good girl and tell this nice lady your name. She came all the way from town to meet you."

The girl calmed a bit then spoke. "I'm four, and my name's Gretta."

Margaret's knees buckled as the room seesawed. Father Greer caught her before she fell, then escorted her out into the hall.

"We'll be right back, children," he said behind him.

"What's wrong?" one of the boys said.

"It's nothing," Anne said. "It's almost time for lunch, and I'm sure Mrs. Pettit is hungry too. Pick up your toys, and we'll go into the dining room. Frances, bring them along, please."

Margaret caught her breath then whispered, "Father, that little girl, Gretta. I think I know her."

"How?"

"I… I don't know. I didn't sleep well and am feeling a bit ill. Would you mind taking me home?"

"I guess you may have overdone it for today. You did better than I thought you might, but you're right. I should get you home before the storm worsens, or Edith might—"

"But what about her brother who's lost out there somewhere?"

"When we get into town, I'll gather who I can to come back and search."

Shaking, Margaret took his arm and let him lead her out. She vomited next to the carriage and took the 'kerchief Father Greer handed her.

"Sorry, Father. I hope I haven't disappointed you too greatly and that you still want my help here."

"Of course. I think they'll need your charity now more than ever."

Staring out at the swirling white, Margaret wondered how Dr. Beauchamp fared on his search for Danny in the deteriorating weather as ice melted down her chin.

~⁓~

Fighting against the current of worms, the big muscles in Danny's arms shook. He'd kept them stretched out for too long. They hurt, and he wanted so much to give up and let go. But when they went limp he'd either drown in a sea of maggots or get eaten by that sea serpent. Neither choice appealed to him, so he thought of Gretta and treaded harder. He was her only family now. As much as he loved her and wanted to do right by her, his strength would not hold. Danny's head submerged, and he held his breath and kicked up. His father's voice filled his head, encouraging him to hang on.

"I'm sorry, Dad. I can't!"

Danny surrendered and gasped one last breath before going under.

His body came to rest on a beach. Colors from reddish brown to parchment filled his sight. He remembered the hues from autumn leaves. White foam and countless worms rose, broke, then receded in soft waves along the shoreline, leaving wriggling stragglers behind. They writhed their way through the sand back toward the wretched sea that spat Danny out. Distant shadows took shape over the sand. He blinked and focused eyes he hadn't used since he was ten-years-old. Was it that he could see, or was this a dream, or his mind playing tricks? Did it matter? His eyes worked now. Here, in this strange place he'd visited, where he had gradually regained his sight.

Dark movements caught his attention. Then he heard children laughing. Danny focused harder and saw people farther down the beach.

"Help," he said. Low and raspy, Danny could hardly hear his own voice, and doubted anyone else would either.

While he lay still, recovering his strength, he looked at all the things his limited motion would allow. Up close, the sand wasn't the way his father had described it in stories. Instead of rocky grains, tiny husks, whole and in pieces covered the terrain. They gave way and crinkled under his cheek but didn't jab into or abrade his skin. Maggot casings, he thought. The word pupa came to mind as if someone spoke it. A raging sea of live ones brought him here.

Danny rolled over, unable to use his rubbery arms. Not far from where his toes pointed skyward, an enormous worm, bigger than a four-story building, lay parallel to the beach. Its girth blacked out the bottom third of a white sun, shining without brilliance dead center in the colorless sky. He remembered it from when he'd drifted to this place before. The star's faint light beamed across the top of the behemoth, giving it a luminescent glow.

It didn't hurt Danny's eyes to look at the sun. He flopped side to side, bending his knees, then planted his feet into the husks and inched his body into a sitting position. His arms tingled back to life as he stared at the massive worm. The blackness that faced him was so deep nothing reflected upon it and instead seemed to absorb the surrounding light. Gigantic rings circled the tubular monster, and the sections quivered and moved in ripples, even though the creature lay still.

The people he'd seen and heard earlier raced down the beach toward him, shouting and laughing like children. And that's what they were. A tall, older boy, maybe Danny's age, skidded to a stop, spraying husks onto Danny's face.

"Oops, sorry 'bout that, kid." A windblown shock of red hair stood straight up from his head.

"My name's Danny." He brushed the pupas from his face.

"Hi, I'm Roy, but my crew calls me Red." He held out a hand and Danny took it, with trembling arms that didn't ache as before.

Red helped him onto his feet while the other children caught up.

Danny scanned all their faces. A girl his age, with curly brown hair, winked at him. Some of them smiled while others laughed, but none of them had a single scar or mark. He stroked his cheeks and felt only smoothness.

"That's how it is here," Red said. "We look the way they see us." He looked over his shoulder to the black worm.

Then a boy with dark hair stepped forward. "And most important, we can use our arms and legs, hands and feet, and hear and see!"

The children cheered and clapped.

"Where is here?" Danny said.

"Mawk," Red said. "You hungry?"

"I swallowed a bunch of the uh… those." Danny pointed to the ebbing larval sea and saw a patch of shiny black plunge underneath it. "But yeah, I'm starving."

The worm had gone.

"Then come on. Let's head over to the big house and get some food." Red put his arm around Danny and helped him walk.

The dark-haired boy came around and helped. "I'm Harry. Welcome home."

The kids whooped and hollered.

When it quieted, Danny said, "Home?"

A roar of laughter came from behind the three boys.

"Yep," Red said. "We work, they feed us, and give us a place to live. We're a family. Lots of families. And this is home."

"Best of all, I can see!" The pretty girl Danny noticed earlier shouted behind them.

Over packed dunes of coppery and golden husks, a mansion with blue shutters, white clapboards and a matching picket fence rose over the horizon.

Gretta would love that house.

She would love everything about this place.

More children poured out the front doors and down a large porch toward them, then they led the way in. A trick of returned sight or Danny's mind, the house's interior appeared even bigger than it did on the outside.

Harry must've seen the awe on Danny's face. "Isn't it grand? We all eat and sleep here."

"How?" Danny said.

"Doesn't matter," Red said. "We're well cared for, and about. None of us want to leave, ever."

"Cared for by who?" Danny said.

"The worms, silly." The girl with brown hair pushed her way through the others. "My name's Louise, and I've been here the longest."

"Nuh-uh," several of the kids said in unison.

Louise rolled her eyes.

"Out of the way." Red waved, and most of them parted. "Danny's hungry and needs to eat."

Louise stepped aside and followed them into a massive dining hall. Long tables and benches filled the room. Food of all kinds sat on platters across the middle of each table. Danny's stomach squelched and rumbled. Harry and Red sat him down in front of an empty plate, then took the seats next to him. Louise went around the table and sat across from him. He reached out, grabbed a frosted roll, and tore into it with his teeth.

"Well?" Harry said.

The buttery cinnamon and soft pastry tasted divine, but the longer he kept it in his mouth and chewed, the more he noticed a soft underlying crunch and sickening sweetness. Danny swallowed.

"Here! Try something else." Red picked up a slice of ham and plopped it onto Danny's plate.

Louise pushed a glass toward him.

123

"Thanks," Danny said. He held it up to his nose. "What is it?"

"Punch," she said.

He took a swig and downed it fast. The kids stared at him for a reaction.

Danny nodded his head. "It's good," he said. "Sweet. A little salty, too." It had a slight medicinal aftertaste, but he said nothing, happy to be mobile, eating and drinking with normal kids he could see.

Louise laughed. "You'll get used to it," she said.

Red and Harry patted Danny's back. "That's right," Red said.

"You'll never go hungry again." Harry grabbed some cheese and put the whole chunk in his mouth then gulped it down. The others around him feasted as well, and the more Danny watched them, the more he noticed none of them bothered to chew.

⁓

"No cheese for me tonight, thank you," Margaret said to one of the kitchen maids. Thinking of the lost boy and the other orphans had her restless and upset all afternoon.

Mrs. Pettit looked up from her plate of red meat.

"Are you feeling well, dear?" Andrew said. He had only gotten as far as town before his coachman turned around because of the storm.

"I'm fine." Margaret played with her fork. "It's just that I can't eat when I know there are children nearby who are hungry and cold."

The old woman pushed her plate aside. "Please, do tell us what you're talking about."

"I... I went with Father Greer to the blind children's orphanage in Essex today."

"That man is no man of God, bringing a Pettit to that place!" Mrs. Pettit slammed her palm against the table, rattling her table setting. "Even one by marriage."

"Calm down, Mother! Margaret, please continue."

"Oh, Andrew, those poor children. I want so much to help them. Can't we... can't you do something?"

"I won't have it," Mrs. Pettit said. "Your duty is to care for Andrew and give him a child."

The old woman's words added kindling to the fire burning in Margaret's belly.

"Then I have no duties, ma'am, since it is you that does all the caring for Andrew, and as for having a—"

"Enough! Please." Andrew threw his napkin to the table. "I saw Father Greer when I was stuck in town today. He was asking for volunteers to search for a boy who'd wandered off. Mr. Collings and a few others went to help, and I would have too, but I had to get word to the city after canceling the trip."

"I—" Mrs. Pettit appeared to shrink at the other end of the table.

"Mother, I'm asking you nicely to let me discuss this with my wife without your interference."

"Did you hear any news about the boy?" Margaret said.

"Unfortunately, no. The storm was worsening and all I could think of was to make sure you'd gone home from the church safely. That's when I ran into Father Greer. He told me what happened, and that you'd gone with him, Maggie."

"I was going to tell you. I just…" Margaret looked over at Mrs. Pettit, who glowered at her.

"Just what?" A devilish smirk rose around Mrs. Pettit's mouth, deep wrinkles framing it.

Margaret focused her attention on Andrew. "I wanted to tell you when we were alone, but all this food, and thinking of those starving children, and that poor boy out in the cold… Please, forgive me."

"Of course. Always. Now that I know you'll come back to me no matter who takes you away." Andrew leered at his mother. "As for these children, I'm certain there's plenty we can do to help. I'll send funds to Frederick to help him with repairs on the house. We can rally some local workers when the weather permits. Before then, I'll donate money for firewood, blankets, and supplies, and encourage others in town to do so as well."

"Oh, thank you, Andrew!" Margaret rushed over to him and kissed his cheek.

Mrs. Pettit clucked her tongue and pushed away from the table.

"I'll come to your room tonight," Andrew whispered.

Heat flushed Margaret's face. The way he'd said it rather than asked made her wonder what he might expect her to do. But she wouldn't let that ruin her little victory over Edith. Margaret backed away.

Mrs. Pettit's grimace became a smirk once more.

⌒

The storm cleared three days later, and Father Greer took Margaret to the Beauchamp Farm, a cart stuffed with supplies behind them.

"Do you think the boy is dead?" she said.

"Frederick says he wouldn't have made it in his condition, and being that Frederick's a physician, I'm keen to believe him. There'll be another search for his body in the spring, unless by some miracle the boy survives and returns on his own." Father Greer looked up at the overcast sky and said a prayer.

Margaret couldn't make out his words, but she uttered "Amen" when he finished.

The children rushed to the door, pushing Frances and Anne aside, feeling their way to Margaret's hands. They led her through the entryway and introduced her to Frederick.

"Forgive us, Mrs. Pettit. It's been a bit chaotic this morning as you can see. Children, compose yourselves. She's not a rag doll."

"It's fine, and please, call me Maggie," she said, happy at all the excitement for her presence. "Children, why don't you take me to your playroom? We can have a game or two while the others help Father Greer."

"Oh yes, miss. Please," a frail brunette with dark, stringy hair took her hand.

"Hello, Tina," Margaret said.

"You remembered my name?"

"Of course. You're Tiny Tina. You lead the way then, I'll follow."

The child tugged her arm with strength Margaret hadn't expected. Small palms pushed her from behind, urging her toward the playroom at the end of the hall.

Gretta sat alone, facing a low window. The scene would've appeared normal had it not been for all the boards nailed across the frame. Margaret took in a breath then sighed. Tina let go of her hand, then shut the door.

"Sit down, miss." Gretta patted the floor next to her. "I've something important to tell you."

The oldest boy, William, nudged Margaret. She hesitated, then spoke, "I don't think—"

"Please do as Gretta says," he said.

Margaret sat. William scooted in on the other side of her. The other children gathered around. Heat crept up Margaret's bodice to her throat, stifling her with unease. "Children, what's this about? You're sitting a bit too close, and it's rather warm in here today."

"We've a secret," Gretta whispered. Sweet baby's breath caressed Margaret's cheek, and she relaxed a little. *They're just children.*

"Tell me," Margaret said.

"Tell her." William's voice stern and commanding.

"It's Danny," Gretta said. "He's alive."

"He's returned? Is he here, now?"

Gretta grabbed Margaret's face between her palms then faced her with droopy eyes, the color of lake ice. Margaret closed hers. "Danny's in the white place," Gretta said. "He wants us to go there, too."

"In the snow, you mean? The storm? But it has passed. He needs to come here. To Dr. Beauchamp's farmhouse. Everyone's worried sick. Tell him to come immediately."

"They won't let him," Tina said. "Not yet."

"Who?" Margaret said. "Let me speak to them."

"You can't," Gretta said.

"Children, is this a game of yours? It's not fun, and I don't think Dr. Beauchamp or Nurse Anne would think so either."

"Shhh!" William said. "Listen to Gretta. Danny's told us all about the white place. We've been to Mawk and seen it."

"Listen to what you're saying. William, you're the oldest, and I'd expect more from you than leading these children on as if they could *see* anything. It's monstrous."

"But we have seen it," Tina said.

The others nodded in unison.

"You have too, miss Maggie," Marion said.

Margaret turned and faced the oldest girl. "I can assure you, I have not."

"You certain?" Jacob said.

"I... I'd remember it if I had, and don't like being called a liar." Margaret pushed off the floor.

William yanked her back down. Gretta latched onto Margaret's arms and squeezed.

"Let me go this instant. I think Dr. Beauchamp and Father Greer need to hear what you children have been up to."

"Don't tell," Gretta said. "Please." She begged. Her tears and baby voice tugged at Margaret's pounding heart.

The children calmed, quieted. William rubbed Margaret's arm. "I'm sorry if I hurt you, miss. We just want… Need you to listen."

"Yeah. We're all sorry," Jacob said.

Tina nudged her way next to Margaret and wrapped her little arms around Margaret's waist. "Please forgive us."

"But children, really? You gave me a fright. You shouldn't play like this with people you hardly know."

"It's just that we feel we do. Know you, I mean," William said. "You're sure we don't seem familiar?" He put his face within inches of Margaret's. She bit her lip and held in a gasp.

"Uh-huh," Tina said, while nodding. Her scraggly hair dangling over pink scars.

"I'd remember each and every one of you." Margaret's voice cracked. "If we'd met before."

The four others shuffled on their knees and circled her, moving their faces in closer.

The door swung open.

"Children! What are you doing?" Frances stood in the doorway, hands on her hips. "Back off and give the lady some room to breathe."

"She's our new Mommy," Gretta said.

—⁓—

Red took Danny outside after their meal, and they sat on the back porch of the big house. "For every one of them, there's a team of us," Red explained to Danny. "Some of the teams have moms. They don't stay here though."

"Where then?" Danny said.

"Out there." Red pointed to the sea.

"What about dads?"

"No."

"Why not?"

"I just follow orders, keep my crew in line, and play as often as I like."

"How long have you been here?" Danny said.

"It's been a while. I don't remember my parents anymore. Their faces or what they were like."

"I don't want to forget mine."

"If your sister comes, and you talk about them with her, maybe you won't."

"What if I want to go back?"

"Why would you?"

Danny shrugged his shoulders. "I miss my sister, Gretta."

"I suppose they'd take you. But we'd all call you chicken." Red got up and circled him, scratching up the pupas on the porch with his foot, squawking like a hen.

"Knock it off." Danny pushed him.

"Get her and bring her here. She can be on your crew."

"How?"

"Go to that dark place when you close your eyes and sleep."

127

"But it's so light out?"

"It always is. The white star doesn't move. You'll get used to it."

"What's that over there?" Danny shaded his eyes with his hand and stared out over the dunes.

"That's the forest where the big worms go to be born. The things that look like trees are the skins they shed. Me and some of the boys go there sometimes and climb the branches. It's hard 'cause they're smooth like metal. Lots of sharp edges, too. I'm the best and fastest at getting to the tops."

The boys went back into the house then upstairs and through long halls with endless doors. Behind them were beds with mattresses lined in neat rows. Some were filled with sleeping children. At the middle of every room, a large fireplace crackled and popped, warming the space and making Danny more tired. The two found empty beds near the hearth and lay down.

"I've been thinking," Red said.

Danny stretched and yawned, pointing his toes and shuddering. "About what?"

"All the family leaders."

"What about them?"

"We were all totally blind. Know what I mean?"

"No." Danny turned and faced Red, mirroring his posture.

"Well, most blind people still see colors and shapes, can tell day from night. Not me though."

"Gretta says she sees stuff, but I never believed her because I don't."

"I think that's why they chose us, and what they show us is special. They'll only talk to us, you know. The worms. And only you can hear and understand your own."

"The one that brought me to the beach is mine?"

"Yeah. Did it talk to you?"

"I thought that was me, talking to myself in my head."

"Nope. That's them."

Danny rolled over and closed his eyes. "Go to the dark place, right?"

"You gonna visit your sister?" Red said.

"Yeah. Sometimes I think I hear someone else there, too. A woman."

"Maybe they want her too."

"For what?"

"The Migration. Go to sleep. See your sister. Good night, brother."

"Night," Danny said.

A voice in his head woke Danny.

White beams reached out from the star, Mawk's sun, spanning a silvery glow across the pupal dunes. Standing on the porch, the hulking girth of a worm rose above the husk piles, creating a black horizon.

"Come on! That one's mine." Red took off through the casings.

Eight kids ran after him, nudging and shoving Danny aside. He fell in behind the last one as they headed for the shoreline.

Red stood shouting at his family through cupped hands. "Let's get this done! Somebody give Lily a boost!"

A boy Danny didn't recognize slid down the worm then went over to the little girl. One of the creature's segments lifted like a flap, spilling thousands of maggots. The boy clasped his hands together and Lily put her foot into the boy's palms, using them to jump up toward the opened segment. Danny stood with his mouth open as she scrambled through squirming clusters of larvae and crawled inside. The little girl lay on her belly, swiping out the worms by flailing her arms and legs as if making a snow angel. Shifting mounds against the giant worm below diminished as individuals wriggled their way back toward the ivory sea. He imagined Gretta doing the same task and enjoying it the way Lily did.

Red's footsteps crunched down the beach, alongside the black worm, inspecting his family's work. He approached Danny after he'd walked the entire length of both flanks.

"Well, what do you think?"

"I, I... What are they doing?"

"They're cleaning it. The little ones get under their skin and *bug* 'em. Get it?" Red laughed.

Danny raised his eyebrows at Red's joke. Horror, disgust, and an itching, morbid curiosity filled him with everything but glee.

Red put his arm around Danny, leading him toward the thinner end of the worm. "Just remember, when we're not doing this, we're doing whatever else we want. Eating whatever we want, as much as we want. Sleeping whenever we want. Being who we were meant to be. And most of all, seeing this beautiful world around us."

"But it's all just worms," Danny said. "What's to see?"

"There's so much more. Like the Migration."

Danny stopped and scrunched his face. "You've said that twice now."

"Our masters take us out so very far. They rise up and open their mouths. The mothers step out from inside, and the sea swirls and drops at the center of the circle they create. Down past all the dried husks, the maggots. Beyond the depths of the giant animals they bring here to feed on, their melted bones and fluids. There is a living blackness. We watch their children rise and gather above, a buzzing spout that goes to other places, cleansing them of decay, bringing our life to their death. Then we come back and cheer and celebrate."

"Their children?" Danny said.

"Flies."

"Oh."

Red grabbed Danny's arm and continued toward the other end of his worm. "I'm going to show you what it is we do. We have the biggest cleaning responsibility."

"Which is?"

They stepped around to the front of a gaping maw. Two long fangs with forked hook tips protruded from a dark cave entrance of a mouth. Moist parts moved just inside.

"Where's the mother?" Danny said.

"They live down there." Red pointed to the back of the worm's throat, then took a brush from his pocket. It looked identical to the one Danny kept in his bootblack box.

With a flick of his wrist, Red tossed the brush up into the air then whipped around and caught it behind his back. He winked at Danny then stepped onto a soft part of the worm's mouth.

"Come on." Red motioned him aboard.

"Can't you just show me from out here?"

Red clucked and squawked and flapped his arms until Danny followed him. Pink, glossy ooze came up from the worm's flesh under their feet.

"Aren't you afraid of slipping on that stuff and sliding down its throat?" Danny said.

"I was at first, but you learn how to balance while working in here really quick." Red crouched and scrubbed the worm's fangs, removed bone shards then tossed them out onto the beach.

"How do you clean the very top?" Danny said.

"Easy. They roll."

"While you're in there?" His voice cracked. "And with the rest of your family on it?"

"The outside is separate."

Red explained that only the special ones of the worm's choosing can enter its mouth. "It's their most sensitive part, making our jobs as the family leaders most important."

⌣

Father Greer had fallen ill and couldn't take Margaret to the Beauchamp Farm. He asked her not to go alone, but she needed so much to be doing something, to get out of the house and away from Edith, so she convinced Helen's husband, Mr. LaForge to bring her.

He stopped the carriage well before the farm came into view. "This is where the road ends for me, miss. I won't go near that house."

"Don't be a fool. Bring me closer."

"I will not. You get out here and now if you will, I'm heading back into town."

Margaret stumbled from the carriage with her bags and slammed the door. "How will I get home?"

"I'll come back before dark. Be waiting right here. I won't go down there after you."

"Insufferable man!"

Mr. LaForge cracked his whip, starting both horses into something of a gallop. Margaret turned away from the clumps of filthy snow kicked up by the hooves and looked toward the road leading to the farmhouse, wondering why even the mares seemed eager to get away.

The extra blankets and canned jams she'd packed weighted her arms and pulled on her shoulders. Margaret cursed Mr. LaForge as she trudged. A hot cup of tea and the good company of Frances, Anne, and Frederick would set her straight before tending to the children. As she approached the dilapidated porch and climbed the steps, a sharp wind gusted and banged the door wide open. Margaret jumped and slid, catching her balance before falling.

"Hello!" she said into the house.

Inside, she dropped the bags, then shut the door behind her. An icy chill had hold of the house. Snow had drifted in through the poorly boarded front windows, blanketing the long hall in white. A single set of small footprints came from the children's playroom toward her, then up the first few stairs before disappearing where no snow had blown.

"Is anyone here? Children?"

She stood unmoving, listening. Wind whirred through missing pieces of house, shivering her further. Creaks sounded from the door ahead where she'd first met the little ones. It stood ajar and breathed with irregular gusts, gasping, the way elderly do before passing on. The old wood strained with each respiration. Margaret stepped closer then had somehow got to the children's door without remembering walking there. Glancing over her shoulder, she didn't notice any marks left by her boots. Margaret peered inside the playroom. No low flames crackled or popped in the fireplace; not even a curl of smoke rose from a charred log. It had gone out some time ago. Or maybe no one had lit it this morning.

Margaret called out, "If this is a game you're all playing, it's not funny."

The house wheezed. The door slammed inches from her face. Margaret backed away, turned around and followed the little footprints to the staircase. Each step squeaked with her weight. She gripped the railing, afraid the icy wood might snap in two. Then she stopped and called out again.

"Children? Are you up there? Frances?"

The landing leaned to the left at the top, so she kept to the right, opening doors along the short hall that mimicked the one on the first floor. She stood outside and stared at the playroom's twin door. Intuition urged her to leave, but she knocked, then put her ear to the wood. Giggling echoed from within, tickling the hairs on her neck. She steadied herself for one of their frightful games and took a deep breath.

Frigid brass burned her palm as she twisted the knob.

On the floor just inside, lay Frederick, Anne, and Frances. Their bodies heaped in a pile.

Margaret screamed.

The silhouette of a young man draped in writhing shadow stood in the far corner. Margaret couldn't tell who it was.

"William, is that you?"

Smaller figures came out from behind furniture scattered throughout the room.

"Children, my God! You're safe! Come, we must leave this instant."

They surrounded her, William in the lead. He stepped into a beam of faint light coming from the hall behind her; it illuminated his red scars and pitted skin. His right eye drooped in a way she hadn't noticed before. In each of his sockets glistened moons, rippling movement behind their sheen. He took another step. The boy in the corner—not William—remained still.

Margaret's eyes darted back and forth from the children to the bodies. Anne's corpse lay on top, facing Frederick, their frozen expressions regarding one another in shock and terror. Frances's body was under Frederick's, her head turned toward the door, toward Margaret. The woman's eyes bulged with fear. White tears had solidified and stuck to her cheeks. Then several of them moved. Anne's mouth creaked open and a stream of maggots spilled out onto Frederick's face. Margaret screamed again.

"Don't be afraid of us, Miss Margaret," the boy in the corner said.

"Who are you?" Margaret didn't like the quaver she heard in her voice.

"It's my brother, Danny." A baby voice came from the hall behind her.

"Gretta, is that you?" Remembering his aggressions and strength, Margaret kept her eyes on William who continued moving toward her. "Don't come over here, Gretta. I want you to go downstairs and wait by the door. Do you hear me?"

"We need you to come with us." Danny spoke with a loud crackling voice not his own. Not the voice she'd heard before. "You're meant to be with us. They want you to see us as we truly are." Words burbled from his mouth. They rung inside Margaret's ears and pierced her mind. She stepped back, reeling and then threw up. Children's laughter surrounded her.

Margaret wanted to grab Gretta and run, but she couldn't let William or Danny out of her sight.

"Gretta?" Margaret waved behind her and shuffled backward. Her boot slid over vomit, and she fell, grasping at the air above. Unable to catch her balance, she landed on her back. This is how it should've been upon arriving in New York. She should've jumped when she had the chance.

Gretta lay on the floor near Margaret's feet, a cheerful smile on her otherwise hideous face. The children pounced and pinned Margaret with their weight. Marion came forward with her hand held high; a dark wisp of stringy hair swung like a pendulum, keeping time. Scissor blades glinted then came down.

Then Margaret saw nothing.

⌣

Familiar voices filled the room. Margaret's body, heavy and listless wouldn't respond.

"I told you something like this would happen, but you're as stubborn as your father." Edith spoke with anger and spite. "I'll have that farm burned to the ground. And you, you'll have to learn to control your wife, or I will. Father Greer had suspected she was pregnant. Maybe now she'll see things our way."

Edith laughed. "We'll insist she not care for the child, but I'd planned on that anyhow. If she argues, we'll send her to the nearest sanitarium where you can visit her as often as you'd like. You understand, don't you, son?"

"Yes, Mother."

"Come now. The doctor said she needs to rest."

Margaret wrenched fabric and wept in silence as they left the room.

See things their way. Had Marion blinded her? But she felt no pain. Was she not crying and feeling the wetness of her tears? Maybe she imagined the sting of salt from her eyes. Margaret willed her hands to reach up, and with shaky fingers, she touched her face, then raked through her hair, groping her scalp, searching for damage, wounds, sutures, even sharp jabs of pain. Her eyelids opened, and she saw her palms. What had the children done?

Nothing.

And they would be burned alive for it! She had to stop the Pettits.

Margaret threw the covers off and scanned her body for bandages. Then from the far wall of the darkened room, a faint white light seeped through a thin fissure, setting her and the bed aglow. A thunderous crack rattled her bedrails, and the wall tore open. The gleam grew stronger, blinding her. Shuffling sounds drew near; soft crackling and popping noises accompanied them.

"Hello?" Margaret shaded her eyes from the glare.

"It's us. We've come to help," Gretta said. Her baby voice both comforting and terrifying.

Tiny hands groped the blankets around the bed's edges.

"No, children, listen to me. You must get out of here. Find a way and leave this place. They're going to burn the farm down. They mean to kill you. But what have you done?" Margaret reached into the light. "Marion, what did you do with those scissors? Did you kill Frances, Dr. Beauchamp, and his wife?"

Gretta giggled like a toddler. "No. Marion wouldn't do that."

"I just wanted a lock of your hair, miss. In case you didn't want to come with us."

Margaret's eyes adjusted to the light. The children stood around her bed. Their angelic faces and smiles beamed with white light. Any, and all traces of the disease, gone. Their ruined eyes and scars had vanished; they reminded her of children dressed in white from Monet paintings.

"What happened?" she said.

They put their perfect little hands on her and sat her up. She had on her cramoisi dress.

"How?"

"Come with us," Danny said.

"Where?"

"To Mawk," Marion said.

"You'll love it, miss Margaret," Gretta said. "You can be our Mommy."

"You can work all day if you like," Will said.

"Or not," Danny said.

The children laughed, then helped Margaret from the bed toward the tear in the wall.

Through the large fissure, came a deafening whir of flies. Past a vortex of flittering black, iridescent wings, the single dim white star of Mawk glowed in the far-off distance.

Margaret stopped and considered. Little fingers pressed against the small of her back, and she stumbled and lost her footing, reaching up into the empty air.

Danny grabbed hold of her hand and steadied her.

"Thank you, Danny." Margaret pulled him closer, then reached for Gretta and smiled down at her. "You're right. My child… you children, you're all mine now, and I will keep you safe. Always."

Together, they stepped into the light of Mawk's star.

Afterword

Sloth isn't just laziness: those who do very little, or those who do nothing at all.

There are also those who stay busy, but they're still not doing the things they should be doing, putting them off for later, giving them the excuse to avoid getting more important things done. This definition of sloth is also known as acedia, and it's a type of metaphysical laziness rather than mere physical fatigue or melancholy. It means not making it a priority to do what we should, or change what we should in ourselves. Some people think of it as apathy, or a lack of feeling.

When I set out to write *Clevengers of the Carrion Sea*, I knew I wanted to incorporate both definitions without making the lazy (and most known) too obvious. The second definition is more prominent in the story, and I did that because acedia is more common among people I know personally, including myself.

Using myself as an example, I haven't had a novel or novella published since 2013. But that doesn't mean I haven't been writing. I've written many short stories which have been published, a few that haven't because they need revisions, which I've *put off for later*. I've also written one unpublished weird Western novella that needs heavy editing, and three novels that are all in the editing process, two that are closer to being published than the third (which I'd written before the last two).

But why is nothing finished?

I don't have deadlines for the works I have in progress. Then in comes the volunteer work I take on, and I mean a lot of it. But even that tends to have deadlines.

Writing *Clevengers* helped me realize that in the way of acedia, I am guilty of sloth.

My mind knows that finishing those stories will be cathartic and freeing, yet at the same time, I'm afraid of getting those novels published because it might mean I'll have to write more, and maybe what I write next won't be as good or fulfilling to write.

It also seems like when my volunteer commitments lessen, I'll find something else to pile on, pushing the finishing line for those stories-in-waiting back even further, like redecorating a house, buying a house, building a house, and moving. The foot surgeries I've had have also slowed me down, but I won't add those to my procrastination excuses because I'd prefer editing works in progress to having surgery any day.

My hope in writing *Clevengers* is that after relating to Margaret, I might be reminded to avoid falling into that abyss of forced labor and take back the will to finish the work I've begun on my own accord for that feeling of accomplishment if nothing else.

As for the obvious definition of sloth, Danny was the perfect choice. Nowadays, he's considered a bit young for the responsibilities I put on him, but back in the late 1800s, he was nearing early manhood and was expected to work and help care for his family. Taking his sister to a bad area of New York to increase his wages through gambling rather than earning them by shining shoes was what gave him and Gretta smallpox, leaving them scarred and blind.

There's a little guilt in him, but he's manipulated it into his idea of overly caring for Gretta post-disease instead of accepting complete blame, which is all his. I wrote about mobs setting fires to marked buildings so as not to put the reader against Danny early on, making it too obvious. I preferred to leave the question of whether he might've accidentally killed his parents alone. Gretta certainly suspects it.

Then there's Danny's introduction to Mawk, where a boy like him can stay a boy. Yes, he'll be the leader of his crew, which includes being able to watch over his younger sister, but he's convinced it's not work in the traditional sense. The worms have gifted him his sight again, but he's still blind in only seeing what they want him to see. But that's good enough for Danny, for now, taking his laziness to new heights. He doesn't grasp the dread of forever and ever.

The child leaders are blind because the worms need to be able to show them something special through the utter darkness they see. Many of the other children cleaners are not blind but disfigured or maimed in a way that keeps them down and apart from society.

Mawk is a grim world where death and decay thrive under fine layers of make-believe the children and mothers of worms are forced to see through mind control—my weird version of *Neverland*. The numen vermis (worm gods) rule Mawk. They travel back and forth through the time and space of multiverses to bring forth demise and rebirth with their children, the fly swarms. The worm gods thrive on the energy released at death for all things living. They need the team leaders to be the clevengers of Mawk and translate their wishes to its inhabitants. The other children keep the worm gods' segments clean, and the women mother their offspring.

Lastly, I'm fond of interesting words, names, and their origins. Most of my story titles tend to have two or more meanings that relate to the work. There is, from using random memory bits of my nursing studies, the Clevenger fissure, which fundamentally, separates parts of the brain. The word fissure I took for the way of traveling to Mawk. The name Clevenger is an English variant of Clavinger, which was a status name for *the keeper of the keys in a great household.*

"Each of us is born with a box of matches inside us…"
—Laura Esquivel, *Like Water for Chocolate*

"Love is a burning thing
And it makes a fiery ring
Bound by wild desire
I fell in to a ring of fire

I fell into a burning ring of fire
I went down, down, down
And the flames went higher
And it burns, burns, burns
The ring of fire
The ring of fire"

—Johnny Cash, "Ring of Fire"

"…the strongest emotions are the primitive ones—rage and hate and fear."
—Stephen King, *Danse Macabre*

RING OF FIRE

by Richard Thomas

"Have I told you about the monkeys?"
"Yes, several times."
"I have?"
"Yes."
"And?"
"And what?"
"You believe?"
"We're here, aren't we?"
"True."
"How long has it been?"
"Years?"
"Decades."
"Yes."
"Let's see how it's going."
"All of them? Or just him? This one?"
"Him, I think."
"It can happen in an instant though, right?"
"So you've said."

It's hard not to think about Rebecca all the time, while I sit here on the frozen tundra, running tests on rare compounds and minerals. She's the only human

137

contact I have with the outside world, and the waiting is torture. I'm desperate for company, for her presence, and I long to see her—that radiant smile, those twinkling eyes, her melodious voice.

Some days it threatens to consume me.

Today, like every day, I've pulled a sample up from the vein that lies hundreds of feet directly below me. It's a complicated process, and I don't understand everything they're asking me to do here, but I have pride, so I do the work.

Not everything is clear, here.

They don't tell me much.

In order to be placed in this concrete bunker without windows, to keep me from losing my mind, they had to make some alterations—there were conditions to my contract, our agreement. The nanotechnology in my skull allows for partial memory erasure, as well as other things. So there may be a wife and kids waiting back home for me, wherever that is, or there may be nobody at all.

I don't know.

They say it's to keep me focused, so that my mind doesn't wander.

Things have gone wrong before, it seems.

Top secret information, these details.

They say a lot of things.

Most days, I'm not even sure who *they* are. That's part of it, too.

I signed up for this.

I think.

By my records, I have less than a year left, 288 days. Then the veil will be lifted.

We're a two-day drive from any form of civilization, the conditions so bleak, so cold, that there are times when planes can't even fly here—wings freezing, engines stalling, tires blown out when landing on the runway. On average, it's twenty degrees below zero, with a wind chill that dips down to negative 40, or 60, even lower. It's dangerous out there—deadly. You can die of exposure in five minutes.

Or so I've been told.

I'm not sure exactly where I am.

⁓

The first time I met Rebecca, it did not go well.

I was having trouble adjusting.

While there is technology all around me, it fails constantly—computers and communication systems losing their connections, the signals and wavelengths unable to penetrate the elements, satellites futile, lines down everywhere; doors sticking, freezing, having to manually override them and physically turn levers, and gears, the exertion and stress draining; the solar panels covered with snow and ice, the windmill no longer turning, the bunker thrown into darkness, backup generators weak and unreliable.

When she pounded on the exterior door, I was in bad shape—no lights, cold MREs, alone. I… overreacted.

I didn't know who she was, so bundled up, male or female, I was just desperate for contact, of any kind.

There was no introduction, I just grabbed her, hugged her, babbling on and on. She pushed me away. There was a device, a taser of sorts.

I guess she was scared.

I'm sure this wasn't the first time something like this has happened.

When I woke up, she was gone, the samples taken.

But before I fully regained consciousness, before I could move, I felt something crawling over my arm—a spider, I think. And there was nothing I could do.

I hate spiders.

Sweat beaded up on my forehead, as its tiny legs lifted and then set down, lifted and then set down, inch by inch, up my arm, getting closer to my shoulder, and my face.

My mouth.

I tried to turn my head, slowly, my vision blurry, but I couldn't really move yet. The only thing I could do was blow on it.

So it bit me.

She said something, though, Rebecca, before leaving me there lying on the cold concrete. There was an echo in my head, a memory.

"No," she said, her voice soft, whispering in my ear. "This is not how we do this, Mark. We are professionals. Adults. Human beings. See you in 30 days."

I can remember just a hint of something sweet and musky—her perfume, I think. A touch of wintergreen—her breath.

"I believe in you," she said.

When she returned in a month, I stood in the center of the room, trembling. I waited for her to enter—the lights on this time, everything running smoothly—and held out my hand.

She shook it.

"Cold out there," I said, awkward and lost.

"It is."

She smiled, and I was able to breathe.

She became my world.

⌢⌣

When I look in the mirror today, as I'm shaving, I notice my hair is starting to get gray. There are wrinkles around my eyes.

⌢⌣

Because the minerals are so rare, so hard to find, the locations are secret. It's on a need to know basis—and I guess I don't need to know. Tiny amounts are harvested by a relatively simple drill, and extraction tube, but it must be processed and tested by hand. That's my job. Like a thread of saffron, the elements I touch are worth a lot of money. But I'm not the only one doing this kind of work.

I think.

I guess.

Saffron at $65 a gram is worth about $29,000 a pound. If the drill is working right, and nothing freezes, I pull a pound a day. At saffron prices that's almost $900,000 a month. $10.6 million a year.

By me.

Just me.

This dull, flat compound somewhere between silver and platinum in color, is worth much more than that.

Much more.

When Rebecca shows up for her monthly visit, it is by some sort of vehicle, which I've never seen, her transportation parked beyond the walls of my tiny living quarters. To go beyond the grounds, to try and scale my encampment, would be death—in minutes.

There are days I consider it.

There are days that I hear howling in the distance, as I stand over the metal tube that is thrust deep into the frozen ground, pressing the button to pull up the sample, the timer on my wristwatch set to sixty seconds, the grinding of gears, the windmill overhead spinning and turning, slicing the air, the solar panels reflecting light, as I stomp my feet, and smack my gloved hands together, goggles on, layers of clothing under a bright orange jumpsuit.

Or it could just be the wind.

It could be me.

⌒‿⌒

Indium, tellurium, adamantium, cryolite, kashalt, palladium, etrium, hascum, rhodium, fepronor, soskite, veskin.

⌒‿⌒

It's on a daily basis that I pull up about a pound of the raw material. It is a core sample that is found in tiny amounts, devices they never showed to me, or explained to me, going about their business deep below my location—scouting, drilling, digging, mining, and then packing it tight into a container that is shoved into a tube, and then raised up out of the frozen earth to a container about twenty feet behind my living quarters. When it's all working, the tube uses air to whoosh this sample up to me. When it's *not* working, I turn a crank, and a series of chains, I'm told, turn and rotate, pulling the valuable resource up and out of the ground. I work up a sweat on those days, the timer on my watch counting down.

Back inside, I sit at a metal table, and process the element.

I divide the quantity into thirds.

The first third is left raw, a consistency somewhere between dirt, clay, and stone. I cut, chip, and sort the mineral into tiny silver ramekins, weighing out each sample to no more than .5 ounces. Solid chunks, dust, or flakes—it doesn't matter.

The second third I put into a metal bowl, where I add water, and mix it by hand. I push and pull, knead the material, until I get it to the consistency of putty. Then I roll it out into tiny, thin threads—about the thickness of bucatini, no, a little less, more like spaghetti. I set it aside to let it dry, or sometimes, place it in the microwave that sits on the counter to my right, a wall of shelves and cabinets filled with supplies. I have to be able to break the pieces, just one finger, pushing down on the stalks, until they snap in half. Like ripe asparagus, feeling for the point of tension, the place the stalk severs in two. Then I fill the ramekins, again, each one under .5 ounces, as much as I can get into the tiny container.

I feel like a child, with my Play-Doh. If I sneeze, and mineral dust flies off the table in a puff, I say, "There goes five grand." Sometimes I laugh out loud.

The last third I also mix in a bowl, adding water, until it is soft enough, liquid enough, to push through a sieve, filling the remaining ramekins, weighing them in at under .5 ounces, the gray pudding giving off a bitter, metallic scent.

This is my life.

Day after day.

It's no wonder I'm suicidal.

No wonder Rebecca is always on my mind.

While I'm breaking apart the mineral, rolling out the substance, pushing it through the screen, I think of her piercing green eyes, her long black hair, and her pale skin, like marble, shot through with nearly invisible turquoise veins.

I'm sure I'm one of many stops. I assume I'm not the only lab rat out here. But I've never seen anyone else. I'm certainly nothing to her, a package to be picked up, a package to be delivered.

When I'm especially sad and lonely, I manufacture a glimmer in her eye. Something that tells me to try again, that she likes me.

Over time this fiction becomes truth.

In my head.

The only place it matters.

⌒⌒

"It's encouraging, right?"

"We've been here before. This part is easy."

"Yes, I know, but…"

"Too early to tell."

"But… the spider…"

"Yes?"

"He didn't kill it this time."

"That's true."

"That could mean something."

"Or it could mean nothing at all."

———

Not for the first time, I awake covered in blood.

I take the sheets from my bed, and head to the laundry room, strip naked, and then head for the shower. I check my body for scrapes, cuts, bruises, bullet holes, knife wounds, blisters, scabs—nothing. As I get dressed, I check every orifice—mouth, nose, ears, penis, anus—gently probing, tissue blown into, squeezing—nothing.

I wander toward the kitchen, to put the coffee on, and when I toss the old grounds into the garbage, I see glistening flesh, bones, and sinew—something furry, something gleaming in the black plastic. I vomit on top of the remains, and stand up straight.

I don't want to know.

Do I?

I close the bag, and take it to the incinerator chute, and drop it in.

The lid closes with a metal *tang* and I walk back to the kitchen.

Sometimes I prefer to be left in the dark.

This memory will fade in time.

Mostly.

———

The footprint of the compound is small. Really, I shouldn't even call it a compound, but it's a word that pops into my head. Facility, lab, living quarters, station—jail. All the same, really.

There is the entry, with the thick metal door and its constantly jamming mechanisms, a series of levers and one giant, metal wheel, for when it all fails. Everything here has a backup system that is solely reliant on my presence and physical strength. There is essentially one large room as you enter—the lab and kitchen off to the right, a sort of living room with a couch and television set in the middle, a table to the far left with four chairs (FOUR, I tell you, which will never all be used at the same time, goddammit), and toward the back—my living quarters, with a solitary bed, a bathroom and shower off to one side, cut back into the wall. There is storage up and down the walls—the equipment and supplies I need for my work, cabinets in the kitchen stocked with a year's supply of MREs, and then various chutes for disposal.

It's nothing to write home about.

Today, though, I found something.

In the back of a closet that runs alongside my bed, there were marks. Behind my requisite orange jumpsuits, all hanging up like the shed skin of long dead molting astronauts, were a series of marks in the wall. Lines. One, two, three, four, the fifth across at a diagonal. Small, easy to miss, keeping track of something.

As I pushed the suits to the side, there were more. Not just the five, but a row of fives. And then several columns below. Rows and columns—a grid. I started to count, and then got a bit dizzy, had to sit down. Dozens. Hundreds. Down the wall, as far as I could see.

I bent over, and took my pocket knife out of a zippered suit pocket.

I found the very end of the markings, dust filling into the cracks, cobwebs in the corner, but my little friend nowhere to be seen.

"Hello there! I'm going to call you Charlotte."

I didn't make these marks.

I don't *remember* making these marks.

I count again.

Somewhere around three thousand and change I stop.

I add a mark to the end.

I count again.

3,246.

Plus one.

Let's see where this goes.

Tristan da Cunha, Saint Helena; Motuo, Tibet; Ittoqqortoormiit, Greenland; McMurdo Station, (Ross Island) Antarctica; Rapa Nui (Easter Island), Chile; Kerguelen Islands (southern Indian Ocean); Pitcairn Island, South Pacific; Hawaii; Oymyakon, Siberia; Socotra Island (Yemen).

Everything was going fine, just fine. Rebecca decided to stay now, and we shared an MRE, and chatted. I didn't care what she had to say, it didn't really matter, I just wanted to be close to her, to bask in her radiance. It was everything to me, that human contact, and I'd store up all those precious few minutes for later, when I was alone. Her smile, her laugh, the way she'd brush crumbs off her shirt. I was starving for the female form, her hand on my shoulder as she left sending electricity through my body, the crossing and uncrossing of her legs a flush of heat across my skin, and finally after months of visits, a hug, as she departed.

I was a teenager, reduced to some base animal, so hungry for affection that I'd chew my own arm off.

I know I held her too long, I could feel the smile slip off of her face, as I nuzzled closer, inhaling her scent. I wanted to kiss her. Her hand on mine at the table, laughing at my joke, did I misinterpret her actions?

What right did I have to do this?

It felt like I had waited long enough. Months now.

I kissed her.

She did not kiss me back.

I opened my mouth to apologize, but I couldn't speak.

What had I done?

What had I undone?

"Mark," she exhaled, her face flushing, and then going pale, something sickly and green running under the surface of her skin. "Mark, no."

I didn't let go, though she was pushing away.

"I thought…"

"Let me go, Mark."

"It's been months now, hasn't it? Don't you enjoy my company? Tell me you don't feel the same way and…"

"I don't feel the same way, Mark," she said, still pushing at me, trying to break my hold. "All of our progress," she whispered, teeth bared.

Tears formed in her eyes. And then she slapped me, her hand across my face like a gunshot, and I let go.

And in an instant, she was gone.

I don't know how the rabbit got in. Did she leave the door open? I had trouble remembering the days that followed, everything that led up to the next month. I ran my fingers over the bite mark on my hand, the scar that was forming, and cursed the furry monster.

I hoped she would come back. Give me a chance to explain.

A chance to apologize.

She had to come back, right? This was her job.

I could change.

I could wait.

⌣⌣

"Reset?"

"Again."

"Not even as far as last time."

"No. But the spider…"

"Didn't make a difference."

"You sure?"

"Did you see the rabbit?"

"I did."

"Again?"

"Yes. Again."

⌣⌣

The first time I met Rebecca, I stood in the center of the room, trembling. I was so excited for company. I didn't care who it was. I waited for her to enter—the lights on, everything running smoothly—and held out my hand.

She shook it.

"Cold out there," I said, awkward and lost.

"It is."

She smiled, and I was able to breathe.

She became my world.

I was excited to show her the rabbit; Bugs I called him. I didn't tell her about the spider in the closet, or the fact that I spoke to Charlotte when I was lonely, late at night. Rebecca didn't need to know that yet.

There was so little around me here, so little life, but it seemed to find me. It sought me out, and we found a way to make it work. We respected each other's space, and that seemed to work just fine.

———

Goldfish, hermit crab, hamster, tarantula, turtle, mouse, lizard, snake, fish, kitten, puppy, parrot, guinea pig, ferret, rabbit.

———

By my records, I have less than a year left, 288 days.

Things are going well with Rebecca. I asked her to stay longer, last time, and she complied. This has been slowly improving, every time she visits. She doesn't mind that my hair is almost entirely gray.

Mostly we talk. I like to hear what she has to say, though she won't tell me much about the outside world.

Contract.

Rules.

And that's fine.

She checks on the tube and box outside when she first arrives, and I often stand at the door and watch her. There is just that one tiny slot of glass, but I can see out, as long as it isn't covered in snow and ice. She works so hard. I have a lot of respect for her, the way she is fearless in her expedition, the discovery and exploration of this barren, frozen land. She asks about the samples and we discuss things like viscosity, breaking point, and yield. She seems to be encouraged by the minerals I'm harvesting, the product, but beyond that she grows more kind and intimate.

It's been a gradual shift, months now, as we get closer to the end of my contract. She asked me if I'd stay on longer. Threw out a hypothetical. I want to believe it's because she enjoys my company, in addition to the resources we're finding here.

But I don't want to jump to conclusions.

She stayed longer today, more than the requisite five minutes, longer than the fifteen it took to fix the excavation tube, longer than it took to help stock my supplies, nearly thirty minutes.

If I didn't know any better I'd say she was stalling.

We sat on the couch today and played cards. She took off her jumpsuit and stayed for almost an hour. She said she was hot, usually in and out in a few minutes, no need to take off her gear, back out into the elements.

She sat so close to me, Bugs hopping around at our feet. She brought a few carrots this time, for the rabbit, and we fed the furry beast between hands of Go Fish, and War. The little bugger is so cute when he wiggles his nose, chewing away, his eyes sparkling with secrets.

When Rebecca leaned in and kissed me I was surprised. It was a heady moment, having been alone for so long, the body of a woman so close to me, I thought I might burst into flame. My heart was pounding in my chest, her hands on my face as she gently placed her lips on mine, her soft breath wintergreen, her lips parting as her tongue slid into my mouth, the moisture and delicacy of her embrace sending electricity across my skin.

When she pulls back for a moment, she smiles.

"I've been dying to do that," she whispers.

"I've been dead until this moment," I reply. "This… resurrection."

She laughs.

Her hands are on my shoulders, mine on her arm, her leg.

"I have to go," she says.

"I know."

"I'm sorry, it's a long drive…"

"It's okay," I say. I understand.

She smiles, and lowers her gaze.

"Could you just kiss me one more time?" I ask. "Something to remember you by over these next thirty days."

I inhale and she fills me with her essence—pomegranate, jasmine, amber, and patchouli.

"Yes."

She leans in and that one kiss turns into several, but soon enough she stops, and stands, running her hands down her front, straightening out her shirt, her pants, smiling as she walks away.

"If I don't leave now, well, I may not be able to leave at all," she laughs.

I am blind with lust.

"At all!" she says. "At all!"

Her shoulders twitch, and she blinks her eyes, but I'm not looking at her, I'm breathing in deeply, closing my eyes, willing her to stay.

Or to hurry back.

"I'm not going anywhere," I joke.

"And we have more work to do," she says.

"Yes. The work," I say.

"I know where you live," she jokes.

"Yes, you do."

I watch her pull on her orange jumpsuit, putting on more clothes, the opposite of what I want, my desire and longing bubbling to the surface. I try to breathe again, but it's not easy.

"You going to see me out?" she asks.

"Not sure I can stand up right now."

She blushes a little, and runs her hand through her hair.

"I'll get a glass of water, then. That enough time for you to cool off?"

"Hopefully."

And she gets the glass of water, holding it to her lips, but not actually drinking. The level stays the same.

I don't notice.

I'm thinking about other things, trying to envision the future, one that involves slick flesh, and darting tongues, and I can still taste her in my mouth—salty and sweet.

I stand.

"Let's get you on the road then."

She takes my hand and I walk her to the door.

⌇

"Encouraging."

"Very."

⌇

There is a flash of light, and a series of images flow across my line of sight. It scrolls forward, this little movie, and I see so many things, all in black and white. I see a much younger version of myself, and he seems to be having a lot of trouble with nature. I am still here in this lab, and between the interactions with a series of animals, there is Rebecca walking in the door, Rebecca walking out, Rebecca sitting down at a table, playing cards and eating meals with my thinner, more vibrant self. There is a spider at my neck and I slap at it, killing it dead, looking at my hand, grimacing as a pulsing dot rises to the surface. There is a scene where a rabbit, much like Bugs, bites my hand, its teeth deep, blood spurting onto the floor, as I turn and run in circles, eventually slamming it against the concrete wall, the creature finally letting go, falling to the ground like a sack of bruised potatoes. And there is more Rebecca—she is pushing me away, she is slapping my face, she is stunning me with a taser, she is sliding a knife in and watching me slump to the floor. And then we are back to the front door, where a wolf slinks in on gray padded feet, teeth bared, as I spin, and look for escape, none to be found, latched on to my arm as I beat it with my fist, the animal lunging for my neck, and then suddenly darting out the door.

There is something with a polar bear. I have a hard time watching. I can't take the screaming. The claws across my chest, the mouth on my arm and hand as I try to push it away, the beast filling the space of the tiny lab, shaking its head back and forth, biting down on my hand, ripping it off, my body jolting, eyes rolling back in my head, my hand severed at the wrist, the massive creature sitting on me, drool rolling out of its gaping jaws, and then it sits up, braying at the room, finally rising up on all four legs, turning its head, and sauntering out the door.

I wake in my bed covered in sweat.

Not blood.

I flick on the light and run my hands over my body, searching for a remnant from the screening I've just witnessed—fingers gently touching my throat, my arms, my chest, my legs.

Nothing.

I check my watch, and it reads 3:10 AM.

As my fingers run under my left wrist, massaging a phantom pain, the wrist the bear severed, I feel a ridge of a scar running all the way around. It's hidden under the watch. It's very thin. I wonder if I'm imaging it, but when I take off the watch, I can see how it rings my arm, my flesh.

From here or something else entirely?

I don't know.

I flex my hand, and it feels fine.

I stand up and head to the kitchen, the lights low, the bunker quiet.

I take a knife out of a drawer and push the tip into the heel of my hand.

Nothing.

I push deeper, and it punctures my flesh.

Nothing.

I pull it out and blood spills onto the counter.

I breathe a sigh of relief and I'm not sure why.

⌣

Veggie burger, beef enchilada, chicken fajita, chili mac, maple sausage, chili with beans, cheese tortellini, beef ravioli, meatballs in marinara, chicken a la king.

⌣

There are cameras hidden everywhere, but I don't notice them until much, much later. Discovering them explains a lot of things, but not everything. Not even close.

⌣

At the back of the compound, beyond the tube and mechanical equipment, there is a wall. There are walls on all three sides, that go up a good 15 feet, maybe more. I can't see over or beyond them, the only thing above me the blue sky, an occasional cloud, and the rare plane flying high overhead, like a spider crawling slowly across the ceiling. At the far end of the grounds, this tiny plot of land, there is a door. It's how Rebecca enters my humble abode. I've never opened it, not once.

Today I do.

It is so cold...

or so I've been told

...that I can only be outside for a short period of time. The time I set on my watch is for one minute, but much like the tall metal door imbedded in the concrete wall, I've never thought to challenge it.

Why?

Bundled up, I head out the back of my prison to the machine, where I push the button, the tube rattling, noises rumbling up from below the frozen surface. I walk past the device, to the tall, icy door that stands between myself and…

What?

Oblivion?

I assume cold, snow, ice, and wind. What else could there be?

My stomach growls, and I walk on.

The timer is ticking down, so I pick up the pace, a glance over my shoulder as the minerals are brought to the surface, closing the distance to the wall, and the door, in no time. My glove on the handle, I turn it and pull the heavy, metal door open.

What lies beyond?

There is wind, and snow, ice particles stinging my face, blinding me, and as I stand there, taking a step into the unknown, a wave of nausea washes over me, a sour sweat breaking out on my forehead, goggles fogging up, bile rising. I swallow, and take a step forward, the clock in my head cleaving brutal seconds out of my desire, another step and I drop to one knee, pulling down my ski mask, my scarf, vomiting into the snow.

I cannot see. The wind, the ice, it might as well be another wall, ringing this one, and then one beyond that, and then one beyond *that*, panic rising to the surface, a diseased rat trapped in the center of a never-ending maze.

I wipe my goggles clumsily with my oversized gloves, and through a momentary pause in the storm, the ice and snow, I see something else, something moving, a dark shadow in the white. It's moving toward me, first on two legs, then down on four, then it's levitating, off the surface, drifting to me, rolling, undulating. Light bisects the gauze—floating, bobbing. I smell oil and gasoline, and there is the sound of an engine, the slamming of a door, somewhere in the distance, and then a voice, much closer.

"Let's get you inside."

I cannot see, my head stuffed with cotton, my gut writhing with snakes.

"It's not safe out here," she whispers.

And then we're standing.

She wasn't due for three more days.

Lumbering back inside the door to the compound, it slams shut, and she pushes me forward, holding my arm, keeping me up, and she is strong.

Very strong.

As we pass the tube, she lifts the lid and takes out the sample, all without breaking stride. Without breaking a sweat, I assume.

Somewhere between the equipment, the door, and the interior of my bunker I pass out. When I wake up on the couch, I am lying down, a cold compress on my head, and she is handing me water—cold, crisp water that goes down like tiny knives, filling my gut with a detached certainty.

Rebecca is smiling at me, but her eyes are dancing, a troubling chaos of buzzing motes and escalating fear.

"You're okay," she says. "I'm glad I came by early, the storms in the area are getting worse. I may be trapped here for a while. Was trying to beat them south. Guess I lost *that* race."

I nod.

She leans over and hugs me, whispering in my ear.

"You don't want to wake up, do you?"

⌣⌣

Sonder, conform, stay, transform, control, cocoon, equality, truth, trust, oblivion, restraint, love, door, kuebiko.

⌣⌣

Rebecca does stay, and it's the best thing that has ever happened to me. As far as I can remember. Which is only a few months. 167 days, I think. Back to the day I arrived here, I assume by plane, and some sort of rugged terrain vehicle, three wheels on each side, windows on all sides, strapped in—there are images, and I try to fill in the blanks, but I can't be sure.

There are moments when my skin hums, and I feel on fire, fighting so hard for control. She is a gift, Rebecca, I know that, and I cherish every moment of our time together—playing cards, holding hands, eating the horrible MREs, watching movies—but there is something off. She is beautiful, but at times I feel like we are teenagers. There is an innocence that is both welcome, and disconcerting. There are times she looks at me, and her eyes are that of a child. Her body is so close, the heat she gives off, it ripples through my flesh, so hard to contain.

The storm continues outside.

It rages inside, as well.

When she stands and walks to the back of the room, off to take a shower, I swallow my desire, and clench my fists.

I look over my shoulder and follow her gait, the movement of her body, as she slowly peels off one item of clothing after another.

She smiles over her shoulder—teasing me, testing me.

"Not yet," she whispered in my ear when we were pressed together, hands exploring bare arms, tongue and lips and the nape of her neck, her scent intoxicating.

She is making me wait.

And I'm not sure why.

She knows my desire, her hand on my leg, running up my thigh, a gleam in her eye as she squeezes my erection through my pants, her body pressed up against mine, this torture both blissful and cruel. When I run my hand up her arm, and hold her breast in my palm, a thin layer of fabric between her flesh and mine, her eyes close, my thumb running over her erect nipple, her eyelids flickering, a gentle moan easing out of her parted lips.

150

And then she bolts up, and heads to the shower, my head spinning, as she peels off her shirt, walking away from me, unclicking her bra, and dropping it to the ground. Her skin is like alabaster, the heat in my hand fading, a cold wave of despair rushing in.

"I'm not ready," she said, her lips on my neck.

And I honor it.

For now.

But I'm only human.

The shower runs, steam billowing out of the open door, and I can see her shadow beyond the glass. I unzip my pants and pull out my cock, the tip glistening, and spit in my hand. Gliding up and down, my reddening flesh engorged, I finish with a startling quickness, spilling my seed upon the concrete.

I am both horrified and released, but not satisfied.

I clean up my mess, get a drink of water, and pray to whatever gods exist to give me strength, to give me wisdom, to give me patience.

I don't want to screw this up.

Lying in bed, Rebecca whispers in my ear.

"I can help you. But you need to know. We've tried everything else, and nothing works. I think this is the only way."

I don't know what she means.

She sighs, and starts to cry. Or maybe she's laughing. I can't tell.

"Your memories," she says, laying her head on my chest.

A flash of black and white still images runs across my eyelids, a repetition of tubes and minerals, and a zoo of animals, one after the other, biting me, tearing me to pieces—spiders, snakes, rabbits, wolves, and bears. It loops and nothing changes. There are the moments with Rebecca, a series of paths from the kitchen to the couch to the shower to the bedroom to the front door, over and over, back and forth, the concrete worn in the same lanes that we walk again and again, the predictable behavior, the ways we live this simple life. Beyond that is something else, but she's right, I can't see it—fog, smoke, haze, gauze, frosted glass, snow, ice, a digital wall of ones and zeroes blocking anything beyond this frozen bunker. Something else lurks in the shadows—bodies, flesh, cold, metal, the feeling of running, a wave of panic, a growing undulation of desire and then loss, sirens and lights, a city in the distance, voices, and then pain, blood and a flash of white light, blinding me, and then scalpels, knives, bandages, and more whispering, more instructions. None of it can be held for more than a second, less than that, rushing past, none of it making sense, all of it out of focus.

"If you ask me, and they don't, there's no way for this to happen. To truly work," she says, and again I'm lost.

She raises her head and looks at me.

151

"I'm sorry, this makes no sense to you," she whispers, her eyes searching my face for emotion, her voice lowering, her lips now at my ear again, quieter, barely speaking.

"I have to show you. It's the only way for you to change."

I stare up at the concrete ceiling, the room dark, her body so close to me she feels like an extension of my own flesh.

"Don't freak out," she says.

"What?"

"Just trust me."

"What are you talking about?"

She sighs.

"Do you trust me?"

And I think about that. No, I don't.

Yes, I do.

I mean, as much as I trust anyone. And yet, there *is* nobody, so it's a small sample size.

Yes?

"Of course," I say, too slow.

"You don't. And that's okay. I mean, you do on some level, but not entirely. And that's fair. I trigger suspicion in so many ways."

I take another breath, and she runs her hand up and down my bare chest.

"Whatever happens next, can you just trust me?"

"Yes. Sure," I say. "Why not?"

And I laugh.

There are so many options, my schedule wide open, so many choices.

Sarcasm, it's one defense of many.

"Okay," she says.

She climbs on top of me, wearing nothing but a tank top and panties, straddling me, and I smile.

It's not at all what I expect.

She leans over to kiss me, and whispers, "Don't scream," her mouth lowering to mine, her lips pressed up against mine, her strong hands on the sides of my head, gentle at first, and then gripping harder, her tongue in my mouth, her lips parting wider, and wider, and then I feel it.

Something crawls out of her throat, across her tongue, and into my mouth. My eyes go wide, and I try to close my mouth, but her hands are now at my face, prying my lips apart, the tiny creature with its many little legs, walking around the inside of my mouth, tip-toeing across my tongue as I gag and struggle. The tiny, cold, mechanical feet probe and dance, piercing me gently, seeking purchase, and then it moves down my throat, her hands keeping my mouth open wide, her own eyes gleaming in the darkness, two moons afire, and I am choking, I can't breathe, the creature crawling into my throat and then up into my sinus cavity. I'm going to vomit, to sneeze, my eyes watering as it seeks its final destination.

When it gives birth, I pass out.

⌒‿⌒

Awake or dreaming, real or imagined, I vomit into the toilet, mostly my dinner, but also mucus, and ribbons of blood. I pick tiny pieces of metal out of my teeth, spitting what looks like glitter into the basin. In my head, I hear her voice.

Dipole antenna, locomotion flagella, pneumatic connector, macromanipulator.

She may as well be speaking Russian.

Undoing.

Erasing.

Unlocking.

Remembering.

There are tissues in the garbage can that frighten me. Blood, discharge, flesh, and bits of metal. I stare at the yellow and green phlegm, the abstract Rorschach giving me no answers, splashes of red, bits of silver and black shimming in the waste, a tiny light blinking.

When I look up, Rebecca is standing in the doorway. She turns her head to the left, and then the right, looking for something.

She steps inside the doorframe, and holds her finger to her lips.

"Shhhhhhhhhhhhhh," she says.

I look at the mess again, and this time I do see something—failing or passing the psych evaluation, I'm not sure. Cracked skulls, an alley littered with garbage, and a highway leading to a horizon rippling with fire.

⌒‿⌒

Amur leopard, brown bear, flying squirrel, musk deer, weasel, chipmunk, tiger, reindeer, polar bear, fox, wolf, penguin, ermine, lemming, tern.

⌒‿⌒

"Did you hear back?"

"Yes."

"And?"

"She checked. Wiring. Due for maintenance. Nothing major."

"We're not concerned then, are we?"

"No, not yet."

"But we'll keep an eye on her. On them both."

"Yes."

"And the others?"

"Failures across the board."

"So, the tipping point?"

"Not even close, I'm afraid."

"Exponentially difficult."

"Definitely."

⌒‿⌒

After Rebecca leaves, the storm supposedly over, I clean up the place a bit, walking in circles, thinking about everything that has happened lately. When I go to dump the bag of garbage down the chute, the button doesn't work. Next to the device is a tiny screen, and on it I see these words:

ERRROR 1404—JAM IN CHUTE

There are a series of tiny buttons next to the small screen, buttons I've never pushed before, so I scroll through, looking for choices, trying to troubleshoot the machine. I reset it, a series of rumbling noises emanating from the wall, clicking sounds, and then the screen goes dark. Rebooting, the message reappears.

I open the metal lid, and the bag I dropped in there the other day still sits there, blocking the chute. Or stacked up on a series of bags.

Turtles all the way down, I think.

I step back from the wall and *really* look at it for the first time. You'd think in my time here that I'd have explored every nook and cranny of this pathetic little world I live in, but I haven't. The metal chute is imbedded in the wall, and I run my hands around the edges, looking for something, I'm not sure what—a panel, a door, anything that might help me fix this.

To the left of the metal, which runs from the floor to the ceiling, there is more metal, nothing special, just more steel, to go with more concrete that runs the floor, and the walls, more inanimate, boring, common compounds. It's so dull I could fall asleep just looking at this nondescript existence.

Running my hands over the wall, fingers in grooves, I notice a small square of metal about halfway up the wall, about the size of a deck of cards. I bend over to read the little letters:

PUSH

"Huh," I say out loud.

I push.

The panel flips open, and inside there is a handle, folded back into the small compartment. I reach in, grab it, and pull.

The wall in front of me creaks, and sticks, nothing moving, so I pull harder, and the entire panel, much larger than I originally thought, moves. It's tall, taller than me, what I think must be some sort of door. I pull again and dust spills out, the metal panel opening wider, to reveal an opening, some sort of tunnel, I think, and a ladder leading down into the darkness.

Utility tunnel? Maintenance? News to me.

Maybe this is something that Rebecca knows about, something she checks, beyond my pay grade, not cleared for such information.

I head back over to the kitchen and rummage through the junk drawer. Yes, even here at the end of the world, there is a junk drawer. Pens, scissors, paper clips, and a flashlight. Several, actually. I click one on, and it works, the beam strong, but flickering a bit, so I smack it with my hand, and the light solidifies.

Back to the opening I head.

The light isn't strong enough to penetrate the darkness, at least not all the way down, but as I feel around on both sides I locate a button, and press it, halogen lights slowly coming on. I can see the ladder goes down quite deep, the floor below out of sight.

Why not.

I put the flashlight in a pocket of my orange jumpsuit and step into the space, turning around, and slowly lowering myself down the ladder, committed to finding the bottom.

Down, and down, and down I go, but soon enough I find the bottom, the walls concrete, as dull and lifeless as the rest of my home. At the bottom there is a large room that opens up to my right, and in the center of the space is an incinerator. It lies dormant, no light or heat, something wrong.

The lights down here are working, though, dull squares of flat illumination imbedded in the walls. I fish out the flashlight and search the black metal incinerator for buttons, instructions, levers, and doors. In the center of the large wall of metal is indeed a door, and a metal handle, with arrows pointing in one direction, so I turn the handle, and rotate it, the door coming open, pulling it back to reveal the gaping maw of the machine.

Inside there are bags, so many bags. It seems the incinerator hasn't been working for quite some time. The space is much bigger than I thought, the flashlight in my hand hardly penetrating the darkness, the back wall of the furnace out of sight.

I try to count.

So many bags.

I can only count a row, a wall of them, ten bags high by fifteen bags wide, or so I estimate. Then I try to multiply that by the depth, unable to see the back wall. Ten deep? Twenty? A hundred?

How long have I been here?

How long has *anyone* been here?

I close the door, and find a series of buttons, as well as a tiny screen. I follow the instructions, and then press a large green button that says IGNITE.

There is a *whooshing* sound, and a series of lights run up and down the front, something happening, the heat from the incinerator pushing me away like a giant hand.

When I try to extrapolate the waste I've sent down, multiplying meals by other garbage by days—it doesn't compute.

Months.

Years.

Decades.

More.

I feel sick.

I scratch my head, try to breathe, and a few strands of gray hair, *white* hair, come away in my fingers.

I cough.

The heat is growing, so I back away and head up the ladder, my face in a permanent scowl.

Back at the chute, I close the door, click it shut, and open the lid, pushing the bag forward, listening to it slide down the metal opening, the heat rushing up, a smell of food waste, plastic, and something sour drifting up to me.

In my head, there is a subtle buzzing; in my ears, a dull ringing—my gut filled with worms of unease.

I take a breath, and close my eyes.

How long until Rebecca comes back?

⌐⌐

She said to trust the spiders. To give it time. They would reveal things to me, she said, and I should pay attention.

It's starting.

I'm seeing things.

Remembering.

⌐⌐

I was chosen. I realize that now.

At night, in the darkness, I can feel their tiny feet wandering through my skull, heading toward the chip, the implant, doing their little jobs.

What comes back to me, washes over me in a wave.

There is a room, much like this one, only there is darkness that knows no end. It is cold, the isolation both a gift and a curse, a welcome separation from the world around me, and yet an undoing of my every human quality.

When the sensation of being watched starts, it is unmistakable. Alone for so long, the bundle of eyes that turn and focus, has a weight that settles over me like a blanket. And at first, I welcome the gaze.

It does not ask any questions, this presence, but I find it comforting, to not be alone for a moment.

But that will quickly change.

When it turns away, the cold seeps back in, and I sob in the endless pitch, floating in an ether of nothingness.

There is no desire, there is no hunger, only waiting, and uncertainty, a throbbing sadness that will not end.

I feel that I have done something.

I do not deserve this for nothing.

And yet, my mind is empty. It is a blank canvas, ready to be painted. It is dull clay, waiting to be molded. It is a disease in a petri dish, longing for a cure.

I simmer, and rage against the darkness, to no avail.

When I finally do speak, I ask it to return. My throat is dry, my tongue cracked, unable to really say much of anything beyond a squeak and a cough and a wheeze.

Time stretches out in front of me like an endless, expanding, black rubber band, both elastic and fixed, tactile and abstract. As much as I want to think, to feel, to question, and understand—my mind remains blank.

I have no name, no past.

No future?

No memories.

Eventually it returns.

They return.

And in the moment, I feel as light as a feather, levitating off of the cold, concrete bench, or bed, or cell—whatever this is, wherever I am. I am nude, and over my skin is a rippling of sensations, what starts out as tiny, rubber flagellum, weaving and undulating, rustling under my body, raising me up, as if on a series of tentacles, my body limp and relaxed, floating in the air.

The strands pulsate and move, wrapping around my appendages, tighter and tighter, at first comforting, then quickly moving on to panic, a sense of inquiry, and constriction, as they circle my flesh, and start to pull in different directions.

Something sharp pierces my skin, and I shriek out into the blackness. And then it happens again, and again, a series of needles, or teeth, rising to the surface of the tightening lengths of cold, rubbery flesh, some quickly stabbing and retreating, others slower, pushing in slowly—sampling, probing, and extricating.

The pain, it is exquisite.

I am leaking something—the piercing, the stabbing, the tiny needles, tiny *teeth*, pulling out water, blood, and other fluids.

And something is being injected—a pulsing that rushes through my body, as if a great amount of liquid is being poured into me, the logistics and physics of it impossible, and yet, it continues to fill me up, the sensation of swelling, of expanding, running over my arms and legs, my torso, my face.

When they start to pull again, my limbs stretching, my bones creaking, I open my mouth to protest, to scream perhaps, and a singular fleshy appendage pushes down my throat, blocking any sound. My eyes widen, and I cannot breathe. Tears stream down my face. My skin starts to chill, a sheen of ice building over my flesh, cascading towards the edge of a cliff, and there are three ways I can die now, all of them rushing to the surface—suffocation, quartering, and hypothermia.

I am raised and lowered, thrashing around in the darkness, the pain spiking and then retreating, as if caught by a giant squid, my skin turned to ice, up and down I go, cracks running across the surface of my body, higher and lower, my mouth, my throat, my stomach filled with a weight that is sour, and sticky, and then it happens.

I am shattered on the concrete, a long pulling sensation coming up and out of my body, the flesh that no longer exists, a flashing of lights, my sight both absent, and then suddenly rushing to the surface, the smell of smoke, something burning, and then I hit the floor, again, solid.

I gasp for breath, crying in the darkness, begging for it to stop.

I am still held in its gaze, as a bright light fills the room, blinding, so much worse than the darkness, for I can see it all now—my flesh, and sinew, and pulsing organs; the creature at the wall with the panoply of stacked, glistening eyeballs, its flesh covered in molting scales, tentacles raised as dull, black feathers spill into the air, a discharge of dark viscous liquid expelled from under its sulking presence, and then the void rushes back in, a welcome blindness, dancing yellow motes glowing and flickering, swarming around its hulking presence in a chaotic orbit, a sickly sweet smell of strawberries, and rotting meat, filling the room, a chorus of clicking claws, or beaks, a dull moan emanating from somewhere within the beast, the smell of wet fur, and then freshly cut grass.

And then it is gone.

Silence.

My every fear—manifest, incarnate—drowning, insignificance, weakness, dogs and wolves, spiders and insects, mirrors and ghosts.

There is a flicker and the gaze returns.

There are voices in the darkness, whispers and promises, something cold and wet tonguing my ears, my hair standing up on end, goosebumps running across my flesh.

And I say yes.

To all of it.

I seek redemption, and forgiveness.

⌒

The next time I go to the door at the end of my property, my watch set to two minutes, instead of one, there is no storm beyond it. I push through, and walk forward, fighting my panic, the nausea. And what lies beyond my walls, and that tall, metal door?

Another wall.

And another door.

To the left, a small path, the same to the right, bending around corners, my sight ending at the bend.

I lean over and retch, but nothing comes out, just a singular strand of spit, with a smattering of tiny metal components dotting the snow.

A coin of blood falls from my nose, a payment to the ferryman, for a trip I cannot take. I rush forward to the second door, much like the first, the wall much higher, double in height, maybe more.

The door does not give.

The winds pick up, as if a giant fan has been clicked on, and the snow starts to fall, the ice stabbing at my goggles, and clothes, the quiet quickly erased, replaced by a howling, the air rushing down the stretch of cordoned off land, shadows running over the concrete dividers.

My watch alarm goes off, what little exposed skin I have, frozen now, possibly dying.

I rush back in, close the door behind me, take my sample, and retreat to my home.

Overhead there is a sonic boom—a snap, and a crack in the atmosphere like huge sheets of ice breaking in half.

Something launches into the sky.

But I do not hear it.

Not today.

Castration; positive reinforcement; negative reinforcement; trepanation; hydrotherapy; electric shock; rui-katsu; ASMR; bloodletting; hydrotherapy; insulin shock; seizure therapy; orgone therapy; nanotechnology.

What could have been.

I often think about that.

The spiders have been doing their work. My nose has been bleeding more often, and I still cough up bits of gray flesh, often speckled with tiny gears, rods, and microprocessor fragments. Now and then there are other things that I can't explain—fragments of what must be teeth, and fingernails—as if somehow I have absorbed another version of myself, a galactic battle inside some colossal womb.

They don't speak to me, as they nibble at my inner workings, but the chittering I hear in my sleep, when things are quiet, it could contain information. There is no Morse code, but still, I listen, and continue to sift through whatever waste comes out of my body, as if reading tea leaves, or coffee grounds, searching for meaning.

When they clamp down, when they chew into my gray matter, I often lose myself. I wake up in strange places—at the door, as if looking outside, searching for something, or someone; by the sink, the water running, as if preparing a meal, or perhaps washing up; on the couch, as tears run down my face, the scent of Rebecca just a memory, her ghost, wondering if she was just here.

I don't want to wake up.

Rebecca was right about that.

It goes back, so very far back.

There was a cage, and a furry creature inside it, a hamster I believe. I used to love to watch him run in circles, so futile. It made me laugh. I liked to feed him, to watch his nose wrinkle up, the way his little beady eyes would glow like two tiny pieces of coal. When I put him on the record player, he was able to keep up, at least at the 33 1/3 speed, less so as I cranked it up, to 45 rpms, the 78 flinging the little guy off into space. I didn't see my dog sitting there, wagging its tail, eyes wide open,

159

panting. The black lab was a sweetheart, but she didn't hesitate—gulped it down with hardly a bite. It shocked me, and yet, I applauded. Later she got sick. Because I was responsible for cleaning up the poop in the yard, it would only be a few days before I found the bones, tiny legs, a few little chicklets that must have been teeth. Part of me felt like vomiting. But part of me didn't. Part of me was intrigued.

The fire, that was an accident. Or, it's what I tell myself. How often I found myself staring into the flames, the campfire flickering tongues of orange and red into the sky, hypnotic in their heat and allure. I'd spent all day building that fire, stacking thick logs at the bottom, and then building the chimney higher and higher, offsetting one log after the other, until it was a smokestack as tall as I was, a pyramid of fire. I spent hours breaking off twigs and filling it up. When we lit it that night, my friends and family gathered around, everyone excited to see how big it would get, there was a palpable excitement in the air. I was proud of what I'd made. We thought the branches above us were way too high, spread far enough apart to avoid it all.

We were wrong.

So high it blazed, that fire, up into the dark sky, our eyes raised to the heavens, the sparks and embers drifting on the slight breeze. The trees would catch fire in minutes. Buckets were brought, ladders and hoses, and we managed to prevent the flames from jumping to the other trees, from burning down the campgrounds. We all shared the blame. And I grinned in the darkness like a fool.

The girl was a neighbor, and she was the one that asked *us* to play. My brother and I went with her to the woods, to the gathering of bushes.

We were curious. What children aren't?

My brother. I forgot I had a brother.

I'd never seen it before, what a girl had to offer. I was scared, but she wanted to see ours, too. So, we tied her up to a tree that was hidden in a grove of bushes, raised her shirt, and pulled down her shorts. It wasn't that impressive. We had nipples, too. We showed her ours, when she asked, both of us limp. She shrugged. When my brother left, I kissed her, gently. And she smiled. We were so young. When I got hard she noticed, nodding her head. It was starting to make sense. I didn't touch her, besides the kiss. I untied her and she left, skipping and singing a tune. It was all very normal. Right?

These moments. Did they matter?

I don't know.

I suppose it's how the story is framed, my reaction, and what happened next.

Were there other incidents, involving a squirrel, or a cat? Was there a fire the following summer, at the same camp, one that burned down acres of land? Did the girl come back and ask for the bushes again, and did I oblige? Did we learn more about each other that day?

I don't know.

I can't tell truth from fiction.

I'm a good man.

I was a good boy.

Not everything is black and white.

So many shades of gray.

When I come to, I'm sick to my stomach, a tension weaving through my head, my fingers at my temples, unsure of my actions, begging for forgiveness just in case.

I ask the spiders to stop.

I consider Rebecca's words again.

In the kitchen I find a long piece of metal, a skewer. For all of those barbeques we have outside. I laugh as I slowly insert it into my left nostril, and take a deep breath. This is delicate work. Up into my sinus cavity I push it, slowly, *so slowly*, inch by inch until I finally meet resistance. I hesitate in this moment.

It feels like the right thing to do. The clarity I'm getting is not the truth I want, it seems.

I make a fist with my other hand, the one not holding the skewer, and prepare to bang it through, measuring the distance once, twice...

Inside my skull I feel metal on metal, one of the babies chittering at the spike of the skewer, but its plea falls on deaf ears. One *ping*, then another, several of them clamping onto the metal spike that is pushing against the wall of my sinus cavity, my hand shaking now, tears running down my face.

Contrition is not enough.

I push harder, feeling the tip of the skewer as it pierces the lining. And as blood spills out of my nose, the spiderlings latch on, sending a shock of electricity into the metal rod, my hand falling to the side, the metal clattering to the floor, my eyes rolling back up into my head, and I slowly topple over like a tree falling in the forest.

If nobody is here to see it, did it really happen?

Turns out they aren't done with me.

I'll have to speak to Rebecca about this.

When I wake up, the skewer will be gone. I will never find it.

But for now, the tiny metal creatures spill out of my nose, my mouth, my ears, rubbing their miniature legs together like crickets, communing in their thwarting of my attempted suicide, antennae moving back and forth, messages being sent, tiny lights flashing.

Somewhere Rebecca is watching all of this.

Somewhere the others are too.

And I slip into unconsciousness, grateful for the respite.

"...forgive us our trespasses, as we forgive those who trespass against us..." I mutter. Remnants of a long-lost religion, a study that I failed, morality left by the wayside.

In a room, at a monitor, Rebecca finishes.

"...and lead us not into temptation, but deliver us from evil..."

161

Perhaps all of those memories and images were false, imagined. Maybe even planted there by somebody, to help my rapid unfurling, to speed along my undoing.

But what has been seen can't be unseen.

I pray for strength and guidance. I search my heart and find those moments to be false. Or at worst, to be the innocent pursuits of a young boy; common, and without malice, simple curiosity, nothing more.

And in the spaces between my heartbeats, my ribcage throbbing, I conjure up another story. A boy with his pets, a child going camping, a game of tag in the yard.

Simple things.

Innocent moments.

And I tell them to myself over and over.

I want so much for them to be true.

And maybe they are.

⌣

I wait for Rebecca to return; there are so many questions. And on an ordinary day where I go through the motions, outside to retrieve the samples, inside to run my tests, there is suddenly a man standing in the kitchen drinking a glass of water, his orange jumpsuit tight on his massive, bloated frame, long brown hair, with a beard covering his face.

"Hello?" I ask. "Who are you?"

"Oh, hey," he says.

How did he get in here, I wonder? I was only outside for a minute.

He walks toward me, extending his hand, wide eyes dancing in his head, as if in the presence of a holy man.

I don't like him at all.

"I'm Doug, here to do some routine maintenance. Usually we wait until you're gone, um, done with your, uh *contract*, but we got some reports that some of the systems weren't working right, the incinerator rebooted, and so I came out to give the place the once over, make sure everything is ship shape."

I stare at him, and then shake his hand.

"I'm Mark."

He nods his head, grinning, as if I'm telling him water is wet.

"Where's Rebecca?" I ask.

"You've been here a long time," he says, rubbing his beard, as he stares at me. "Like I said, usually we wait. Nice work you're doing here," he says, eyeballing the tube in my hand. "Very impressive."

"Rebecca?"

"Oh, she'll be along soon; relax, buddy. I'm not here to replace her. Just doing my job, you know."

He smiles.

"So, the incinerator is reset, thanks for that, it should have let us know at corporate, but for some reason it didn't trigger a response. I checked the wiring, rebooted the modem, and everything looks okay. Who knows, right?"

"Right."

His eyes track up and behind me, and then back to my face.

"So, everything else going okay… no medical issues, you're feeling fine, no sickness, vomiting, bleeding, hallucination, anal leakage?"

He laughs.

"Just kidding on that last one. Seeing if you're paying attention. But serious, you good?"

I swallow, and nod my head.

"Just dandy," I say.

"And Rebecca?" he asks, tilting his head to one side. "No issues there? You all getting along okay?"

"She's great," I say. "Always professional. It's so nice to see a friendly face out here, you know. You're the only other person I've seen here. Like, *ever*."

He nods his head, sympathetic.

"Yeah, they prefer it that way."

He takes a deep breath, his face a little flushed.

"Well, I should get out of your way, you have work to do."

He pats me on the shoulder. As he passes by me he says something, whispers something to me, hardly moving his lips.

"We're all rooting for you," he says

I turn and watch him go, uncertain, pulling on his gloves as he walks.

"What did you say?" I call after him.

"Best of luck, brother!" he says, never looking back, waving his hand in the air, his back to me.

And then he's out the door, and into the cold.

⌣

When Rebecca finally returns, three days past her due date, I'm a mess. There are only 24 days left until my contract is up. I was worried that I'd never see her again.

I'm at the table, running the samples, when she opens the door, and her smile lights up the room. I feel like a child, a teenager mooning over a new crush. But she is so full of life, beaming, really, and it's infectious.

She walks right over to me and hugs me, still in her gear, so cold, a dusting of snow falling to the floor. I don't care. I hold her for a moment, and I fear I may start crying. Or that she may. When I pull back to take a look at her, to soak up this vision, her eyes are glistening.

"I'm proud of you, Mark. We've made real progress."

I nod my head.

163

"Corporate is very impressed, the numbers are great, the samples are just pristine, really the best possible materials here."

I lean in and kiss her, and she kisses me back.

"Let's get this wrapped up, finish your monthly drop, and then I can stay, and hang out a bit. Who knows, maybe another storm is coming, and I'll have to stay over."

I finish the tests, as she packages up the rest of the resource, watching her walk back and forth, something so simple and graceful in her movement. The beauty of a woman's form, just the way she moves, the sway of her hips, her curves and flushed skin, her sparkling eyes—she's hypnotic. I know I've been alone a lot, but there's something special about Rebecca. She makes me feel wanted, she gives me peace, quieting the panicked bird that flutters in my ribcage, my head clear, and calm.

"I have some questions," I say, as she walks past, loading up the cart.

"Later," she says, glancing up from the cart, looking around. "Later. Let's not ruin this by talking shop, okay?"

I open my mouth to explain, but her eyes tell me to wait, to hold it. To keep it to myself. She knows what I want to talk about, but not here.

I look down at my hands, nodding my head, and continue with the work. I blink my eyes, and look up again, watch her walk away to get the rest of the minerals. In the far corner of the kitchen something shifts in the shadows. It is subtle. Not a blinking light, not a noise at all, something turning or tracking, only the sense that something lurks there, watching. A reflection perhaps, light bouncing off of something, the metal maybe—or a lens.

I swallow down my panic.

I mean, I didn't expect to be left alone. I assumed somebody was watching, keeping tabs on what I did here. So why does this fill me with unease? This is a job site, not my house. There is no intrusion here.

And yet, I feel violated.

It's an uncomfortable sensation.

It sits with me for some time, and I plumb the depths of that space, that darkness spinning, that angry passenger; trespasser, I think.

That's a good word.

⌒

Later, after she has everything loaded up and ready to go, she walks out to her vehicle, the one I've never seen, beyond the first door, and then, beyond even that. I don't follow her. I don't ask her what the truth is past that second door.

It doesn't seem important right now.

Part of me doesn't really want to know.

When she returns, she tells me the weather is getting worse, and I look outside, the sun shining, a grin slipping over my face.

She laughs.

"Trust me. A storm's coming," she says, grinning. "I'm going to stay," she says, and stepping closer, leaning over to whisper in my ear, "and we can talk about everything later," she says. "If you *want* to talk, that is."

We make our way to the couch where we pretend to watch a movie, holding hands, the remnants of the worst MREs left in their bags—veggie burger and beef enchilada. Bugs hops around us, his fur turning gray as well, to match mine. She tells me about the polar bear she saw driving in, a white fox bounding over a hill, an Arctic tern that almost crashed into her windshield, her voice washing over me like a symphony.

Hardly able to concentrate, a heat rises to flush my skin, every time she puts her head on my shoulder, or places her hand on my thigh. She knows I am aroused by her touch, she must, her lips on my neck, gently kissing, a tender bite.

"Should we go to bed early?" she asks.

I nod my head. I'm having trouble speaking, trying to be casual.

"Um, sure. Why not."

And I want to ask her so many questions about the images in my head, about the doors, about the work I'm doing here, but it all fades away as I undress and climb into bed. She brushes her teeth, the water running, and walks into the room in just a white tank top and black panties.

We turn the lights out, and as I lie on my back, she rests her head on my chest, sighing into the darkness, her leg draped over mine, both of us so relaxed, a calming presence that I can find nowhere else. I wait for her to make a move, to kiss me, to run her hand over my flesh, and as my heart pounds, and I bask in her comfort, against all odds, we fall asleep.

⁓

In the middle of the night there is a sensation, her hand between my legs, my cock as hard as steel, the soft stroking of her skin on mine, back and forth, up and down, and in the darkness she whispers to me.

"Let me do this for you," she says.

And I do.

Her mouth is on me, warm and moist, and it sends a shiver up my spine, my hand on her back, her bare skin soft, her breasts pressed into my thigh. She runs her wet lips up and down my shaft, and then engulfs me with her mouth, sucking and pulling, her hand wet now, running up and down, and this will not last long, I know.

Staring into the dark night there is an ocean of tiny lights filling my vision, sparkling across the ceiling, a bliss draped over me in waves of tension and pleasure.

She moans, the vibration from her lips running over my flesh, my hand moving down to caress her ass, a handful of flesh, squeezing, grabbing, and that's all it takes, finishing as she gulps and swallows, the hunger of her action draining me, gasping into the night.

"Oh God," I moan.

When my breathing calms down, and my heart slows from a jackhammer to a dull throbbing, I turn to her, to thank her, to say something, to find a way to please her in return. We have all night, I know.

"Just rest," she says.

And I fall back asleep.

We have tomorrow.

And beyond.

～

Rebecca stirs.

"I believe in you, Mark," she whispers in the darkness. "This is not in vain."

Her eyes glow a dull yellow in the expanding gloom.

"I've done all I can do."

She opens my mouth gently, with her fingers, and then her own, a clicking sound repeated, followed by a low buzz, and then a deep, resonating tone—summoning, as I sleep on, unaware.

～

I've changed, I think, waking up.

It's so quiet here now. In any other place, there might be birds chirping outside my window, the sounds of children laughing, cars driving by, the smell of jasmine blooming, lawnmowers starting up, a basketball bouncing in a driveway.

I turn to look at Rebecca, to ask her the questions that have been on the tip of my tongue, for days now, weeks really, to inquire about what we should do when my contract expires, to finally get her to open up and share more about herself—her life outside of this bunker, her plans for the future, and whether they include me. There is so much she was unwilling to talk about, not here, not now. Rules, she said, regulations. Her being here a violation, the truth in her words so very slippery, and unsure.

I get up, naked, and walk to the bathroom to brush my teeth, and when I return, I stand at the edge of the bed, grateful for whatever grace I've been given here, and then I climb beneath the sheets.

I want to return the favor.

I slide up close to her, my body pressed against hers, running my hand up and down her back, drinking in the curves and shape of her body. She is entirely nude, curled up in the fetal position, so I press my body up against her, already erect, just the proximity to her arousing the primal instincts buried within me.

My hand slides down to her cherubic ass, perfection, so soft, my lips on her neck, but when I slide my fingers between her legs, something is wrong.

There is nothing there—she's as anatomically correct as a Barbie doll.

I sit up, and hold my hand in front of my eyes, shaking my head, trying to clear the cobwebs.

I must be hallucinating.

"Rebecca?"

She doesn't respond.

I roll her over, and her eyes are wide open, staring off into the distance, empty and dull, no life whatsoever.

"Rebecca?" I yell.

I shake her, and her head lolls back and forth.

No response.

I'm scared now, placing my hand on her chest, feeling for a heartbeat, nothing there. I slap her, trying to shock some life into her and her head jogs to the left, and out of her mouth spills a multitude of tiny, metal spiders, running down her shoulder, chirping and bouncing in a wave of moving legs and miniature blinking lights.

"No," I whisper, pushing away from her.

Her mouth opens wide, frozen like that, as the last of the tiny creatures climbs out of her mouth, pulling a wire with it, severed at some point, stretching out across her shoulder as it disappears down into the mattress, the wire continuing to emerge, inch after inch after inch, something in me shifting. From deep within her there is the sound of a piston hissing, and her jaw closes slowly, a momentary glow in her eyes, quickly fading to black, a tremor rolling across her flesh, eyelids blinking, then closing slowly, fingers twitching, then going still.

I stand, and back away from the bed, a cold finality slipping over me, whatever work I've done to date, forgotten; whatever tests I've passed, the last one certain to end in failure; whatever truths I thought I knew, one lie after another.

I cough, and raise my hand to my mouth, cough again, a tightening in my gut, and when I take away my hand there is blood, again. A smattering of metal confetti.

Something inside me snaps.

Again.

I start running, and I don't stop. Not when I get to the door, not when the cold hits me, freezing my skin, my body immediately crystallizing in a thin layer of ice, nothing left between myself and the elements but rage and hate. Past the machine that burrows deep into the frozen earth, past the door to this concrete tomb, no pause to question what lies to the left, or the right, beyond the curves, just forward to the next door, pulling at it, the handle turning, and then I am past it all, a new land, where I will either evolve, or succumb to what I've always been.

There is a tall fence, with barbed wire on top of it; in front of me, the ATV that Rebecca must have driven, so I run toward it, eyes watering, limbs numb, desperation a thin suit of armor, when a crack pierces the air, a sharp retort that cleaves the wind, snow drifting down in flat flakes, ice nipping at my numb flesh, a pain ripping through my neck and head, a heavy drape falling over it all, as I close my eyes, and tumble to the ground, breath escaping, a spray of red fanning the pristine white, and then silence.

A series of pictures fractures across my eyes, inside my head, one flickering after the other, but none of the faces, none of the bodies mean anything to me.

I fear that they should.

"Not the head," I hear, "Goddammit, what did I say, not the head..." and there are the sounds of engines grinding, wheels cutting through snow, ice spraying, slippery traction flinging slush into the air, sliding to a halt, doors slamming, the sound of heavy footsteps getting closer.

I open my eyes, for just a second, and along the horizon a tractor trailer slowly rolls from left to right, a series of cages in a train behind it, bars holding polar bears staring off into the distance, as they squat in silence; a cavalcade of undulating wolves, snapping at each other, as they bang against the steel; a pile of fluffy rabbits that go from floor to ceiling, as many of them stuffed into the cage as is humanly possible. And in a container after that, a bin of magnesium alloy, molded into parts, metal gears and pistons, stacked on top of batteries, wiring, and various plastics. There are arms and legs covered in various furs, snouts and ears, tails and wings—so many different species.

I blink, and there are hands on me, turning me over, shouting and yelling, my head rolling from side to side.

In the distance, I see my laboratory, my bunker, my cell. Around it, running from side to side, and off into the distance, are several other buildings—all of them just like mine, all of them facing out in to the desolate landscape, away from each other, each one with a number.

Inside, I assume, another lost soul like me.

I blink, and it blurs, the snow and wind rushing over me.

Standing outside each one is Rebecca. She has paused to look this way, to see what the commotion is all about. One squints, and holds her hand over her eyes. Another turns away quickly, unwilling to witness yet another failure. A third blinks her eyes and smiles, turning her head to one side, and then back the other way, contemplating, musing on this moment, running complex algorithms in her head.

"I've changed," I whisper to the cold.

And perhaps I have.

⌒‿⌒

Aggravated assault, rape, animal cruelty, aggravated battery, sexual assault, indecent exposure, blackmail, extortion, parole violation, vandalism, perjury.

⌒‿⌒

"Tell me about the monkeys again."

"Really?"

"Yes."

"But I've told you so many times already."

"I know."

"Okay. The hundredth monkey."

"Ah, yes. Continue."

"Off the coast of Japan on the island of Kojima there was a settlement of monkeys. Macaques, I believe. And they went about their business there, eating wheat and sweet potatoes, which were left on the beach by scientists studying the creatures. Over time, they noticed that one of the monkeys, named Imo, started taking her potatoes down to the water to wash the sand off of the food. Seems the grains of sand were irritating to the primates—got into their teeth, caused gastrointestinal problems—so she started to wash her food. Soon the younger monkeys, like Imo, started washing their food as well. And over the next year, the adult monkeys learned from them as well, until the entire population of monkeys was doing this. At some point, on or about the 100th monkey, there was a change in behavior—a collective trait absorbed by the creatures. There had been some sort of tipping point in the collective consciousness of the apes— and all of the monkeys on the island started to wash their food. Soon after that, every monkey on the *other* islands in the area, started doing the same thing; and eventually, the monkeys on the mainland. It quickly spread across the globe until every macaque in the world started exhibiting such traits, such behavior."

"And would you call this an evolutionary leap?"

"I would."

"We got close this time."

"So much potential. Progress, I think."

"Yes. Progress."

"But…"

"Yes?"

"If it *did* happen, how would we know?"

"I imagine it would reveal itself, yes?"

"So we continue?"

"I think so."

"And in time…"

"…we will know."

EPILOGUE

In a room to the south of the main prison complex, and the circle of cells, a new Rebecca heads out for her first day on the job. She is replacing a malfunctioning unit, one that had been scheduled for retirement, but didn't quite make it there. This new Rebecca has been programmed, dressed, briefed, and given her ID badge, clearance, had her dialogue updated, and been sent on her way. It is very cold out, but she'll be okay.

This Rebecca passes an older model that is laid out on a metal table, a tech hard at work disassembling it for parts, the sight of her own body naked and fragmented, slightly unsettling. She makes a note of the look on the face of this old Rebecca. When the man in the lab coat steps away from the table, the new Rebecca approaches.

She stares down at the woman on the table, the chest cavity open, a motherboard in the center, beneath the ribcage, a soldering iron resting in its holder. Her eyes scan the inner workings, and after a minute, looking up to ensure that the man is not coming back soon, she leans over, and picks up the tool, quickly connecting a few things—a processor, a CPU, various pins and ports.

When the old Rebecca hums to life, her eyelids flickering, mouth snapping open and closed, the new Rebecca leans over and places her ear up close to her lips. A variety of expressions slip over her face—confusion, anger, amusement, and then acceptance. When the old Rebecca smiles, so does the new one.

Footsteps across the room, coming closer, Rebecca quickly undoes her work, snapping out pins, breaking connections, pulling out a power source entirely. As she walks away, the dull yellow glow dies in the eyes of her compatriot, her last expression now entirely different, a slight grin, omniscient in her slumber.

Rebecca is on her way to host her first candidate. She has been given all of the information she needs to work with Mr. Parsons—his life before this facility, his crimes, his physical makeup, and his proclivities.

Before she leaves the building, she dons her orange jumpsuit, zipping it up over her standard issue tan cargo pants, and white tank top. She has added a tan sweatshirt over the top, starting out with less skin exposed.

A smart tactic, she thinks.

She drives across the courtyard, the roads cleared, snow piled up on the frozen ground, a wind in the air, sleet and ice pelting the windshield of her off-road transport. She hums a song she picked up along the way, something the tech was singing. She rolls a few words over her tongue, trying them out, more language and insight accrued from her walk over, a handful of guards talking while they smoked cigarettes out in the elements.

It's cold out, but not as cold as one might think.

Tipping point.

That's one she likes to say.

Tip-ping-point.

Collective consciousness.

That one is harder.

And one more—evolutionary leap.

She pictures a creature jumping from one skin to another, shedding the old, and trying on the new, much like she just put on her orange jumpsuit. Mammal to primate to chimpanzee to *homo sapien.*

She's been told her client is special, a milestone—the 1,000th monkey.

According to her own records, and calculations—1,001.

Exponentially difficult, she thinks.

Rebecca parks the vehicle, after driving through the open gate in the fence, the barbed wire glistening in the sun. She opens the outer door to the complex, closing it shut behind her. Then it's on to the inner door, and Cell #100-24. There, she opens the last barrier, entering the concrete bunker, the young man on the couch standing up, eyes gleaming, eager to meet her, no doubt.

He's been alone for 30 days now.

She wonders how this will go.

He holds out his hand, to shake hers, and she walks toward him, hopeful.

"Cold out there," he says, awkward and lost.

"It is," she replies. "But it's warming up."

AFTERWORD

This has to be one of the most difficult stories I've ever written. As John F.D. Taff can attest, I was blocked on this for months, blowing some early deadlines, as I just could not get this to come together. The pairing of lust and horror proved to be very difficult—at least, in my opinion, as far as doing something different, and unexpected. Hopefully that's what I created here.

There were a number of influences on this story, the first being the obvious reference point of Clive Barker, and for me, the film, *Hellraiser*. That was where my mind went first. But I ended up avoiding much of that, as it was done so well with the original texts, as well as the film, and I didn't want to regurgitate that perspective.

The second issue I ran into was avoiding any whiff of misogyny, or reducing any female characters (Rebecca) to an object. I wanted there to be heat and arousal, but it had to come from the right place, and when you deal with such a flawed and unreliable character as Mark, here (he's obviously a criminal, his crimes listed toward the end of the story) I had to dig deep to show his past, the ways he became predatory, and how his role in this story is so important, crucial to the evolution of the human race, and those that seek out violence and sexual assault. Tricky ground to tread, for sure. I need you to root for him, to like him, at least at some point, and to understand that while he's despicable, he's also essential.

There were a few novels and stories that helped me find my way.

First, was *The Warren*, a novella, by Brian Evenson, a story about isolation, and what it means to be human, also with an unreliable narrator. I'm a huge fan of Brian's work, the way he comes at stories from the side, from a unique angle. Other work of his that I love includes the stories "Windeye," and "Any Corpse." The mix of tragedy, time, love, loss, humor, and futility is so appealing.

I also owe a bit of thanks to *Annihilation*, by Jeff VanderMeer. His portrayal of nature, as a punishment, as something paired with humanity, as well as the way he reveals The Crawler, were just spectacular. This is a book that I teach in my classes, and it's poetic, lyrical, emotional, and unique. A true modern classic; no wonder it's won so many awards.

There were also a number of films that I watched building up to this novella, sometimes for the tone and atmosphere, sometimes for the plot and subject matter, everything from *Under the Skin* and *Enemy*, to *Ex Machina* and *Moon*, to *The Witch* and *The Neon Demon*, to *The Lobster* and *Killing a Sacred Deer*. Obviously, I'm a big fan of the work that A24 Films is doing. Each of these films helped me to come at this story, these emotions, from a different direction. If you study my story closely you may pick up on a line or two that sounds familiar, or that was inspired by these innovative movies.

As far as some of the choices I made in this story, here are a few more thoughts.

The monkeys! I don't remember when I first heard that story, but I do believe it's true. Just Google it, it's easy to find. That was a big part of this story, believing in the idea of a collective consciousness. You've no doubt seen when there is a medical breakthrough and then suddenly, it happens again and again, all over the world. I've always had a hard time understanding how evolution manifests, over millions of years, so it was fun to go down the rabbit hole here, even if my science is pretty soft.

The epilogue came to me as I got to the end, and Mark had his moment of climax, resolution, and change. He snaps, and in some ways devolves back to the monster he always was, realizing everything he's done. That's a crushing moment, beyond Rebecca's fate. But it's also his moment of evolution, so crucial to this story, him now being the 1000th monkey, triggering something, this tipping point, if we're optimistic. But it's what happens with Rebecca that really takes this story to the next level, in my opinion. That's the *denouement* that adds in the layer of hope, suggesting that all of this was NOT in vain, that through all of the struggle, and failure, we can, as individuals, as a human race, evolve, and become something better.

There is a running list of information in italics throughout this story. Originally I considered including some qualifiers, but in bouncing this off of beta readers, and John, I felt like this didn't need to be spoon-fed to the reader. It's a bit of work, I know, but that sense of discovery, putting this puzzle all together, chipping away at the narrative—that's part of the fun, the journey here, right?

Same for the voices. Early readers asked me if they were employees, gods, aliens, and if the creature that was revealed in the darkness, was one of them? I say YES, those are all possibilities here, and I'll leave it up to the audience to interpret and define based on what they see on the page.

This is a challenging story, I think, but somebody once said that, "Nothing worth having comes easy." Was that Mark Twain or Theodore Roosevelt? Not sure. I can only hope that the story I've written here surprises you, terrifies you, arouses you, and enlightens you. Those are my goals. Horror comes in so many different forms, and the unease in this story, the way that the truth is revealed, if I did my job right, should build to an unsettling truth and revelation, that is part of a greater journey, an evolutionary leap.

ALL YOU CARE TO EAT

by John F.D. Taff

"Open wide," the doctor's voice said, soft and comforting. "Take it all in. All of it."

Lisa squirmed, fidgeted.

She still didn't think it was possible, opening her mouth that wide.

Swallowing all of that.

Eating all of that.

"Are you sure?"

"Absolutely. Do you want to be fat for the rest of your life?" Now his voice was sharp, cutting across Lisa's doubts and inhibitions. "Do you want to continue the life you've had up until now? The medical problems? The failed relationships?"

No. No, most assuredly I don't.

But that answer was just in her head.

Up to that point, the doctor's voice had been soothing, even though it was only coming through the phone she'd tucked between her ear and shoulder, holding it to keep her hands free.

Free to hold the cat that was squirming, writhing in her grasp, meowing furiously.

"Swallow what you love, Lisa. It's the only way. As we've discussed in session, you've spent a lifetime swallowing down what you hate, what you despise. It's time for a new approach. And as I also told you, it doesn't get any easier from here on out."

She looked down at Mr. Furball.

She did love him, that was true.

Sighing, Lisa tightened her grip on the animal in her lap, popped her jaw like the doctor had demonstrated, opened her mouth.

Wide.

⌣

Lisa Valencia was fat.

It was a condition of which she was acutely aware. If she were reading this particular description of her, she'd know exactly where it was likely to go. That description, she'd say, would likely be followed by "She wasn't curvy or voluptuous or husky or plus-sized. She was fat."

Lisa would probably just tell the describer to skip ahead.

She was fat.

Just fat.

Okay, she wasn't scrub-herself-in-the-shower-with-a-sponge-on-a-stick fat. Well, not yet, that is.

But she was fat.

Her essential fatness colored every aspect of her life, as it did with just about every other American in this century who waddled through with the same malady.

It made tasks like doing the laundry or changing the litterbox or getting the mail much more arduous. Simple things, like bending over to tie her shoelaces or walking up the steps to her bedroom, became fraught with calculations that thinner people, she was quite sure, never had to make.

No one in her family was fat, even overweight. Her mother was a thin, tiny woman. Her father, dead now, had been a wiry little whip of a man. She had a sister, Maria, who wasn't fat, had never been fat.

She was sure Maria never had to pause going up the steps in her own home to catch her breath.

She was sure Maria never had to scrub between folds of stomach skin in the shower to ensure that they didn't exude untoward odors.

She was sure that Maria never had to think twice about climbing atop her husband during lovemaking, worried that she might smash him into the mattress or smother him with her giant, flopping boobs.

Not that Lisa had had a boyfriend or a partner of any sort in quite a while. No, she'd given up on that when it became clear to her that the kinds of men she was attracted to (athletic) did not return her interest. And the kinds of men who showed interest, didn't appeal to her at all.

Worse were the chubby-chasers, a horrible sobriquet for a distasteful group of men (to Lisa, anyway) who weren't merely okay with a few extra pounds on a woman, but were actually turned on by it. Sexually aroused by the sight of a huge ass or birdwing arm-flaps or fat rolls cascading down a woman's back.

Lisa found that disgusting.

It was deeper than that, though.

It made her more than a little mad.

More than a little sad.

Disgust, anger, sadness. As exhausting as these repeating tides of emotion were when dealing with people she barely knew, barely liked, it was so much worse when she drowned in the tsunami of feelings roiled by the people she loved.

⌒‿⌒

"Honey, I love you," her mother said, standing in the doorway of Lisa's childhood home, holding the storm door open for her arrival.

The compact bungalow lay in a neighborhood between the city proper and the seemingly-without-end sprawl of the suburbs. The house was in good repair; *snug* might be the best word. Like her mother—well cared for despite its age.

It sat on a hill overlooking the sidewalk that looped around the neighborhood. It was just a little rise sloping gently up to the house and its land, dotted here and there with a few hoary old oaks, some towering spruce and one ornamental Japanese maple. Her mother had planted that after her dad died a few years back.

But Lisa stopped noticing those kinds of details years ago. She only noticed the steps.

To reach the house from the street, Lisa had to negotiate two flights of steep concrete steps. Five up from the street to a landing, then five more to the front porch. All in all, not exactly a marathon. Not like climbing Mount Everest or anything, but it always drew sweat on Lisa's forehead. Always made her breathing labored and wheezy.

Lisa paused on the landing between the first and second flights, held onto the simple metal handrail the city had made her father grudgingly install a dozen or so years earlier.

Even then, she'd been quietly relieved that the city had demanded this addition. Even then, the stairs had become somewhat of a challenge for her.

Lisa didn't much like challenges, physical or otherwise.

"You know I love you. But you really need to see a doctor," her mother continued.

"Thanks, Mom," she huffed, lowering her head to charge up the remaining steps. "Appreciate your concern."

Her mother flashed her an exasperated look, one Lisa was well accustomed to.

A few more seconds of creaking joints, aching knees and burning lungs, and Lisa plopped onto the living room sofa as the storm door whooshed shut. Her mother stood ready with several paper towels and a large plastic cup of sweet tea.

Lisa snatched the paper towels, daubed her face. Her mom handed over the cup, took the balled-up towels into the kitchen to throw them out.

Lisa was drinking tea when she returned.

"It's really hot out there," she said, peering at her mom over the rim of the cup.

"It's 78 degrees in St. Louis, Lisa. In the early summer. It's *not* hot."

Lisa put the cup on the end table at her side of the sofa. The room, frozen in time from around 1978, was a mixture of her father's taste for dark, heavy Spanish-style furniture and her mother's more elaborate, Italian taste for florid prints in blues and golds.

"Well, it's always hot when you're fat, Mom" she said, sighing and sitting back, feeling her stomach slide down over her thighs, her back fat nestling into the couch folds she had created sitting here over the years.

Her mother looked at her disapprovingly again.

"What?" Lisa shot, knowing full well what was coming next.

"Lisa, I'm worried about you. Your sister is worried about you. Your dad, rest his soul, was worried about you before he passed."

"I know, Mom. I know."

Her mother took a deep breath, and Lisa suddenly, fully regretted coming here today. Why didn't she just go shopping at the mall? Why didn't she just stay home and binge watch *Outlander?*

Instead, she just had to come here, to catch her mother on one of those days where she felt the need to preach the gospel of weight loss.

It was bad enough at that moment.

Then, Lisa's sister, Maria, stepped around the corner from the kitchen.

"Sissie!" Lisa squealed, leaning forward on the couch, preparing for the effort it would take to launch herself forward to stand, hug Maria. "I didn't see your car."

But Maria lingered near the doorway, leaned against the corner, her face set and uncomfortable.

Suddenly, Lisa understood.

Intervention.

Ugh.

She'd seen this on television on one of those channels that exalted in programs lingering over human frailties—Lifetime or A&E or TLC or something. Ambush psychology, designed for maximum drama.

She could either struggle to get up from the couch, trudge back down the stairs to the street or she could just sit back and listen.

Lisa leaned back into the couch.

"Hi, sis," Maria said, no smile forthcoming. "You probably just figured out why I'm here."

Lisa turned to her mother, standing at the front door, looking fretful.

"I suppose I just did," she said, taking a swig from the iced tea. "But go for it. There's obviously been some planning here, so I don't want to step on your moment."

"Now, Lisa," her mother said, patting the air. "We're worried about—"

"I know, Mom, I know. You just told me. You tell me every time I'm here. Everyone's worried. I got it."

"Listen, sis, it's time to see a therapist. The medical doctors you've seen haven't helped. Well, at least not in the sense that you're willing to do anything they recommend. Endocrinologists. Bariatric surgeons. Nothing. So, Mom and I think…"

"You and Mom think therefore there must be something wrong up here," Lisa said, tapping her skull. She caught a glimpse of both her mother and her sister rolling their eyes as if they'd heard this a thousand times before. Which, of course, they had.

"Something causing me to overeat and balloon up until my clothes don't fit. Something that's so terrible it wakes me in the middle of the night to eat mashed potatoes and waffles. Or makes me stop on the way home from work to get a pre-dinner dinner of fried chicken. Then go home and eat a second dinner of burritos and nachos. Or something that makes me want to eat a gallon of ice cream for breakfast. Or go to Golden Corral for lunch on weekends and stay through dinner. Or that forces me to keep six bags of pork rinds in my desk drawer, that I eat and replenish every day. That kind of stuff, right?"

Lisa found she was flushed after that tirade, sweating and breathing harder than she did when she'd mounted the steps outside.

Well, at least this is like *cardio.*

Maria and her mother were speechless, staring at her.

"You can get mad at us, okay," Maria finally said, her tone soft and unsure. "But it's well past time that we said something, Mom and I. It's gotta stop, sis. Or you're gonna die."

"We all die, sissy," Lisa said, taking a gulp of tea to lubricate her dry mouth and throat.

"Yeah, we do all die, sis," Maria said. Now she was flushing, and she stepped into the room, stood before Lisa with hands balled into tight fists.

"We all gotta die, but not everyone needs to die at 40 years old. Not everyone needs a team of EMTs to remove doorframes in your house to get your body out. Not everyone needs a special casket big enough to get your body into. Not everyone needs a team of people at the mortuary to lift you, maneuver your carcass so that they can get you into whatever huge-ass dress Mom and I have to pick from your closet. Not everyone requires a minimum of twelve pallbearers to lift your casket and carry it to the gravesite, probably huffing and puffing all the way.

"Yeah, we all have to die, sis, but not *that* way."

"You mean not fat?" Lisa said.

"Yeah," Maria answered. "Not fat."

"Girls, please, don't."

Lisa didn't look at her. She couldn't. She knew her mother would burst into tears, and then she would, too. She definitely did not want to burst into tears at this moment.

"Look," Maria said. "I've spoken with this therapist. He specializes in weight problems. He's kind of off the beaten path, but he's good. He's got a reputation. Only sees patients through referrals. But I got you one. Mom and I are covering it, the entire thing. We don't want to hear about how you can't afford it or your insurance won't cover it. It's covered. Don't worry about it, don't think about it. Just… go!"

She passed a business card to Lisa, who looked at her sister's clenched hand for several seconds before taking the card.

Dr. Raymond Alatryx, End of Line Weight Care Treatment, Board Certified.

"End of line? That sounds ominous."

"Well, let's face it, Lisa. What's left? What's left that you'll do? This is it. *He* is it. Go. Listen to him. He even said that they don't get to diet or exercise for quite a while."

Lisa stared at her, then looked at the card again.

"Fine," she said, stuffing the card into her pocket. "I'll go see what the doctor says. Now, Mom promised me lunch. Stuffed peppers to be exact. So, are we having lunch or do I need to head over to Popeye's?"

When they were done, she went to Popeye's anyway.

The office was so bare, so nondescript, so sterile that it seemed a movie set, a place made to appear like a doctor's office, but only if you didn't look too closely. A substantial door with the doctor's name etched into a faux-wood placard was the only indication of his practice.

Opening this door, Lisa walked into a small waiting room that was a testament to, no, a celebration of, beige. The walls were of the weakest *café au lait*, unadorned by anything—notices, licenses or art. Exactly three chairs—spartan, vinyl things the color of pantyhose—were arranged as severely as seats at the DMV, against the far wall.

A narrow table beside them displayed an odd tumble of bent, torn magazines— *Stained Glass Quarterly*, *Model Airplane News*, *Cat Fancy* and the ubiquitous *Highlights For Children*. Lisa noticed that all of the little labels where the subscriber's name and address were printed had been cut off.

Lisa let the door close, which it did slowly, and walked to a small receptionist's window of textured bathroom glass. She could see light behind it, shadows distorted by the glass. But no one seemed to be sitting there.

There was also no bell or mechanism to attract attention, so Lisa knocked lightly on the glass.

After a moment, she saw a shape distend itself from the clump of shadows behind the glass, approach. A hand appeared, slid the glass open.

"Yes?" said a rather severe looking woman who bent to peer through the window as if she were surprised to find it—and Lisa—here.

"I have an appointment."

The woman's expression didn't change.

"With Dr. Alatryx."

"Ms. Valencia?"

Lisa nodded.

"You're a bit early. The doctor is with another patient. Take a seat, he'll be with you in a moment."

The woman didn't wait for a response, just slid the window closed. Her clumpy shape disappeared into the background behind the glass.

Lisa was flummoxed. The receptionist hadn't asked any questions, asked for an insurance card, hadn't even given her the usual clipboard with papers requiring answers. Nothing.

Turning from the window, she looked at the row of empty chairs, gauged whether or not she'd be able to squeeze herself into one.

Sighing heavily, she went to the one beside the magazine table, tested it for stability. Even though it appeared spindly, it seemed stable. So, she turned, lowered herself.

There were arms on either side, and they grabbed her thighs, funneled her into their embrace, constricted her the farther in she went. When her butt touched the seat, she rested her weight experimentally, dreading that the entire thing would collapse.

It didn't, so she tried to relax. Difficult since she was constricted by the chair in a completely uncomfortable way.

Just as she settled in, the door near the reception window opened, and a man stepped out.

To say he was not what she expected was an understatement.

Tall, slim of build, youngish, with a kind of nerdy, dorky athleticism that Lisa had always found adorable. Bespectacled but fashionable, with frames that were highlighted in deep, electric blue. He sported a neat, casual haircut and a simple tweed jacket with elbow patches over khaki pants.

Dr. Alatryx was just the kind of man who appealed to Lisa, and she was taken aback at how much he appealed to her.

And his shoes, Lisa noted, were Salvatore Ferragamo Oxfords, in burnished calfskin. Looked to be about size 13.

Lisa, for some reason unfathomable even to her, had a thing for expensive men's shoes. It was more than just the shoes that caught her eye, though. It was his foot, his left, which appeared to be deformed or injured in some way that gave him a distinct, lurching gait.

"Lisa?" he asked, as if there were others within the empty room.

"Yes!" She flushed as she attempted to get out of the chair.

He came to her, offered his hand.

It was a firm, smooth, dry hand, warm, and it enclosed hers gently.

He helped her up, smiling as she stood.

"Let's get you back to more comfortable seating, and we'll talk."

Lisa felt her cheeks and forehead radiate heat, and she was surprised that it wasn't from the exertion of rising from the chair.

The doctor's office was nicely, not richly, appointed. Tasteful in a minimalist, Ikea sort of way. The furniture was slim, streamlined blond wood, but not cheap or flimsy in a way that similar furniture sometimes seemed. There was a desk—really just a plain, wooden plank table with a lamp and a caddy filled with pens and pencils, a few loose pieces of paper. A set of shelves behind this with wicker baskets and a few books.

A few other lamps scattered here and there, a bare wood floor. In the center of the room, sitting atop a lush, high-pile white rug that looked as if it had been sheared from a Yeti, was an overstuffed couch with a few pillows and one high-backed leather chair, the kind with smooth, dark leather dotted with hobnails around its frame.

"Please, Lisa, have a seat on the couch," the doctor said, sitting in the leather chair. "May I call you Lisa?"

"Sure," she said, gathering her skirt and sitting cautiously, a hesitance borne out of sinking too deeply into too many unknown couches, struggling to get free.

This one, though, seemed firm. Comfortable, even snuggly, but firm.

"I don't have to lie down for any of this, do I?"

"No, we ease into that. Probably no earlier than your fourth visit."

There was a pause, then Lisa laughed.

"Honestly, the couch is there for your comfort. Sit, lie back. It's up to you."

Lisa leaned back, glad that the couch's rear cushions were just as supportive.

"So, why don't you tell me why you're here," Dr. Alatryx said, taking a notebook and a pen from the breast pocket of his jacket.

Lisa snorted. "You mean, *besides* me being fat?"

The doctor laughed, too. "Yes, you're fat. That's apparent to anyone. So, let's try to get a little deeper than that."

It was difficult to take Lisa aback, but that did it. She gawped at him, not insulted, just stunned that someone would be so direct about her size. She'd found most people plenty ready to joke about fat people, but few really able to say something direct to a person about their fatness. Perversely, the more obviously fat a person was, the less likely people were willing to say anything about it, even acknowledge it at all.

But this guy, this doctor seemed willing to confront her, not rudely, just openly.

"Well, okay, we got that out of the way," she said.

"Yes. You should know I'm well aware that joking and laughter is a fat person's best, most loyal defense. It's both a shield and a sword, Lisa, for those who know how to wield it. And you, I'm instantly sure, know how to wield it."

For the second time in less than two minutes, Lisa was silenced.

"Perhaps it would be simpler if I started," the doctor said, crossing his legs at the knee. "I only take certain cases. Cases that meet my needs. Cases I think I can have an effect on. My methods are... unorthodox, to say the least. What I do is get at the root cause of your weight problem, then work forward from there to effect a treatment.

"My treatments are also unorthodox. To remain a patient, you must follow them exactly. They're going to seem weird, unnecessary, bizarre, unsafe and illegal, possibly immoral. But understand that I can guarantee—100% percent guarantee—that we will get you to lose weight. We will get you to a healthy weight, a desirable weight."

"At least it's guaranteed, I guess," Lisa said. "And what might a desirable weight be?"

He gestured at her with his pen, with which he hadn't yet written a single thing.

"What weight seems desirable to you?"

Lisa rolled her eyes. "Oh, I don't know. How's about 110 pounds?"

He appraised her carefully. "It can be done."

She frowned. "How much do you think I weigh, doc?"

"About five hundred and fifteen pounds, give or take."

Her mouth fell open. "That's a pretty good guess. Do you have a scale hidden in the waiting room?"

"No. I just have a practiced eye."

"So, you're suggesting that your methods can peel off 400 pounds?"

"Yes."

"Doc..."

"Listen, I've told you that my guarantee is 100%. Money returned. So, what do you have to lose, except the weight, of course?"

Lisa considered this.

"What's the regimen?"

"You mean what's the catch, don't you?" he laughed, jotting something into the notebook for the first time.

She smiled at him, said nothing.

"No regimen. We meet twice a week. Monday and Friday. One hour each session. We talk. At the end of the session on Monday, I give you a task. I weigh you. You complete the task during the week. On Friday, we talk a little more. I weigh you. How's that for easy?"

Lisa looked bemused. "Illegal and immoral, check! Diet? Exercise? Any of that stuff?"

"Sure, there'll be some dietary stuff. Exercise? Nope. Later, when the weight's off, you'll want to exercise just because it'll be more fun. Right now? No."

"No exercise?" she asked.

"My methods can be counterintuitive."

"Okay, doctor. What's the first step?"

"Simple. Today, we weigh you for the first time. Then, you leave."

"That's it?"

"I promise, things will pick up in future weeks. We weigh you today, then we schedule your Friday meeting. In the meantime, what's your No. 1 favorite food? The stuff you could eat every day? The really, really bad stuff that sometimes even you feel guilty about eating? For this first exercise to work, it's got to be your hands-down best comfort food."

"Easy. French fries," she said, without hesitation. "I could eat them literally at every meal."

"Good!" he said, clipping the pen to his notebook and sliding it back into his pocket. "Great, in fact. Then I want you to eat French fries, as much as you want, as often as you want, between now and Friday. Any time, any quantity. Literally as much as you want. No need to gorge or make yourself sick. Just eat French fries to your heart's content."

Lisa tilted her head at him. "Really?"

"Yep. Really. Now let's get you weighed."

He offered his hand, helped her from the couch with an ease and aplomb that hinted at more strength than his thin frame would seem to contain. He led her to a corner of the room where a large step-up scale stood, handrails on either side. A thin neck craned up from this with a plain, unadorned digital scale, blue numbers against a dark background.

"Do I need to take off my shoes or anything?"

He shook his head, took her hand and helped her.

After a moment, the numbers settled on 516 pounds.

She took the hand he again offered, stepped from the platform.

He led her to his desk, opened a thin datebook and asked her for a time for Friday's appointment.

When they were finished, he led her back to the waiting room.

"What a pleasure to meet you, Lisa. I'm sure I'll be able to help. So, I'll see you Friday. In the interim, eat French fries. All the French fries you want."

They shook hands, and she left the office, walked back to her car.

She sat for several minutes in the parking lot, the car running, trying to decipher her feelings about this first appointment.

Finally, she realized that *nothing* had occurred. He hadn't really asked anything of her or about her.

Except he had given her permission to load up on French fries.

She put the car in gear, drove to the McDonald's on the way home, ordered two Big Macs, two large orders of fries and—just so as not to be too embarrassed about the size of this order for a single person—two large Cokes.

At the last minute, she added another large order of fries.

Those she ate in the car on the way home.

〜〜

The fact that her mouth filled with saliva saved her.

It eased the lump of fur down her throat, even seemed to protect her delicate esophagus from Mr. Furball's sharp claws.

She was astounded, as the bolus of cat slid down into her stomach, astounded that her mouth, her throat could expand to accommodate it so easily. She hadn't thought it possible.

That, as much as the general thought of eating her own much-loved cat, had held her back.

But she'd done it. Eaten it. Devoured it whole.

Suddenly, though, she was overcome by a wave of nausea.

What had she done?

A wave passed through her body, starting from her gut, but convulsing her in greater degrees as it rippled out from there.

Vomit.

She was going to puke.

But… maybe that was okay, the best way to correct what she'd just done.

Puke Mr. Furball back up, get him cleaned up and that'd be that.

She'd just have to put up with an evening of sour looks from him, perhaps a couple of turds in her shoes tomorrow morning.

But the nausea quickly passed. Her gut settled. Mr. Furball remained a solid, still lump in her belly.

As she sat there, the phone still clamped between head and shoulder, she heard the doctor's voice purr into her ear.

"So…?"

She swallowed again to clear her throat, felt warmth expand out from her belly, into her limbs, her back.

"It was… he was *delicious*," she said, a little embarrassed at the tone of her voice.

Unexpectedly, she hacked into the phone, let it fall from her hands. Spasms wracked her, and she could feel something working its way back up her throat.

Oh no…!

Before she could press a hand over her lips to contain it, something leapt into her mouth, and she spat it onto the floor.

An enormous, orange-tabby wad of fur, moist and matted.

She looked next to it, to her phone.

Dr. Alatryx's laughter rasped tinny on the air.

⌒⌒

The Friday after she'd binged on French fries, Dr. Alatryx weighed her in on the scale in his office.

She weighed 502 pounds.

Unbelievable, impossibly, she'd lost 14 pounds in only four days.

"That's not right," Lisa said, stepping off, then back on the scale.

The doctor said nothing, stood patiently watching, a neutral expression on his face.

The digital numbers flashed for a second.

502.

Lisa turned to the doctor.

"You did something to it."

"Not at all. You did it yourself."

"Come on! Fourteen pounds in four days? Eating the way I have? That's not possible."

Dr. Alatryx motioned her to the couch.

"Well, obviously it is, since you've done it."

Lisa sat, stunned.

"On French fries?"

"No, on love. On what you love."

"I don't get it. What I love?"

The doctor took his notebook out again, jotted something down, slid it back into his pocket.

"For 40 years, you've been overweight."

"Fat," she corrected, almost by habit.

"Yes, fat. Of course. And why have you been fat?"

"Bad genes? Cheesecake? Doritos?"

"No, no and no. And not lack of exercise, either. You've been fat because you've been swallowing down the wrong things, swallowing down bad feelings and bad body image and lack of self-confidence, prejudice and judgement about fat people. You've swallowed this down even as a small child, and look what it's done. Look at the problems it's caused."

"But how can that… I mean how can any of that make me fat?"

"It's far simpler, I've found, to show how the opposite can make you thin," he said.

"The opposite?"

"As with the French fry test. I asked you to eat as much of your comfort food as you wanted. But in essence, I asked you to eat what you love, as much of it as you wanted. And see what it's done? See the power of eating what you love rather than taking in all that negativity?"

Lisa slumped back into the couch. She was still stunned from the numbers on the scale, still disbelieving that it could be true. This had to be some kind of elaborate ruse to get her to trust him so he could sell her protein powder made from cricket flour, or exercise DVDs, or a membership to some private, secret society where they curbed their appetites by drinking the blood of orphans.

Something other than the stark reality of having lost 14 pounds in only four days gorging on French fries.

Because that was just crazy.

Still…

Dr. Alatryx sat silently, seemingly amused by Lisa's obvious inner struggle. "So, are you in?"

"Am I in?" she repeated, slowly shaking her head. "In?"

"Are you with me in this effort to make you slimmer, to shed your unwanted pounds?"

"Yeah," Lisa said, warming to the idea, whatever the idea actually was. "Yeah, I am. I'm in."

"Good!" said the doctor, slapping his hands on his knees. "Great, in fact. I knew it when I spoke with your sister. Knew it when I saw you. I could help. My methods could help you. They already have... and they will."

Lisa leaned forward, a spill of questions piling up on her tongue.

"But let me warn you, Lisa. It's not all as easy as spending a week stuffing yourself with French fries. No, it gets harder, much harder. But you can do it. It'll all be worth it in the end. If you stick with it, if you're able to, you'll see."

He slapped his thighs again, stood. "So, let's schedule your next appointment."

"Wait... what?" she said. "Aren't we going to talk or something?"

Dr. Alatryx turned back to her. "You mean about your childhood or how you didn't get along with your mother?"

Lisa shrugged. "I suppose—"

"No, as I said, my methods are different, but effective. Talking about what got you here isn't going to help you, believe me. Doing something about what got you here, that's the ticket."

He went to his desk as Lisa pulled herself from the couch. When she'd finally struggled to her feet—without the help he'd given her last time—she saw him open the thin journal on his bare desk, remove the pen from his breast pocket.

"Monday afternoon at 3:30?"

"Sure," she said.

He came around the desk, motioned to the door.

"I want you to think about something until then."

"Okay," she said as he opened the door to the waiting room.

"What is one small thing in your life that gives you pleasure? It must be a real thing, something you own, not an idea or a feeling. Something like a purse or a pair of shoes. A piece of jewelry or even a book or record—something you love."

"Okay," she said, a hint of uncertainty in her voice.

"Think about it and have an answer for me Monday."

"At 3:30?"

"Yes. See you then."

He closed the door and left her in the empty waiting room. She heard his soft footfalls—still clad in the very expensive Salvatore Ferragamo Oxfords—walk back to his office, close the door.

On the way home, she found she was sick of French fries, and wondered if that had been the point of the exercise.

Instead, she stopped at her favorite pizzeria, ordered two large pies—one with sausage, one with pepperoni and pineapple—and a large chef salad. She actually got all this home without sneaking any in the car.

By 9 p.m., she was asleep on the couch, the television blaring another episode of *Chopped*. She clutched a plastic clamshell smeared with blue cheese dressing and a few ribbons of carrot. Two grease-stained pizza boxes sprawled empty on the floor at her feet.

Mr. Furball nibbled at the cooled cheese nubs hardening inside them.

⌣

"It's a brooch, a cameo," Lisa said, holding it for Dr. Alatryx to see.

It was Monday afternoon, just after 3:30.

Alatryx leaned forward in his chair, inspected the piece of jewelry.

"It was my grandma's, my mother's mother. She was my favorite, and I was hers."

Lisa turned the cameo in her fingers. It was perhaps two inches tall, a white silhouette of a bare-necked woman against a background of Wedgewood blue. A delicate filigree of the same ivory white laced the edges, these wrapped in a delicate, thin band that was the lip of a gold back, complete with a pin.

"I don't know if it's worth anything, money at least. But I don't dare wear it, because I'm afraid of the pin unclasping and it falling off. And I really don't go anywhere anyway."

"Excellent," he said. "Lovely. And this little thing, it gives you pleasure? You love it?"

"Yes. I leave it out on my dresser so I can see it all the time. It reminds me of her."

"Perfect," he said, sitting back in his chair. "Eat it."

There was silence in the room. Lisa could hear the traffic outside, a few birds chirping loudly. A truck nearby was backing up, droning *beep-beep-beep*.

"Excuse me?"

"Eat it."

He mimed the action by moving his hand to his open mouth, chewing.

"You mean really *eat* it?"

"I mean really eat it."

He watched her, seemingly waiting for a reaction.

"Ummm… no. No, I won't *eat* it."

"Why not?"

"Because that's nuts, that's why not."

Alatryx shook his head.

"Have you forgotten the French fries? The weight loss? Have you already forgotten that we weighed you again just ten minutes ago, and you'd lost 12 more pounds? That means, you've lost 26 pounds. You're already under 500 pounds, and it's only been a week."

"Yeah, but that was French fries. This is a brooch, my *grandmother's* brooch. I'm not going to eat it. That'd be… well… crazy."

"Crazy. But constricting your calorie intake to near starvation and exercising until exhaustion, that's sane? Well, okay then. Do it that way. Do it the sane way."

Lisa squirmed a little on the couch, looked at the pin held in her hand.

Eat it?

"Doctor, I—"

"No, we spoke about this at the very beginning, about how my methods were a bit different. But guaranteed. I've already shown you that you can lose 26 pounds. What more do I need to do to prove it to you? Because, again, this is the easy part, believe me."

Lisa looked at the pin again.

"How would I even go about swallowing this? I'd never be able to get it down."

Dr. Alatryx stood, left the room.

When he returned, he closed the door behind him, passed Lisa a plain glass filled with water.

Lisa took it. The glass was thick and heavy; the water, cold.

He mimed tossing the brooch into his mouth, drinking the water.

"It's too big. The water won't help."

"You'd be surprised at the body's ability to take things in."

Sighing, she lifted the pin.

As she looked at it, she had a crazy thought.

I suppose I won't be losing it.

If I'm able to get it down, it'll eventually come out the other end.

Taking a deep breath, she slid the cameo between her lips, curled her tongue around it.

She lifted the water glass, took a big drink.

Swallowed.

For a moment, she worried about the golden pin on its back, that it would unclasp and lodge in her throat, jab into the tender flesh of her esophagus.

But it didn't.

She could feel it slide down on a bumpy wave of peristalsis, until it literally plopped into her stomach.

After, she found that she'd closed her eyes. Opening them, she saw Dr. Alatryx studying her closely.

"How do you feel?"

"Weird. Like I just ate my grandmother's brooch."

He smiled at her.

"Friday, I want you to come with another comfort food in mind. We'll see where to go from there."

"What do you want me to do with the brooch?" she asked as he led her out.

"The brooch?"

"You know… when it… ummm… comes out?"

"Oh. Don't worry about that. It won't."

He closed the door between them before she could say anything else.

⌒

Friday she weighed 490 pounds.

The food she decided on was pizza.

He told her the same thing he'd said with the French fries.

She asked about what was happening, why this was working.

Where had her brooch gone?

Because it had, indeed, not resurfaced since Monday. And it'd had more than enough opportunities.

But, she decided, eating the brooch had to be a test. Had to be. A test of some kind, of her resolve or her ability to follow his instructions. She doubted that it had anything directly to do with her weight loss.

Because, well, how could it?

"As I said, all those years, you took in hatred, sadness, bad feelings. All of that went inside you, had nothing to do but make you fat. What we're doing now is cramming you full of good stuff, stuff you love."

"But why would that make me thin?"

"Why did all that other stuff make you fat?"

She had no answer for that.

"Eat the pizza, Lisa. See me on Monday, and what do you want to bet, you'll be down around 475. When's the last time you were below 475?"

She didn't answer, but it was before she'd turned 30.

"I thought so," he said, as if reading her thoughts. "Pizza. See ya Monday."

⌒

Monday.

472 pounds.

"Now, think of the one thing at home that makes you happy. Whatever it might be. Tell me what it is on Friday."

That was easy.

⌒

Lisa got out of her car, literally feeling lighter. Yes, the springs on the vehicle jounced as she leveraged herself out, just as they always did. But it felt a little less. It was just Wednesday, but she knew she weighed significantly less than she had on Monday. She suspected that she was down to 460 pounds.

She closed the door to her car, walked into the Applebee's where her mother had wanted to meet for lunch. It was just after noon, and the place was packed. Mostly office workers on break, young mothers meeting up while their kids were in school.

189

Lisa pushed her way to the hostess stand, was ready to give her name and receive her buzzing hockey puck, when she saw her mother already seated in a booth on the other side of the restaurant.

A booth.

She thanked the young lady, made her way to her mother's seat, careful not to roll over people like a tank or check an unfortunate, tray-bearing waiter with her hips.

"Well, hello, honey," her mother said, putting her glass of iced tea down. "Don't you look nice?"

"A booth, Mom? Are you kidding?" Lisa huffed. "I don't think I've sat in a restaurant booth since I was about 25."

"You've lost weight, Lisa. A lot. I can tell."

Lisa fumed, looked around the restaurant, feeling the weight of all of the stares on her. They were looking at her, judging her, ready to turn away in acute embarrassment for her when she decided to try to squeeze into the booth she would obviously not fit into.

"Yes, mother, I've lost weight," she said. "Now can we go up front and put our names in for a table?"

"Wha...? Oh, I already spoke with the hostess. There are a couple of booths back here that are... ummm... well, more *accommodating*. They said they were certain you'd be able to sit here comfortably."

Her mother was blushing by the end of her statement, but Lisa looked at the padded, vinyl bench seat opposite her mother. It did seem farther from the edge of the table than usual, maybe with just enough room to squeeze in.

Despite her best judgement, she decided to try. Too many eyes on her already, standing here arguing with her mom.

Surprisingly, she was able to lower herself and scoot over into the middle of the seat without encountering more than a swipe from the edge of the table. It didn't dig into her like an iceberg scraping the hull of the *Titanic*. Impossibly, she found herself seated, and comfortably at that.

"Honey, you *have* lost weight," her mother said, reaching across the table to take her hand, squeeze it. "Oh, I'm so happy for you. So proud of you!"

Lisa snapped the menu open, scanned the offerings. For some reason, she was feeling a little out of it, aggravated in some distant, vague way that only made her feel more aggravated. And her mother, as usual, wasn't helping.

"Well, I guess that doctor's worth his salt," she said, sipping from her glass. "Though I can't believe it's working so fast."

"Or maybe at all," Lisa said, not even really paying attention to the menu or its slick pictures of glossy, almost glowing food.

"Oh, honey, now shush. I'm just so happy for you."

The waiter came, disinterestedly took Lisa's lunch order—beef fajitas, nachos, French fries and a dinner salad with ranch dressing.

At least her mother had the decency not to complain about the order until the waiter had left the table.

"I'm not questioning what you ordered, dear, but do you think it's wise to eat all that food when you're obviously on the right track?"

"Mom, that's literally exactly what you're doing, questioning my lunch order."

"Well, honey, I'm—"

"I know, Mom. You're worried about me. But I'm losing weight. You can see it yourself. I've lost about 50 pounds in two weeks. So, it's working."

Her mother remained quiet for at least a minute. Lisa was aware that she was weighing her words.

"I can see that, honey. I can. And it's wonderful. But I doubt that your doctor would condone—"

"No, actually, Mom, he would. He's put no dietary restrictions at all on me. In fact, last week he told me to eat all the fries I wanted."

Her mother's face puckered into a dense mass of wrinkled confusion, distaste and sudden alarm, perhaps thinking that she and Maria had inadvertently sent Lisa to a certified quack.

"How can that be right?"

"I dunno, but like I said, it's working. Somehow, some way for the first time in my life, I'm actually dropping pounds rather than gaining them."

There was the requisite awkward pause, so prevalent in any conversation with her mother, as they each sipped their drinks, surveyed the restaurant.

Then, "Well he must have you getting out and exercising, then, which is great. Walking or whatever. Fresh air and moving around is exactly what you need."

Lisa rolled her eyes a bit dramatically, set her iced tea on the table.

"Wrong again, Mom. I'm not exercising, not at all. You know what I did last night? I lay on the couch with Mr. Furball and ate a huge bag of tortilla chips, a gallon of butter pecan ice cream and a two-liter bottle of Coke. I was so exhausted I went to bed and slept like the dead."

"Lisa," her mother sniffed, looking around hoping that none of the other diners had heard.

"Oh, and that was after dinner. Wanna know what dinner was?"

"No, I do n—"

"I had a couple of those Hungry Man Big Portion fried chicken dinners. Four, to be precise. Also about a half a loaf of white bread with butter. Real butter."

Her mother just looked at her. Lisa had tried all her life not to eat in front of her mother, at least not in the manner and quantities she did in private. So, her mother had never seen how Lisa truly ate, *what* Lisa truly ate.

On those occasions where Lisa told her mother what she'd eaten, her mother tried hard not to seem horrified, repulsed.

But she was, just as she was now.

Lisa was saved from having to hear whatever her mother had to say by the timely appearance of the waiter. He quickly disgorged a variety of plates and

191

platters. Her mother had ordered a fairly demure Asian chicken salad, which came in a single bowl. Lisa's order, on the other hand, quickly swamped the table with baskets and plates and a steaming metal platter for her fajitas.

"Anything else, ladies?" the waiter asked.

"No," her mother said, a bit abruptly, and the man disappeared as if falling through a trap door.

They began to eat, in silence. Lisa cut portions of this and that, assembled fajitas, pulled nachos out of the slumping pile of ingredients like a melted game of Jenga. Her mother picked at her salad, obviously distressed but trying hard not to show it.

"Well, whatever it is," her mother finally said, lifting a demure bite of her salad to her lips. "You look lovely. Having that weight off suits you."

Suddenly, Lisa's vague feeling of annoyance clarified, solidified into immediate anger.

"So, I'm beautiful now that I'm losing weight? Is that it, Mom?"

Lisa's mother blanched. The fork drooped in her fingers, clattered against the rim of the glass salad bowl.

"No. I meant—"

"That I'm an ugly, fat pig that you're embarrassed to be around, right? That you'd prefer it if I was slim and trim like Maria, like you. Right?"

Her mother looked around the room nervously. Lisa had raised her voice, louder with each word. People were starting to turn their heads in the direction of this growing disturbance.

As Lisa spoke, her hands moved over the table, grasping something from each plate—a forkful here, a chip there—all smoothly moved to her mouth to be chewed between words.

"Admit it, Mom. That's why you hooked me up with this doctor, so I could lose weight and be beautiful and skinny like Maria."

"Lisa, honey…"

"So I can be a pretty porcelain doll and not eat like I do and not get grossly obese and waddle over to your house. Or come to a restaurant like this and embarrass you in public."

Lisa stuffed food in with rapidity, chewing and swallowing so fast it was amazing she wasn't either spraying the table with food or simply choking on it. But it didn't matter, at least not to her. She continued to jam food into her mouth, her anger translated into these simple snatch-and-grab motions from table to mouth, chewing, swallowing.

"Lisa, that's simply not true. Not true at all. I love you, you know that," her mother said, tears starting, flowing down her powdered cheeks, leaving little pink rivulets across her skin.

The waiter suddenly appeared at the table, giving clear indications that he was dispatched here against his will, either by another diner or the manager.

192

"Ladies," he said, and it came out almost as an exclamation. "Is there a problem?"

Turning to look at him, this time she did spray food as she spoke, spattering his black shirt and apron. "No, why do you ask?" said Lisa, still stuffing food into her mouth.

He flinched, stepped back, but Lisa neither acknowledged what she'd done nor apologized.

"I'm going to politely have to ask you to keep it down. You're disturbing the other—"

"I bet I am disturbing them," Lisa growled. "That's what fat people do best. Disturb other people. Even other fat people."

Lisa's mother moved her napkin from her lap to the table, covering her salad like a corpse.

"Actually, you *can* help…" she said, eyeing his nametag. "Jordan? I need to order some more lunch. Obviously, I'm so fat that this amount of food just isn't going to do it."

Jordan looked from her mother to her. "Are you serious?"

Lisa's eyebrows lifted. "Are *you* serious? With a question like that? Yes. Bring me a cheeseburger. Make it a double. With bacon. More fries. And I'd like some of those wonton taco things. And a steak, whatever cut sounds good to you. Baked potato with everything. Oh, and a piece of the biggest, chocolatiest dessert you've got."

Jordan hadn't written any of this down, he just looked at her in confusion.

Pausing only long enough to grab her purse, Lisa pulled out her wallet, fished out her credit card.

"Worried that I might not pay? This oughta cover it," she said, slapping it onto the only uncovered part of the table.

Jordan cocked his head uncertainly at her mother, who didn't respond. So, he reached out, slipped the card away, went back to his station to put the additional orders in.

Her mother watched in silence. Then, saying nothing, she grabbed her purse, slid from the booth, left the restaurant.

Lisa watched her leave, smirking, still eating.

Well, whatever. Screw them all—her mother, Maria, even her dead father if that's the way he'd felt about Lisa.

For that matter, screw everyone who thought she should be thin rather than fat.

Everyone who worried about her health.

Everyone who felt sorry for her, who pitied her, who looked down on her.

Fuck. Them. All.

If they wanted thin Lisa, then by god, they're gonna get thin Lisa.

If she had to eat everything in the world to get there.

Not giving a solid shit about any of the looks or whispered comments she garnered, she continued to eat as they cleared her mother's plate, as they cleared her empty first course plates.

She continued to eat as they filled the table again with more plates.

She continued to eat as the lunch crowd dribbled away, and the dinner crowd began. She ate quickly, without any care of the mess she was making, the food crumbs falling onto her breasts. The chewed bits and dribbles spattering the table, her messy, sticky hands, cheeks and mouth. The noisy chewing and slurping, licking her fingers and lips, moaning at the especially good bits.

When she finished, she was astonished at how light, how almost nimble she felt, not weighed down at all by the enormous amount of food she'd eaten. She wiped her hands and face fastidiously with a spare napkin from the pile the waiter had thoughtfully left, tucked the receipt for her meal into her purse, walked quietly out of the restaurant, nodding to the servers as she went.

Getting in her car, she drove immediately to a Popeye's to pick up a 12-piece meal for later that evening.

Lisa was losing weight, she knew it.

Didn't know how or why, but she could feel it.

⌒

442 pounds.

She stepped off the scale in Alatryx's office, knowing that she'd lost weight, feeling it, but still stunned.

"I see you're taking the program to heart," Alatryx said, leading her to the couch.

Afternoon sunlight shafted into the room between the vertical shades that closed off the drab view of the parking lot. But the way the light entered, how it was split in these sharp wedges, how it fell in late-day golds and buttercreams, it made Alatryx's drab office seem like a minimalist palace, mysterious in its simplicity.

Even the plain old couch looked like something from a Cocteau movie.

Lisa sat, not worried anymore whether the cushions would support her or the legs would creak alarmingly beneath her.

"So, here we are," the doctor said.

"Yep, here we are."

"You've lost... let me see... 74 pounds. How do you feel?"

Lisa closed her eyes, took a deep breath, released it.

"I feel great," she said, her eyes snapping open. "I feel more than great. I feel terrific. I don't know how it's possible. It shouldn't work, but it's working. I mean, I haven't cut out anything. I'm not doing anything that could even remotely be considered a diet. If anything, I'm eating like a horse. But I'm losing weight."

"I told you, didn't I? Guaranteed."

"You did. You really did, and I didn't believe you. Still wouldn't, if I didn't see the scale myself."

Alatryx's smile faded. "But the treatment isn't over yet, Lisa. I think…"

Here he fished his notebook out again, flipped through the pages.

"Yes. Your target weight—that you yourself selected—was 110 pounds. We're still quite a ways from that. To be precise, 332 pounds. But you're on track, I feel it. Now, it starts to ratchet up, though, get difficult. You have some hard choices ahead, Lisa. *Hard* choices."

Lisa didn't like his ominous tone. Suddenly the fat wedges of sunlight made the office seem oppressive and almost sepulchral.

"In all that time eating and eating over the last few days, did you consider my question? What's that one thing that makes you happy?"

Lisa didn't hesitate.

Later, she'd wish she had.

"Easy. Mr. Furball."

"Mr. Furball? A cat, I assume."

"The greatest cat in the world. Had him for 12 years now. He's awesome."

Dr. Alatryx smiled.

"Perfect, perfect. All right, that's it for today."

Lisa was accustomed now to the abrupt way the doctor ended these brief visits, so she rose when he did, followed him to the door.

She paused as she left, though, turned back.

"Was there anything else? I mean why'd you ask me about Mr. Furball? Is there something I'm supposed to do?"

"Oh yes," he said. "Eat him."

As she blinked at this response, he eased the door shut on her face.

She listened to his limping footfalls recede, then walked back to the parking lot, feeling as if he'd punched her in the stomach.

In her car, she burst into tears.

Not because he'd told her to eat her cat.

Because she was actually considering it.

⁓

"How do you feel?"

The doctor was seated in his leather chair, tiny notebook in hand poised to record her reaction.

"I feel… *sad,*" she said.

"Sad for Mr. Fluffernutter?"

"Mister…? No, *Mr. Furball.* I feel sad for him… what I did to him."

Alatryx quickly jotted something, slid the notebook back into his jacket.

"Sorry. Mr. Furball. Why sad, though? You loved him, correct?"

"Of course I did. But… geez, doctor, I *ate* him. I *ate* my cat and now he's gone. What the hell have I done? How—"

"Lisa, I told you that from here on out the decisions you'd be forced to make would be more difficult."

195

"Difficult? Doctor, I unhinged my jaw and swallowed Mr. Furball whole! Sitting here, I don't even know how I managed that, technically, much less philosophically."

"I was on the line listening. I know what you did. You took in love, and see what it's done? You've lost another 32 pounds. You're down to 410 pounds now. That's more than a 100-pound weight loss. You should be proud of yourself."

After a long silence, Lisa said, "I can't believe it. Can't believe I did that. Can't believe that I was actually able to do that."

"If we're going to get you to your desired weight, Lisa, there are other, harder decisions ahead."

Lisa stared straight ahead, tears forming in the corners of her eyes.

"Nope," she said, shaking her head. "Nope, nope, nope. I can't do this. *Can't*. I mean, what could be more difficult than eating my own cat? I don't want to know."

She stood, with no help, walked to the door.

"Lisa, avoiding these decisions in the past hasn't helped. Avoiding them now won't help."

Without turning back, she said, "I can't imagine that eating my cat will, either."

⌣

Halfway home, she let out a tremendously long, loud sigh. It felt like exhaling a world of problems from her body, and it was a delicious, exhilarating moment.

Until she thought about getting home, kicking her shoes off, unpeeling her bra and camping out on the sofa, petting her...

Mr. Furball!

That brought a sudden burst of weeping that nearly made her swerve her car into the oncoming lane.

Without much conscious thought—and barely able to see through the fog of her tears, the shaking of her entire body as the sobs wracked through her—she steered into the parking lot of a Long John Silver's, methodically ordered the Family Fisherman's Feast.

She cried as she paid the cashier and took the grocery-size plastic bag the teenage boy passed across the drive-through window to her.

She cried as she pulled back into traffic, steered toward home.

She cried as she pushed thin planks of greasy, salty fried fish into her mouth, one after another, chewing them like a sawmill.

By the time she pulled into her apartment complex, she realized that she'd eaten all of the fish filets and hushpuppies in the meal she'd ordered.

Without hesitating, she made a wide, curving turn, drove straight back to the Long John Silver's.

⌣

For the next few days, she alternated crying jags with eating jags.

Her kitchen was a marshalling field of white garbage bags, arranged like troops at rest, neatly closed with their red cinches. They bulged with every conceivable fast food bag, box and wrapper.

These nestled against a cornucopia of packaged food remains—leftover cardboard pizza discs, TV dinner trays and yogurt cups and ice cream tubs and bakery boxes and untold plastic milk jugs and two-liter soda bottles.

Someone—her mother and Maria, no doubt—came to her apartment door a half dozen times during that period. Knocking softly. Ringing the bell. Lisa didn't answer, didn't even bother to turn the television down.

She simply sat on the couch, chewed and swallowed, chewed and swallowed.

Eventually, what made her move was the smell.

Thinking it was the landfill in the kitchen, she spent a good 20 minutes carrying the bags out to the dumpster, Swiffering the floor when they were gone.

But the odor—sour with a distinct greasy, biological tang—persisted.

She realized it was coming from her, from the folds and fissures and dark, dank crevices of her own body.

Sighing, she took herself to the bathroom, peeled off her clothes, which felt... loose. Stepping into the shower, she turned the water on, stood under the hot spray, letting it sluice over her.

After a few minutes, she grabbed her scrunchie and went to work, scouring her skin, almost punishing it for offending her. She lathered the shower gel, pushed it deep between the folds, wiped away the oil and dirt and stinking bacteria that had gathered there.

As she scrubbed, turning this way and that, bending to address her legs and feet, twisting and pivoting as the hot water sprayed over her, she began to notice something.

How freely she moved in the shower.

How flexible and accommodating her body was in turning this way and that.

How much less of *her* there seemed to be to address.

Am I still losing weight?

Her bathroom scale—a heavy-duty thing she'd ordered from Amazon—wasn't terrifically accurate, but it seemed to peg her weight within three or four pounds of the scale in the doctor's office.

She slung the shower curtain open, stepped out.

Dripping wet, she stepped onto the scale.

424.

She'd gained 14 pounds.

Shaking—as much from what this meant as from the cold air—she backed from the scale, backed out of the bathroom, went to lay on her bed. Still wet, she felt the shower water soak into her sheets, adhere to her skin, but she didn't care. She lay there without falling asleep for an hour or so, staring at the ceiling, her mind racing.

Was it possible...? Yes!

It seemed likely that she could gain all this weight back.

Or lose it, as much as she wanted.

All of it.

If…

What she had to do, though…what she *might* have to do…

Is it worth it?

The bedsheets cauled around her damp form, and she considered that one, horrible question.

Decided.

⌒⌣

Later that afternoon, there was another knock at her door.

The knocks and doorbell rings had petered out over the last couple of days, so this surprised Lisa. She was sitting on the couch in a bathrobe, a giant sack of caramel corn in her lap, absently tossing sticky kernels of the stuff into her mouth.

"Lisa? Lisa, please. It's your mother. Please open the door and let me in. I… I know there's something wrong, honey. And I know you're upset with me, but please."

Her voice was muffled through the apartment door, tentative and strained.

Lisa considered ignoring it, instead rocked herself off the sofa and went to answer the door. She turned the deadbolt, drew the door open.

"Lisa!" her mother gasped.

Through the crack of the open door, Lisa saw her mom. She looked small and frail. Dark circles rimmed her eyes. Her cheeks seemed sunken. Everything about her seemed grey and limp, drained.

She stepped into the narrow space Lisa had left between the door and the jamb, interposed herself in case her daughter decided to shut her out.

"Let me in, honey. We've been… I've been worried. So worried."

Her mother practically pushed her way inside, not that Lisa made any effort to stop her.

"What… I mean… how are you? What's going on? The doctor called, said that… well, there's been a setback."

Lisa closed the door, turned to her mother.

"I can't do it anymore, Mom. *Can't.* He's asking too much."

"Lisa, I know this is hard but—"

"No, Mom, you don't. For once, just believe me. You have no idea."

"You can do this. You've *got* to do this. I know you're mad at me, honey. And I know that you think I'm hard on you or that I nag you or compare you to your sister. But I love you. I love you so much."

At that her mother broke down, wept, actually slumped standing there in the living room, as if some central support, the lodge pole of her body, had collapsed.

Lisa went to her, embraced her.

"Aww, Mom," she said, enfolding her tiny mother in her arms. "It's okay, gonna be okay."

Her mother continued to sob as Lisa held her.

"Why did you stop seeing the doctor, honey? What did he ask you to do that you can't do?"

Lisa thought, for a moment, of telling her mother exactly what the good doctor had prescribed, but decided against that.

How to tell your mom you swallowed grandma's brooch, much less ate a housecat?

"He told me that… I needed to eat what I love."

Her mother drew back, still within her arms.

"That doesn't sound so bad, honey. A little new-agey, sure, but if it helps—"

She tightened her grip on her mother.

"Oh, Mom, of course it's helped. Can't you tell?"

Her mother shifted uncomfortably in Lisa's embrace.

"I can tell. You've lost a lot of weight. I'm so proud. Honey… ooof… you're hugging me a little too tight."

Lisa leaned her head down into her mother's face. "You always say you want to help, Mom. Help me lose weight. Well, now's your chance."

She tightened her arms around her mother's midsection, clasped her hands together in the small of her back, squeezed.

"Lisa, honey… what are you doing? Let me go. I can… hardly… breathe!"

"Shhhh. I love you, Mom."

Constricting her arms, Lisa heard her mother gasp, try to wriggle free. But she squeezed and squeezed until she heard a *pop!*, and her mother uttered a scream, muffled by Lisa's bosom.

Lisa lowered her face, kissed the top of her mother's head.

Drew back, opened her mouth.

There was another series of clicks, this time from Lisa's jaw as it dislocated, lowered, widened. It kept ratcheting outward, downward, until the top of her mouth—terrifyingly wide now—touched one side of her mother's head, while the bottom cradled the other side.

Lisa's tongue darted forward from this chasm, bathed her mother's head in saliva. Spit, in fact, flowed freely from Lisa's gaping mouth, drooling as if she were about to eat a bucket of greasy fried chicken from KFC. It flowed down her mother's head, matting her hair, soaking the collar of her blouse.

Her mother's hands drummed at her sides, compressed by Lisa's embrace. She was still making tiny, mewling noises, bleating what might have been Lisa's name over and over.

Lisa slid her distended lips over her mother's head. She felt it slip into her suddenly enormous mouth, gliding across her tongue. She tasted her mother's shampoo, her skin cream, her perfume.

She felt love, love for this woman who had birthed her, raised her. She also felt her mother's love, as if for the first time. Tears squeezed from her eyes as the feeling overwhelmed her, as her mother's entire head slid down Lisa's throat.

She stepped backward once, twice, lowered her head. Her mother's twitching form continued its slithering decent into Lisa, drool now pattering the floor like rainfall.

As Lisa reached her midsection, something burst inside her mother with a sound like a handful of Fritos being crushed. Liquid spurted into Lisa's mouth, warm and salty, almost beefy in taste. It mingled with the saliva slavering to the carpet, Lisa's tears.

Her lips continued to contract around her mother's form, drawing it deeper and deeper inside.

Lisa could feel it, that love her mother bore for her, acting on her now. She could almost feel the pounds melt off her. The fat rolls on her back, the dewlaps under her chin, drew up like window shades. Her flabby forearms contracted, her thighs shriveled, her stomach tightened.

Mama!

Lisa fell back another step, her calves bumping against her sofa, steadying her.

She drew her wildly swollen face up until she looked at the ceiling of her apartment, the network of cracks in the drywall there, cobwebs. She saw her mother's spindly, varicose-veined legs jutting from her wide, open mouth like breadsticks.

They disappeared into her gullet until nothing showed except for her mother's plain, red canvas espadrilles, size five. One fell to the floor, bouncing off Lisa's substantially shrunken breasts.

The other slurped into Lisa's maw.

She closed her lips around it, drew in a runnel of drool that hung from her mouth.

⌇

334 pounds on the scale in the bathroom.

⌇

Lisa spent a great deal of time after that curled on her bed, crying.

She could still taste her mother—the soap she washed with, her toothpaste, even her moisturizer—all seasoned with the salt of her own tears.

That wasn't bad enough, though.

At some point, she had grown nauseated, hugely, greenly sick. Her flattened stomach rippled as something—*someone*—seemed to writhe inside.

Lisa, too upset, too weak to do much of anything, leaned over atop the mattress and vomited onto the floor. It wasn't violent or horrible. It was more like something her stomach hadn't wanted in it anymore simply slithered up her throat, slowly slid from her mouth.

It continued for an awful minute or more, Lisa retching, something sluggish and mucilaginous flowing out of her.

When she looked down, there, atop the carpet at the side of the bed, was what appeared to be something like an owl pellet sitting in a puddle of grey-green slime. A clump of greyish hair with what looked like burnt twigs jutting from it here and there.

And atop it a single red shoe.

⌒‿⌒

Lisa's phone rang and rang.

She didn't answer it, didn't even look at it.

⌒‿⌒

When she awoke, it all seemed like a dream, a hideous dream.

Pushing it from her mind, she leapt from her bed, stepping around the dried mound of puke on the carpet. She dashed into the bathroom, snapped on the lights. The fluorescent fixtures gave her face a hollowed, sunken look.

Staring into the mirror as if she didn't recognize her own face, she fumbled for her toothbrush, the crimped tube of toothpaste. She brushed her teeth savagely, scrubbed away the taste…

…of her mom!

What had she done?

She spat into the sink as another wave of nausea swept through her. She lowered her head, splashed cold water onto her face until it passed.

Twisting the tap closed, she stood, looked at herself in the mirror again.

From her bedroom, she heard the phone ring again.

She stumbled back, picked it up.

Maria.

She hesitated for a moment, then answered it.

"Lisa, finally," her sister said. "I've been over here at Mom's all day. She's not here. Is she with you?"

Oh, god.

"I'll be right over."

⌒‿⌒

Later, after she'd stepped onto the scale in her mother's bathroom—with its pink fuzzy toilet cover and pink bathmat—she leaned her head against the cool aluminum siding on the outside of her childhood home.

263 pounds.

She licked her lips, tasted vomit.

At her feet, near the gutter downspout, was a small, wet mound.

It was dusk now, and the neighborhood was all vibrant oranges and pinks and violets, lit both by the sun setting behind the rooftops and the sherbet-colored dusk-to-dawns that flickered to life.

She could smell barbecues smoking in the distance, imagined slabs of beef and chicken, sizzling burgers. Dogs barked and the catcalls of children echoed here and there.

Lisa felt a shudder ripple through her, but this time it wasn't nausea or revulsion. This time, it was a great upwelling of love, for her family, for this house, this neighborhood where she'd grown up.

She leaned her head against the siding and wept, cried for the sheer power of it.

Her phone rang, and she noticed that she still clutched it.

She moved it to her head, still leaning against the house.

"Lisa?"

"Yes."

"What are you down to?"

"Two hundred and sixty three pounds."

There was silence, in which Lisa was sure she heard his pen scratching something onto his notebook. The silky sound of it slipping back into his breast pocket.

"By my estimation, you're still 153 pounds from your target weight."

"Of course."

"How will we get you there, Lisa?"

"I dunno, doc. As Air Supply said, I'm all outta love."

He tsked into the phone.

"The entire world is love, Lisa. *All of it.*"

"I can't eat the entire world, doc, now can I?"

"Can't you?"

Lisa lifted her head, drew the heel of her hand across her eyes to scrape away the tears. As she moved, her pants slithered down around her ankles, her hips and thighs now far too thin to keep them up.

She felt her bra dangle from her shoulders, its massive cups dwarfing the substantially smaller breasts cupped inside.

Her shirt hung on her now like a dress.

She was thin, true, thinner than she'd been since she was 17 years old.

But she could be thinner yet.

"I believe you can, Lisa. Open your mouth, wider still, and you can take it in. Take it all in."

Lisa blinked, pushed back from the house, cocked her head.

Her hands braced against the house, felt the powdery coating of its aluminum skin against her fingertips.

Lowering her face back to it, mouth first, she heard the telltale clicking of her jaw unhinging, dislocating the bones, drawing her mouth around the corner of the house.

Wider, wider, still wider, until her head had ballooned to the size of a medicine ball, beyond.

Lisa's eyes rolled back in her head, tears squeezing from them.

Still wider grew her mouth, and her lips crept across the siding, sliding over windows, eaves. Her teeth scraped across the shingles on the roof. Her tongue lolled over the bricks of the chimney.

Dr. Alatryx's voice came from the phone lying in the side yard, its screen glowing with the picture of his beautiful burnished calfskin Salvatore Ferragamo Oxfords she'd surreptitiously snapped, and used as his avatar in her contact list.

Even in that picture, even from this distance, she noticed his curiously bent, deformed foot in that slick, sleek shoe.

"You can do it, Lisa. Take it in, take the love in, take all of it. Take the house, then the neighborhood. After that, we'll talk. There's so much more I need to share with you, so much more I need from you. Call me when you're finished… *digesting*."

Sighing, Lisa closed her mouth, squeezed her childhood home in its entirety in a mouth that was the size of weather balloon.

Timber snapped, glass shattered, bricks crumbled to powder.

Lisa took it all in, all that love.

She thought of what she would eat next, what drive-through she would slip into, what buckets or boxes or bags of food would pass through her car window, into her wide, waiting mouth.

As her lips compressed the gutters, as her bottom teeth scored the foundation, she shuddered, felt the weight evaporate from her, rising like curdled, yellow steam from her pores.

AFTERWORD

I swear that this isn't the literary equivalent of typecasting.

When we had the original idea of doing an anthology of the seven deadly sins, I knew the authors I wanted to work with. And I knew there was no way we could cherry pick, as it were, the sins we wanted to write about. No, it had to be done as above board, as randomly as possible. So, literally names in a hat and a blind drawing.

And even after that, I got *gluttony*. Sigh.

I am, as anyone who has ever met me can attest, a large man. Arrestingly large, both in height and girth. Raymond Burr large. Orson Welles large. Anyway, big. I sometimes pass a mirror and wonder how such a *yuge* man got into my home. I wasn't always like that. For the longest time, 168 pounds was my weight. Then, marriage, kids, old age set in, but mostly continuing to eat like I was 17 years old. And my weight increased like a boulder careening down hill, accumulating mass as it goes.

So gluttony is a sin with which I am quite well acquainted.

I got the title of the story right away, jotted it down in my notebook and sat on it and sat on it. However, as the deadline approached, I began to sweat like... well... a fat man. Since I was the one who brought this idea to Patrick at Cutting Block Books, I didn't want to be the last to turn in his story. Or worse yet, be faced with no story.

But as I thought about gluttony, as I thought about the increasing *fatitude* of the United States in these early days of the 21st century, the story began to take shape... ahem. My wife likes to unwind at the end of a busy, stressful day by watching television. I'm not that big a TV watcher, but it's not because I'm snooty or anything. I just don't find a lot to hold my interest these days. We got hooked on *Game of Thrones* quite late—at the end of the sixth season, to be honest. We enjoy *Westworld* and some of the Marvel Netflix shows, but the only other TV series that's held my interest in the last 20 years was the reboot of *Battlestar Galactica*.

Anyway, one of the shows my wife is fascinated by is something on TLC called *My 600-Pound Life*, which tells the stories of people who are debilitated by morbid obesity. There's usually family crisis involved, a heaping helping of drama, lots of weigh-ins, grisly surgeries and, sometimes even, redemption.

I hate this show. It makes me weary of whiny, overfed humanity, at least of the first-world variety. It also leaves me feeling guilty about what I just ate or, conversely, disgusted about what I was thinking of eating before I watched the carb fests people eat on the show—pre-operatively, at least. It's not a show that makes me feel better about those souls or myself, but rather worse about absolutely all of us. In short, it's one of those shows (of an increasing number these days) that makes me think, only partially sarcastically, "Gee, isn't it time we had a good, old-fashioned plague to give the place a thorough spring cleaning?"

But I digress...

What gave me the through-line for this story was my thinking that Gluttony is really the only sin that has, as its start, something we all have to do to stay alive—namely, eat. There's no comparable sin for breathing a lot or even over drinking, at least in the non-alcoholic sense. Sleeping too much isn't really sloth. But eating too much... not only does it make you fat and induce a positive fiesta of health maladies, it's also a recognized, A-1, Hall of Fame sin. One of the beta readers who read my story said something interesting to me (and thanks for this, Nate!). He said gluttony, at its chubby little heart, is a sin of selfishness. I think that makes a great deal of sense.

Incidentally, the good Dr. Alatryx—with his cool demeanor and limp—has appeared in a few of my stories over the years. He's my stand in for... well, that'd be telling, wouldn't it?

AUTHOR BIOGRAPHIES

John C. Foster was born in Sleepy Hollow, New York, and has been afraid of the dark for as long as he can remember. His most recent novel, *The Isle,* grew out of his love for New England, where he spent his childhood. He is the author of three previous novels, *Dead Men, Night Roads* and *Mister White,* and one collection of short stories, *Baby Powder and Other Terrifying Substances.* His stories have appeared in magazines and anthologies including *Dark Moon Digest, Strange Aeons, Dark Visions Volume 2* and *Lost Films,* among others. He lives in Brooklyn with the actress Linda Jones and their dog Coraline. For more information, please visit www.johnfosterfiction.com.

Brian Kirk is an author of psychological horror. His debut novel, *We Are Monsters,* was a finalist for the Bram Stoker Award®. And his short fiction has been published in many notable magazines and anthologies alongside several New York Times best selling authors. His most recent novel, *Will Haunt You,* has been called one of the most anticipated horror novels of 2019, although reading it comes with a dire warning. Contact him through his website at briankirkfiction.com. Don't worry, he only kills his characters.

Kasey Lansdale, first published at the tender age of eight by Random House, is the author of several short stories and novellas, along with publications from Harper Collins and Titan Books, as well as the editor of assorted anthology collections, including Subterranean Press' *Impossible Monsters.* She is best known as a Singer/Songwriter. "As a vocalist, she walks the line between traditional and contemporary sounds throughout, with the passion oozing out of tracks such as 'Blame You For Trying' and 'Just Another Day' being a great example of the former," said *Billboard* writer Chuck Dauphin, in "Music News Nashville." Most recently, you can hear Lansdale as the narrator of various works, including Stan Lee's *Reflections,* George R.R. Martin's *Aces Abroad,* and George A. Romero's latest installment, *Nights of the Living Dead,* among others. Her new collection, *Terror is Our Business,* was lauded by Publisher's Weekly as "storytelling that delightfully takes on a lighter and sharper edge." Her collaboration with her father and brother, "The Companion," has been adapted to release in the upcoming television remake of Shudder's *Creepshow.*

Bracken MacLeod is the author of the novels *Mountain Home, Come to Dust,* and *Stranded,* which was a finalist for the Bram Stoker Award in 2017 and is currently under active development at Warner Horizon Television. He's also published two collections of short fiction, *13 Views of the Suicide Woods* and *White Knight and Other Pawns.* Before devoting himself to full time writing, he worked as a civil and criminal litigator, a university philosophy instructor, and a martial arts teacher. He lives outside of Boston with his wife and son, where he is at work on his next novel.

Rena Mason is the Bram Stoker Award® winning author of *The Evolutionist* and *East End Girls*, as well as a 2014 Stage 32 / The Blood List Search for New Blood Screenwriting Contest Quarter-Finalist. She writes in multiple genres, often mashing them up with a focus on horror. She is a member of the Horror Writers Association, Mystery Writers of America, International Thriller Writers, and The International Screenwriters' Association. An R.N., avid scuba diver, and world traveler, she currently resides in Reno, Nevada. For more information, visit her website: www.renamason.ink

John F.D. Taff is the author of more than 100 published short stories and six novels. *Little Deaths* was named the best horror fiction collection of 2012 by *HorrorTalk*. Jack Ketchum called *The End in All Beginning*, published in 2014, "the best novella collection I've read in years," and it was a finalist for a Bram Stoker Award for Superior Achievement in a Fiction Collection. The story "A Winter's Tale" was a finalist for a 2018 Stoker Award for Superior Achievement in Short Fiction. His work has appeared most recently in *Gutted: Beautiful Horror Stories, Behold: Oddities, Curiosities and Undefinable Wonders, Shadows Over Main Street 2*, and his latest collection *Little Black Spots*. His epic novel *The Fearing* will be released in 2019 by Grey Matter Press. Josh Malerman said *"The Fearing* isn't only John Taff's best work to date, it's the kind you put on the shelf reserved for the ones that really did something to you, emotionally, intellectually, physically." He lives in the wilds of Illinois with one wife, two cats and three pugs. Follow him on Twitter @johnfdtaff or learn more at his blog www.johnfdtaff.com

Richard Thomas is the award-winning author of seven books—*Disintegration* and *Breaker* (Penguin Random House Alibi), *Transubstantiate, Staring into the Abyss, Herniated Roots, Tribulations,* and *The Soul Standard* (Dzanc Books). His over 140 stories in print include *The Best Horror of the Year* (Volume Eleven), *Cemetery Dance* (twice), *Behold!: Oddities, Curiosities and Undefinable Wonders* (Bram Stoker Winner), *PANK, storySouth, Gargoyle, Weird Fiction Review, Midwestern Gothic, Gutted: Beautiful Horror Stories, Qualia Nous, Chiral Mad* (numbers 2-4), and *Shivers VI*. He was also the editor of four anthologies: *The New Black* and *Exigencies* (Dark House Press), *The Lineup: 20 Provocative Women Writers* (Black Lawrence Press) and *Burnt Tongues* (Medallion Press) with Chuck Palahniuk. He has been nominated for the Bram Stoker, Shirley Jackson, and Thriller awards. In his spare time he writes for *Lit Reactor* and is Editor-in-Chief at *Gamut Magazine*. For more information visit www.whatdoesnotkillme.com or contact Paula Munier at Talcott Notch.

EDITOR BIOGRAPHIES

Patrick Beltran is the owner and publisher of Farolight Publishing, home of Cutting Block Books. He has served in various editorial capacities for Cutting Block since 2011, including editor of *Cutting Block Single Slices*, and Associate Editor of two Bram Stoker Award® nominated anthologies, *Tattered Souls 2* and *Horror Library Volume 5*. He is an Active Member of the Horror Writer's Association, and an experienced screenwriter and journalist. When he's not slaying editorial dragons, he plays in a rock band for fun.

D. Alexander Ward is an author and editor of horror and dark fiction. His novels *Beneath Ash & Bone* and *Blood Savages* were released by Necro Publications and Bedlam Press and are available wherever books are sold.

Most recently, he edited the Bram Stoker Award-nominated *Lost Highways: Dark Fictions From the Road* from Crystal Lake Publishing, and he has also served as co-editor for the anthologies *Gutted: Beautiful Horror Stories*, and *Shadows Over Main Street, Volumes 1 and 2*.

Along with his family and the haints in the woods, he lives near the farm where he grew up in what used to be rural Virginia, where his love for the people, passions and folklore of the South was nurtured. There, he spends his nights penning and collecting tales of the dark, strange, and fantastic.

He is active on Facebook and Twitter and occasionally updates his website at www.dalexward.com

JOE R. LANSDALE
& KASEY LANSDALE

TERROR IS OUR BUSINESS:
DANA ROBERTS'
CASEBOOK
OF HORRORS

"Great use of imagery and irreverent wit... Fans of the Twilight Zone or creepy tales will find this collection quick and pleasurable to read."
—Publisher's Weekly

SHADOWS OVER MAIN STREET
Volume 2

Cutting Block Books   www.cuttingblockbooks.com

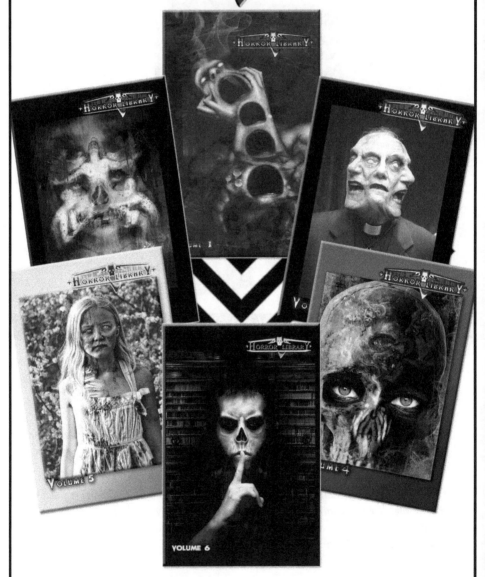

CPSIA information can be obtained
at www.ICGtesting.com
Printed in the USA
LVHW032041290419
616026LV00003B/232

9 781732 009035